Beryl Chalmers, writing under the pseudonym Julia Bayer, is a former journalist with a passion for sailing and the sea. As a freelance writer, she won various awards, including a Cabinet Office award, for creating simple English local authority publications.

She lives on an island off the east coast of England with her husband and has one daughter. *Fighting Back* is her first novel.

Dedicated to my daughter, Steffy Goodwin, whose enthusiasm for this book encouraged me to find a publisher, and to my husband, Simon Palmer, who fostered my love of the sea.

Julia Bayer

FIGHTING BACK

Who Will Win?

AUSTIN MACAULEY PUBLISHERS™

LONDON * CAMBRIDGE * NEW YORK * SHARJAH

A CIP catalogue record for this title is available from the British Library.

ISBN 9781398415164 (Paperback)
ISBN 9781398415171 (ePub e-book)

www.austinmacauley.com

First Published 2021
Austin Macauley Publishers Ltd
Level 37, Office 37.15, 1 Canada Square
Canary Wharf
London
E14 5AA

Chapter 1

He was dead. Two simple words had ended her torture.

Cara got up, walked to the window and looked out at the damp, grey morning greeting London. A homeless man lay in his soggy cardboard box in a shop doorway on the other side of the street. *What will his day bring? Nothing like mine,* she thought. She had a plane to catch.

She showered, dressed in the clothes she had planned to wear, applied her make-up carefully and meticulously. She had to look the part. The grieving widow. All in black. Dark eye-shadow to make her eyes look heavy and tired.

The phone call had ended her years of torture. She had been through it a thousand times in her head. Let it ring eight times and then pick up. Sound groggy as if she had just woken up. Let the news be told. Sharp intake of breath. "No! It can't be. How? When? Why? Not Ian. Not my Ian." Sob.

When she hung up, she felt her performance had been good. She hadn't overdone it. She had let her sister-in-law console her. Had let her talk. Had let her go through the details of the 'incident'.

But why had she longed for this moment? Why could she not live without it anymore? She pondered this in the taxi to Heathrow, in the departure lounge, and eventually in the plane.

Had she been weak? Was he such a monster? But then she remembered how her hell had begun, how she thought she would welcome death, the years she suffered at the hands of her husband—repeatedly raped and beaten; how fear gripped her whole being.

The flashbacks came—the times of terror, to the day she found herself joining a guided tour at the Tate Modern just killing time until the deed was done.

Her phone had rung, causing others on the tour to tut and glare at her. It was Ian.

She walked away from the group and pressed the green button.

"Where the fuck are you?" he yelled at her. "And don't lie. I know you are not with Janine."

Cara shook and let out a sound like an animal caught in a trap. She tried to speak but couldn't get any words out.

Ian's onslaught continued. "It took me a while to work out you were not in Belgium and then I got it out of Mike that you were in London. You will never escape, Cara. You must know that by now. Janine and Mike see me as the over-caring husband and that's exactly how it is going to be. I am coming to get you and bring you back."

Cara felt the blood rush to her head. She was sweating and freezing at the same time. As she crumpled to the ground, two people in the group were at her side, just stopping her from hitting her head on the cold, hard floor.

Cara woke up to see a lot of strangers' faces peering down at her. Her head was in someone's lap and the contents of her handbag were on the floor next to her.

Her lipstick was still rolling across the polished surface, quietly escaping between the feet of the onlookers.

"You okay, dear?" Cara's gaze followed the sound to an old lady standing above her. "You just fainted. It's hot in here. Always is. I've told them before to turn the air-conditioning up."

Cara got to her feet, thanking her rescuers and confirming that she was okay and would go to the Café 2 to sit down with a cold drink.

She edged away from them, slowly picking up her bag and its contents as she did so.

When she sat down with a glass of water, she fumbled in her bag for her mobile phone but couldn't find it. Then she remembered what had happened just before she collapsed. She ran back to the tour, desperately searching for her phone. She could not communicate with anyone, especially Mr Smith, if she couldn't find it.

It was no-where to be seen. She caught up with the group and asked all of them if they had seen it. She was greeted with blank looks.

Cara began to panic. She had to speak to Mr Smith, had to warn him Ian was on his way to London but she couldn't. She cursed herself for not writing his number down anywhere else, but she thought she was doing the right thing, not leaving anything to chance to connect her to him.

She ran from room to room, almost shrieking to the groups of people looking at the exhibits. "Have you seen a phone? I've lost my mobile."

The people seemed to be in a trance, none of them answering her, just staring in amazement at this highly-strung, screeching woman disturbing their peaceful visit to the gallery.

Eventually, Cara ran out of rooms to search. She sat down on a chair, trying to take in her new situation—again feeling Ian was getting closer and closer to imprisoning her for life. She tried to think logically but the fear creeping through her body prevented her from rational thought. She couldn't fail now, not for the sake of losing her phone.

Her flight announcement brought her back to reality—back to the day she had been told her husband was dead and why she was catching a plane to Cape Town.

Chapter 2

At first New York had been good for Cara, although she had been nervous of travelling around the city, unsure of which areas were safe and which were not. She decided it was just like any other city in the world—good and bad. She bought a tourist guide and a hop-on, hop-off bus ticket and decided that was the best way to find her way around.

Cara felt excited as she walked around the city, through Central Park, across the Brooklyn Bridge. From her parents' small house in England, just a few months ago, she was now a New Yorker. Well, almost.

She loved Fifth Avenue, Bloomingdales, Manhattan, Broadway and Times Square. And Central Park was out of this world. Ian was very generous and encouraged her to buy whatever she wanted. He would pick up the tab.

Cara and Ian were invited to a couple of dinner parties and they, in turn, invited their new friends to their new apartment. Life, at last, seemed good. Ian had been right to insist they move to New York after her parents died.

Until, one day when he came home late from the office very drunk and in a bad mood.

"Are you all right?" Cara asked, very concerned. Ian didn't really drink. She wondered what had happened.

She walked over to Ian and put her hand out to stroke his cheek. But before she had touched him, he swung his right arm and punched her on the right side of her face. She reeled backwards, losing her balance and fell, hitting her head on the edge of the coffee table.

"Wake up, you stupid cow. I don't want your silly molly coddling. God, your parents have a lot to answer for. You think the world is sorted out with hugs and kisses."

Cara's vision was blurred. His voice struck her as hard as his fist. "Ian, what's wrong?"

"We're out of here," Ian said. "Now, tonight. Pack the cases."

"But why? Where are we going? What's happened," pleaded Cara.

Ian walked over to her prostrate body on the floor and kicked her in the stomach. "That's for asking too many questions. Just shut it, unless you want more where that came from."

Cara curled up foetal-like on the carpet. Where had this nightmare come from? What had she done? She didn't recognise this monster as her husband. She stayed silent, not even daring to groan with the pain shrouding her body. Slowly she got up, but as she did so, the blood from her head dripped on to the carpet. Cara stared at it as if it was dripping from someone else. Her head spun and she thought she was going to fall. She grabbed the back of the chair and hung on until the feeling had passed.

Eventually, she staggered across the room, giving Ian a wide berth just in case he lashed out again. *Was this really happening,* she asked herself. *Where had her loving husband gone? What had turned him into this bully?*

Gradually she got the two suitcases down from the top of the wardrobe and began to fill them. She heard Ian in the sitting room, heard the whisky bottle pouring into a glass and dreaded the consequences.

She didn't know how long they would be away or what she should pack but she didn't want to ask so she packed a mixture of clothes and shoes and then dragged the cases into the sitting room. Ian was staring into his empty glass, motionless, like a strange art class model. Still she said nothing, just waited for the next instruction, or worse, the next assault.

After ten minutes, Ian looked up, growled something Cara couldn't understand and hurled his glass at the wall. It smashed, scattering shards of glass everywhere—like a fountain spraying outwards with the light from the table lamp glinting on every droplet. But this was far from beautiful.

He strode across the floor, picked up his car keys and told Cara to follow. She struggled to pick up the cases but she was not going to complain or ask him to help. Her thoughts drifted through events in the last year—happiness, sheer joy, shock, sadness, desperation, love. So much had changed in her life but this was the most shocking—even more than her father dropping down dead in front of her. She had never been struck by anyone before—not by her parents, not teachers, not even in playground fights. Her head throbbed. The bleeding had stopped and, as she felt her head, she could feel the congealed blood in her hair. Her face was swollen and she knew she would have a black eye—but that was the least of her worries. It was the kick in the stomach that sent her into a panic.

She was pregnant but had waited for the right moment to tell Ian but there hadn't been one. She had been so thrilled when the nurse at the surgery told her the news and she was sure Ian would be overjoyed. But now she was in turmoil. She didn't know what to do—to say something and risk another onslaught from his fists, say nothing and irritate him with the silence, or to try to talk to him. Tell him about the baby and maybe that would make him feel better and diminish the anger he was obviously feeling. But she didn't know this man. He was a stranger so she didn't know how to treat him.

Eventually, it was Ian who broke the silence. "You drive," he growled. "Head north to the highway." Cara had never driven through New York before, only just around their neighbourhood. She was terrified and the shock of Ian's attack on her, as well as the thought of driving through one of the busiest cities in the world, made her begin to shake. Her teeth chattered, her knees shook and her whole body became a mass of uncontrollable movement. Her breath came in gasps and she found she couldn't speak if she had wanted to. Shock gripped her body and she could do nothing. No tears came and no words. Ian stared at her quivering in the driver's seat and the realisation of what he had done to her started to creep over him. His drunkenness subsided as he looked at his wife. Out of all the wheeling and dealing, high life and fast pace he lived at, there really was only one person who mattered to him. Cara. She was his only rock in the tide that carried him from business deal to business deal. She mattered to him, and for the first time since their early days in Sheffield, Ian looked at Cara and felt sorry. She was so innocent, so loving to him, so forgiving. She took nothing from him and gave everything.

Today, he had lost everything; all the money he had accumulated from trickery and deception, and yes, from murder—all the millions he had conned out of his rivals. Someone had beaten him at his own game.

He could only build his empire again and get back in the world league with Cara as his mainstay. If nothing else, he had to be seen as the respectable family man—dinner parties with the right people and networking among the attorneys and politicians around the world. If he looked the decent, respectable citizen, he could get back. And if he could get back, he could get revenge.

He held Cara's shoulders and pulled her to him. "I'm so sorry my darling. How could I have done this to you? You, the only person I love in the world, or have ever loved." At first, Cara didn't know what to do. She held herself rigid in his arms, unsure of whether he would hit out again. But Ian knew what he had to do, and he would do it, whatever it took. He broke down and sobbed on Cara's shoulder. "My darling, I am so sorry. You will never know how much. It was the drink. I never drink, do I? It just took over from my bad day. Please forgive me, Cara. Please. It will never happen again."

Cara finally began to relax. This was yet another side to Ian she had not seen before. He had always been strong, self-sufficient and confident. What had pushed him to behave like an animal? No, she corrected herself, no animal hits out without a reason. Ian continued to stroke her hair and hold her, telling her over and over again that he was sorry and could she ever forgive him?

They sat there in the car in the underground car park below their apartment for over an hour. Neither of them had said anything for the last half hour. Eventually, Ian said, "I'll navigate you through the city—it'll be easier that way." Thoughts raced through her mind but she couldn't articulate any of them. She started the car and backed out of the parking space. As she moved the shift into drive, Ian said, "We'll have a holiday, gather our life up and begin again. I've lost everything today, Cara, but I never want to lose you. I'll explain tomorrow."

As she began to pull out of the car park, he suddenly yelled and said, "Shit! My phone. I'll be back in a minute." With that he had run from the car and sprinted into the building. It was ten minutes before he returned but Cara was calm now and just sat motionless until they were on their way, driving out on to Interstate 495, following the northern bank of Long Island Sound for a while. She then turned left towards the Interstate 684 to avoid the 87-toll road until she reached Highway 9. From there, she headed north towards Albany and then picked up Interstate Highway 87, until she crossed the New York state border and on up towards Maine. As she drove through the night, Ian slept fitfully. At one point, Cara sobbed and said, "Why Ian?" but Ian was back in control now. He knew he had won her around and she would forgive him. He just had to play the doting husband for a while and his marriage would be back on track.

After more than 300 miles Ian and Cara were approaching Portland in Maine. The sun was just coming up and although Ian's head was throbbing with a whisky, hangover, he felt the greater distance he put between his enemies and him, the more he could concentrate on his next move.

Cara was still very tired but awake enough to feel the aches and pain from her attack. She touched her face and felt the warm swelling around her cheek and eye. She folded the sun visor down and looked in the mirror. The bruising had come out and her eye was almost closed with the swelling. But that didn't matter;

it was superficial. She put her hand down on her stomach and prayed the baby was all right. Ian reached out to her and whispered, "You'll never know how sorry I am. I just hope that one day you will forgive me." Cara remained silent. She decided to tell him about the baby when she was more in control and less likely to cry. Ian followed the signs to the port and directed her to pull up outside the ferry ticket office.

He got out of the car and looked through the window to see if there was any sign of life. It was not quite fully light—the power buttons on the fax machine and photocopier glowed their green tinge in the dim office. Ian read the notices on the door and windows. It would be another hour before it was open but the first ferry out was just half an hour after that.

"Let's go and get breakfast somewhere," Ian said as he returned to the car. "There must be somewhere open around here."

They found a small diner at the edge of the port car park and ordered a full breakfast and a pot of coffee.

As Cara ate, her face hurt. Each chew made her wince. "You should see the other guy," Ian joked to the waitress. He sat opposite his wife and put his hand out to her. Gently, he stroked her cheek and said, "I'll make it up to you. I promise."

Before Cara could stop herself, she blurted out, "I'm pregnant. I'm so scared I'll lose the baby." If Ian was shocked, angry, devastated or annoyed, he didn't show it. He gave her his big broad, wide smile, took her hands and said, "I told you it was a new start. We'll be a proper family now."

Cara didn't know why she had dreaded telling him. Everything was going to be okay. He was over the moon. And so, she was too. For the time being, she forgot all about the drunken attack and melted all over again at the man she adored. She walked into the ticket office and bought the tickets as Ian got their bags before driving on to the small ferry. By this afternoon, they would be well away from danger, well away from his enemies and well on the road to a new start. Again!

When the ferry docked, Ian could see his next move. He drove straight to the marina, suggested to Cara that she enjoy the view in the sunshine from the balcony of the local yacht club and set off on his next mission.

Chapter 3

It didn't take Ian long to find the perfect way to escape. "Know anyone who does charters," he said to a very smart looking man sitting in the cockpit of one of the biggest yachts in the marina.

John, dressed in pristine Chino navy shorts, a white polo shirt with Buccaneer, the name of the yacht, embroidered on the front, and very expensive looking Dubarry leather sailing shoes, replied, "Depends where you want to go and how much you're prepared to pay," replied a very articulate voice.

"South east from here. Possibly Caribbean," said Ian. "Warm, blue skies, chilled. Money depends on what's on offer."

John suggested Exuma, to the west of Fort Lauderdale—a long trip down the east coast of America, but with some interesting sailing. "Went there last year. Great trip. I took eight weeks out of work and ended up extending it to 12. Exuma is the up and coming Barbados. Unspoilt, great walks, fantastic sailing. The perfect getaway."

"Sounds good, just what we're looking for," Ian replied. "Would you be interested for five grand one-way?"

"U.S. or Sterling?" John asked.

"Sterling, if we leave today. U.S., if we have to wait."

"Today it is then," John said. "Be back here at 7 pm. Sail at 8. Boat's ready anyway."

"See you at 7 then," said Ian as he walked back up the jetty.

Ian painted a perfect picture for Cara. The romantic sail into the sunset. Blue seas, dolphins crossing the bow. What more could she want? He dropped Cara into town to pick up some shorts, tee shirts and swimming gear and drove off telling her he needed to get to the bank to pick up some money. He would meet her back at the marina late afternoon.

There was just one more trace Ian had to get rid of before he had true anonymity. The car. Everything else had been taken care of—the New York apartment, all fuel and ferry tickets had been paid for with cash and the velcroed number plates had hidden the ownership of the car. He drove out of town until he found a dirt track at the side of the road. He turned down it and pulled up. He found the chassis and engine numbers and mangled them enough to be unrecognisable. He then removed the original number plates and put them in his small backpack to be dealt with later. He removed the Velcro and bolted the new number plates on. He was ready.

He tore a hole in the upholstery of the driver's seat and then lit a match. The foam took hold instantly and soon the inside of the car was engulfed in flames. Thick black smoke poured out of the driver's door Ian had purposefully left open. He picked up his backpack and ran back to the road, flagging down the first car that came along.

"Too late," said Ian. "The whole thing's gone up. Could you give me a lift back into town, please, so I can report it to the police and organise moving it?"

Back in town, Ian found a quiet corner of a park to sit and contemplate his next move. He still had £15,000 Sterling and $20,000 U.S. dollars left—nothing could trace him and he could escape from the U.S. and lie low for a while.

He returned to the centre of town and found a mobile phone shop where he bought a couple of sim cards with cash. Before he replaced his old one, he checked for messages. "You can't escape. There's nowhere we can't find you," said the American accent. *That's just what you think,* thought Ian. Things had gone badly wrong in such a short time. Just last week he had $5million. He was a respected businessman meeting the right people and being accepted as the great English gent' wherever he went.

But his fortune had not been amassed through hard work. His scams with drugs, paintings, and jewellery—in fact anything of significant value—had left him a few enemies. But he had taken one big step too far. He had withdrawn all his money to be paid over to a drugs cartel in southern Florida. $5million would bring him at least $15million on the street. He had set up a deal with five separate dealers in the Bronx, each of whom would be handing over $3million. He met the dealer from Miami, tested the goods in a back warehouse and handed over the cash. He had been careful to hire the truck using a different name and had bought a passport, claiming he was Danish. Ditching his English accent, he had been practising his Pidgin English with the higher tones throughout many sentences for months. The Miami dealer knew nothing of him except he was from Esbjerg in Denmark and was known as Karl. Then, in turn, he became

Australian—the blonde, blue-eyed hunk look always came in handy. The Bronx was a difficult area for someone so blonde to be in without standing out, so he met his five dealers on the ferries going between Staten Island St George's terminal and Manhattan's Whitehall terminal in New York. Each time he used a different van, dressed in very different clothes—a suit one day, shorts and tee shirt running gear, the next, jeans and leather bomber jacket another. Even as a woman in long skirt, jacket and wig once and finally in tweeds and brogues. He made sure he travelled at different times of the day and night to make sure he was never on the same shift on the ferries. In just three days, he had delivered his haul and collected $15million that he had paid into a variety of accounts.

But then, very rapidly, his luck ran out. He had stashed the cash in different accounts in six separate banks worldwide. In total he had 18 accounts in three separate names in the banks, all set up swiftly and efficiently on-line. No one knew a face to link to an account. He was totally anonymous and thought he was 'laughing all the way to the bank.'

But he hadn't been quite clever enough. He had done all his planning and preparation on his laptop, using his broadband dongle. Sitting outside a café on the edge of Central Park, he had worked on-line for months with no-one knowing from his office, home, gym or anywhere Ian was known, that he was one of the biggest dealers in Cocaine. He had the perfect set-up. Total anonymity and he left no tracks for anyone to follow. Or, so he thought.

On his way home, just two days earlier, his mobile had rung. It was one of the dealers from the Bronx. "This had better be a joke," snarled the voice. It didn't take Ian long to realise that his entire Cocaine shipment from Miami was nothing but flour and talcum powder. Worthless. The white powder he had tried was the only packet worth anything and he didn't even know if that had been taken out of the haul. He had used his entire fortune built up through many scams and frauds to pay for this deal and now he had five of the hardest drug dealers from the Bronx out to kill him. He had to move fast.

Early the next morning he went to the coffee shop on the Fifth Avenue side of Central Park. When he went to pay for his coffee, he put his laptop bag on the ground while he searched his pockets for change. At that moment, the owner of the coffee shop ran through to the shop from the kitchen with a fire extinguisher, saying the stove was on fire. Panic set in making everyone in the shop dash for the door. Two minutes later, the fire was under control and peace returned to the early morning coffee drinkers. But it had been enough time for the computer hacker to switch laptop bags and disappear into the crowd outside.

It was another ten minutes before Ian opened the laptop bag on the bench nearby and reality slowly sunk in. It looked the same until he tried to log on and his name and password were rejected. At first Ian thought he had merely mis-keyed but at the third attempt he knew it was not his laptop.

Meanwhile, the hacker had not only bypassed his log-on details but had also accessed all his accounts' details, transferring every cent of the Bronx dealers' payments to his own accounts. For a few hours' work the hacker had cleaned up $15million and had then shut down all of Ian's accounts.

There was nothing Ian could do by the time he had found an internet café and logged on. He had been so stupid. All of his account details were on his laptop with no copies of account numbers anywhere else. What he had thought was the most secure way, had been the least secure. Over the months of planning, he had not noticed the hacker watching him as he worked outside the café. He had also not noticed him following him around the city—watching his meetings with the Bronx dealers. And now, all of Ian's planning, dealing and distributing had not only left him virtually broke but also a wanted man—and these men don't give up. He could never return to New York.

Chapter 4

Cara's retail therapy had made her feel better. By the time she was back at the marina with armfuls of new summer-wear, she was tired but relaxed. The thought of sailing off into the sunset with Ian took her back to the first few months with Ian when love, passion and happiness outweighed all else. She had just ordered herself a coffee sitting on the balcony of the yacht club when she saw Ian down on the jetty at the southern end of the marina. He was talking to a man who she assumed was the yacht's skipper. As he left the man and turned to walk back up the jetty, she saw him do a very strange thing. He looked at his mobile phone, kissed it and threw it in the water. There really were strange sides to Ian she knew nothing of. Although, she had relaxed during the day, the memories of last night were still very raw. She automatically put her hand to her cheek and felt the swelling around her eye. Her other hand was on her stomach, subconsciously protecting her unborn baby.

As Ian approached the yacht club, he looked up and saw Cara sitting on the balcony. He waved up to her and then took the stairs two at a time to be with her.

"All set," he said. "The boat's ready for the off. I see you've had a good time spending my money." Although Cara knew he meant it light heartedly, something inside her felt a stinging—why 'his' money? She had given up her life and her degree at his request. Surely, everything they had was theirs, not his. After all, she thought of her parents' house as theirs, not hers, to return to whenever they were back in the UK. Cara said nothing and just let it pass. After all, this was nothing compared to last night. Was it really only last night? Such a lot had happened in less than 24 hours.

She leaned across the table and kissed him tenderly. "We really need this holiday," she told him. "It's so long since we had time to do anything together. I can't wait."

"Well, you don't need to any more," Ian replied. "Drink up and we'll head down to the boat. I've already put our bags on-board. You'll like John, the owner—from around here but has spent a few years in Cowes on the Isle of Wight."

He squeezed Cara's hand and said, "I told him you had a fall yesterday. Best to forget it all, don't you think?"

Cara didn't reply. She didn't trust what she might say to him. Although, he persuaded her his fists came to life with the whisky, there would always be a small part of her that would remember and make her fear him.

Cara liked John instantly. "Ian tells me I have a crew of three, not two," he grinned. Ian patted Cara's stomach and said proudly—"The two most important people in the world." Cara was going to enjoy this holiday.

John showed Cara and Ian around the Buccaneer, a beautiful 68ft sloop with teak decks. He had given them the master cabin in the stern that had its own bathroom—Cara would never get used to the nautical terms. How can the bathroom be called the 'heads'? The cabin was luxurious although Cara thought she would find it difficult living in such a cramped space. John showed her how to pump out the loo and the shower tray and then showed her around the rest of the yacht. He told her it was probably best if she went to bed soon after sunset as she might feel a little seasick as she was not used to sailing. "You can't watch the horizon at night," he explained, "and that's the best way to get your sea legs."

Cara was very happy with that suggestion as the previous 24 hours had left her feeling drained. Ian, too, was beginning to look forward to rest, but not until they were well away from the U.S. mainland. John introduced them to a young man whom Cara thought to be about 18—not much younger than she was. "This is my younger brother, Tom, my crew. Doing a gap year before Uni. Tom and I can sort the boat out to leave you two to relax and enjoy your trip."

The sunset was everything Cara had hoped for. She and Ian took themselves off to the foredeck and sat down on a couple of cushions on one of the hatches. The boat's motion was like a baby's cradle—a gentle swaying from side to side as the wind followed them down the coast. Ian, too, was impressed, and for the first time in what seemed like weeks, began to relax. He put his arm around Cara's shoulder and told her he loved her. She cuddled into him and watched the waves tumbling along next to them until the bright orange sun was almost kissing the horizon. "Why have we not done this before?" Ian broke into Cara's thoughts. "This is what life is all about. This is what we should be working for—our own yacht to escape the storms of life."

"Could we really do that?" said Cara. "Could we really sail off and leave our friends behind?"

"No," said Ian, "I don't mean forever, I mean to spend our weekends and holidays on. Maybe when we are old and grey…"

Ian and Cara soaked up the beautiful sunset and felt closer than they had in a long time. When the orange glow was finally replaced with a black sky, Ian and Cara got up and without saying a word, went back to the cockpit, said goodnight to their hosts and slipped quietly to their cabin.

They made love for the first time in many weeks and drifted off to sleep with the soporific rhythmical sound of the waves on the hull.

Ian and Cara slept for many hours—Cara woke first at 6 am and looked across the bed at her husband. He looked peaceful and at that moment she knew she could never love anyone else. He was her world. Whatever had led to the awful attack just 36 hours earlier was a different life. A different man. She felt so much love for him at that moment she thought she could not contain it.

She leaned on one elbow and stroked his hair and then his face. He murmured in his sleep. She kissed his eyelids and then his mouth. Her hand moved down his body, stroking the hairs on his chest and then his stomach. He was awake now and moved on to his side, finding her mouth with his. His tongue explored her mouth and then moved down her body. She thought she would explode as his tongue searched her. She couldn't wait any more; she wanted him so badly. She pulled at his shoulders and steered him back up to her mouth, her body lifting off the bed to meet his. As he entered her, Cara almost screamed with pleasure. Their lovemaking was fast and furious—neither wanting to wait for the climax. They had not made love like this for a very long time. Their combined finish left them groaning and breathless as they lay in each other's arms and again they drifted back into a deep sleep for another two hours.

When they got up eventually, the sun was up, the wind a peaceful Force 4, and they were nearly 100 miles away from their enemies. John and Tom had taken it in turn through the night to helm and navigate. Tom showed Cara their position on the chart and explained their course while John cooked breakfast. While the autopilot whirred away, the four sat companionably in the cockpit and ate their breakfast. Cara and Ian were ravenous—they ate hungrily and realised they had not eaten properly for two days. Life was again great, thought Cara.

Over the next three days, Cara and Ian learned a lot about sailing, navigation, tides and boat handling. It was a completely new world to them and they loved it. Neither suffered from the motion of the boat and were able to helm, keep a good compass course, change sails and put plots on the chart.

Their course took them past Newport and New York—but well offshore—and down towards Florida. On the third night, Cara woke up at 3 am to find Ian had got up. She pulled on her clothes and staggered through to the main saloon. No one was around. *They must all be up on deck,* she thought. As she climbed the companionway steps she saw John sitting in the cockpit, his eyes closed. The autopilot had control. She knew he was just catnapping so she moved past him quietly to the stern deck. The sea looked beautiful, sparkles of phosphorescence jumping on the quilted sea. She sat mesmerised for a long time, forgetting she had got up to find Ian. As she sat and stared at the wake of the yacht, she saw something in the water—a number plate from a car. What a strange thing to see so far from land, she thought. She turned around to see Ian's silhouette up at the bow. He was bending over the toe rail holding his backpack. In his hand was a long flat shape—another number plate—he had obviously thrown the first one overboard. What was he doing? Why the number plates?

She moved forward, grabbing at the rigging as she did so. She had no lifejacket or harness on so she tried not to trip and fall overboard. She reached Ian just as he turned towards her. "Why are you throwing these number plates overboard, Ian? Where are they from?" Ian felt anger well up but controlled himself. He didn't answer, just took her hand and eventually said, "Come on, you'll get cold out here at night. You have to look after yourself for the sake of the baby."

"But Ian, what were you doing?"

"Nothing you need to worry about. Drop it!" was all he said. Cara knew the matter was closed.

They reached the cockpit as John looked up. "What are you two doing out here? Can't sleep?"

"No, just a wonderful night," replied Ian. "As you're up, would you mind putting a plot on the chart for me? Tom's still asleep and I didn't want to wake him," asked John.

"I'll do it," said Cara before Ian could answer. "And I'll put the kettle on too."

"Sounds good," said John. "You can be my crew, any time."

Ian felt a pang of jealousy. Cara and John were very easy with each other and he didn't like it. He had to be top dog, but after his attack on Cara, he knew he

22

must continue to be the caring husband. He had won her back and he didn't want her to ever doubt him again, whatever it took.

Cara went down below, checked the GPS and put a plot on the chart. They had done a few hundred miles already. She then checked the weather report on the Navtex, put the kettle on and reported back to John.

"Bad weather coming from the south," she said. "Force 7-8 in the next 24 hours."

"We may have to put into Miami for a day or so, if it's bad. We'll keep an eye on it. Thanks, Cara," replied John.

"Is that really necessary," said Ian. "Can't a boat this size handle it?"

"The boat can but I'm not sure about the crew," said John. "Better to be safe, especially in Cara's condition."

Ian was not at all pleased. He wanted to be anywhere but Miami at the moment. He knew the Bronx brothers would be looking for him and Miami was the obvious place they would be—they knew that's where the drugs had come into the US and although he wanted to deal with the man who robbed him of his $5million, he would deal with that later. Now was not the time to take his revenge.

He went below to have a look at the chart. Fort Lauderdale was nearer than Miami. Maybe that would be better. He returned to the cockpit and said Fort Lauderdale was just 30 miles away so perhaps it would be better to head there now instead of waiting. John felt Ian was now being over cautious.

"We'll be okay today," he said. "I'll check the forecast during the day and make a decision tonight."

"I don't want you putting Cara in any sort of danger," said Ian. "I'd never forgive myself if anything happened to her."

John noticed Ian's change of heart in just a few minutes, but said nothing. He was a strange one, this man; changes mood at the drop of a hat. He was like a cat on a hot tin roof when he first met him at the marina. Then he was calm and the doting husband. Now he was uptight again. *A few skeletons in his closet,* thought John. Cara, on the other hand, was delightful. Calm, friendly, intelligent. *Had she really fallen over to get all that bruising?* Whatever John thought, he didn't say. It was none of his business.

The Buccaneer passed the outer harbour wall of a very big marina in Miami at 11am the next day. The wind had strengthened considerably and was now a Force 7 on the nose with more to come. As the wind had got up, so had the seas, making the boat's motion very uncomfortable. Cara had been sick and was lying in her bunk. Ian was on the stern deck hanging on to the guardrail. He was not as worried about feeling sick as he was about whom he might bump into in Miami, especially around the port. He had not shaved since they left Portland so had the beginnings of a beard. The blonde-ginger stubble coming through made him look a little unkempt but that was better than the very recognisable fresh-faced look.

John and Tom moored the boat with expertise, putting out extra ropes to cope with the wind. They topped up the diesel and water tanks and stowed the sails. As soon as the bad weather had passed, they would set off again for Exuma.

Cara appeared on deck looking relieved they were safely in harbour. She noticed Ian was looking agitated and said, "It's okay. We've never been to Miami. Let's go and explore. When the weather's better, we can resume our trip to paradise."

"Do you have to prattle on?" replied Ian. "Everything's always so bloody rosy with you, isn't it?"

Cara was stung by his harsh words. "Sorry, darling, I'm just trying to make the best of it."

Ian decided at that moment to head for the warehouse and get his $5million back. He had no idea how, but he was going to do it. But first he had to get a gun. He left Cara standing on the boat as he jumped on to the jetty and disappeared up the ramp.

He bought himself a baseball cap, big trainers, a hoody and jog pants and then went to Downtown Miami to a bar where he had first met the cartel member. Just across the road from there, he went to a basement flat where he had 'bought' his alternative passports. This time, he bought himself a gun—with a silencer.

He returned to the bar and sat down at a table in the corner, not knowing what he would do. He just needed to do something.

He could not be in Miami and feel he was a sitting target. The Bronx brothers would not be far away and he meant revenge on the cartel. He was not the stupid naïve 'little man' they thought he was. They were going to pay for their cheat.

After changing, he hid his usual clothes in a toilet compartment in Miami Central railway station. He then went to a coffee bar near the warehouse. He had been there for just a few minutes when a black teenager came in. He recognised him from somewhere but wasn't really sure where. He knew he was connected to the dealers. When the teenager left carrying a carton of coffee, he decided to follow him. With baseball cap peak pulled down and hood up, his face could not easily be seen.

The boy led him through a few streets and down a narrow alleyway. He disappeared into a doorway, leaving Ian feeling very vulnerable outside. Ian listened at the door and gently pulled it open enough to sidle in. His heart was beating very fast and sweat trickled from his temples. He edged his way around the dark hallway until he reached a door at the far end. He listened for a few minutes and heard two voices—one was young—the teenager—the other one, the man he had handed over his $5million to just a week before.

Ian had to think fast. What madness had brought him here? Why had he come? Was he really going to take a whole drugs cartel on? *But then,* he thought, *they are the reason he has five of the worst killers from the Bronx on his back.* Suddenly, there were footsteps just on the other side of the door. Ian had nowhere to hide—he instinctively reached for his gun and screwed the silencer on. As the door opened towards him, he pushed his back into the wall behind it. The teenager ran through the doorway letting it slam behind him and in a flash, had reached the outside door, and was gone.

Before Ian could realise what the consequences of his actions would be, he had opened the door and gone inside, the gun pointing ahead.

"What have you forgotten now," said the small, dark man sitting at a table, his back to the door.

"I never forget," said Ian, and as the man turned, Ian aimed the gun at him.

"I've come to collect the $5million you cheated me out of," growled Ian. But the man wasn't about to enter into a conversation. In an instant, he had pulled out a gun, but before he could level it at his target, Ian pulled the trigger.

It was not like killing Cara's mother. That was simple. This was completely different.

The man reeled back in his chair, knocking his coffee cup off the table, blood pouring from his chest. Ian panicked. He dropped the gun and tripped in his haste to escape from the room. He was about to pick it up again when he heard the outside door open. He hid behind packing boxes near the door when the teenager came back in. His heart pounded and sweat poured out of him. At first, the teenager didn't appear to notice, but as his eyes focused around the room, he saw the coffee spill on the floor that led him to the bleeding man. He rushed over to him and said, "Christ George, what the…" and then realised that whoever did this must still be nearby. He turned and fled, not looking back and not noticing the gun on the floor. Ian crept out of his hiding place and grabbed the gun. He didn't give himself time to see if he had killed George, just got out into the street and away. He went straight back to Miami Central, changed his clothes and found a bin for his incriminating ones. Ian was desperate. He needed a drink. He went to a bar just outside the station and ordered a large whisky. He downed it in one and ordered another.

"Wow," said the barman. "You okay?" Ian ignored him and drank the second glass. He was beginning to calm down. He sat in silence for more than an hour, taking in the enormity of what had happened in just a week. He would never be caught out again.

Chapter 5

When Ian left, Cara stood in the cockpit wondering what on earth had happened now. Everything had been fine since they had got on the boat. Now, he was showing signs of the aggressive bully again. Fear began to crawl all over her again.

John had heard the conversation between Cara and Ian and felt sorry for Cara. He was a bully, that husband of hers. But why did she put up with it?

"Why don't you let me show you the sights," said John. "The boat's safe now so we've got all day."

Cara wasn't sure what to do. She didn't want to upset Ian, but she didn't feel safe to explore on her own. John read her mind. "I don't bite, you know," he said. "If Ian's got business to deal with, let me look after you. I'd be honoured to." How could Cara refuse?

John called down to Tom that they were going sightseeing and told him to lock the boat if he went anywhere. "Yup, will do," was all that came back.

John helped Cara down from the side deck to the pontoon, putting out his bare arm for her to steady herself. She noticed he had a tattoo on his forearm and wondered who the Karen was inside the heart. John hailed a taxi and he and Cara set off to explore.

By 4 pm, Cara was feeling tired so suggested they went for a coffee. They soon found an internet café so Cara decided she would e-mail a couple of friends—her friend and neighbour in New York and Julia she had started her law degree with and who was just finishing her second year at Sheffield.

She found she had a lot to say, but obviously kept quiet about Ian's attack on her. She told them about how beautiful the Buccaneer was, how she was learning to navigate and how she and Ian were closer now than for a long while. "This trip is just what we needed," she said.

"Once we reach Exuma," she said, "We plan to chill out on the beach for a week or so and then maybe explore some of the islands to the south before heading back to New York. I could really get used to this life on a boat."

Cara and John returned to the boat at around six and were surprised Ian was not back.

"Haven't seen him all day," said Tom.

"Let's go and have a drink at the yacht club," John suggested. "We can see the boat from there so we can see when Ian gets back."

The three left the Buccaneer, locked up with a note on the main hatch telling Ian where they were. It was difficult walking along the pontoons as the wind was so strong. Cara was afraid she might be blown to the edge of the pontoon and fall in. John put his arm around her shoulder, as if reading her thoughts, and steered her protectively to the yacht club. "Glad we came in," he said. "It would have been a bit of a pig out there in this wind."

"So am I," said Cara. "You can get too much of a good thing." They both laughed.

Sitting in the warm shelter of the yacht club, Cara began to wonder where Ian was. She tried his mobile but it was switched off again. Two orange juices and a coffee later, Ian walked through the door. He looked dishevelled and tired. And worse still, he smelt of whisky.

"Where have you been, Ian?" said Cara. "I was really worried about you. I tried to phone you but you had it switched off."

"God, this wind," he said. "So hard to do anything. Look at my hair," he joked to the expectant three. "But Ian?" Cara continued.

"Oh, don't fuss, darling. I told you I had a bit of business to sort out," was all Ian told them.

By the next morning, the wind had calmed down and the sea state was easier. The Buccaneer left harbour at 7 am with John at the helm. The engine starting had woken Cara who had not slept well. She dozed through the night wondering where Ian had gone to in the afternoon. Why was he so agitated before he left and in such a state when he returned? As she lay next to Ian she knew he was still troubled. He tossed and turned and shouted in his sleep but she could not make out what he was saying. She decided to do a little investigating.

She got up, dressed and climbed up to the cockpit. She was pleased John was alone and Tom was still asleep. She was at ease with John and felt as if she had known him all her life. Neither of them said anything for a while, both enjoying the morning sun and gentle breeze. The Buccaneer sliced through the waves with full sails up—a perfect sail. Cara knew she would go sailing for the rest of her life. It gave her a peace she could not find anywhere else. John was the first to speak. "All okay with you and Ian?"

"Yes, I think so," Cara replied, not feeling at all confident of her husband's well-being.

"He just seemed out of sorts yesterday," continued John, "not the relaxed holidaymaker I had seen before."

"Yes, he was a little distracted, wasn't he? Takes his work too seriously," Cara replied.

"What does he do," asked John.

"Always big business deals," said Cara. "An entrepreneur," she went on. "Always chasing the big one."

For the first time Cara suddenly realised she had no idea what deals Ian got involved in. She knew it was buying and selling and she had heard property conversations, but she didn't actually know. Whenever she inquired, Ian had dismissed the subject with a nonchalant air. Yes, there was a lot of investigating she had to do. She and John chatted over a cup of coffee as he described Exuma and Great Exuma to her.

Tom was the next to appear on deck with his usual 'just got out of bed' look. He had a look around the horizon, noted they had already put Miami at least ten miles behind them and went down to put a plot on the chart.

"Anyone for a coffee and croissant?" he asked.

"Sounds like just what I need," said Ian as he appeared from the stern cabin. He, too, looked a little unkempt as he hadn't shaved for a few days. His stubble, Cara noticed, was beginning to show the odd signs of grey here and there and yet he wasn't even 30 yet.

She found she was a little wary of saying the wrong thing this morning after Ian had snapped at her yesterday so sat in silence. Ian came and sat next to her, kissed her and said, "Good morning, darling. Great to be back on the water."

Their sail to Great Exuma took them through turquoise seas glinting in the sunlight. Cara spent her time studying the charts and learning how to trim the sails. John was a very good teacher and he enjoyed showing Cara how to handle the Buccaneer. Ian was quiet and seemed distant to the other three. He knew they had noticed and occasionally excused himself by saying, "You don't know how tired you are until you have time to rest."

The Buccaneer's arrival at Exuma was uneventful. The wind had eased, making mooring the boat much easier. The island seemed very quiet after the metropolitan feel and chaos of Miami. They all went ashore and while John paid the mooring fees and sorted the paperwork, Ian, Cara and Tom jumped on a local pick-up truck taxi to explore. They went into the small town not far away where Tom and Cara sat and had a coffee while Ian went to find an internet café. He was just about to walk in to one on the edge of town when he saw two of the Bronx brothers inside. He quickly ran down an alleyway between buildings and hid in a doorway until he decided what he would do next.

How did they know he would be there? he thought. No one knew. Maybe it was a lucky guess as it was on a direct route from Miami to the Caribbean and only 35 miles southeast of Nassau in the Bahamas. Or maybe that's where they picked up their cargo?

Whatever the reason, he had to hide and had to leave Exuma as soon as possible.

As he was pondering how to escape, the brothers left the internet café and stood on the pavement outside. They exchanged a few words and then each went off in a different direction. Ian tried desperately to think how he could get away. There was only one road, so he couldn't run in any direction. He squeezed between a wall and a large bin overflowing with rotting garbage, trying to see where the two men were. He could see one walking in the direction of the marina but he couldn't see the other. He stayed put.

After a few minutes, he crept out of his hiding place and tried to see where the other man had got to. Just as he got to his feet, he felt something in his back and heard the words, "Don't try anything. It will only take a split second to end this now."

Ian froze and tried to look over his shoulder, but the gun was pushed further into his back.

"Right, let's go. Walk straight ahead of me and take me to the marina. I know you are on a boat so don't even think of telling me otherwise."

Ian walked slowly, his mind racing, desperately trying to work out how he could get away. But he would not leave Cara behind. Whatever happened, she would be with him.

As they walked, the man called his brother and just said, "I've got him. We're heading to the marina. Wait for us."

The five minutes it took to reach the Buccaneer seemed in one way like hours, and in another, like seconds to Ian. How could he do anything with two murderers holding him. They were thugs who would stop at nothing. Ian didn't think of himself in the same way.

As they reached the boat, Ian saw Tom at the other end of the pontoon and was glad he would have no witnesses. As they each climbed on to the side deck, Ian knew he had a chance—the killers were thrown off balance as the boat tipped with their combined weight. He snatched at the mainsheet holding the boom central to the boat and let it go. The boom swung violently towards the pontoon, hitting both men in the face. They fell over the guardrails and landed in a heap, both unconscious. In a split-second Ian had vaulted over the guardrails and down to the pontoon, grabbing the gun and using the handle of it to make sure both men would not wake up. Checking no one had seen, he then shouted in a frenzy for help.

The ambulance arrived, stretchered the two men off the pontoon and left the marina long before Cara and John had returned. Ian hit the whisky again, desperate to be away before any authorities came asking questions.

Chapter 6

It was another three hours before they arrived back at the boat, by which time Ian was apoplectic. He shouted at John to "get this fucking boat out of here" and forget about being 'Mr Nice Guy' with his wife. He was being paid to do a job and that is what he would do.

The others stared at him in amazement. It was Cara who spoke first.

"What on earth has happened now, Ian?"

Ian caught himself before he lashed out at her. He couldn't risk John throwing them off the boat. "God, sorry, Cara. Things are just very bad at the moment. Had some very bad news about the deal in Auckland."

He turned and apologised to John and Tom and asked quietly if they would be leaving soon.

John began to open his mouth to tell Ian he had had enough of his behaviour when he caught Cara out of the corner of his eye. She was looking at him, silently pleading with him not to do or say anything. He stayed quiet and prepared the boat to leave as Ian stayed down below and Cara sat in the cockpit, not daring to risk another onslaught, either verbally or physically, from Ian.

Once underway, Ian spent a lot of time up at the bow watching the bow wave, deep in thought. Was this how life was going to be—running away all the time? Making enemies and escaping? He needed this trip more than he had realised. He needed time to plan his next move. He was starting again with very little money. He had lost so much by his naivety. It wouldn't happen again. Cara was his rock and he had only just started to realise it. He needed her in his life, whatever he was doing. He was glad they were having a baby, if only because she would never leave him now.

Over the next five weeks, the Buccaneer took them to beautiful islands surrounded by beautiful blue seas. Coral blue. They swam and they snorkelled and forgot all their stresses. Well, almost. Ian would never forget his New York downfall. John taught Ian to scuba dive which he was fascinated by. He dived each day, exploring an underwater world he had never ever thought about. Cara didn't join him and he was happy in his wanderings among the thousands of colourful fish. Instead, she used the time to do a little bit of investigating, but she was terrified by what she found.

It took her a long time to find Ian's backpack, despite the boat being a mini world with not too many hiding places. She wondered how long it had taken Ian to lift their bunk top and find the small hiding place behind the bulkhead next to the steering quadrant. She knew, as she began to search, that she could find something she would regret for the rest of her life. But she had to know. Otherwise, why would Ian have to hide it?

She pulled out the backpack and was surprised at its weight. As she began to open it she found herself trembling and breathing heavily. Her fingers fiddled with the buckles, her hands shaking at the expectancy of what she might find. Eventually, she pulled open the top and put her hand inside. As she slowly emptied the contents on to the bunk, a fear gripped her so strongly, she felt the baby inside her react. Kicking and moving as if he or she, too, could see what was making Cara so frightened. When she got to the heavy, hard object wrapped in an old pillowcase, she almost dared not look. She knew immediately it was a gun, but why? Why did Ian have it? She unwrapped it slowly and as she did so, the silencer rolled out across the bunk and fell on to the floor. It clattered heavily, waking Cara from her racing thoughts. She picked it up and held the gun in her hand, wondering if Ian had ever used it. There must be some reasonable explanation. After a few minutes, she put the gun down on the bunk and looked through the rest of the contents of the backpack, each package bringing greater fears. Bundles of money, both dollars and pounds, four passports, two with Ian's photograph and different names, and two with her own photographs and different names. Then she found a small envelope folded and wrapped up tightly—various mobile phone sim cards. Was this the stash of a criminal of some sort? What was it all about? She needed answers but she had no idea how to get them. Just as she was deep in thought the hatch above her head suddenly opened. John slowly took in the spread of objects on the bunk—the cash, the gun, the silencer, the passports. Cara panicked and tried to gather them all up. In an instant John had jumped down through the hatch and was standing next to her.

"What's going on?" he demanded. "Who are you two?"

"I don't know," Cara spluttered. "I have never seen this lot before. I just wanted to try to answer some questions about my husband I was worried about so I started searching for his backpack."

John knew she was telling the truth. "Look, he'll be back in a minute. Put this lot back where you found it and we'll talk later."

Just then they heard a noise from the bathing platform. Ian was back. John instantly closed the hatch above their heads and locked it.

"I'll keep him up on deck," John said. "Get this lot put away."

Cara repacked the backpack quickly but carefully and hid it where she had found it. She was back up on deck just as Ian had got his wetsuit off and was about to go below. It was another 12 hours before John and Cara could talk. Either Tom was with them, Ian, or both. Eventually, as they sailed through the inky black sea below the stars, Tom went below and Ian took up his usual position at the bow.

The sea was calm, just a swollen mattress lumbering along with no breaking waves.

"Well, what do you think now," said John.

"I just don't know," replied Cara, and she really didn't.

"Do you think he used that gun when we stopped in Miami," John suggested. Cara shuddered.

"You don't think he really did, do you?" said Cara, all her worst nightmares at the point of coming true.

"Well, you obviously know him better than I do, but he was definitely very upset about something."

"I love my husband and up until now that love was blind. I believe he loves me but I have discovered in the last few weeks that I don't really know him.

"When we are together with no thought of work and everyday life stresses, we can be just as close as we were in the early days, but those times are getting fewer and fewer. I think I need to give him more attention. I have been so wrapped up with the baby that I haven't really given him any time lately. If nothing else, this trip has stopped us in our tracks to take stock," Cara finished.

John took in what she had said, thinking that she was still blind to the reality that her husband was not the man he showed her he was. But he didn't say it.

"Just promise me you will be careful," he said. "Don't give him yourself totally; keep a little bit back. That way you will survive, whatever happens," he said. Cara was surprised. How dare this man who had only known her and Ian for just a few weeks dare to suggest how she should live her marriage. But she didn't say it either. Deep down she knew he was right, but she couldn't admit it. Yet. She changed the subject.

"Where to next?" John knew the subject was closed. He didn't try to reopen it, but made himself a mental note that he would keep an eye on Ian. Cara had touched him—her warmth, honesty and perhaps even her naivety. He would look out for her if he could and if she would let him.

The Buccaneer sailed further south and east, heading for the Virgin Islands: US islands first and then British. As they rounded St Thomas, John explained how different the US islands were compared to the British. There is even an old red phone box on an island at the southern end. After mooring the Buccaneer and clearing immigration and customs, the four went ashore to the local yacht club and enjoyed their first taste of Caribbean rum. They received a very warm welcome from the Commodore and staff.

"Nice to see a few folks from home," said the man in charge. "First time in the BVI?"

Within half an hour they had been told which islands offered what, where to trek through the rain forest, where to victual the boat and the best places to eat.

Ian and Cara enjoyed the old Colonial atmosphere. The Commodore even wore a silk cravat.

After a couple more rums, Cara suggested getting something to eat. As she was not drinking alcohol she noticed far more how drink affected Ian. She didn't want to risk another upset, so they left John and Tom and wandered off to find a restaurant.

"I love this place," Ian surprised her. "It feels like home but it's warm."

"Yes," Cara agreed. "I think I could even live here. Great place to bring up a child."

"Do you think so?" said Ian.

"Maybe we could…" He trailed off, losing himself in thought.

"Maybe we should investigate a little," said Cara. "Find out about houses, schools, work, visas etc."

"You don't need a visa," said Ian. "It's British."

"Oh, yes, of course," said Cara. "Even better. We could really learn to sail and buy a boat."

Now Ian was getting excited. Cara loved him even more. That was the Ian she knew.

By the end of their meal, they had decided to get out of New York—not a place to bring up a child they decided—and to set up home here in the BVI. They would have persuaded themselves anywhere else in the world at that moment was not the place to bring up a child. They had fallen in love with the islands.

Ian persuaded Cara he could work from anywhere in the world. He just needed an internet connection.

"We don't even have to go back to New York," said Ian. "We could start again here."

"But we've got to go back to pack up all our things in the flat and say goodbye to our friends," said Cara.

"I could fly back, close the office and pack our things," he replied. "You could stay here and find us a house. Then we could invite our friends to come for a holiday."

Cara wasn't sure but Ian was so excited, she didn't want to spoil the moment.

"Let's go and tell John what we've decided." Cara was caught up in Ian's enthusiasm. And just for the moment she had put the gun, cash, passports and backpack to the back of her mind.

They paid the bill and left the restaurant, their arms around each other as they wandered back to the marina.

If this was what made Ian happy again, this is what they would do, thought Cara. It will be fun looking for a house and making all their plans.

John and Tom seemed very happy for them and said they could leave the Buccaneer in the marina for a month or so until they had found a house. They would fly back to Portland and maybe return to sail further down the Caribbean chain of islands later.

So it was all set. The three would fly back, leaving Cara in paradise to organise their new home. After dropping them off at the island's airport, Cara's first stop was to the yacht club. They had made a few new friends there in the past few days so she thought she would ask their advice on where to find a house, sort out residency and prepare themselves for a lifetime in the sun.

Cara arrived at the club just as the restaurant was opening. She realised she had not eaten breakfast in the rush to get to the airport and to see the others off.

She ordered a full English breakfast which surprised the waiter, but she suddenly felt ravenous.

As she ate, she looked out of the window across the marina. The water sparkled with the overhead sun. She felt a warm glow of happiness wash over her. She felt she had come home. No more flitting from one place to the next. New York was an experience but she had never felt at home as she did now.

As Cara ate her breakfast, the restaurant began filling up. It was now late morning and the early lunchers were tucking in. As usual, the rum poured freely but Cara declined. She didn't need an alcohol fix; she couldn't be happier. All thoughts of the gun and numerous passports had left her.

In just a couple of hours, she had the names of two letting agents, one very good contact for buying an apartment and had even found out the name of a good school. A little early, she thought, but it might matter with the location of the apartment. She also knew where the local medical centre was, the dentist and good supermarkets. All that over one lunch.

Ian had left her more than £10,000 in cash—she had wondered why he had so much on him—but she needed it now as she couldn't find her credit card. It was always in her purse, but she had not been able to find it for a week or so. She had had no need for it on the boat so had not worried. Ian had said he would cancel it and report it missing so she could get a replacement sent to the yacht club. He really could be so thoughtful and caring.

She paid her bill and set off for the centre of town—not a big place—but had most things she might need. She came across an internet café so thought she would check her e-mails and send one to Julia telling her all their plans.

As she logged on to Hotmail she was pleased to see she had three e-mails, one from Julia, one from her neighbour in New York and one from someone she didn't recognise.

Her thoughts drifted back to her carefree days at university when she first met Julia.

She was on the same law course as she was and had a room on her floor in halls. Julia came from Southern Ireland and had a warm, friendly accent. Cara and Julia became lifelong friends.

One evening, the two caught the bus into town and went to a wine bar they had heard other students talking about. Money was short so they would have to make their drink last all evening unless they were lucky enough to 'pull' and have their drinks bought for them.

They bought their wine and settled themselves on bar stools to have a good view of the rest of the local talent. They had been there an hour and had just about managed to make their drinks last when the barman put two more full glasses in front of them.

"From him in the corner", he explained in as few words as he could be bothered to utter. They turned to find out who 'him in the corner was' only to find the back of Ian's head as he left the wine bar. "That's him just leaving," said the barman of few words. "Why would he bother if he wasn't on the pull?"

Cara and Julia sipped their wine as Cara told Julia about how she had met him. He was the one who stood out on the first night in the university bar. Tall, strong, quiet, yet he had a presence. He didn't need to do or say anything. You noticed Ian. She was intrigued and chose her moment to strike—not to a mushy or slow song on the jukebox, but to an upbeat, lively one—Scissor Sisters—Ain't no dancing tonight. How could he say no? But he did. "Not my rhythm," he said, dismissing her nonchalant, but pushy plead for a dance. "Well, what is your rhythm," she responded. "Depends on my mood, and as you have no idea what mood I'm in, you'll never know what to put on!"

Despite his arrogance, she was even more intrigued. She had always been the belle of the ball at school and A-level college. She was used to handling men situations. But this one was interesting, if a little irritating. She decided she would wait. And make him wait. She looked around the bar, saw an athletic-looking student surrounded by girls. He would do.

She waited until there was the ideal slow tempo and walked over to him. She pushed her way through the gaggle waiting for him to ask for a dance, took him by the hand and led him to the dance floor. Not quite the venue for romance with drunken students, empty cigarette packets and beer cans littering the floor, but still room to show Ian she was a force to be reckoned with.

Jack was a cool dancer, enveloping her in the way she wanted Ian to see. But Ian had gone—nowhere to be seen. Her efforts were wasted. She kissed Jack on the cheek and said, "See you around," and disappeared into the warm September night. As the door closed behind her, she heard Jack, "What was all that about?" But she was on a mission. She went back to her room and planned her next move.

In the morning, she went to the new admissions office and said she had accidentally picked up a pen in the bar the night before and thought she should return it as it was a silver one of obvious value.

She scanned the list of the new undergraduates until she found what she was looking for. Ian Campbell or Iain Dickinson. Luckily, only two Ians in the new intake; one was studying physics, one business management. Both in Block B in halls.

On her way to Block B, she spotted Sir Arrogance going into the lift up to the refectory. She went straight to Block B, knocked on the door of Room 87 and was greeted by a very sleepy, hungover Iain Dickinson. She made an excuse for knocking on the wrong door and went to Room 32. No answer. *Must be his room,* she thought. Just as she turned to leave, the double doors at the far end of the corridor crashed open and two students in tracksuits came laughing through the door, followed by Ian. She was caught. She turned to go the other way, when she heard, "Still after me then? Did your homework well to find my room number so quickly. I'm impressed."

She wanted to run, call him an arrogant pig. But instead, she coolly replied, "If I see something I want, I go for it and if I find it's not something I want after all, I drop it dead. Time will tell." God! Where had that come from? Now, she was impressed with herself.

She turned, walked slowly to the double doors and was gone.

"Just playing hard to get, obviously used to doing things his way in his own time," said Julia.

Cara went back to her e-mails. She opened Julia's first, eager to hear her friend's news. Her southern Irish accent even showed through her writing. Cara could imagine her friend talking fast and furiously about University, about others they had got to know in Sheffield and about how her course was doing. She said she was jealous of her friend's lifestyle—sailing, popping down to the Caribbean, New York, what next? Cara had a sudden pang of homesickness. She would have loved to have met up with Julia, gone to a bar and relived their times together. Such a lot had happened in such a short time. One day soon, they would meet again. Maybe Julia would come out to see them.

Cara then went on to the next e-mail from her New York neighbour, Karen. Karen was a New Yorker, through and through, bold and a little brash but good fun with a kind heart. She had taken Cara under her wing, introduced her to friends at the gym and had generally been a good neighbour.

As Cara began to read, she felt that old fear creeping over her again.

Dearest Cara,

I have been so worried about you. I tried so many times to call you and even tried Ian's mobile but I don't think I have the right number. Where are you now? I got your e-mail about your trip to Exuma but that was ages ago. I don't know if you have heard about the fire. There was an awful blaze in the apartment block late one night. They think it was arson but I haven't heard the results of their investigations. Your flat was completely destroyed, same as the one above. We all had to be evacuated as the building isn't safe. We're now living around the corner in Philadelphia Square. The police were trying to find you—at first they thought you might be in the flat but then realised your car had gone. I am so sorry to have to tell you this by e-mail if you didn't know.

Some men came to the apartment block, too, the morning after it happened. They were looking for Ian but I said you were both away. I don't know why, but they didn't seem very nice. They left me a mobile number and asked me to call if I heard from you. When I eventually got your e-mail saying you were going to Exuma I called them and immediately wished I hadn't. They were really awful. Very threatening and said they would find me if I wasn't telling the truth. They made me give them your e-mail address. I hope I did the right thing telling them about Exuma.

I feel so sorry for you. All your possessions gone. Nothing left and then these hard nuts after you both.'

"Nothing left," said Cara, out loud to herself. "Why? What is going on? Who are these men?" The questions poured out of her.

Karen continued, *"Please let me have a phone number so I can call you. Mine has changed because we were evacuated. Take care, Cara. I miss you."*

Cara immediately tried to call Ian but couldn't get through. She suddenly felt very alone in an unfamiliar place. There wasn't anyone she could talk to.

Without her realising it, tears rolled down her cheeks. She had never felt so alone, co completely lost. She felt the baby kick inside her. Could he or she really feel her emotions?

She then felt a hand on her shoulder and a soft voice. "Can I help?" said Joanne Clark. "I'm sorry, I couldn't help but notice your sadness."

Cara felt the woman was genuine and kind but she was wary. She wasn't sure why she was wary, but she didn't really know who or what to trust any more.

"I'll be okay," she replied. "Just homesick and my husband's away on business."

Joanne knew it wasn't the truth—she had heard Cara talking out loud—but she didn't pursue it.

"Fancy a coffee," she asked. "I'm Joanne. Joanne Clark. Been living here for 20 years. Almost a local."

Cara relaxed a little, accepted her offer of coffee and spent a pleasant hour chitchatting, giving nothing away. Her experiences since she met Ian had changed her. No longer the easy-going, loving life young girl just starting university.

The only thing she gave away was that she was pregnant and that she and her husband were hoping to set down roots on the island.

"Great," said Joanne, "We can be friends."

Yes, but for how long, thought Cara. Every time she had settled down and made friends they had to move again. *This time,* she thought, *I want to stay put.*

The day was disappearing fast and all she had managed to do was eat and find an internet café. She had already forgotten how good she had felt before reading her e-mails. But what was the rush? Ian wouldn't be back for at least a week.

"Why don't you come to my house for supper?" Joanne had interrupted Cara's thoughts. "I can drive you home later."

Home? thought Cara. *I don't even have a home. Come to think of it, just at this moment I don't have a husband, a house, any friends or a base. I am completely alone.* The tears started again.

Joanne sat quietly for a while and then said, "You have me as your friend," as if reading her thoughts. "I'd like to help, whatever it is."

This time Cara wasn't so wary and smiled at Joanne. "Thank you, Joanne. You don't know how much that means to me just at this moment."

Joanne drove Cara to the south of the town. As the road climbed up the hillside, dusk started to fall. The lights of the boats at anchor looked beautiful against the black sea. Joanne pulled in to a tiny drive outside a small house built into the Cliffside.

"Welcome to my little bit of paradise," she said. "Come in and make yourself at home."

Joanne showed Cara around the very modest house. The rooms were very small and the décor minimalist. Just the odd painting, a vase and lots of books. Cara loved it. As she wondered around, Joanne pottered about in the kitchen preparing supper. When Cara reached the kitchen, she saw why Joanne lived here. One wall of the kitchen was all glass—window and double doors opening on to a balcony. The balcony, Joanne explained, hung over the cliff side giving her a panoramic view, north to the town harbour, east across the beautiful Caribbean Sea and west towards the furthest tip of the island.

At night, it was beautiful with all the lights on land and boats at anchor, and during the day the scene changed to greens and blues—just as beautiful.

Maybe this place really would become home, thought Cara. *If she could find somewhere like this...*

The two new friends ate their meal on the balcony and Joanne explained how she had come to leave England and settle in the Caribbean.

"I was married to a Merchant seaman and when he left the Navy, he decided to come here and try to set up a ferry service between the islands. Just a small business with a boat taking up to ten passengers.

"It was great for a while but he never did anything properly. He skipped the paperwork and regulations until the authorities caught up with him and shut the ferry service down. It was a shame because the islands needed something like that. Rob, of course, blamed everyone but himself, including me and after a couple of years we split up and he went back to England.

"I had fallen in love with this place so stayed on and here I am 20 years later."

"But how do you live?" said Cara. "Do you have a job?"

"To begin with, I had three or four jobs at once. Delivery driver for a supermarket supplying the cruise ships, cleaner for the marina offices early in the mornings and bar work in the evening. It was a bit tiring but I was happy. Then I started to paint, just watercolours of places around the island. I sold them at the local market and found the tourists loved them. I eventually got enough money to rent this place and then ten years ago I was left some money so I bought it."

Cara thought how strong Joanne was to cope on her own and make a life here. She didn't think she would ever be so strong.

"This place is so beautiful," said Cara. "Just beautiful. I hope I can find somewhere like this for Ian and me to rent."

"There are a lot of beautiful places on this island and on some of the other islands nearby," said Joanne. "I tell you what, why don't we go to the agents' offices in the morning and we can go and see a few. I'll show you around this beautiful island."

"That would be lovely," said Cara. "Yes, it really would."

The two women sat and chatted late into the night, Cara eventually let her barriers down and opened up to her new friend. She then told her about the fire in New York and the fact that all hers' and Ian's possessions had gone. Burnt in the fire.

When Cara said goodbye after Joanne drove her back to the Buccaneer, she knew she had made a new friend. A real friend who seemed to understand Cara's sadness without needing to know more. She got into bed looking forward to the next day; maybe she would find another little piece of paradise, just like Joanne's home.

She had not heard from Ian and presumed he must be preoccupied with finding the burnt out building which was their home. *What a shock for him*, she thought. At least she didn't have to see it. Her thoughts began to turn again to Karen's e-mail, but she chose to close her mind to it, just for the moment. She would deal with it in her own time. And then she remembered the third e-mail that she hadn't opened. She made a mental note to go back to the internet café after looking at houses with Joanne.

The next morning, Cara was up early. She had showered, dressed and tidied the boat before 8 am. Joanne arrived just after 9 and the two women headed for the estate agents' offices in town.

They picked up details of four apartments and houses within a few miles of the town. If Ian was going to open a new office, he would need to be central.

The first apartment was in the main town, great for Ian, but not for her. "There is no peace here," she said to Joanne. "No view, just noise."

"Okay, next one," said Joanne. "It's about five miles away. Should be much better."

The two women got back in the jeep and headed towards the airport. As the car climbed the winding road, Cara knew it was the wrong direction.

"Sorry Joanne," she said, "This one isn't right either."

"But we haven't even got there," Joanne laughed. "This is where a man would say, 'Women!' Where's the logic?"

They both laughed and Joanne turned the jeep around and headed back towards the town. She didn't need to ask why it wasn't right.

The third was better; a little two-bedroomed apartment with a small garden along a track a few miles from town.

"I know I'm being fussy," said Cara. "But I need space, not inside, but out and this one is too tucked away in the trees."

Joanne pulled out on to the main road again. "We're not far from my house. Shall we stop for a coffee?"

As Cara walked out on to the balcony she knew this was what she wanted. Space and the air to breathe.

Joanne noticed Cara enjoying the view.

"It's great, isn't it?"

Two completely different views by night and day, but both just as beautiful. Just at that moment Cara's phone rang. It was Ian.

He said nothing of the fire or the burnt-out apartment. Cara assumed he didn't want to shock and upset her but she really wanted to know if anything was left. Had they really lost everything—her photographs, books, pictures, address book, CDs, everything? She said nothing. That was the way she dealt with everything now, as far as Ian was concerned. She was no longer sure of the man she adored, the man she had thought she would spend the rest of her life with.

Joanne noticed the resigned look and the 'small talk.' She was surprised Cara had not mentioned whatever it was in the e-mail which had upset her so much, but then thought that perhaps the bad news had actually been about Ian.

The two women got back in the jeep and drove on for another few miles, with just one more apartment to see. Joanne's mobile phone broke their silence. As she stopped at the side of the road to take the call, Cara could tell by Joanne's excitement that it was good news. As she flipped her phone shut, Joanne said, "That was my neighbour. I saw her early this morning and asked her to let me know if any apartments became available. The one just 50 yards up the hill from me will be vacant in three weeks' time. The tenant gave notice last week—he's going back to St Thomas in the US Virgin Islands. Isn't that great?"

Cara couldn't believe it. In just 24 hours her life had turned around again and was back on track. She knew Joanne would become a very good friend.

"Can we go and see it?" she asked.

"I'm sure we could. The tenant's still in it but I've met him a couple of times. I'm sure it will be okay."

Within less than an hour, Cara had not only seen the apartment and loved it but had signed up for a year's lease. She called Ian and this time got through. He was quiet and seemed subdued at first but soon joined her excitement when she described the apartment and told him all about Joanne.

"Better find us a car next," he said. "And make sure it's big enough for a buggy! I love you Cara. You're just great."

Once again, Cara felt as she did that night just a year ago at the Savoy.

Her mind went back again to her early days with Ian. He had drifted in and out of her life, each time crumbling the foundations of her existence. He had disappeared again with no contact for five weeks. Just as she had decided she needed to forget about him and catch up with all the studying she had skipped, she had a text message. "Darling, dinner tonight. The Savoy Banquette Restaurant. 8 pm. Ian."

She, at last, had his number. She called it immediately but it was switched off. She knew she shouldn't go and knew Julia would not approve, so she didn't tell anyone. She left her room at 2 pm with a small suitcase, her credit card and make-up bag. She went straight to the railway station and caught the next train to Waterloo. Just three hours after receiving his text message, she was handing over her credit card to pay for a black dress and strappy sandals in a very up-market shop in Knightsbridge. No, Julia would definitely not approve. But she was sure the Savoy would not approve of the usual student gear of jeans and baggy jumper. By 7.30 pm she was in the toilet of the Strand Palace just opposite the Savoy. She changed and did her hair and make-up and then packed her old clothes, including her student duffle coat, into her suitcase. As she left the hotel, she quickly crossed the street, entered the Savoy and climbed the stairs to the first floor. She then took the lift back down to the ground floor, which opened opposite the reception desk. As the concierge looked up, she handed him her small suitcase and said, "Please, keep this in your secure storeroom until I return. I don't want to leave it in my room."

Then she turned and headed for the Banquette Restaurant before the concierge could ask for her room number. As she entered the restaurant, she saw Ian's smile look across the room at her. He was here, on time and waiting for her. It was all worth it.

She had not seen or heard from him for five weeks but there was no explanation. As she approached the table he held out his hands, took hers and kissed her—just like at the tearooms. She melted immediately and all her fears floated away.

Cara did not want the evening to end. He was warm, gentle and loving; told her about his childhood, growing up on a tea plantation in India run by his parents. He went to school in England and spent long summers and happy Christmases in India with his sister, Janine. He grew up wanting to build an empire; his own empire, buying and selling whatever was wanted. His business studies course at Sheffield was just a step his father had made him take, not one he felt necessary. He was already a player in the global markets.

He told her he loved her, had fallen in love with her that first night in the university bar. He knew she was the one for him for the rest of his life.

Cara forgot everything; forgot Julia's warnings and her lonely nights in the past five weeks thinking she would not see him again. She forgot about the warnings from her lecturers that if she didn't sort herself out she would be thrown off the course by the summer. She hadn't even thought about how she would get home that night.

At the end of the evening, Ian called the waiter and told him to deliver his order to Room 507. He stood up, took Cara by the hand and led her to Room 507 where the champagne bucket had already been delivered.

As he undressed her, she felt she had never experienced such love before. His touch on her breasts left her pleading for more and as he slowly undressed, Cara felt her world ignite—a longing for him she had never felt for anyone before.

When he finally opened the champagne at 4 am Cara knew her world was complete. They drank their first glass thirstily, sipping between kisses, and as he poured more over her breasts and stomach, Cara did not want him to stop. She eventually fell into a deep sleep feeling full of good food, good champagne and above all, love.

But when she woke up at 9 am he was gone. There was no sign of him, just a note saying he had been called away. No 'love, Ian,' no kisses. But Cara was not going to let those fears creep back in. Last night had been the best night of her life. She showered and dressed and left the room. As she walked out of the lift on the ground floor, she heard someone mention room 507 but as she still didn't even know much about Ian or his business, she didn't want anyone asking her questions. After all, it didn't look good; still dressed in evening wear and leaving alone. What might they think?

She hurried out of the door and out into the Strand, diving onto the nearest bus to take her back to the train station. It wasn't until she was on the train to Sheffield that she realised she had not picked up her suitcase. All her favourite clothes—jeans, baggy jumper, trainers, duffle coat were all in there. Perhaps she could phone the hotel when she got back and ask them to send it on.

A mixed bag of emotions filled her on her journey north. He loved her. He had chosen her. Hadn't he?

Back in her room in halls she wrote herself a letter. She explained to herself why she felt as she did, why she had gone and why he made her feel so good. She excused his sudden departure.

Over the next month, Cara read and re-read the letter to persuade herself she hadn't dreamed her night at the Savoy—her night of pure love and passion with Ian. But still there was no word. She couldn't talk to anyone, not even Julia because she knew what she would say, but Cara knew he would come back to her. No one could pretend that much and spend so much on dinner and the room if he didn't feel what he said he did.

Exactly five weeks to the day, Cara had taken the train to London, Ian turned up at Uni. She came home from lectures one afternoon to find him in her bed with his usual big smile she had grown to love. "Hi sweetheart, have you missed me? Got called away on a business deal," was all he explained. She felt a mixture of anger, love and confusion. Love won. He took her in his arms and all was forgotten.

Then, as suddenly as he had appeared back in her life, he went down on one knee and said, "Will you marry me?"

A week later they were husband and wife, marrying in a register office in Pinstone Street, Sheffield. They called two strangers in from the street as witnesses. No pomp. No ceremony. Ian didn't like that.

Chapter 7

The days and weeks that followed, changed her life forever. No longer was she the girl from a working-class background whose parents had given her an education, a solid background, and an ambition to be a lawyer.

Cara didn't know how she was going to tell her parents. Ian had to go away the day after the wedding to finalise a good business deal he said would bring them a secure future together. She was so proud of him. She went to find Julia and face the music.

Julia was in the library surrounded by case studies relating to business and contract law. Cara sat down next to her and whispered, "I just got married."

"WHAT?" exploded Julia. The two almost ran out of the silent library and went to the square outside the university bar. "Who, how, when?" Julia rattled off a dozen questions.

Cara simply said, "Ian, yesterday." She explained the London trip and how she had felt with him and slowly Julia realised there was no point in saying anything. It was too late. Cara returned to her room and organised all her books and notes. She then wrote a letter to her tutor explaining that she had to go home for a few days to deal with a family matter but that when she returned she would catch up on her work and knuckle down again. She was happy. She would finish her degree and then she would be able to join Ian in his business. Maybe be the company lawyer. What more could she ever want?

As she walked up the garden path leading to the familiar old green front door, Cara had a sudden pang of guilt, panic and terror all rolled into one emotion. Her parents had worked hard all their lives and had gone without over the years to make sure she could get the best education to lead her to law school.

How would they take the news? It mattered more than anything to her that they would be happy for her and above all, would like Ian. But he wasn't even there for them to meet him and she wasn't even sure when he would be.

She walked up to the front door and rang the bell. Even though she still had her key she felt it would be too much of a shock for her to just walk in. Her parents were over 70 and were beginning to show their age. Her father had been a greengrocer all his life, leaving school at 15 and running a market stall with his father. When his father died, he used his very small inheritance as a deposit for a tiny corner shop in Market Harborough. He married Cara's mother four years later and they lived a happy married life, working all hours.

For many years, they were childless and thought that was their fate until Cara came along as a great surprise. The three were happy together, living and working until her parents retired last year. They sold the shop and bought a small Victorian terraced house just off the Kettering Road which they said would be Cara's one day when they passed on.

Cara heard the familiar sound of her mother's footsteps approaching the front door. She could imagine her mother drying her hands on her pinny as she was bound to have had her hands in the sink doing some domestic chore. Her mother opened the door and her face lit up at the sight of Cara, but soon turned to concern as to why her daughter had come home unexpectedly in the middle of term. "Don't worry, Mum, it's nothing bad. I just needed to see you." *Well, it was almost the truth,* Cara thought to herself.

"Where's Dad? Is he home?" Cara asked. "He's just popped to the library; he'll be back soon. Have you eaten? Have you had lunch? Shall I get you some soup?" Her mother was straight back into maternal mode and Cara hadn't even reached the kitchen.

"No, I'm fine," she replied. "Had a sandwich on the train."

After the usual 101 questions from her mother, Cara felt panic beginning to well up inside her. She was about to shatter her parents' dreams. How would they take the news? Would they be too disappointed they weren't at the wedding? Just as her panic was beginning to spiral out of control, she heard her father's cheerful voice in the hall. "Who's here, Mother? Whose is this suitcase?" Cara rushed down the hall and threw her arms around her father's neck.

"It's me, don't you recognise the case you bought me?" After the questions her mother had asked were repeated by her father, the time drew near to come clean. She could never hurt them, but would her news be good or bad for them?

Without another word, Cara blurted out, "I got married yesterday." But at the same time, she burst into tears. Her parents sat there at the kitchen table as she had seen them a hundred times before, but this time they said nothing. Their mouths were open as if they were in mid-sentence, but there was no sound.

Cara tried to fill the silence telling them about Ian, how successful he was, how he loved her, about being brought up in India, his parents' tea plantation. But still they said nothing. A tear rolled down her mother's cheek as her father banged his fist on the table. "You are 18," he roared. Cara was shocked. She had never heard her father even raise his voice before. "You are just starting out. You can't possibly know this man."

"But I love him," Cara explained, as if that would put their minds at ease and answer all their questions.

"You don't know anything about love. You are just a schoolgirl. Why have your mother and I worked all our lives to give you a good education? For you to throw it away on the first man you meet."

"I'm not throwing it away," Cara yelled back.

"But of course you are. The next thing is you'll be expecting his baby…or is that why you've rushed into marriage. I can't believe you've been so stupid with some smooth-talking fly by night." Cara had never heard her father shout; had never known him to lose his temper. She looked at her mother whose eyes had filled up. What had she done? But she loved Ian, loved everything about him, including the mystery about him.

"I am not stupid," she retaliated. "I love him and he loves me. You don't even know him. How can you judge him?"

"Well, where is he?" shouted her father. "If he had an ounce of decency about him, he would be here with you now; here to support you, here to meet his new relations." Deep down Cara knew he was right, but how could she agree. She had made her bed and…

Instead, she said, "He's completing a very big business deal that will buy us our first house."

"But this is your house. You know your mother and I will leave it to you. This is your home. We are putting the deeds in your name."

"But we can't live here, not with you."

Her father misunderstood. "So we're not good enough for you now; too working class. My god, you've only been at university for a few weeks. How could you have thrown away your background, your upbringing already?"

"I haven't," Cara replied. "You just don't understand."

"Of course, I understand. He's bedded you and now you're eating out of the palm of his hand—throwing away your education, your degree…"

But before he could finish, Cara shouted back, her anger rising at this dismissal of her love, her man, her husband! "I'm going to finish my degree and be his company lawyer, and…" But before she got it all out, her father's face turned purple and he staggered backwards, trying to grip the edge of the table. As he fell slowly to the floor, Cara knew her news had killed him. Her father died of a heart attack right there on the kitchen floor.

Over the next few days, Cara and her mother tried to take in what had happened. Her father had been her rock all her life; was always there when either she or her mother needed him. And now, she had killed him.

The funeral came and went and her mother slowly began to wither. The life had gone out of her. Not even Cara could bring a smile to her. Cara tried to talk about her happy childhood to remind her mother of all the happy times they had enjoyed as a family. But it was no use. Her mother felt the only two people who had ever mattered in her life had passed on—her beloved husband to the grave and her beloved daughter to some man who somehow had killed them both. She thought whatever happened, she would never find a place in her heart for Ian. She couldn't even bring herself to say his name. What had she to live for now?

Cara had tried desperately to call Ian since the awful day she had arrived at her parents' house but his mobile was either not on or not working. It didn't even ring. Where was he? Could she cope with married life like this?

After a couple of weeks Cara returned to university and resumed her course. She buried herself in her work and soon caught up with the many weeks she had either missed or dawdled through lectures. She went home every weekend to see her mother, organised a home help, gardener, cleaner and meals on wheels, but as the weeks went by, her mother became more and more withdrawn, more resigned to the inevitable.

Ian returned a month after they were married and as he walked back into Cara's life for the fourth time, was taken aback by his wife's distraught tears as she clung to him. She told him all about the visit to tell her parents, the row with her father, the emotional blackmail about him putting their house in Cara's name and how he had misunderstood her reply. She went on to describe the awful moment when she knew her news had killed her father and about the weeks which had followed.

She waited for his response. There was nothing at first. She didn't see the faint smile appear on his face as he stared out of the window.

Chapter 8

"Coffee's ready." Joanne brought her back to reality.

Cara hoped more than anything that their new life in the British Virgin Islands would bring them total happiness again, especially with their baby.

Three weeks later, Cara and Ian were moving in to their new home with Joanne and Ian nagging Cara to take it easy. So she did exactly that, sat out on the balcony and soaked up the sun and view.

As she sat there, she could hear Joanne and Ian chatting. She was pleased they got on. It was important to her.

"Thank you so much for finding us this apartment," said Ian. "We have been so excited about moving in. It's so good we will be settled in and sorted in plenty of time for the baby. I've found an office in town and I'm hoping to get a new contract in the next week or so."

"What line are you in," asked Joanne. "Cara never did say."

"Buying and selling," replied Ian. "Whatever anyone wants, I'll get it and sell it to them. It's an interesting business, one day you're dealing with fine art, the next properties in Spain. Never a dull moment."

"Sounds good," said Joanne. "Not something you could ever get bored with then?"

"I'll cook for you both tonight as you won't have time."

"That will be great," said Ian. "We should have this place sorted out in no time. We don't have much stuff."

"Yes, Cara said you had lost everything in the fire. Must have been awful," said Joanne.

Cara felt the baby kick as her stomach lurched. She had never mentioned the e-mail from Karen to Ian because he had never mentioned the fire to her. What a mess. How can this happen? Why is she so scared to talk to her husband about such devastating news?

Ian said nothing. Nothing to Joanne and nothing to her. Just carried on unpacking the few possessions they had. Joanne noticed the conversation shut down and immediately felt the tension. She walked through to the balcony, squeezed Cara's hand and mouthed, "Sorry" to her though she didn't know why. She then left to go and prepare dinner.

"What sort of wife are you?" Ian growled. "How did you know and why didn't you tell me you knew?" With that he lashed out at her, knocking her off her chair. He was careful not to leave bruises this time as he punched and kicked the prostrate Cara.

"How the fuck did you know?" he yelled, "and why the silence?"

"Because you didn't say anything, I didn't know what to do," she whimpered. "I checked my e-mails and there was a long one from Karen. It made me scared. She told me about two men looking for you and how when she phoned them to say we would be in Exuma, they threatened her if she was lying. Who are they Ian? Who burned our apartment? Why are they after you?"

"YOU!" He exploded. "You are the one betraying me."

"What am I doing Ian? How am I betraying you?"

But she didn't hear an answer. The blow from Ian's fist knocked her out.

When the ambulance arrived, so did Joanne. In the stillness of the evening she had heard the shouting, had heard Ian, and although she didn't see anything, she knew her friend was being attacked. She had called the police and the ambulance. Would the baby survive what was obviously a vicious attack?

"I saw the ambulance go past," she explained, "and when it stopped here I thought I should come," she lied.

Ian had composed himself and played the caring, loving husband. "She tripped and almost fell over the balcony. I think she hit her head on the railings."

"Oh God, I hope the baby's all right."

Joanne noticed the fear in his voice, the slight tremble. At that moment, she hated him. She really knew very little about these two, but she knew enough to know Cara needed a friend. She followed the ambulance to the hospital trying to work out what had happened. When she had first met Cara in the internet café, she knew she was a 'victim'. There was a fear in her eyes and a lost look which brought out Joanne's maternal side. She was more than 20 years older than Cara, but saw herself in her new friend. A young woman in a strange country trying to find her way.

Cara had regained consciousness in the ambulance, but her vision was blurred. She could make out Ian's shape sitting next to her as she lay on the trolley but that was all. No features, just shapes.

She put her hand to her head and felt the throbbing bulge. She ached everywhere—her legs, her arms, her head, and her stomach. *Oh God!* she thought. *Please, let the baby be alright.*

She couldn't remember what had happened, she just knew it was bad. Ian held her hand and stroked her forehead. "Ian, where am I? What happened? Did I fall?"

"Shhh, darling," said Ian, trying to decide if he could get away with this latest attack. "You had a terrible fall. Almost fell over the balcony."

"I can't see properly, Ian. What's happened? Is the baby ok? Oh God, please let the baby be alright."

Just for a moment Ian felt desperate. How could he have done this to the only person in his life who really mattered? But she had betrayed him. She was the one who gave his enemies the path to track him down. He regained his composure and said he would go and find the doctor. "Don't leave me Ian, please," she sobbed. "I need you." But he was gone, ignoring her, his mind set to find out if Cara and the baby would have any permanent damage. He had to know—he was back in control of himself.

Over the next few weeks, Cara's sight returned to normal and the baby continued to grow inside her. When Ian was working Joanne was there for her. Cara didn't notice Joanne was never there any more when Ian was.

She thought she would perhaps like to go home to see old friends and her old home before the baby was due so told Ian her plans when he came home one evening. She thought he would make a big fuss about her going. On the face of it, they had just had a wonderful sailing holiday for a few weeks.

Instead, he just said, "Of course, you must go. I'll miss you but take your time while you can. Once the baby's here it will not be so easy."

"Thanks, Ian, I'd really like to go and, as you say, once the baby's born it will not be so easy to travel."

But whatever happened, Ian was not going to let her leave the island. He came home the next day and said he had sorted the flights. They were booked for the following Thursday, leaving at 4 pm, changing in Antigua and then straight to Heathrow. She would have two weeks there and then return within a week of the deadline for her not to fly until after the baby was born.

55

Then, while she was busy in the kitchen, he took her passport, made an excuse to go out, and burnt it.

Cara was excited even though the darkest doubts she had about Ian began to creep back in. Was he really the monster she had decided he was? Now he was the caring, loving husband, buying her flowers, taking her out for romantic dinners, and being very concerned for her and the baby's welfare.

She went to see Joanne the next morning to tell her the news.

"That will be so nice for you," said Joanne. But Cara knew she was holding something back. She wanted to ask her friend if she knew exactly what happened the night they had moved in, but she couldn't because she felt as though she was betraying Ian if she did.

Was she giving Ian yet another chance? She had certainly softened towards him the previous evening and had not resisted when he reached out for her when they went to bed. She just couldn't understand how he could be two totally different characters.

Joanne said she could do a bit of decorating for her while she was away.

"I'll enjoy that," she said. "Unless, of course, I'd be treading on Ian's toes."

"Of course not," said Cara. "Ian's not exactly Mr DiY. He'd be really pleased."

"Well, check it out with him before you go, choose the colours and I'll do the rest."

"Fancy lunch today," said Cara. "I sort of feel like celebrating."

The two women sat watching the antics in the harbour as two big yachts vied for the same berth. The American skipper, who had arrived first, was attempting to berth stern-to, but was having difficulty as the afternoon breeze was blowing the boat sideways.

Cara and Joanne sat bemused at the spectacle, not quite understanding what the problem was. Then the German boat decided to seize the opportunity and tried to go into the same berth bows-to.

All hell let loose. The American skipper took great exception to this, shouted a few insults and ended up ramming the stern of his boat into the bow of the German's.

Cara and Joanne smiled. "Just men," said Joanne. "They can't do the decent thing and give way."

The two women laughed and then Joanne said, "Are you okay, Cara? I sometimes worry about you."

"Sure," said Cara. "Why shouldn't I be? My fall the day we moved into the apartment is well behind me now and the doctors have given me and the baby the all clear."

"Just wondered," said Joanne, quietly deciding Cara would talk when she was ready.

"My ex-husband was a charming 'Jack the lad' to all but me. After five years of beatings, I had had enough. That's why we split up. I couldn't take any more. My self-esteem was rock bottom. It was always my fault."

"I'm sorry," said Cara. "I didn't know."

"But I'm strong and resilient now. I don't let anyone, or anything, bring me down."

Cara was surprised by her tone but let it pass.

"I lost a baby after one of the beatings. That's when I decided I had to get out. I started drinking, even slept around as I wanted to treat all men badly. I would snare them, make them love me and then dump them. I'm not proud of it."

Cara was shocked by the news from her friend.

"But Ian's not bad," she began to say. "He loves me dearly. It's just that he's had such bad luck with his business."

"Yes, Cara," said Joanne. "It's great you are able to go home for a couple of weeks." Cara began to realise Ian's story of how she ended up in hospital was not the same as Joanne's. But she had lied to Ian by not telling him she knew about the fire. She would be more open in future and try to get more involved in Ian's business so she could share his downfalls and celebrate his wins with him.

She still adored him but she knew there was a side to Ian which she did not understand and from which she had to protect herself. They would have a baby in just over three months and that would cement them together as a family.

On the way home, she stopped off at the supermarket and bought all of Ian's favourite food and a special bottle of wine. She also bought him a little card to tell him how much she loved him.

She spent the afternoon tidying the apartment and filling up all the tea light holders on the balcony. Ian phoned to say he would be home at 7 pm so she prepared the evening to show him she was not leaving him but going to England was just because she needed to get some of her personal things and a few of her parents' mementoes before the baby arrived.

Ian came in and dutifully kissed her on the cheek. As he looked around the apartment she knew he was pleased. "You've been busy," he said as he wandered out on to the balcony.

"Looks like my wonderful Cara is back from the blues."

He took her in his arms and kissed her for a very long time.

"You are beautiful," he said finally. "How could I live without you?"

She went to pull away to get him a drink when he lifted her up and carried her to the bedroom.

"I was about to start dinner," she protested mildly.

"Dinner can wait," he said firmly, as he laid her on the bed.

He slowly made love to his wife and took delight in listening to her moans of pleasure. It took them both back to the night at the Savoy.

By 11 pm they had still not eaten so they decided to get up and have a light snack on the balcony. The stars twinkled on the water and the still night was just for them. They sat holding hands and staring out across the bay, needing nothing and no one else.

"I will miss you so much when I go home," Cara broke the silence. "Will you come with me?"

Ian was irritated to be brought back to reality so suddenly but didn't show it. He didn't want to think about what lay ahead. More lies. More deceit. He wanted this night to go on forever.

"I can't, darling," he eventually said. "I have lots happening over the next few weeks to give me time with you and the baby when he arrives."

"He?" replied Cara. "She will be here very soon."

They both smiled, thinking very different thoughts, got up and went to bed.

"Shit, Cara. It's nine o'clock," Ian shouted as he got out of bed. "How can you have let me sleep in? I had a conference call at eight. For Christ's sake," he roared.

Cara awoke with a start, thumping back to reality from the depths of a contented sleep.

"What?" she asked. "What's wrong?"

"You've let me sleep in you stupid bitch. How can I possibly run a business when you do everything to ruin it?"

With that he stormed out of the bedroom and into the shower. Cara followed him, meekly uttering "sorry" after him.

When he came out of the shower, he threw some clothes on and ran out of the house, grabbing his briefcase as he went.

As Cara heard the car start, his mobile phone rang on the balcony. She rushed to get it and go after him but the car had already sped off, spinning its wheels in the roadside gravel as it did so. Cara looked at the phone. 'One missed call' showed on the screen. She pressed the 'show contact' key and saw the letter J come up.

Must be Julie, his secretary, she assumed. Just as Cara was pondering the situation, the phone bleeped again, this time with a text message.

"Where were you last night? I waited up and kept the bed warm for you."

Cara reeled with the shock of the words. Her loving husband, her only world in this unfamiliar place, was cheating on her. Was that what was happening? Could she have misinterpreted the message? She read it again and felt nauseous. She walked to the sink and was sick. She just didn't understand. Ian had shown her last night how much he loved her and told her he could not live without her. How could he betray her and hurt her so much? What was wrong with her? Cara's first instinct was to go straight to Ian's office and confront them. But what good would that do? She must be subtle so she made herself a cup of tea and sat down to contemplate her situation. His anger this morning was understandable, because he was late for work. But nothing else was understandable.

The more she thought about Ian and Julie together the worse she felt. Her stomach lurched and she was sick again. If Ian could lie about this, what else could he lie about? Her thought went back to the Buccaneer and finding the gun. The man she married was someone else. Two people—one her loving husband and one the lying cheat who was capable of something she feared the most. John came into her mind and she suddenly wanted to talk to him. He had said she could call him at any time. She looked up his number and called him. He took a long time to answer the phone and when he did, he sounded very sleepy.

"John," she wailed, and before he could say anything, she sobbed and sobbed and tried to get her story out.

"Cara," John said. "Hold on, I can't understand you. Slow down and take a deep breath."

Cara poured it out—how she had lost everything in the fire in New York, about her hospital stay and now finding out that her husband and his secretary were lovers.

"I'm so sorry, Cara," John said. "I could come down to the Caribbean and see you if you like. I'm in Sydney at the moment but I'm back in Portland tomorrow evening."

Cara wanted him to come but felt it was too much to ask. She needed him to come. He was the only person who knew about the gun, about Ian's mood swings—about so much.

She cried again.

"I'm supposed to be going home to England next week," she said. "I wanted to go home to my parents' house and get some family mementoes before the baby arrives. Now I don't know if I'm strong enough to make the trip on my own."

"Look, I'm due to fly to London next Tuesday after settling a few things in Portland. Why don't I postpone a few days and fly with you," John offered.

"Would you?" Cara replied. "Thank you so much. I just feel so awful at the moment. I can't seem to cope with anything and now all this with Ian and Julie."

"Of course, Cara," said John. "It would be great to see you anyway. Leave it with me and I'll organise my flights. When did you say you were flying out?"

"Thursday afternoon," replied Cara.

"I'll try to be on the island by Wednesday, at the latest. I've got your number so I'll call you when I've sorted it out."

"Thank you so much, John, you are a good friend."

When she put the phone down she felt a little better until her gaze found Ian's phone again. How was she going to cope knowing what she knew.

She went to see Joanne and poured out her sorry story. "How can he?" she pleaded. "He's such a Jeckyl and Hyde. One day, he's so loving and caring, like last night, and the next I find out he should have been in his secretary's bed."

Joanne was obviously shocked by her friend's news as she seemed distant to begin with, deep in thought. Eventually, she said, "What a bastard. How could he do this to you, especially in your condition?"

Cara cried again and let her friend hold her. She needed a prop and Joanne was her only real friend on the island.

"It's good you are going home next week," she said. "It will give you time to work all this out and decide whether to stay here with him or leave and settle back in the UK."

Cara tormented herself re-reading the text message in her head. It didn't make sense. Ian adored her. He told her that and he told her couldn't live without her. Nothing seemed real any more. She drove into town and went to the internet café where she had first met Joanne when she arrived. She needed to return to what she knew. Get back to reality. She checked her e-mails and was very pleased to find one from Julia. Cara wished with all her heart she could be with her friend now—to chat into the early hours as they used to. No cares. No worries. Just a bright future. She read Julia's e-mail, greedily hanging on to every word and re-reading it to try to transport herself back to Julia's room at Uni. Everything was simple then. All they had to think about was getting up in time for lectures and who they might find in the university bar that evening.

Julia told her all about her life, how she was panicking about her exams, how she was applying for post graduate jobs and most of all about James, a third year PE undergraduate who had taught her to play tennis and squash, but most of all, he had taught her how to have fun and not work so hard. She was in love and as happy as she had ever been. They planned to spend the Easter holiday in a secluded stone cottage on Brandon Point, the most western tip of Ireland, and so of Europe. They would take their books and combine exam revision with pure indulgence. There would be just the two of them.

As Cara read Julia's e-mail, she didn't realise tears were pouring down her face. She felt a whole mix of emotions—happiness and love for Julia, jealousy that her life and love seemed so simple and almost anger because Julia would not be in England when Cara was going home. She needed Julia—she didn't really have anyone else.

Although Cara had planned to e-mail Julia and pour her heart out, she no longer could. Her own story was so negative, so bleak and so full of despair.

As she logged out, she turned away from the screen to find a few of the people in the café looking at her. She must have looked a mess with her tear-stained face and blotchy eyes. And not for the first time there. She stood up and walked out into the street, her head buzzing. Scooters, trucks and people filled the street—old men sat in doorways drinking the first of the day's rum. Their black faces lit up when they smiled; the whites of their eyes gleaming, but their yellowing teeth giving away years of decay and neglect. But to Cara, even they seemed happy—even they didn't appear to have a care in the world and yet they had so little. She wandered towards the sea where the cruise ships docked and browsed around the spattering of market stalls nearby. The colourful bandanas, shoulder bags and strings of beads did nothing to brighten her spirits.

The throngs of people pouring out of the bowels of the cruise ship smiled and chatted, excited to be visiting a new town in the Caribbean jewel of the British Virgin Islands. Had Cara felt like that when she arrived on the Buccaneer? It seemed like a lifetime ago when it was actually just a few months. After a little while Cara decided she had to pull herself together, if only for the sake of her unborn baby. She would go to Ian's office in town and pretend she and Ian were the closest and happiest couple there ever was. She would show Julie she couldn't just take Ian away from his wife and soon to be family. She would be strong and battle it out.

As she walked into the outer office she heard laughter coming from Ian's office. Suddenly, the bright, white-walled office with colourful paintings on the walls, seemed to be screaming at her. The paintings now garish. Okay! She would catch them out and force him to choose here and now. She marched into his office and found Julie leaning over Ian's shoulder. They were both looking at something on Ian's desk and were obviously amused by it, whatever it was. "What the hell's going on here?" she bellowed at them. They both stared at her as if she had just landed from Mars. "Do you think I am stupid just because I am pregnant?" she raged on.

"I know all about you two—cosy little set up you have here. But Julie, I am telling you now, I am a force to be reckoned with and you are not taking my husband away from me!"

With that she walked out of the office and back out into the street. She was shaking and crying and wishing Ian would come out to console her and tell her she had got it all wrong. But he didn't. And he didn't come home that evening. Cara found her way to her car and drove away up the long hill. As she sat waiting up for him she persuaded herself she really had got it all wrong.

She had mis-read the text message; she had mis-read the scene in Ian's office. She was just hormonal and emotional because of the baby. Now, she felt very alone and scared. By midnight, Cara was beside herself. She couldn't go through the night like this. She decided to go and see Joanne. It was only a few yards away and she knew Joanne wouldn't mind; she had always told her to call on her whatever the time of day or night.

Cara went out of her front door and into the darkness of the night. It was difficult to focus after leaving the lights of her house. She edged her way along the side of the road, wishing she had brought her torch. It was a still night with only the cicadas for company. On any other night, she would have stopped and looked up at the stars but not tonight. Tonight her eyes were puffy and sore from crying.

She could see in the distance that there was a light on in Joanne's house. It immediately made her feel better. She carried on walking along the edge of the gravel, too scared to walk further into the road. Drink-driving was a matter of everyday life on the island—no-one thought anything of spending an evening drinking rum and Ting, rum and Coke, in fact rum and anything and then getting in their cars to weave their way home along the dusty roads.

As she approached Joanne's house, she could just make out a car or jeep-like vehicle parked outside just beyond the dim light of her sitting room. Just as she thought she should perhaps go home again as Joanne obviously had a visitor, she heard voices through the open windows. She couldn't quite make out any words, just sounds. And then, within the space of a split second, Cara's life was changed forever.

What she saw would live with her for the rest of her life. As a car came up the hill, its lights shone into Joanne's house, and there it was. The sight of her husband, Ian, making love to her only friend on the island, Joanne. The sounds were their groans of ecstasy.

Cara stumbled with the shocking sight of them and fell backwards into the path of the car. The drunk behind the wheel had no chance of avoiding her. The front of his jeep hit her straight on, folding her torso over the bonnet and breaking both her legs.

Chapter 9

It was four weeks before Cara woke up in hospital and the second she opened her eyes, it all came back to her. The text message, the confrontation in Ian's office, the desperation of her situation, seeing Ian making love to Joanne and then total blackness. No pain, just the black memories.

She looked around her hospital room, saw the pale blue curtains with little boats and seagulls on, the whitewashed walls, the numerous monitors next to her bed, and then the neatly folded sheet lying across her legs and body. It was only then that she screamed. She knew she was no longer pregnant.

Her scream brought two nurses into her room, their dark blue uniforms, starched caps and aprons gave them an official look. "Hey Mamma, it's okay. We've been waiting for you to wake up. You sure took your time."

"My baby, my baby," screamed Cara.

"Mamma, he's been waiting for you to wake up, too."

"He", said Cara questioningly. "He?"

"Yes, he, Mamma. He's just up the corridor."

Cara tried to get out of bed to rush to see her son. It was only then that she began to realise her injuries.

"Hey, slow up there, Mamma. We'll get you there just as soon as you've seen Dr Jenkins."

Dr Jenkins was called and was by Cara's bedside in just a few minutes.

"Well, you've given us all a bit of a scare," she said.

"My baby, I want to see my baby," wailed Cara.

"Of course you do, and I'll take you to him in just a few minutes, but first I must carry out a few checks and tell you what happened."

After Dr Jenkins had looked in Cara's eyes, ears, checked blood pressure, temperature and reactions, she told Cara about her son.

"When you came in, we all thought you and the baby could not survive. The car hit you head on and knocked you 50 yards up the hill. You immediately went into labour. You had blood pouring out of you and your legs were twisted and mangled.

"We performed a Caesarean immediately but your baby was in a very bad way. He was born with all his limbs broken and part of his chest crushed, but his head survived injury. Bit of a tough nut, he is.

"He was on a ventilator after we operated—in all he had four operations in the first week, but he slowly began to improve.

"He's still in intensive care and the next couple of weeks will tell us what his future holds.

"At the moment, the only thing we know for sure is that he is profoundly deaf—probably caused by the impact. His inner ear was shaken very severely, or maybe the trauma of his first week."

Cara stared at the doctor unable to take it all in.

"And as for you, Mrs Campbell, mechanically we have fixed you up, but it will be a while before you're are up and about on those pins."

"Please, let me see him now," said Cara quietly.

"Okay, but until we have run thorough checks on you, we'll take you in your bed."

When Cara saw little Richard, an overwhelming feeling of joy enveloped her. She desperately wanted to hold him and never let go, but all his tubes and monitors prevented her.

She could see her dad in his tiny crumpled face—the way her dad looked as he got older. It was then that she thought of Ian and her repulsion for him. The reality of little Richard lying there helpless in a tiny incubator because of him, made her physically sick. She could and would never forgive him this time.

Ian arrived at Cara's bedside an hour later, just as she arrived back from more tests.

"Darling, I've been so worried about you. You gave me such a scare and our little man has been waiting for you to wake up," he said as he tried to cradle her in his arms. She was cold to him and pushed him away.

"Just don't, Ian. Enough is enough. I can't take this life with you any more. I don't know you and I don't really think I ever did."

"But Cara, darling. I know you've had a bit of a shock and little Richard isn't quite what we hoped for…"

"A bit of a shock! Richard not quite what we hoped for…who are you, Ian? Wake up to the real world. I nearly died and so did Richard and all because of you!"

"Me?" he replied. "What do you mean? I know you thought Julie and I had something between us, but you were wrong. You jumped to conclusions because you were a bit, well, hormonal. And we'll see how Richard goes. If he doesn't pull through properly, maybe we could have him adopted and try again. You see, one day we'll have a proper family."

Cara opened her mouth to reply but nothing came out. She knew then that she had to get away from this monster. But how?

It was another six weeks before Richard was well enough to go home. Cara had been discharged within two weeks of waking up. Ian had come to see her every day and talked to her as if nothing had happened. He rarely asked after Richard and seemed to be able to ignore the fact that he was a father. He never went to see him in the nursery and never asked the doctors about his future.

As time went by, Cara struggled to keep hold of the reality of her accident—to remember exactly why she hated Ian so much. He acted as if nothing had happened and so did Joanne. They both visited her in hospital. They both talked about the accident as if they were not the reason she had stepped back in shock into the path of the car. But Cara knew what she had seen and she would never trust either of them again. They tried to make her believe she had seen nothing—or at least had not seen her husband, Ian, making love to Joanne.

Joanne had intimated she had been entertaining an old friend on the night of the accident and had admitted nothing of her affair with Ian. And Ian had said he had been in a bar on his own after work for the whole evening and only knew of the accident as he was driving back up the hill to their apartment and saw the emergency vehicles' flashing lights.

Little Richard was her focus in life now. Whatever happened between her and Ian would not matter anymore. She could and would cope with anything. Richard was the important one now.

By the time he came home, Cara had decorated the nursery for him, bought a cot and lots of colourful mobiles and friezes to brighten his room. Even if he could never hear the nursery rhymes the mobiles played, he could see them and as he focused on them spinning round, his face lit up.

Cara would spend the rest of her life making it up to him for his violent and traumatic birth.

She joined a mother and baby group and made new friends and so did little Richard. He was a happy and contented baby with Cara, but became irritable and unsettled whenever Ian was around.

Ian continued to almost ignore his son, apart from telling Cara to 'shut the brat up' when he cried. But Cara didn't care. Richard was her life now and one day when she and Richard had the strength, she would go home. Home to England. Home to her parents' house. And she would try to forget she ever knew Ian. But Ian had other ideas. He wanted Cara back and he would do anything to get her. But he wasn't stupid enough not to realise that getting Cara back also meant having the little brat around, so after a few months he decided he would play it her way. He would deal with the 'brat' later.

He came home one day with a little push along trolley with plastic building bricks in for Richard. He also had a bunch of red roses for Cara and a bottle of champagne.

"Sorry, I've been so distant," he told Cara. "I'm not very good with babies and I just don't didn't know how to handle a disabled one. Now he's crawling and almost walking I can relate to him more. I'm so sorry, darling."

Cara was very surprised, but also very wary. She had shunned him in every aspect of their lives since the night Richard was born, including in the bedroom and had begun to wonder how they could go on living under the same roof. But this was a bit more of the old Ian, the charmer, the little boy lost in the big bad world. Did he mean it? Could she love him again?

Then Ian brought in another bag full of clothes and toys for Richard.

"I've been shopping," he said. "There's a whole world of stuff out here for kids that I never knew about."

"Look at this," he said, as he pulled out an activity centre with bells and whistles and a siren. "Isn't it great?"

He got down on the floor and showed it to Richard, ringing the bell and making the siren blow.

Cara felt anger burning up inside her. It was all for show. Ian hadn't thought about Richard. This was all for Cara. All to get her back. Richard couldn't hear any of the bells, whistles or siren, but Ian hadn't even considered that.

She decided to say nothing but to pretend she was pleased. She never wanted Richard to witness his father's temper or ever see what a battered wife his mother was.

"That's so great, Ian," she managed to splutter. "At last, you are seeing Richard as your son."

Ian beamed, thinking to himself how easy it was to get around Cara. She never could resist his charm.

That night after Richard had gone to bed, Ian opened the champagne and toasted, "Richard, our little man who one day will do great things."

Cara went along with it, all the time wishing she was on her way home, but she knew it would not be easy getting away from Ian.

She looked at him now, sitting on the balcony, wondering how their lives had changed so much in such a short space of time. How had it? He was still the good-looking, confident man she had met on that first night in the university bar.

She remembered back to their carefree days when she saw him playing tennis one Sunday morning—the day she knew she would never be the same again.

It was a cold Sunday morning in November when the winter sun was shining, Cara decided to get some fresh air from her studies and go for a walk. She watched the usual rugby team battling it out on the touchline and walked on towards the lake. As she saw the ducks waddling at the side of the lake, a tennis ball landed at her feet. She bent to pick it up and heard his voice. Ian, his unmistakeable voice. He was dressed in a very expensive-looking tracksuit and trainers as he bounded up to her and said, "Thanks, my serves are always a bit OTT." His wide smile endeared her even more to him. He was still a little tanned from the summer and looked healthy and fit as he stood there with his equally expensive Wilson in his hand.

"Do you play often?" The words were out before she could stop herself. What a crass thing to say. Why did this man make her feel awkward, inadequate and like a blushing schoolgirl? He decided to ignore her awkwardness and invited her to afternoon tea in the village tearooms.

"4 pm, I'll see you there," and then he was gone, back to the court to dish out yet more punishment to his opponent. He didn't even wait for an answer.

She returned to her room, determined not to go. She would finish her essay, prepare her work for tomorrow's discussion group and send e-mails home.

At 3.55 pm she found herself outside the tearooms having got no more work done. Why did this man have this effect on her? From his accent and his clothes, he was a silver-spooned spoiled brat; not the background she was used to, or even liked.

She was shown to a table by the window where she sat and waited for him. By 4.15 pm she wished she hadn't come. There was no sign of him. By 4.30 pm she was ready to shout abuse at him from the rooftops. But by 4.45 pm she was stunned into silence as he walked through the door, walked over to her with his big, wide smile and kissed her a long and lingering kiss on the lips. She couldn't think of anything to say and was too afraid to try in case she came out with another crass comment, or even worse, her voice wobbled.

They sat and drank their tea and enjoyed their cream scones without much conversation between them. When they had finished and she had recovered her composure, she asked him how the tennis had gone. *That was safe,* she thought. But his reply threw her completely again. This man was different. "Well, as we are now an item, I suppose we'd better swap mobile numbers." She was again lost for words–something that rarely happened to her. She was used to being in control, calling the shots, handling her men well. But this one was like no other. Just as he had keyed her number into his phone, his phone rang. "Be two minutes," he said and with that, stood up and left the tearooms. No goodbye. No 'call you.' No goodbye kiss. Just the bill for her to pay!

As she wandered back to her room, she hoped Julia would be home. She wanted to talk. Was this normal? Was it her? Was it him? Exactly what was "it"? But Julia wasn't there so Cara just carried on and finally sent her e-mails home.

The next morning she got up very early. She hadn't slept well and she still hadn't done any preparation for today's discussions. But she found she couldn't concentrate. That kiss had changed her forever. Nothing would be the same again. That was the only thing she was certain of. As she left her room she was determined she would not let Ian take over. She was at university because she had always wanted to be a lawyer—she had fought hard to get there—state education, no family money, no old boys' network to help her. She got there by sheer hard work. She would not throw it away on some arrogant self-assured pig.

But there was no word from him for two weeks. No phone calls, no notes. She didn't even see him at the tennis court on Sunday—not that she was really looking! But then the flowers arrived. An enormous bouquet of two dozen red roses with a card which simply said, "To our future, Ian."

She raced to Block B and knocked on door 32. No reply. She was about to write a note when the door opposite opened and Steve said, "He's not there. Left two weeks ago."

"What do you mean, he left two weeks ago?" Cara said.

"Dunno, he just said he'd had an offer so was jacking it in."

"But, do you know where he is? Where can I find him?" said Cara.

"Nope, no forwarding address." And with that Steve closed the door and returned to his pit.

Cara didn't know what to think, or how to think, for that matter. Where was he? Why had he left? Why did he send the flowers? For the next two weeks there was no word. Nothing again. No contact. Cara was slowly grinding herself down. She couldn't sleep properly. She couldn't remember the last time she had eaten properly. She had begun to skip lectures and this was only her first term.

Julia was worried. "You have to get a grip," she said. "You don't even know where he's from or even what course he was on and you're letting him take over your life."

"I just can't help it," said Cara. "There's something about him. I think I'll be with him for the rest of my life."

"Give me strength," said Julia, in her strongest Southern Irish accent. "One kiss, a few flowers and you're growing old with him."

"Where do his parents live?

"Where did he go to school?

"Has he got brothers and sisters?

"How old is he?

"What does he want to do with his life—the same as you?

"You know nothing about him except he didn't swoon at your feet on the first night. He didn't call, AND he didn't pay the bill at the tearooms. Not the best CV for your lifetime's partner."

Although Cara knew Julia was right, she was irritated by her bluntness. She had never felt this way before. Was it love? A part of her wished she would never see him again and the rest longed for him. No, she had never felt this way about anyone before.

She remembered how she used to love to run her fingers through his hair, how his fringe still dangled across his right eye. His nose and square chin gave him that all American good guy look, and when he smiled his small dimples could still almost melt her. But only almost.

She looked at little Richard sleeping and after one glass of champagne, Cara began to wish with all her heart she could still love Ian. That he could shed all those awful things about him she had grown to hate. There she sat, feet up on the balcony railings, the stars making the sea below sparkle, but he was just a mirage.

The vision she had was of someone she could love, not the man who had somehow made her life complete and then ripped it apart, bit by bit.

She came back to her senses as Ian poured her another glass.

But this time she wasn't wearing it. "No, Ian, I don't want any more champagne," she said. "I've had a bit of a headache today—it's the weather, I think. So stormy and close. Do you think the locals are right—could be a hurricane coming?"

Ian wasn't listening. He had one thing on his mind and he was going to have it.

He moved across the balcony towards Cara, moving his hands over her as he embraced her. His lips parted hers, despite her attempts to say 'no' and as he picked her up, she knew she could not stop him.

He carried her to the bedroom and kicked the door shut behind him. Cara was desperate. She had sobered up instantly but as she tried to wriggle out of his arms, he lay her on the bed and pinned her down. "No, Ian, no", she cried out. "Please, no."

"Shut up you stupid cow. You are my wife and I will do as I damned well please.

"Don't worry, the brat won't hear you anyway," he laughed a callous, cold laugh that made Cara freeze.

He held her by the throat as he pinned her down.

As he raped her, Ian continued to laugh and shout at her. "Do you think I'm stupid? Don't think you'll ever leave me, because you never will. And if you ever try, just think about Richard."

As he reached his climax, he grunted like a wild animal. Cara lay rigid, unable to cry, unable to say a word. She knew this was her life…

Chapter 10

Over the next year, Cara grew more and more tired and weak. Her resolve to leave and start again in England with Richard, weakened as each day went by. She tried her best to be a happy, smiley mum for Richard, but he, too, began to disappear into his silent world. She had been determined to give him words, to give him communication from the start, but she grew weaker and weaker. To the outside world, Ian carried on as if he had the best home life there could be. But behind closed doors, he treated Cara as his slave, ordered her to clean his house, cook his meals and keep 'the brat' out of his way. And when he felt like it, he raped her. And each rape left her less able to cope with anything, even Richard. The worst was when he came home drunk. He muttered something about 'crack' and went to the safe for his gun.

"They will never get me," he slurred. "I'm far too clever for them."

At that moment, little Richard came into the sitting room and Cara feared for their lives.

"Come to daddy," roared Ian. "Come on you stupid little bastard, come here."

Richard looked terrified. He didn't know what to do. He knew his father was ordering him to do something but he didn't understand. He looked pleadingly at Cara to help him but Cara could do nothing. "Just watch this Richard. This will show you daddy's in charge." And with that he swung the gun at Cara's head. She reeled backwards, falling across the armchair. Richard made a pitiful sound as he ran to his mother's rescue, but Ian pre-empted his move and the next blow sent Richard across the room, hitting the doorpost. Fortunately for him, he didn't see his father rape his mother again.

In the morning, Ian was gone. Cara woke to the sound of Richard whimpering. He was sitting in a puddle of his own urine, shaking and making sounds like an injured animal. Cara went to him immediately, cradling him to her breast. She didn't know how much he had seen of Ian's assault on her.

As she held him, she looked down at herself—her torn dress, her bruises. Then she caught sight of herself in the mirror. Her congealed blood matted in her hair. It was only then that she saw that Richard, too, had suffered an assault by his father. There was blood in his blonde hair at the back of his head. His little Bob the Builder yellow tee shirt was dark at the back from bloodstains. As she held him to her, his little body shook again against her chest. He was having some sort of a fit. In an instant she was on her feet and on the way to the front door. As she opened it, her heart was racing. No! She couldn't lose Richard. What did she have to live for if he wasn't there?

She was shaking as she struggled with the latch to open the door. She clung to Richard, shouting at herself to get a grip, sort it out and save her little boy.

Finally, the door was open and there stood John.

In an instant, John understood the situation. He took Richard from Cara, put him on Cara's lap in his car and raced round to the driver's seat.

"Where's the hospital—in town, where?"

"Yes, turn around, back into town. Please, hurry John, I think he's fading…"

By the time they reached the hospital, Richard was limp. No sound, very shallow breathing and very, very white.

John grabbed Richard from Cara and ran into the hospital, shouting as he went. "Help! Emergency, please."

Over the next hour, John held Cara tightly at Richard's side as doctors and nurses worked to revive him. At times, he seemed to open his eyes and murmur but then fall back again into his quiet world. Cara's mind was on a roller coaster. "Richard," she screamed. "Don't go. Richard, hang on."

Eventually, the doctor told her he was stable and he thought he could be okay.

Cara was too tired to cry. Too exhausted to even utter a reply. It was then the doctor noticed her torn clothes, bruises and congealed blood. "What happened, missus? Who did this?"

"Is that what happened to your little boy?" Cara couldn't reply. She turned and sat down on a chair next to Richard's bed. She picked up his hand and noticed how clammy, but cold, it was.

She had to be strong for him. Somehow, she had to.

John said nothing but sat next to her and waited.

Chapter 11

It was two days before Richard had come around fully. He had drifted in and out of consciousness. And for two days Cara was rooted to his bedside. She didn't notice the colour of the walls, the pretty curtains, the pictures on the wall. All she saw was her helpless little boy. She refused food, sleep or relief from her vigil. By the evening of the first day, John thought Cara was calm enough for him to leave her. He looked at her pitiful state and felt nothing but love for her. He had abandoned her when he had vowed to look after her. He knew she had suffered at the hands of Ian, but he had no idea of the extent of her grief. He saw her torn dress, her cuts and bruises which were beginning to turn a dark purple colour. He saw her listless eyes, once bright and full of hope and optimism and he saw scars on her legs. How could the beautiful English woman who had arrived on his boat in Portland be so wrecked now, so devoid of life and so utterly helpless?

He stood up to go and told her he would be back in an hour. She didn't look up. In fact, she didn't even seem to be aware of his presence.

John drove into the main shopping street and parked the car. He got out and joined the crowds ambling along. Why was everyone moving so slowly? He had errands to do and then he had to get back to Cara. She needed him now more than she had ever needed anyone before. He didn't really know her but he knew that as a certainty.

He walked into the first clothes shop he came to. He wanted to buy her new clothes and burn those torn, bloodstained ones which told nothing but despair. He walked up to the counter, not knowing her size or taste, and asked the young assistant what size she was. Apart from her hips she looked similar to Cara. She seemed a little taken aback until John explained he needed to buy a dress for a friend.

She went to the racks of dresses and picked out three for John to choose from. "Yes, I'll take them," he said, to the assistant's surprise.

"All of them?" she asked. "Yes, all." He then asked her to choose underwear and then handed over a wad of US dollars without asking the price. The assistant was delighted—her bonus would be very good this week.

As John left the shop with bags full of clothes for Cara, he looked up and down the street looking for a children's clothes shop and a supermarket. As he was about to cross the road he saw Ian striding along as though he didn't have a care in the world.

His first reaction was to clench his fist and knock seven bells out of him. He knew Ian was the cause of Cara's trauma, but he realised in time that thumping him would do no good. In fact, in the long run he would probably cause more harm to Cara, but he couldn't greet Ian as an old friend and pretend nothing was wrong. Not now.

Instead, he went back into the clothes shop, much to the surprise and delight of the assistant who could foresee an even bigger bonus.

"Do you know of a children's clothes shop?" he asked. "He's a toddler," he said, trying to work out how long it had been since he had brought Cara to the island.

The assistant pointed across the street to an alley which she said led to a square. John was across the street before she had finished her sentence, but this time there was no sign of Ian.

As John walked back into the hospital, he heard a familiar voice. Ian was talking to a doctor. "I've informed the police," he said, "but I should think he's long gone by now."

"And with my laptop," he added. "Will my little boy be all right? And my wife, will she be okay?"

The doctor said Cara was not harmed physically, but mentally he feared she had many scars.

"I think you should sit down, Mr Campbell."

"Why? They are going to be okay, aren't they? I'll hunt him down whoever did this to them."

"I'm afraid it looks as though your wife was sexually assaulted, too," said the doctor. "We haven't been able to get her to talk very much but we examined her because she had so many cuts, bruises and torn clothes."

"Oh my God," said Ian. "My Cara. How? Who?"

"Maybe you can get her to talk. Whoever did this to her and your little boy should be locked away for good. He is nothing but an animal," continued the doctor.

"A vicious, callous, dangerous animal."

Ian sat down and hid his face in his hands. To all the world, he looked like the devastated husband and father. But to John he was the animal the doctor described. He walked past Ian and headed for Cara's door without Ian seeing him. As he walked in, the sight of Cara melted him. A frail, pathetic woman who looked 30 years older than her age.

He whispered to her, "He's here. Ian."

He felt her shudder as he laid his hand on her shoulder. As he began to say, "I'm here too, and will be for as long as you need me," Ian walked in and in an expansive gesture, ran over to Cara, cradling her and saying, "Darling, who did this. What happened? Is Richard all right." Cara didn't look up at him, just continued to stare into nothing.

John broke the silence. "Hello, Ian," he said, trying to keep his voice calm.

Ian put on an even bigger show of pretending he hadn't noticed John. "Hello," he said, "Terrible business this," not knowing how much, if anything, John knew.

"What happened, Ian?" Ian knew he had to be careful. He must not say the wrong thing.

"I've been away on business for a couple of days and got home to find the place a mess and bloodstains in the sitting room. I came straight here. When did you arrive?"

"I brought them to the hospital," John said, not giving anything away and managing to resist the urge to attack Ian.

They both looked down at Cara and Richard, both feeling opposite emotions—Ian despising his wife for being such a victim, and John desperately wanting to hold Cara and make it all right for her and her little boy. He didn't want to go and leave them with this monster who was the cause of all their pain, but felt awkward standing there when it was obvious Ian wanted him gone.

"I'm staying near the yacht club, the apartment across the road," he said. "Please, let me know if I can do anything."

Ian turned and shook his hand and replied, "Good of you, John. Be in touch."

Cara looked up and looked pleadingly at John. She didn't want him to go. She needed him. But John knew he could do nothing for her while Ian was there.

He tried to intimate with his expression that he would be back but couldn't tell if Cara understood. How could he leave her now? But how could he stay? What could he do while Ian was there?

As he left the room he realised, Cara meant more to him than anyone ever had before in his life.

Cara felt her world was dying. Richard lay lifeless and there was nothing she could do. Ian was back in charge and always would be. John had gone and there was nothing she could do to change anything. She couldn't even cry any more. If Richard didn't survive, what was the point in her carrying on? She sat staring at her son, almost wishing he would die so that she could end her misery, too. Then Ian said something to her which would change her mind.

"I killed your mother and don't have any doubt that I couldn't kill you and Richard too, if you say a word."

Cara's head was spinning. Her mother! How could that be? She had died from hitting her head falling down the stairs, hadn't she? She turned and looked at Ian, venom in her eyes. She would make herself strong again. She would take control of her life and Richard's life again. Ian would pay!

Still, she said nothing, just looked from Ian to Richard and felt her whole being change.

"Stay with your son and call the doctor if there is the slightest change. I'm going for a shower."

She picked up the bags John had brought in and walked out of the room. As she went she thought she saw a slight glimmer of fear in Ian's face.

Ian immediately regretted telling her about her mother. While she was a victim, he was in charge, but he had felt the change in Cara when he told her.

He thought back to his first murder. How he had planned it from the day Cara told him her father had died at the shock of hearing his precious daughter had married him. When she had told him the news, he had put his arms around her and pulled her to him. "I'm so sorry Cara. It must have been awful for you and your mother. I wish I could make it all better for you."

"But how can you?" said Cara. "He's gone and it's because I hurt him so much. How can I ever forgive myself?"

"You can't see it like that, Cara. We got married because we loved each other. It was right and always will be. I will always love you and be there for you. Let's go and visit your mum today, see if we can make her see we did the right thing. I love you, Cara."

Ian knew Cara had felt better and was surprised that he had understood so well, as he knew she would. She had never thought he would be the sort to get into family visits—he was far too much of a high flyer for that. It had made her love him even more and he knew it. As they left the room, Julia was just returning to hers. "Hi Cara. Things any better with your mum?"

"We're just off to see her," Cara replied. "Hope things are beginning to pick up for her. Give her my love," said Julia.

Julia didn't acknowledge Ian; he knew she didn't like him so maybe one day he would have to deal with her, too.

As Ian's Porsche Boxster had pulled out of the campus entrance, Cara had seen her tutor. She waved and although she knew he saw her, he looked the other way. "Why would he do that," she had asked Ian.

The two-hour journey passed quickly. Ian had told her how much his latest deal would make, how they would be able to buy a house within a year and how he couldn't wait to carry her over the threshold. Cara forgot all about her sadness and revelled in Ian's excitement over his latest deal. He knew how to manipulate her. She told him she couldn't wait and asked whether they should buy in Sheffield centre. She had prattled on about some nice Victorian semi's in the trendy area—or whether they should buy somewhere outside the city where they could breathe, enjoy country pubs, walks and fresh air. She really had no idea. Her parents had molly coddled her and wrapped her up in cotton wool. She thought the world would always be nice to her.

As they had turned off the motorway and headed for Market Harborough, Cara had gone quiet again, no doubt her thoughts returning to her mum. It was then that he decided he needed to get rid of his mother-in-law. She was too much of an inconvenience and he wanted no-one taking Cara's attention away from him.

They pulled up outside the house and as they walked to the front door, she let him know her thoughts, *Please, please god, let Ian win her mum over. Let him be the one her mum leans on and then everything will be all right. Won't it?*

Her mother took a long time to answer the door. No more the busy housewife rushing to the door to see who it was. Eventually, when her mother opened the door, she looked from Cara to Ian and back again and simply said, "You are not welcome here. Please leave our daughter alone."

It was time for him to play the doting husband, caring son-in-law and use his charms to sort it all out. Easy.

"Mum, please," said Cara, but Ian intervened.

"I know how you must be feeling, Mrs Wallace."

"How can you have any idea how I must be feeling, young man? Please, don't patronise me. I know why my husband died and I hold you responsible."

Cara had taken a sharp intake of breath. "Mum! Don't be so cold. You have always welcomed my friends, including boyfriends. I can't take this. There's a wedge between you two—the two people I love and I have to break it down."

Ian came to her rescue. "I do know how you feel, Mrs Wallace. My parents were both killed in the London tube bombings in 2005. They were on their way to see me at my boarding school. I have no brothers and one sister who married and now lives in South Africa and since I had spent most of my childhood in India, there was no one I could turn to in this country. I felt very alone until I met Cara. I love her dearly, Mrs Wallace, and I promise you I will always care for her and be there for her."

Cara had looked at him, shocked. She knew he had been brought up on a tea plantation in India but she didn't know his parents had since died. He could see her mother, too, was shocked. It was as simple as that—a couple of lies and he had them eating out of his hands.

"You'd better come in," her mother said to both of them eventually, "And have a cup of tea."

Over the next few hours, he had won her mother's affections and Cara saw her mother change from victim to maternal protector again. By the time they left at midnight, her mother was insisting they came for the weekend so she could feed them both up. Cara had told him she was happier than she had been for a long time. "At last something was going in the right direction," she told him.

Cara settled back into her studies and felt life was going well. Ian had gone back each weekend and they drove south to be with her mother. Her mother seemed to be picking up the pieces of her life again and spent her weeks planning all sorts of treats for them both. As Christmas approached, they had planned to go home as usual, but late on December 23, his phone rang with a business deal he couldn't refuse. He had to go, he told Cara, catch the first plane to New York and then on to Auckland, New Zealand—his business demanded it. He couldn't let this one go, Christmas or not!

He knew Cara felt hurt at missing their first Christmas together, but she had got used to saying nothing when she felt like that. She knew he just wouldn't like it. And he wouldn't.

Instead, she cheerfully said, "Of course, you must go. You've got to get that money for our house."

She was so easy to deal with. He had left her a bag of the sort of presents to keep them happy—a cardigan, slippers and nightdress for her mother plus a pair of pearl earrings—very simple but very expensive. He made the effort to write a card to Cara, "I love you, Cara, more than I can say. I am so sorry I can't be with you for our first Christmas together. All my love, Ian xx."

Her present was a large diamond ring—a sure winner for both Cara and her mother.

He phoned them at 2 pm. "Good morning, Marcia and happy Christmas," said Ian. "I hope you are enjoying your day with Cara."

"Thank you so much for my beautiful earrings. You really shouldn't have spent so much," Cara's mother replied. "Only the best for the two ladies in my life. Is my darling wife there?"

"I've just got up," Ian went on. "So I thought I'd call you before I had breakfast. The hotel here in Seventh Avenue is very nice but not like being at home with you."

Cara told him how much she loved the diamond ring and how much she loved him and wished she was with him—as he knew she would.

After a few minutes, Cara's mother said, "You'd better not stay on too long; it must be costing him a fortune." So Cara said her goodbyes, but not before pleading with him to come home soon.

When she put the phone down, it didn't occur to her to dial 1471, but then Ian knew that.

Christmas and New Year came and went and Cara went back to Uni. Her mother seemed to be coping far better and had made a new friend at the local flower arranging class. He knew how to get around her; he called in frequently and had taken her out to lunch, despite her pleas that she was not dressed up, and once, even stayed the night when he had a business meeting the next morning in Leicester.

He told her he was thinking of opening an office there as it was fairly central to his business activities. If he did, she said, "Of course, you must come and stay with me and think of 89 Gorse Lane as home."

Within a month, he had moved in. Cara couldn't be more pleased. Everything was going well. Very well. Until that conniving bitch, Julia at university with Cara, interfered, Ian remembered.

She had dropped a bombshell asking how his sister was and had she got over her operation? They had bumped into each other in the Café Royal in London a couple of days after Christmas—just at the time he was supposed to be in New York and then Auckland. He didn't return to Cara until January 2.

She had phoned him in a panic, crying and suggesting all sorts of things. Ian had had to stay calm. "Don't be silly, darling," he said. "You know I was in New York. I remember bumping into Julia in the Café Royal in Regent Street but that was after I got back in early January. I was with my sister. She had come to London from her home in Cape Town to have an operation on her foot and I took her out for dinner. I remember Julia saying she was heading back up to Sheffield the next day for the start of term."

Cara immediately felt stupid as he knew she would. "How could she have doubted him," she said.

"Sorry, Ian," she said. "I was being silly. I just love you so much I don't want anything to go wrong."

After she had rung off Ian decided he had to move his plans on a pace… He had had enough of all these stupid women complicating things.

He began coming home from the office earlier to help with the cooking. Each evening he would sit and chat to Marcia, telling her about his childhood, his life in India and his schooling in England. He had felt very alone in this country until he had met Cara.

"It was love at first sight," he said. "I am working very hard to get the money for a house, maybe somewhere between Sheffield and here."

One evening, when Ian came home Marcia told him she had made a decision. She would pass the house over to him and Cara, as her late husband had always planned, and she would move into sheltered accommodation. "But you can't do that. This is your home."

"But I can and I will. I have enough money left over to buy a one bedroomed flat in a sheltered accommodation block in Market Harborough."

"You and Cara need a home to yourselves. You are young and you don't need me getting in your way. As I get older, I don't want you two having to look after me. It's best I move while I am still able."

Over the next few days, Ian and Marcia talked more about it and Marcia said she had been to look at a sheltered accommodation flat near the centre of town. "That way I can always get public transport," she said.

Ian said he, too, had been thinking about it all and thought it would be a great surprise for Cara. They agreed to keep it a secret and say nothing until it was all sorted out legally. Marcia was very excited. She liked this plan. And so did Ian.

When Cara came home that weekend, she told Ian she could see the friendship between her mother and Ian was even stronger. She was so pleased; now she never had to worry about her mother during the week because Ian was there to look after her.

Within a couple of weeks Ian had all the legal papers drawn up to sign the home over. In effect, they would be buying it for a minimal amount. Marcia would then be buying her flat with the remaining money and to wrap it all up neatly, her estate would be left to them on her death. What Ian did not mention was that Cara was not mentioned in any of the papers.

Marcia duly signed all the papers where Ian showed her and went to bed feeling very happy, totally oblivious to the fact she had signed her daughter's inheritance away. She was set up for the rest of her life and so were Cara and Ian. Her husband would have been proud of her. "What a shame he never got to know Ian," she had told Ian.

Ian told her it would still take a few weeks to sort out and he would call the home to let them know she was buying the flat and everything was in the hands of the solicitors.

He asked Marcia to arrange the cheque to buy the flat but not to fill in the payee details as he wasn't sure whether it went to the original owner of the flat or to the sheltered accommodation service company. All was in place—all he had to do now was move on to the next part of his plan.

Over the next few weeks, he called Cara a few times a week telling her he was a little worried about her mother. She had been feeling sick, lethargic and not herself.

Cara was worried but was reassured by Ian that she was in good hands. He knew Cara wouldn't ask her mother because she wouldn't want her mother to think she and Ian discussed her in private, and if she did, Marcia would deny any illness. After all, there was nothing wrong with her and Cara would just think her mother didn't want her to worry. Mind games! Ian's speciality.

Once the house was completely his and the cheque for Marcia's flat was safely deposited in an offshore bank account, Ian moved on to the final stage of his plan. But a call to Marcia one day from the service company, telling her another flat had become available and they wondered if she might be interested in that one as the first didn't overlook the gardens, threw him into a panic.

He had to activate his plan earlier than he had anticipated.

He phoned Cara and said her mother was in bed feeling very unwell so he had called the doctor. There was no need for her to come home as he had cancelled his business appointments and would be with his mother-in-law 24 hours a day.

He put a stew on the stove to slowly simmer. Marcia was upstairs. He took the stairs two at a time. He had to deal with this quickly before anyone called by or phoned.

This was it. Now or never, to take him into a league even he never imagined he would venture into. He grabbed Marcia from behind and dragged her from the bedroom to the top of the stairs. She was too shocked to scream. She stared at him with pitiful eyes and mouthed, "Why, Ian, why?" He held a knife above her with his left hand and told her to be silent. She was too scared to move. Her breathing became fitful as Ian growled at her to be quiet. He couldn't back out now but could he really do it? He began to shake and sweat poured from his face dripping on to Marcia's pinny. As he held Marcia rigid at the top of the stairs, he battled with himself that he had to go ahead with it. Seconds ticked by. One, two, five, ten. But he knew he couldn't move forward with his plans with her still alive. He moved his right leg in front of hers, steadied himself against the bannister, and with all his strength, pushed. Pushed his mother-in-law forwards, down the stairs and to her death. Her body seemed to float in slow motion as she left his grasp, but at the same time, each thump on the stairs pounded in his head. He leapt down after her, kneeling next to her lifeless body. Her eyes were still open but there was no pulse when he put his fingers on her neck. She was dead. Was it really that easy to kill someone? He had to get a grip; get himself back in control. He ran to the sitting room and grabbed the whisky bottle from the cupboard. As the cold liquid hit the back of his throat, Ian choked. His eyes filled up and his nose felt as if it was going to explode. He wasn't a spirit drinker but he had to calm himself.

After a few minutes, he slowly returned to the hall; this time he had time to dread the sight of Marcia. She lay there very peacefully as if she was in a deep sleep. He checked her pulse again. Nothing. *Good, job done,* thought Ian.

He then made a cup of tea with cold water and placed the cup and saucer on her bedside table. He scrutinised the bedroom to make sure everything was in order. The bed was unmade, her clothes were laid on the chair so that it seemed she had been in bed all day. By the time he had finished, it was after 6 pm. He then phoned the local surgery and said he had left a message earlier for the doctor to call but no one had been and his mother-in-law seemed worse. The frosty receptionist said she had not received the message and why did he think it necessary for the doctor to call. Couldn't he bring Mrs Wallace into the surgery? Ian put on his exasperated voice and said he was very worried about his mother-in-law—she had been in bed all day which was not like her at all. He said he had taken her a cup of tea about an hour ago but she had seemed worse—not really able to communicate. He wondered if she had had a stroke.

Eventually, the receptionist said she would put him on the list for a home visit but she had no idea when it would be as it was already the evening and the doctor had three other visits before her.

Ian put the phone down, waited three minutes and phoned back. "Oh my god," he spluttered. "She tried to come downstairs when I was making dinner, but she fell. It's bad. She feels cold and clammy. I think she might be dead!" The frosty receptionist told him to calm down and explain the situation more slowly. He said he had gone to cook her dinner after telling her the doctor would come later and he heard her calling from upstairs. He came through to the hall as she fell from the top of the stairs. "She must have hit her head. She's not moving—and I don't think she's breathing. I think she might be dead."

The doctor pronounced Marcia dead at 6.52 pm and said he thought she must have hit her head when she fell down the stairs. He signed the death certificate, made a few phone calls, and left. Ian phoned Cara, put on his best grieving son-in-law act and broke the news.

It had been very easy to kill.

The sound of a nurse coming back into the room brought him back to the situation before him—his son lying almost lifeless in the bed, wires and monitors everywhere and his wife's cold voice telling him she was going for a shower. He didn't know this Cara.

She had gone to the nurse's station and told a nurse to go straight to Richard's room and to stay with him until she returned from the shower as the man with him could not be trusted. The nurse was about to ask Cara a question, but as she opened her mouth, Cara turned and walked very determinedly to the shower room.

Chapter 12

As the days went by Richard seemed to improve but he never smiled. Cara knew he had seen too much that night, though she would never be sure how much. He seemed disinterested in anything. His doctor said he had shut down as a result of trauma and may never be able to come back from it. Any toys, DVDs or even his favourite television programmes brought no joy to him. He had been home for two weeks and Cara had been determined to make everything better for him. Then, one day, John took Cara and Richard sailing. He chartered a boat from a marina and sailed to Cooper Island, a couple of hours away. Cara sat up at the bow with Richard who was fascinated by the bow wave. He stared at the white frothy waves bouncing off the hull and running back to the stern, and slowly Cara felt his little body relax. When they anchored off the beach, John suggested a swim and produced a little pair of goggles for him. Richard wasn't sure if he wanted to put them on until John brought out another two pairs, one for Cara and one for him.

Richard climbed down the boarding ladder hesitantly but John held him tightly and signalled to him to hold his breath and look under the water. In an instant Richard popped his head up, squealed at Cara and had a big smile on his face. The hundreds of colourful fish under the water had swum around him as John tipped a few breadcrumbs out of little container. Cara then jumped in from the bathing platform at the stern and the three of them spent half an hour swimming around the boat and searching for more fish.

They went ashore for lunch but Richard was keen to get back to the fish. John took him into the only shop near the beach and bought three snorkels. After that Richard's whole world opened up and Cara finally knew he was going to be all right.

Each day, Cara took Richard down to the beach and they snorkelled, looking for any kind of sea life. There were very few fish so close to the island but there were all sorts of treasures Richard found. In a very short time Richard had learned to dive down, pushing water out of his snorkel. The sea had become his playground where he became confident and content. His lack of hearing didn't matter here. He was just a normal little boy at the seaside.

John had to return to the States a few days later, but before he went he asked Cara if she could leave Richard at a nursery for a morning and meet him at the marina. He took her out on a boat and they motored round to Coral Cove, just north of the marina. He picked up a mooring, turned off the engine and said, "Tell me all about it, Cara. I know I have to get you and Richard out of here but I need to know what I'm up against."

He sat quietly, listening to the most sordid tale he had ever heard. He said nothing, just let Cara pour it all out, and when she eventually cried, he held her tightly. Still she talked, her words sometimes inaudible through her sobs. When she eventually told him what Ian had confessed to in the hospital, she stopped crying and her voice turned to steel. "I cannot let him get away with any of this. And that's probably just the half of it," she said. "Remember that gun I found on the boat? Well, not long after that I heard there had been a shooting in Miami. A drugs' killing. I might be putting two and two together and making five, but I don't think so. I think it was Ian."

"When I arrived here I had a strange e-mail from someone I didn't know. It was very threatening—wanted to know where Ian was. I deleted it and never replied."

John listened and knew that all her suppositions were right. He knew Cara had to decide for herself to get away; he could not take control, but he would do whatever it took to help her.

Before he left, he gave Cara a mobile phone and said he would take care of the bills. He also gave her a credit card with his PIN so that she could do whatever she needed to in a hurry if things got any worse. He said he would be in touch as soon as he had worked out how he could keep Cara and Richard safe and well away from Ian. For the first time in many months, Cara felt optimistic and positive.

She thought about how to get away; planned to return to England to live in her old home and bring Richard up. She would get a job, make new friends and try to study in the evenings. One day, she would be back on track with Ian, hopefully, just a distant memory. Ian came home each evening and continued to behave as if nothing had happened. He treated Cara as his servant and was totally in control of her. Cara pretended to live as she had for so long—the victim, subservient to her husband and she endured his demands in bed, saying nothing, but now sure she would not have to endure it for much longer.

She drove into town one day, seeing for the first time in almost a year, the beauty of the island. The trumpet flowers were in bloom, hanging down between expansive green leaves. The cicadas squeaked their song and the gentle wind whispered in her hair. She was going to make it. She was on her way home.

She parked the car, took Richard's hand and set off for the internet cafe. How different she felt today from the time she read Julia's e-mail and thought she had no future. As she logged on, she waited almost with excitement to see if there was any word from John. There was. And there were also e-mails from her neighbour in New York and two from Julia. She eagerly read John's who laid out his plan for her and Richard. He would bring the Buccaneer to St Thomas in the US Virgin Islands and she was to take a day trip down to the south of the island and then take the ferry to St Thomas. He thought she shouldn't join the ferry in Palm Tree lagoon as it would be easy for Ian to follow. He also suggested she bought tickets to Virgin Gorda and leave the receipt in the house to send Ian in the wrong direction as soon as he realised she had gone. John said he could be in St Thomas in six weeks' time.

Cara's excitement grew as she read every word over and over again. Six weeks—that would be around the middle of April. She would work out all she had to do when she got home. She then opened her other e-mails. Her New York neighbour said there had been a lot of activity recently with the police, drugs' squad and fire investigators searching the remains of Cara and Ian's apartment. They had concluded the apartment had been torched and they wanted to talk to Ian. She didn't know if she should say anything to them so didn't tell them their new address, e-mail or phone details.

Cara was grateful for that. She wanted to keep a low profile until she could escape. She knew Ian had burned their apartment when they left in the middle of the night. She knew he was mixed up somehow in drug dealing. And she knew the Miami murder was part of it all. How could that beautiful man she had met at college become this criminal? Julia's e-mails were full of life and optimism although she said she was worried she had not heard from Cara for such a long time.

Cara decided it was time to tell Julia some of the truth. She sent her an e-mail, telling her friend that she and Ian had split up and that she was coming home with Richard. She wasn't sure when she would be back, but it would definitely be before the summer.

She also replied to her New York neighbour, thanking her for the information and saying she was grateful she had not passed on any information as to their whereabouts. She told her briefly she was going back to England but nothing else.

As Cara set off for home, she felt a slight apprehension creep over her. What if John's plan went wrong? She was now sure Ian would have no hesitation in killing her, or even worse, Richard.

She had to dot every i and cross every t to make their plan secure.

Her first move was to book Richard in to a nursery school for three mornings a week—for two reasons. Firstly, Ian would never guess what she was planning if it looked like she was setting Richard up for his entry into school. And secondly, it would give her time to sort things out if she was on her own. At first, Richard was not very happy; he was very clingy to Cara and unsure about anything at all. But then the nursery had a trip to the beach and Richard was back in the place he loved. None of the other children at the nursery could swim so they played with the shells and broken pieces of coral on the beach while Richard spent his whole morning in the water. At first, nursery staff were worried about him going out of his depth and one of them tried to coax him back to the beach. But within minutes, the quiet little blonde boy showed he was a good swimmer and was even diving down to pick up bits and pieces from the seabed without a snorkel or mask.

Next, Cara had to think through their plan—every minute detail of it. She had to be one-step ahead of Ian at every move; had to think the way he did. She could leave nothing to chance.

She decided she needed to take her passport, money and a few essentials away from the house and hide them somewhere she could access them at a moment's notice. After dropping Richard at nursery, she bought a waterproof holdall and went home to pack a few clothes for her and Richard. It was then that she realised her passport was not there. And neither was Ian's. She searched everywhere she could think of in the house but found nothing. She realised then that it would be obvious to Ian she would leave if ever she had the opportunity, so he must have taken her passport. The more she thought about how to resolve the problem, the more she realised it was useless. He had either locked it in his office safe, kept it in his briefcase, or simply destroyed it. Whatever he had done with it, Cara would never be able to get to it.

How was she going to be able to leave and get into US territory at St Thomas without a passport? US immigration was a stickler at the best of times, so she knew she could never be let in without everything being in order. She wondered about contacting the passport office in the UK and ordering another one, but that could take weeks and she might have to use local authorities to verify her address and residency on the island. She could not risk that. Ian could find out from an innocent remark.

What were her options, get into St Thomas illegally by paying a local fisherman to take her and Richard to a quiet bay but in the long run she would be stuck at every port or airport where she had to show her passport. Or, find some other way.

Just as Cara had begun to feel desperate again, and thought she would never be able to leave, she remembered her plan—she had to think the way Ian did, or she would not survive. What would he do? She felt muddled and confused. The previous year had taken its toll on her; she no longer had a fast, efficient brain which could analyse problems and formulate solutions. She felt old, weary and resigned—but then she thought about Richard and knew above all else she had to work it out.

She needed a passport for herself and for Richard. She couldn't apply for one in the conventional way because it was unsafe. There was no option—she had to steal one. But whose? She thought about all the people she knew, which was not very many. In the past year, she had become reclusive—rarely meeting anyone outside of the house. The only people she ever had any dealings with were from the hospital or the nursery, but how on earth was she going to be able to access a passport, steal it and get away without the owner realising? It seemed impossible, but she had to find a way.

When she arrived at the nursery to collect Richard, she got there early to try to chat to some of the other mums and nursery staff. She was not going to get anywhere remaining such a recluse. She smiled and found it hard trying to communicate with other people. It had been a very long time since she had just chatted with anyone. Soon she found she was scrutinising the other mums— looking for any similarities between how she looked and how they did. There were two mums with brown hair—the others all seemed to be blonde, vibrant and confident-looking. Had she ever looked like that—too much had dragged her down to even remember.

She saw Richard—as usual sitting on his own, but he seemed content with his picture of the seaside, colouring in the fish and the boat in the background. When he looked up, he saw her and immediately ran to her, wrapping his little arms around her legs. He buried her face in her legs and clung to her—she was his total world and only she could bring him happiness and a future. As she took his hand and pulled him away from her, she noticed another little boy sitting quietly, not mixing with the others. His mum had brown hair.

Within a few minutes Cara had introduced herself, made a fuss of the little boy, and suggested they meet for a coffee sometime. And two days later, she found herself sitting on the beach with Richard and Kevin, slowly accepting each other, although at a distance, and she and Kevin's mum chatting about life on the island. Her plan was slowly working.

A week later, Jane invited Cara and Richard for tea. As the day drew near, Cara became equally nervous and excited. Could this be her chance? She tried to think how she could search for Jane's and Kevin's passports—hoping there would be a bureau, filing cabinet or some obvious place they could be.

She took Richard into town in the morning and went to the local toyshop—that could waste at least an hour. She then wandered around the market—remembering how she loved the bustle of it when she first arrived, looking at the colourful homemade crafts and clothes. She loved chatting to the market stallholders—intrigued by their yellow crooked teeth from years of chewing tobacco.

It was still only 11.30 am—how was she going to fill the next six hours? She found her way to the internet café and sat Richard at a table with his colouring pens and his new colouring book bought that morning. As she logged on, she decided she would e-mail John and tell him what she planned to do. The more she wrote, the more excited she became and the words spilled out—she never gave it a second thought that what she planned to do was wrong, illegal and could lead her to a court of law. She could only think positively now—no point in dwelling on what had happened or what could happen. She needed to escape with Richard—and this was the only way she could get there.

As she hit the send button, she looked at her inbox and saw another e-mail from her New York neighbour. She wished life had been different for her then—she would have liked to have stayed in the city and made a nice life for her and

Richard there. There seemed to be so many more opportunities in America—if you worked hard you could secure a solid future. But there was no point in dwelling over what could have been.

She opened the e-mail and immediately felt fear again creeping over her. The hair on the back of her neck, she knew, had stood up and her hands became clammy. As her heartbeat quickened and her breathing came in short gasps, she realised time was running out—not just for her and Richard, but for Ian, too.

The fire department and New York police had visited her neighbour again and had told her a warrant had been issued for Ian and Cara's arrest. They had sufficient evidence to show their burnt-out apartment had been the result of an arson attack and they had also told her they knew Ian had bought ferry tickets in Portland the following morning—his English public-school accent had been remembered and security cameras in the port had picked him up. A burnt-out car had been found nearby, and although all identity had been removed, it was the same model car as registered in Ian's name, so they had put two and two together.

They had also mentioned a big drugs swoop which had taken place in Brooklyn and that they thought Ian was involved. Although, her neighbour knew Cara would not want her to give any information as to Ian and Cara's whereabouts, she felt she could end up in trouble if she did not help the police. She had told them Ian and Cara were living in the Caribbean. Her e-mail had been sent two days ago.

Cara knew it would not be long before the police arrived.

She returned home and packed a few things, including food, into the holdall for her and Richard and then drove east towards the airport. She drove on until she arrived at a small bay where she turned off the road and followed the dirt track down to the water's edge.

Cara grabbed the holdall and ran into the trees behind the beach. The bay was deserted with only an old fishing boat bobbing on its mooring in the middle. There were no houses or apartments nearby and no-one to see Cara hiding the holdall in the undergrowth behind the biggest tree on the shore. She returned to her car and reversed at speed back up the track and out on to the road going south. Now, she had to get those passports.

She returned home to compose herself, change and prepare for the only crime she had ever committed in her life. She sat on the balcony breathing deeply and thinking through the job ahead. Her handbag had a good zip so she could easily hide the passports if she could find them. She was ready.

As Cara turned the key in the ignition, a car drew up behind her. It was Ian.

Chapter 13

Cara knew as Ian got out of the car that he was in a foul mood. She had seen it too many times. "Where the fuck are you going?" he growled. "Get out of the fucking car, bring the brat and get back into the house."

"I'm just going to pick him up from nursery," she said. "And then we were going for tea to a friend of Richard's."

"No, you're fucking not going for tea," he spat back very sarcastically. "Get into that fucking house."

What could she do? If she went into the house it would be another beating, another onslaught—maybe another rape. Was she strong enough to escape—NOW? There would be no going back. In a second, she had locked the car doors from the inside, slammed the car into gear and hit the accelerator. The wheels spun on the gravel and threw up dust and debris, creating almost a smoke screen between her and Ian. As the wheels touched the Tarmac, the car lurched forward and she was away up the hill, leaving Ian running back to his car, grabbing for his car keys in his briefcase.

She didn't take her foot off the accelerator as the car reached the top of the hill and disappeared over the other side. She knew Ian would be close behind her but where could she go and how could she stay ahead of him? As panic replaced the adrenalin rush, she saw a possible hiding place. A row of more than ten second-hand cars were lined up at the side of the road. She slowed the car enough before she hit the dusty roadside. She then freewheeled into the car lot, joining the end of the line, turning the engine off and hiding below the dashboard just in time before Ian roared past and around the bend in the road. She counted to ten before starting the car again and tentatively looked out of her side window to make sure Ian hadn't already guessed her move and turned around. She pulled out across the road and headed back towards town, passing her home one last time. As soon as she could, she turned off the main road and followed the back streets around the town.

She had very little time, but she knew she had to get those passports. Again she composed herself and again she started the car to head to the nursery to pick up Richard and then on towards Jane's house.

As Cara sat making polite conversation with Jane, she wondered how she was able to cope with her life. There was only going to be one way to go and that was up—for Richard's sake if not for hers.

As Jane went into the kitchen to make the tea, Cara looked around the room, desperately hoping for some clue. She could tell by the orderly way the books on the shelf were arranged that Jane was tidy and efficient. Big books next to the end wall, moving along to smaller books at the other end. The top shelf had a trailing plant with no sign of dust or spider's web and there were a few small ornaments dotted about in front of the books which showed Jane's like of unusual island pottery.

On the other side of the room was a table and three chairs with a map of the island on the wall next to them. The window at the far end had shelves on each side with lots of photographs of Kevin, a man Cara presumed to be Jane's husband, and family portraits of people who looked both, like Jane and her husband. An insignificant display of family life.

It seemed unreal to be sitting with a cup of tea and teacake watching Richard and little Kevin playing on the floor after the past few hours.

Eventually, Cara asked where the toilet was and made her way down the hall to the last door on the right. As she went, she glanced to the left and right, peeking through doors in search of some sort of office or study. Finally, opposite the bathroom was a door partly ajar with a desk, laptop computer and various books and papers in neat piles next to it. Cara was sure this was where she would find her treasure, but how could she do it? She returned to the sitting room and formulated yet another plan. She had noticed the study's window had overlooked the garden so asked Jane questions about how long she had lived there, did she do the garden and other nondescript queries. Jane offered to show her around the house—the first part of the plan worked.

Richard, forever worried if his mother was out of sight, immediately got up and followed them, trailing behind as Jane opened doors and showed them around. At last, they reached the study and as Jane and Cara entered, Cara had a sudden fear come over her. What was she doing snooping around trying to steal from her new friend? But then she saw it—the box file on the desk marked

'Personal Documents'. So close, but how on earth was she going to be able to open it, leave alone steal some of its contents?

Richard came to her rescue. He needed the toilet. As she pointed Richard towards the bathroom door, Jane said she would go and make another cup of tea. Now was her chance.

She dived back into the study, opened the box file and right on top were two passports. There was no time to look in them to see whether they were Jane's and her husband's or Jane's and Kevin's so she snatched them up, shut the file and then realised she had left her handbag in the sitting room. She swiftly put them down her shorts just as Richard emerged from the bathroom. Almost there.

Cara almost choked swallowing the newly made hot tea but she had to get out of there. In just a few minutes, she had thanked Jane, grabbed Richard and almost run out to the car, leaving Jane looking a little bewildered on the doorstep.

She tried to drive away casually without kicking up dust on the unmade road, but her nerves were almost giving out. She just needed to get away and hide with Richard until she could work out what to do and where to go next. She drove north again and turned off the road, hiding the car off a track. Just in case the car had been seen, she took Richard's hand and led him away from the track into a more hidden area behind trees and bushes. At last they sat down. Cara began to shake uncontrollably until eventually she was sick. Could she take any more? Richard picked up her handbag, opened it and took out a packet of tissues and gave her one. Yes, of course, she could go on.

Cara sat for a long time not moving, not speaking and trying to think what she should do next. As she sat, she suddenly felt exhausted, unable to do anything, except curl up with Richard and sleep. They slept in the forest for almost two hours by which time it was dark, but when she woke, she felt able to think more clearly. She took the mobile phone John had given her out of her bag. She had never needed to use it but had made sure the battery was always charged—just in case. Now she was grateful she had done it.

She dialled John's number and waited for the single tone to ring—six times, seven times, eight times. "Please, John, you have to be there," she pleaded in her mind.

Eventually, she could hear his voice saying "Cara, is that you. Are you safe?" In a rapid fire of words, she explained briefly what she had done and how she had to get off the island and away. It would not be long before Ian, or even the police, found her and Richard.

John said he would call her back, within the hour, with some sort of plan.

Cara got out a notebook and wrote down her options.

Get to the airport and try to get the first flight out to anywhere. No, that wouldn't work. She had very little money on her and hardly any food.

Go back to town and try to get a ferry to the next island. Not far enough away and too conspicuous—a woman and a little boy would be too visible.

Go back to town on her own and get some money—she would have to leave Richard in the forest on his own in the dark. A horrible thought, but there was nothing else she could do.

She tried to explain to Richard what she needed to do but in the dark she could not make him understand. She just had to hope he would know she would be back for him.

She crept away back to the car, leaving her young, vulnerable son, hidden in the bushes. How could she do this to him? But then, she remembered it was not she who had done it to him; it was Ian. She felt anger and hatred which gave her the strength to see her plan through. She reached the car and slowly reversed back to the track and on to the road, not putting on the lights until she was on the road. She drove slowly and carefully back down the road to the town, pulling into a side street near the harbour. She parked her car on a piece of rough land not easily visible from the road and quickly walked in the shadows to the cash machine. She had two cards—one from John and a joint one she and Ian had. She withdrew the maximum she could from both cards and then ran into a small supermarket near the harbour, snatching anything she could from the shelves before running back to the car. When she got back to Richard he was crying silently where she had left him, his little body shaking with each sob. Cara knew then that whatever else she did in her life, she would care for him until her dying day.

Now, armed with food and money, Cara felt more in control. Then she remembered the passports. For the first time, in as long as she could remember, luck was on her side. She opened the first passport that belonged to Jane's husband—but her heart lurched as she thought she had no passport for Richard. She opened the second one to find Kevin was included in Jane's passport and the photograph was not too dissimilar from Cara's. Jane's hair was longer and she was more tanned but Cara could maybe just get away with it if the immigration officer didn't look too closely.

Cara then drove to the airport and bought two tickets to Trellis Bay on Virgin Gorda on the North Sound Express. She paid with a credit card and made a point of chatting to the person selling the tickets. Once she thought the person would remember her, she and Richard then went to the public toilets and from there through the service door to outside the terminal building. Leaving her car prominently parked in the public car park nearby, she and Richard then walked for two hours towards the town, hiding in nearby undergrowth if they heard a car coming. They turned off the main road and found the track leading to where she had hidden her holdall, picked it up and then continued on back to town.

They arrived at the Far-Off Island ferry point just as the sun was coming up. There were very few people around so Cara felt safe to buy tickets and board the ferry, hiding in the enclosed cockpit until the ferry left. It was hot and smelly and the rolling motion of the moored ferry made both Cara and Richard feel sick. Large coils of damp rope lay around with dented cans of old engine oil and ancient yellow oilskins growing mildew lay in a corner. As the skipper began to prepare to leave for his first trip of the day, the two passengers felt it was safe to come out into the fresh air but a commotion on the dockside took their attention. The St Thomas ferry had just docked nearby with three very officious-looking armed American policeman stepping off with great speed. Cara's heart sank as she pulled Richard back into their hiding place, willing the skipper to throw off the mooring warps and set off.

The skipper took another drag of his cigarette, sat down and watched the events unfold on the dock. Eventually, when the policemen had moved away and got into a car driven by the local constabulary, he flicked his dog end into the harbour, threw off the warps and put the engine into gear. Cara didn't dare look out of the cockpit—anyone might remember seeing her and a blonde little boy going off on the early morning ferry.

It was less than an hour's trip to the island and Cara felt very unsure she had made the right choice. There were very few places to hide on the island, with only one very large resort hotel, but that was where she and Richard would stay until she could think of what to do next. It was then she remembered John was going to call her back. She had turned the phone off to save her battery so now switched it on again to find she had six missed calls—all from John.

She immediately phoned him and started to apologise before he interrupted her with dozens of questions about where was she, how was she, was she safe, how had she got away?

John knew Far Off Island and suggested she and Richard walked around the island to the other side, well away from the many tourists around the hotel. He would then fly to St Thomas and somehow get to the island, hopefully persuading one of the water taxi drivers to take a detour from his normal route. They arranged she would switch her phone on at 6 am and 6 pm each day—BVI time.

Now all Cara and Richard had to do was wait; they didn't know how long for, but at least they were away from the island and in relative safety. They found an old hut and hid themselves away to sleep.

Chapter 14

John knew he could get to St Thomas within 24 hours, but finding a water taxi driver who was willing to be bribed was another matter. What he couldn't do was waste any time. Cara must be exhausted and she needed to be safe. Far Away Island was just not far enough away from Ian. What he could hope for, he realised, was that Ian was arrested before, he, too, got off the island.

He booked a flight to San Juan and flew south later that day. He took with him as many American dollars as he could easily access, his passport, yacht qualifications and bought clothes for Cara and Richard. They had fled in haste so probably only had the clothes they stood up in.

On landing, he made his way to a local water taxi company and spoke to a couple of ferry skippers. Each said they couldn't help him and sent him off to other ferry companies who all said the same. He was just beginning to despair and try to charter a yacht when the first skipper he spoke to appeared and beckoned him to follow him along a small alley. A deal was struck and they would leave as soon as it got dark. It was still only 5pm. An hour later John spoke to Cara and said he was on his way and would hopefully be there before midnight. He suggested she and Richard ate dinner in the hotel restaurant overlooking the small ferry terminal and yacht moorings. They could mingle with the other guests and hopefully remain anonymous.

Cara felt it was too dangerous but went along with the plan. She and Richard made their way back around the island while it was still just light enough to find their way and then sat down at a table near the waterfront where they could see all the boats coming and going. They ordered their dinner and both faced away from the restaurant to avoid having to speak to any of the other diners. Cara felt tense during the whole evening and felt sure something would go wrong. Richard sensed this and fidgeted so much at the table that he spilt his drink over the tablecloth and Cara. Her reaction was out of character. She shouted at him and raised her hand to slap him before regaining her composure and calming him down—but not before the other people in the restaurant had noticed and tutted.

Just after 11 pm, Cara heard the motor of a small boat approaching the ferry terminal and prayed it was John. The boat moored briefly to let a single passenger off, and then headed out again into the darkness of the night. Was it John? She couldn't see. She got up to walk towards the terminal and then stopped dead. It wasn't John at all. It was Ian. His distinctive confident gait was obvious.

Oh my God, she thought. *How on earth had he tracked her down so quickly?* She swung around to see if Richard had followed her to see him standing next to the table with a puddle around his feet. He had already seen his father.

Without a second's pause, Cara pushed Richard into the restaurant and led him through the tables to the toilets at the back. She didn't look round until she was going through the door. *Had he seen them? Where was he now?*

She couldn't see him which worried her more. Her mind raced to think what she should do and then she noticed a waiter watching her, thinking perhaps she was trying to leave without paying. She gave him a half smile and beckoned him over to her, all the while looking out towards the beach. She snatched a fistful of dollars from her purse and thrust them into the waiter's hand, He could see instantly it was a lot more than her bill would have been, and sensed at the same time she was in trouble. Without a word, he pulled her and Richard out of the restroom and pushed them through the door leading to the kitchen.

From there, he quickly spoke to a colleague and then led them to the back of the building and out into the dark night. He asked no questions and started to head back into the kitchen. Cara touched his arm and mouthed a 'thank you'.

She hid Richard between the very large bins and crept out to try to see around the corner of the building. Instantly she saw Ian, this time not striding confidently but moving surreptitiously in the shadows as if hiding from someone. She kept her distance and realised instantly that he, too, had escaped—he from the police—and had gone to the nearest island. It was the fastest way out and both of them had chosen the same route.

While she was pondering her next move, a very big, fast boat appeared at the ferry terminal, its big search lights trained on the shore. As it docked, six men in uniform jumped off and ran ashore. They were carrying guns and shouting to everyone in the restaurant to stay down. Cara froze and stayed in the darkness, creeping back to Richard's hiding place at the back of the restaurant. She saw Ian crouch down too but he was still near to the front of the restaurant. In an instant a shot rang out and big torches appeared around the side of the building. The police were on top of Ian in a second.

The kitchen door opened and the waiter came out, took Cara's arm and led them back into the building. He knew she must be connected with the police activity outside, but asked no questions. He walked in front of them to the shore and pointed at a small beach bar, now closed, suggesting they could hide there well away from the restaurant but still be able to see what was going on.

As the shouting died down, Cara saw the police dragging Ian towards their boat, his hands cuffed behind his back. At the same time, she heard an outboard motor and looked around to see a small boat following the shoreline. As the police boat prepared to leave, their lights shone along the beach, briefly illuminating the small boat. It was John. She and Richard ran to the water's edge and waded through the silky black water towards the boat, and towards safety. As they reached John he leaned over the side and lifted Richard up out of the water. He then bent forward to reach Cara and as he did so, the police boat passed them. Cara, John and Ian all saw each other at the same time.

Chapter 15

As Cara perched herself in the boat, she sat Richard on her lap, and stared into the darkness after the police launch. She felt a mixture of emotions. She was exhausted and drained but at the same time almost euphoric that the one person she could no longer cope with could not get to her or Richard any more. As the gentle humming of the engine took her further and further away into the night, Cara finally felt she could sleep. She gave herself totally to the security of John, closed her eyes and drifted into a deep sleep.

John asked the water taxi driver if he knew where the police launch was based—wherever they were to go to now needed to be in the opposite direction to Ian. They headed north to Virgin Gorda and decided to stay there for a couple of days to recover and make sure Ian was firmly in the custody of the United States authorities before they ventured further.

They booked into the nearest hotel to the small jetty where the water taxi docked. Cara and Richard had slept soundly throughout the trip and were still asleep. John felt bad about waking them; they had been through hell and back, but just another few minutes and they could sleep safely in a bed.

The next morning John sat drinking coffee on the terrace overlooking the turquoise sea. The sun turned patches of the water almost white, giving it an ethereal look. He tried to imagine what had been going on, what had really happened to make this beautiful, gentle English woman flee with her son. He just couldn't.

Every half hour he wandered past their room and listened at the door. He could just make out calm but deep breathing. "They must be exhausted," he thought. They had been asleep for many hours and there seemed to be no sign of them waking. He decided to go and get breakfast for them to have in their room... As he returned from the hotel shops, he saw the handle turn on their door. He quickly assured them it was him and that everything was safe and they would be all right. Cara opened the door, clutching a hotel dressing gown around her. John could see the little hump of Richard's body still curled up in the bed.

That afternoon while Richard paddled at the shore just a few feet from his mother, Cara and John thought through their options. Cara's immediate wish was to return to England straightaway to her parents' home and from there begin to rebuild her life. She needed to get away from the paradox of this beautiful prison in the Caribbean—no longer did the twinkling sea, the friendly smiles of the locals or beauty of the rainforests give her any joy. She would leave here and never return.

John wasn't sure it was the right thing for her to go back to England so soon. She would be alone again and after all she had been through, she may not be strong enough to deal with whatever she needed to do. The police would also need to talk to her. He knew she was the totally innocent victim in this lifetime drama, but would they believe her? He was also not sure he wanted her to leave him so soon. He had grown to love her in a caring, fatherly sort of way, but occasionally he thought perhaps there could be something more. When he held her close to him in those dark, terrifying times, he never really wanted to let her go. He would also miss Richard—the quiet little boy who said nothing, heard nothing, but came to life in the sea.

He suggested they flew back to America, live in John's house until they could sort everything out with the police, and then return to England. He would look after them until they were both strong enough to cope on their own and he would help her to deal with the police. Cara was not at all sure; she wanted to get as far away from Ian as possible and he would be in America.

"America is a very big place," said John. "And apart from that, Ian will be locked up for a very long time. They'll probably throw away the key." Cara was not so sure. She needed normality in her life, if not for her, but for Richard. She wanted to go home, catch up with Julia and just live a normal, quiet life. She wouldn't have to worry about money for a while—her parents had a little put by for a rainy day which she could live on until she found a job.

After a while, she agreed to stay with John for a month before flying home— he had been so kind to her. Without him she and Richard would not have survived; she was absolutely sure of that. She knew they would be lifelong friends, even if they rarely saw each other.

John's house near Portland overlooked the Atlantic Ocean—a beautiful house on stilts with miles of sand at the bottom of the steps. In a different life she could have stayed there forever, but not now. Not at this time in her life. She had to leave. He had been left the house by his grandmother 15 years earlier and lived there between charters. "The balance between the house and the Buccaneer was perfect," he said, although he had never found the right partner. It was the first time Cara had ever thought about John's life. She had been so wrapped up in her own sordid existence, she had never wondered if John had a wife or partner, whether he had been married, or what his life was. She felt guilty now. He had unselfishly put his life on hold to save hers, without question.

Now she looked for signs of a past life in the house—a photograph, clothing, just things. But there was nothing. John's house was a very male house—no ornaments, no bits and pieces, everything in order. All the coats hanging in the hall were male, the shoes on the rack below, even the umbrellas near the door. She found herself watching him when she hoped he didn't notice. He just got on with whatever needed to be done—no questions, no dramas, just did it, whether it was emptying the bins, making dinner or ironing his shirts. And occasionally he would take Richard's hand and suggest they go looking for clams in the sand at the water's edge. Cara could see Richard was at ease with John—he knew it was John who had saved them, and without him, they would still be running from his father.

Within a few days of moving into John's house, Cara knew she must face the police soon, but would she be strong enough to deal with them, to prove her innocence. She had, after all, gone along with Ian at every move—the midnight flit from New York, the strange route south from Portland, finding the gun in Ian's holdall but not doing anything about it, hearing about the shooting in Miami but still doing nothing about it. Would they believe her?

She let John lead her—make the decisions as to how she should go about it. He went to the police on his own first and asked to speak to the most senior officer. At first they tried to palm him off with the desk officer but once he mentioned drugs, Miami shooting and a cartel, they started to take him seriously. He had been at the police station for almost three hours before he was finally shown to a large office with lots of framed photographs on the wall, books and files stored neatly on the shelves, and a very tidy desk with a large uniformed officer sitting behind it. He knew this would have made Cara run and was glad he had decided to try to see the police first before she had to face them.

He first of all explained how he had come to know Cara and Ian and had thought they were an ordinary, but very nice, couple from England. Cara had a very nasty bruise on her face but he had believed the story of her fall without question. He described their journey south towards Exuma trying to remember as much detail as possible to make Cara's eventual story more credible.

When he had finally told as much as he thought he knew he explained why he had come to the police first, not wishing to put Cara through her recent history again without giving the police the background.

At first the senior policeman said nothing, just sat with his forearms on the edge of his desk, his fingers entwined. Apart from an occasional blink, he made no facial movements, just stared straight ahead at John. He said his story was quite incredible but he could see no reason why John had come in to see him if there wasn't some truth in it. He wrote down John's address, pressed the intercom button on his phone and asked another officer to come in. He then instructed the officer to go and collect Cara and Richard immediately. John started to object, pleading with the officer to allow him to go and get Cara, but his demands were waved away and the senior officer made it clear he did not want John to say any more.

John's heart quickened and he could feel anger well up inside him. What was about to happen to Cara was exactly what he didn't want—she would feel she was arrested and he would not be there to help. He was helpless—this time there was nothing he could do for her.

As the police car drew up outside John's house, Cara immediately jumped— she knew things were not as they had planned, but she also knew, she could not hide, run or escape. She had no choice but to open the door and let them take her. She took Richard by the hand and walked out to the police car. A policewoman immediately took Richard's other hand and escorted them. Richard looked up at his mother questioningly and Cara tried to reassure him but she had no idea what to do or say. She had run out of excuses for their situation.

At the police station John was sitting in the foyer waiting for her but as they walked through the door, he was stopped from going to her. When he tried to object, he was forcibly held and told to sit down. The look in Cara's eyes and Richard's young face broke his heart. How could he have got it so wrong?

Chapter 16

Cara had been questioned by the same people who were holding Ian in Miami and then by the local police in Portland. She was separated from Richard whom she was told would be 'looked after.' She thought this could not have been happening; it was yet another nightmare where she was playing out a scene. She told her story over and over, giving details of her neighbours in New York, the hospital staff in the Caribbean—in fact anyone who could verify any tiny part of her story.

She described over and over how she met Ian, how she had fallen for his charms and had ignored her conventional upbringing. She got it all wrong and now she just wanted to go home.

"Don't think you'll be doing that for a very long time," was the only response she got from her questioners. She could not understand why they didn't seem to believe her. She was innocent. She had done nothing wrong, but fall in love with the wrong guy. Hadn't she paid enough penance?

After 72 hours, she realised it was going to be a long haul to get herself out of there. And then she saw him. Ian.

Slowly she realised why she was not being believed. He had laid a trail of deceit which put her totally in the wrong and him in the caring, hard done by, hurt role. After all, she was the one who drove out of New York in the dead of night. She was the one who paid for the ferry tickets in Portland. She showed herself to be the unstable one in Ian's office in town—his secretary would vouch for that. She had stolen passports to help her escape. And she was the one who ran to Far Off Island when the US police arrived—he had merely followed her to try to help her to give herself up.

The months that followed led Cara to depths she had never before seen—not even the year she was repeatedly beaten and raped by Ian. Richard was taken from her and she was told at first he would be put into care, but later, the worst possible scenario played out in her life. Ian was released from police custody while Cara was charged with drug dealing, fraud, murder and more. And worst of all Richard was given to Ian as he was his paternal father—nothing Cara could say would change anyone's mind. She was held in custody at a women's penitentiary while her son was in the hands of the real monster.

Cara faced more monsters in prison—women who had 'sold' their children, women who had battered their husbands, and women who went to any lengths to feed their drugs' habit. She tried to keep herself to herself and away from people she didn't even recognise as womankind, but that wasn't easy. She made herself more visible to them by alienating herself. One warder seemed to look on her a little sympathetically and made sure she was not on her own in the boiler room, showers, or anywhere some of the more maniacal inmates might get to her. Cara felt everything which had gone before was not greatly significant—just excessive domestic upsets. This was more real than anything and she knew she had to get through it to get out and find Richard. She couldn't imagine how he was—he would have reverted into a totally silent world with Ian. "But, please God, don't let Ian hurt him any more."

John was told to leave the police station—there was nothing more he could do for the time being, but he was told not to leave the country as he would be needed for more questioning at a later date. He tried to work out what would happen to Cara, but his imagination didn't run to the depths she and Richard would find themselves in eventually. When he heard Ian had been released and knew instantly Richard would be given to him—he had to protect the little boy while Cara couldn't.

He tried to find out where he had been taken into care so that he could watch out for him. It took him four days to find out, by which time he didn't know if Richard was still there. He sat in a café across the road from the so-called safe house and waited. He drank coffee after coffee, not even thinking about eating. He saw a few women coming and going from the house at different times of the day, some with young children, but there was no sign of his little friend. He, too, was beginning to fear for Richard's safety. Eventually, he could stand it no more so he crossed the road and stood to one side of the big, heavy door. It was an old building with a metal fire escape staircase up the outside, the windows dirty and the paint peeling from years of neglect. This house served a purpose and it wasn't as a home. It was just a temporary haven for women and children who had nowhere else to go which was safe. The women looked unkempt, even dirty, with unwashed, unbrushed hair, ragged clothes and faces which had seen too much heartache and despair. He immediately thought of Cara and realised that one day she, too, might be holed up in here until she could get her life back together, if ever she could. John felt for the women—no hope in their eyes, no one to look after them and care for them. How had they come to be living here; what did their stories tell?

When the door opened, John swiftly stepped across the threshold and into the hall. No nice hall dresser, coat hooks, stair runner or niceties here—just bare floorboards and rickety stairs which creaked at every footstep. Now he was in, he didn't really know what he should do next. Before he had time to think his next move through, two tall men appeared either side of him and took hold of his arms, manhandling him towards the front door again. "I'm sorry," said John. "I didn't mean to alarm anyone. I'm looking for my nephew. His mum has been mistakenly arrested and I am worried Richard will be too scared.

"He can't hear, you see, he's profoundly deaf, so he won't understand what is happening if anyone tries to explain to him."

But the two bully boys, who supposedly looked after the vulnerable women in the house, were not listening. One opened the door as the other threw John out into the street. He landed in the gutter, hitting his collarbone on the edge of the kerb. A shooting pain went through him like a dart—he knew it was broken. The door behind him slammed firmly shut.

A few passers-by stared at him as if he was an old drunk rolling around in an alcoholic stupor, but no one stopped to help him up. Each time he tried to get on to his knees, the pain seized him again. Then out of nowhere a woman whom he had seen before, but was not sure where, was beside him and taking his weight to get him up. An ambulance arrived and he was helped inside. All the time people in uniform were asking him questions, but he didn't want to answer; he just repeated Richard's name—"Richard, little boy. Blonde. Deaf. Taken in here. Nephew. I must find him. He is in danger."

Just before the ambulance doors closed, the women from nowhere said, "I've seen him. I'll try to watch for him before you come back. Meet me over there." She pointed to the café.

It seemed like hours and hours before John was discharged, his shoulder and arm firmly held in a sling. The hospital had given him painkillers and told him to go to his own doctor the next morning. John wasn't listening. He had to get back to the café.

It was very dark when he got there and there were no lights on, except for the tiny purple glow from the insectocutor at the back of the café. He tried the door but it was locked. All he could do was sit outside and wait. In just a few seconds the lights were switched on in the café and the woman who had helped him was there in her dressing gown.

"Come in. Quickly," she said. "Don't let anyone see you."

He struggled to his feet and almost ran through the café door. In seconds, she had locked up again, pushed him through to the staircase at the back of the café, and turned the lights off again. At the top of the stairs she ushered him into a sitting room over the café which faced the 'safe house.'

"I've seen him," she said. "This morning. He was brought in an unmarked cop car. Don't know why they try to hide the car. You just have to look at the cops inside to know it's them. He was taken inside but only for a short while before a man arrived in another cop car and took him away."

"What did he look like, the man?" John asked the question almost as a formality. He knew full well it was Ian.

"Not the usual sort of bloke who turns up there," she said pointing across the road. "Didn't really look like the normal down and almost out."

"Was he blonde, about my height, sort of English gent-type?"

"Yes, that was him, but I could tell from the look of the boy he didn't want to go with him. In fact he looked terrified."

It was not what John wanted to hear.

"Don't suppose you know where they went," he asked, already dreading the answer.

"Well, obvious," she said. "Where they always take them. The motel just off the highroad out of town. Supposed to be the next step from a safe house but you only have to ask anyone round here and they'll tell you. They put them up there until they get themselves a train ticket to wherever and that's them."

John was down the stairs in a second, forgetting about his broken collarbone. "How do I get there," he yelled at her. "Please, I need to know now."

"Well, you go past the cinema in Orange Street, down past the police station. No, just a min. You go past North Street first, then turn into Orange Street. Oh, it'll be quicker if I take you," she broke off, rushing through to her bedroom to throw some jeans and sweater on.

John knew this was his only chance of keeping track of Richard. By the morning they would be gone and he would have no hope of finding Cara's only reason for living. On the way, the woman from the café finally asked him why. "Who is he? He's not your nephew, is he? He's not even related, is he?"

"Hard to know where to start," said John. "No time anyway. Let's just say a woman's life is at stake, as well as the little boy's. I have to ask, though, why are you helping me?"

"Two reasons," she said. "You seem a genuine guy."

"And the other?" said John.

"It's exciting. Nothing ever happens in my life. I knew you were watching the house from the café."

If it hadn't been such a traumatic evening John would have probably smiled.

When they reached the motel, Rosie drove up the steep drive with the lights off. John opened the car door and began to thank the woman, whose name he didn't even know.

"Oh, no you don't," she whispered. "You're not dispensing with me now, not just as it's getting interesting. Anyway, if they came out now, how could you follow them without a car?"

This woman was becoming very interesting.

"Okay, what's your name and how do you want to help?"

"It's Rosie," she said. "That's why the café's called Rosie Lee—you know Cockney slang. Tea."

John had no idea what she was talking about but she had helped him a lot and he knew he couldn't really go much further without her.

"I'll be your driver," she said. "No-one will know me or my car. Just fill me in a bit. Who's the man and who's the boy?"

John merely told her the boy's mother had been arrested when it should have been the man, the boy's father. He was dangerous and was capable of anything.

Just then, they saw a light come on in one of the ground floor rooms nearby It was the nearest to reception. John got out of the car and crept along in the shadow of the bushes at the edge of the car park to try to get a better look. The door opened and a gruff Ian told the boy to get out and go to the car. Richard stood rigid in the doorway, not moving, not knowing what he was supposed to do. Ian's hand soon showed him.

Richard tumbled out towards the car park, picked himself up and moved towards a dark green Ford. Ian went back into the room, picked something up, turned the lights off and stepped out into the darkness. He caught up with Richard, unlocked the car and opened one of the back doors. Richard meekly climbed in and lay down on the bench seat. Ian threw his holdall in after him but then returned to the building and walked around the corner towards the reception. At that moment, Rosie let the handbrake off and free wheeled backwards down the drive towards the road with the car lights off, swinging round to face the right way as she picked up speed. John realised he had to catch up. He crawled back through the shadows as quickly as he could, caught up with the car and got in. Rosie had already started the engine by then, so she moved out into the road, not quite joining the traffic flow. By the time Ian had got back to his car, started the engine and moved down the drive, Rosie had pulled into the traffic, travelling as slowly as she could to let Ian catch up. *She's a pro,* thought John.

Ian's car roared past and Rosie put her foot down, staying one car behind all the way down the highway. The chase was on.

As the highway signs sped past and the sun came up, Rosie and John talked about where they thought Ian was heading.

"My guess is, they're heading for the airport," said Rosie.

"But that's back the other way," said John.

"No, the aero club one with all the little planes," she explained. "It's just got a dozen or so light aircraft and a small flying school. Bet that's where he's heading."

Rosie was right. Ian turned off the highway after an hour or so and drove straight to the aero club. By this time, it was after 9 am and the place was buzzing with small planes, fuelling up, taking off, landing, doing circuits, and loading and offloading students and instructors. John could not afford to be spotted by either Ian or Richard.

Rosie read his thoughts, pulled up outside the clubhouse, told John to stay low and slowly strode inside. She seemed to be in there for a very long while but returned full of information. Ian had chartered a small plane to fly him south to somewhere around the Cape. They would be leaving at 12 pm; Rosie, too, had chartered a plane, but for a lesson, charming the instructor in her Rosie Lee manner. She needed to hand over the $120 for the lesson, plus another 'wedge' to get them to the Cape before Ian.

She drove out of the aero club car park at speed, spraying gravel and dust behind her. John saw in his door mirror the groundsman shaking his fist, and again, in other circumstances, would have smiled. They withdrew as much cash as they could get and returned to the planes, to find Ian and Richard sitting in the clubhouse. John stayed out of sight but watched as Ian seemed to become twitchy and impatient. Richard sat motionless, a resigned, but terrified, look on his face.

Rosie went inside with the cash, returning a few minutes later with a flying helmet and goggles. "There," she said, "no-one will recognise you in this. Your lesson starts in five minutes."

John only realised then that it was his lesson, not Rosie's. She was leaving him there.

As soon as they were airborne and the instructor had explained every move and got John to follow all his movements, John came clean and produced a handful of cash.

"I'm really sorry about this, but I have to get wherever that Englishman is going with that little boy. I'll give you whatever you want."

The instructor began to question John and shake his head but John produced another handful of cash and the instructor just nodded. He called the aero club on his radio and asked what other traffic was about. Within a few seconds, he knew Ian was heading for a flying club at the Cape and he would be taking off in ten minutes.

"Okay," said John. "We have to get there before him, please."

Less than two hours later, John was hiding in the men's toilets watching the planes through the window. Right on cue, Ian's plane landed and he and Richard went into the clubhouse. He saw Ian make a phone call and realised he must be calling a cab or a hire car. John followed suit and told the driver it was urgent. Thankfully, John's car arrived first and he quickly dived into the back seat and shielded his face from the window.

"Just drive out of the aero club and wait, please," he instructed the driver. "Now, follow that cab but don't stay too close. The young driver liked this; it was just like the movies."

"Who are we following?" he said. "Anyone famous?"

"No," said John, "no-one famous." The driver was a little disappointed more information was not forthcoming, but he did as instructed and kept the other cab in sight but stayed back.

Ian was headed for a hotel where he could rest. He had been on the move for days and needed to think through what he should do next. Richard was the problem—what was he supposed to do with the brat? But he knew it was his ticket to Cara. It wouldn't be long before the police realised their mistake and she would be released. The only thing on her mind would be to come looking for Richard. Then he would sort her out.

Chapter 17

Cara lived her days existing only to answer more questions, avoid trouble in the prison and think of Richard. She lost even more weight and looked gaunt and only half-alive. She explained over and over to the police what she thought Ian had been involved with. She had no proof of anything illegal, just a whole lot of coincidences which led her to believe he was involved in drug dealing, plus what he had told her.

But then she would say that, wouldn't she? Her situation was hopeless. She pleaded with them to contact her neighbour in New York—they had already been there and nothing could be proved or disproved there in Cara's favour. She pleaded with them to contact her tutors at university—they had nothing good to say about her; she had wasted her time there, given up and run after a man. She pleaded with them to contact the sheltered home her mother had planned to move into—they hadn't even heard of her mum, let alone her. And the address she gave them of her parents' home told them nothing. The people living there had never heard of her. Her life was desperate—she had no future.

Slowly Cara was dying. She couldn't eat or drink and her body was just giving up. John visited her in prison one day and almost didn't recognise the person on the other side of the table. A crumpled being who looked twice her age. She didn't even ask about Richard.

John asked to see the prison doctor and the governor. He tried to tell them as much as he knew but they were bound by the court which said she must stay there until all police inquiries had been completed and she appeared in court to face charges of first-degree murder, drug dealing, fraud and theft. They did agree though that Cara was not the average inmate accused of such crimes. There was no fight in her, no aggression and no manipulative traits—no, not the average murderer, if ever there was one.

He left knowing that unless he could think of something, Cara would die.

John had followed Ian and Richard from hotel to hotel and eventually to a small house he rented north of New York City. There, he kept Richard prisoner, rarely taking him out. John saw Ian take delivery of takeaways, saw him with bags of McDonalds, but never with bags of groceries. He watched from a petrol station just along the road. Once he was satisfied, Ian intended to stay there for a while and that he wasn't about to do anything with Richard, apart from just keeping him alive, he thought it was safe to start trying to really help Cara.

He returned to Portland and went to Rosie's café. She was pleased to see him and asked him a dozen questions at the same time. Although, he didn't know this woman, he knew one thing. He could trust her. He told her he knew where Richard was and that he had been to see Cara in prison. He told her there wasn't much time left; Cara could not survive in the state she was in. And then he told her his reason for coming.

"I need you to hide Richard for me. This is the last place Ian, or anyone else for that matter, will look—right opposite the 'safe house' the police used. He would pay her whatever she needed and would try to keep in touch, but he had no idea how long he would need her to keep Richard. Rosie agreed at once."

"I told you before, my life is so dull, but ever since you sat in the window of Rosie Lee's, things have picked up." And then added, "Even though it does seem desperate circumstances," just in case John thought she was a little callous.

John caught the shuttle to JFK, made his way to Central Station in the city and caught the train towards Yonkers. He didn't want to hire a car because he wanted no trace of his route from the airport. He had paid cash for his flight and to the taxi driver into the city. He took a bag of clothes for both him and Richard, and after dying his hair dark blonde, hoped he could get away with looking like Ian for a while. He sat in the petrol station café again, watching Ian's house. He didn't have to wait long. Ian opened the door and stepped out within ten minutes. John saw him shout back into the house and for once was glad Richard couldn't hear anything. Ian walked in the direction of the railway station, carrying a light briefcase with, no doubt, a laptop inside. John followed a fair distance behind to make sure Ian got on a train.

As soon as the commuter shuttle moved out of the station John ran back to the house, through the gate and round into the back garden. The grass and weeds were knee high and John had to wade through them to reach the back door. He wasted no time in smashing the window and letting himself in. He ran through the house looking in every room and then took the stairs three at a time, searching for what he knew would be a very sad sight. Eventually, there he was, the little blonde boy tied up, gagged and covered in excrement and urine, half empty food cartons strewn around the floor. The smell was overpowering.

John choked and put a hand to his mouth. How could a father do this? He slowly and gently walked towards Richard who at first didn't appear to recognise him. John showed him the tattoo on his forearm and the panic in Richard's eyes started to disappear. As he untied the little boy's bruised and grazed wrists and ankles, Richard threw his arms around John's neck and clung to him. What a sorry sight.

There was no time to waste; John had to get Richard out of the house and away, but they couldn't draw attention to themselves. The smell was too great. He quickly stripped the little boy, wiped him all over with a pack of baby wipes he had in his rucksack and dressed him again. He then tried to cover the smell on him with the congealed food on the floor and dabbed a sachet of tomato ketchup on stains on his trousers from Richard's lap. He then picked Richard up, stroked his hair away from his eyes and tried to tell him he would look after him but he didn't know if he understood.

They left the house by the front door—Ian had not locked it with a key, just the Yale lock—walked down the path and headed for the station. Wherever Ian was going, John hoped it wasn't a brief visit a couple of stops down the track. Their lives depended on it. As they approached the railway station a roadside seller was touting Yankees baseball caps—hopefully it would cover Richard's head and most of his face with the large peak.

John had never before felt so tense, so scared and so almost out of control. He looked sideways, in front of him, behind him, even above as they emerged from the train in Central Station. Ian could be here. He could be anywhere. They could be caught at any time. John ran, carrying Richard and his bag, up the stairs and into the rat race outside; what seemed like hundreds of yellow cabs and the throng of people of all shapes, sizes, colours and creeds, going about their business, without, what seemed to John, a care in the world. The open-topped hop-on hop-off buses with the tour guides telling their stories, some a monotone drone giving dates in history no-one was listening to and others excited and animated about the exciting city they were being shown. Was this the same world he was in? The same world Cara was dying in? The same world Richard had been held prisoner in? Nothing made sense.

John dived for the first free cab, opened the back door, pushed Richard in and jumped in beside him. "La Guardia, please. Soon as you can." John was careful not to give a round-trip route. If security cameras were checked, he didn't want to appear on the same ones twice. Was he now becoming paranoid or was all this necessary? Arriving in La Guardia, he then jumped on a Blue Shuttle minibus just as it was setting off.

"Got your piece of paper mate?" said the driver. "Yeh, in my wallet. Let me just sit my son down," John replied. "It's okay, mate, give it to me at the other end. Heading for Manhattan?"

John mumbled so the driver couldn't hear and sat down, pulling Richard in to his side.

"Just got to pick up at JFK and then we're on our way," said the driver. When the driver got out at JFK to go and find his new passengers waiting at the Blue Shuttle desk, John and Richard hopped off and disappeared into the crowd. He knew the driver wouldn't think about them for more than a second on his return.

They made their way to the flight desk to take them back to Portland, bought their tickets and sat watching the departures screens. Almost away.

Chapter 18

By the time John and Richard arrived at Rosie's café, John was exhausted, mentally and physically. Rosie could see he was, so took Richard's hand and led him upstairs. John trudged up behind them, walked over to the armchair near the window overlooking the street outside and the safe house, and fell into a deep sleep. For a while anyway, Richard was safe.

Rosie ran a bath for Richard, got out the biggest, softest towel she could find, and gently bathed him, washing the grime and nightmare out of his little body. She then lifted him out of the bath and wrapped him in the towel, sitting him on her lap. While she dabbed the towel over him and stroked his head with the towel to dry his hair, she felt Richard start to soften, his rigid body weakening in her arms. Before she had finished drying him, he slumped on to her chest and was asleep.

It was almost 9 am before John woke up. He woke with a start, not realising initially where he was. Rosie had put a blanket over him and on the other side of the room Richard lay on the settee, curled up under a duvet, only his blonde hair showing. The events of yesterday came back to him and he realised it was far from over yet. He still had to get Cara out of jail.

There was nothing to link him to Rosie and for that he was grateful. It put Rosie and Richard under less pressure. They were safer. He got up and walked through to the kitchen at the back of the building and made himself a coffee. He realised then that he hadn't eaten the day before, and neither had Richard. He suddenly felt very hungry. Rosie had heard his footsteps from the café and appeared at the top of the stairs.

"Let's have your order, then, sir. Bagels, sausage, onions, beans? How do you like your eggs—poached, fried or scrambled?"

"The whole lot," John said with a broad smile across his face. "You are a good woman, Rosie Lee, and I will always be grateful to you."

As John munched his way through the biggest breakfast he had eaten in his life, he looked across at Richard and felt good he had managed to get him out of the house and away from his monster father. No child should experience what he had been through. John felt more positive now than he had for weeks and felt more able to try to help Cara. His first move was to return to New York and speak to her old neighbours. Next, he would go back to the Caribbean and try to speak to as many people as he could who knew Ian or Cara and then maybe Miami, but that was a long shot.

He waited for Richard to wake up and then tried to tell him he would leave him with Rosie who would look after him and keep him safe. He said he needed to go and try to help his mum and might be away for a few days. He also told him he must not go out.

Later that night John was back on a flight to New York. And the following morning he was standing around the corner from Ian and Cara's old flat. Over the next few hours both Karen and John swapped notes on what they both knew had happened. They both tried very hard not to exaggerate or assume—because they realised that would not help Cara. They could only deal with the facts. Karen said she had been visited about five times by New York City police and others she thought were the drugs' squad. She had also had a visit soon after Ian and Cara left from two men who wanted to know where Ian was.

"Did you tell the police that," said John.

"Of course, I did. I told them these men came looking for them within a couple of days of them moving out."

"No, I mean did you tell them they were looking for Ian, not 'them'?"

"Oh, I see," said Karen, drifting into thought. "No, I think I said them, but I can't be sure."

"Well, that's a start," said John. "Okay, you say you didn't tell the men anything and didn't say where Ian was?"

"No, I didn't because at first I didn't know where they were but then Cara e-mailed me to say they were on their way to Exuma. I was worried and thought I should tell them so I phoned the mobile number they gave me. It was then they became very threatening and told me I would 'get a visit' if I wasn't telling the truth."

"Do you still have that number?" asked John.

"I don't think so," she said, "but wait a minute, I think I e-mailed the number to Cara in case she or Ian recognised it."

An hour later, Karen had printed out half a dozen e-mails written to and from Cara.

John went to a nearby office supplier and photocopied all of the e-mails. He then put them in an envelope and posted them to Rosie. Everything he did had to be known by someone else, he realised. He was up against an evil he had not come across before in his life.

His next trip was south to Miami. The flight landed at 6 pm, giving John enough time to make his way to the marina where he had moored the Buccaneer and find somewhere to stay nearby. After that, he wasn't sure exactly what he would do. He just knew he had to try to find out what Ian had done.

He sat in the yacht club bar for the evening chatting to the barman, offering to buy him a drink each time he filled his own glass. Within a couple of hours, he had the barman's ear. John steered the conversation to drug smuggling through the marina and asked if there was much going on with boats coming in from Cuba. Soon the barman was sharing his wealth of knowledge about how the Miami vice squad often visited the marina, how it was easy to get drugs and what sort of boats brought the stuff in. Eventually, John brought the conversation round to the shooting in Miami a while back.

"Wasn't that something to do with drugs?" he asked.

"Yeh, it was. Always is. They never got him though. A killing at point blank range. Just held the gun up, aimed and bang. That was the end of one of the middlemen. He was insignificant though, just a messenger really between the big boys and the smaller dealers. I felt sorry for the young kid—they reckoned he missed the gunman by seconds."

"What young kid?" said John.

"He was just in the wrong place at the wrong time. At first the police thought he'd done it because his prints were all over the place, but they soon realised he was just a go-for for the dead guy. They soon let him go."

"Who was he?" said John.

"Dunno, just a kid. Think he hangs out at the drop-in centre in downtown. Usual, almost homeless kid, living off doing anything and everything."

John realised there was no more information to come, and although he hadn't really got much, there were a few threads to go on.

The next morning, he headed for Downtown Miami and wandered around trying to find the drop-in centre. He stood out as a white man in a very black area. Why hadn't he taken the time to wear some sort of disguise? Too late now; he was there.

He found a coffee bar and thought he would stop for a while and think about how to go about things. He knew he was out of his depth, but the sight of Cara looking near death spurred him on. It was not the sort of place to pass the time of day with the other coffee drinkers, so he picked up a newspaper from the table next to him and pretended to read while trying to listen to others' conversations.

This was going nowhere. He had been there nearly two hours and hadn't got a clue what to do next. This was a stupid idea. He got up to leave and as he did so, a young black kid sidled up to him and said he could help him. John didn't know what to say or do—how could he help him? What did he know and how did he know he needed help?

Outside, it became clear. The kid put a tiny packet into John's jacket pocket and suggested he could get a lot more. How much did he want?

John realised at once maybe this was the only way he was going to move forward.

"I'm not interested in the small stuff," he said. "I need something a lot more. I already have a network."

"Yeah, well, need to see your money first."

"Here, tonight. 11 pm. Bring me someone I can talk to. Not a kid," said John.

With that he shuffled away, turned a corner, and disappeared, making his way back to the marina, his heart beating fast and his palms sweating. When he reached his room he lay down and thought through the conversations of the past 24 hours and what he had arranged for 11 pm that night.

This was madness. He knew nothing about drugs, dealers, networks or any of that. He just had to find some link to Ian and pass it to the police.

He decided he couldn't go through with it. They were serious drug dealers who would see through him in an instant. They might even think he was a policeman and kill him. What he would do, though, would be to go there in disguise to try to see who turned up. He would find some hiding place and just watch.

At 10.30 pm John was lying in a filthy old sheet in a dark doorway, head almost totally covered, his face and hands smeared in dirt. It was not easy to see the doorway, leave alone him, but he could see the café where he had met the kid. As he lay there he wondered if anything would come of this strange scenario—his thoughts raced through all of the events that had happened since that sunny day when a blonde Englishman turned up at his boat and asked if he could charter it. He thought through the trip, the stop in Miami, the journey down to Exuma and on to the BVI. And then, like a bolt of lightning, it struck him.

Why hadn't he thought of it before? It was obvious when he thought about it now. Nothing had led the police to Ian because there was no evidence, nothing to link Ian to anything. No gun!

John realised that the gun which could be the one which killed the dealer in Miami was possibly right under his nose. On the Buccaneer. If Ian wanted to hide it for possible use later, where better to hide it than somewhere he could always return to and where no one would think of looking because they didn't really know anything about it. It was a moving hiding place, rarely in the same place for very long.

He wanted to leap out of his hiding place and run. Run back to the room, collect his things and head back to the airport. But just as he was thinking it all through, a car pulled up and two teenagers got out, one of them the one from the café, and the other he hadn't seen before. The teenagers looked all around them but shook their heads. Then an older man got out of the car and started arguing with the first teenager, hitting him in the shoulder.

Seconds later, the man got back into the car and it sped away but not before John had memorised the number plate.

Now he had a couple of things to go on.

Chapter 19

John was desperate to return to the Buccaneer to see if the gun was there, but he also realised time was running out for Cara and he needed to find out more just in case he was wrong and the and gun wasn't there. His next trip was back to the Caribbean, back to Ian's office and back to the hospital.

The office was obviously closed but there was a sign in the window with the letting agent's phone number and address. John went straight there and spoke to the woman sitting at the reception desk.

He was then on his way to Julie's home, Ian's secretary who Cara had mistakenly thought had been having an affair with Ian. John found her very willing to spill whatever beans she could about Ian—when he had fled he had gone without paying her, paying any of the office bills, and had also taken her mobile phone.

"It was a new one," she said. "An iPhone. Thieving pig. He had loads of money. It took me nearly a year to save up for it." John wasn't really listening; he just wanted to know as much information as possible on Ian's contacts on the island, who he did business with, where he went on his business trips and what she really thought of her boss.

Julie listed a lot of local people but nothing really stood out as anything out of the ordinary. John decided he would try to feed her snippets of the sort of monster Ian really was, to see if she could be more forthcoming. He mentioned his physical attacks on Cara. Julie looked shocked but then drifted into thought. He then mentioned his running away from almost every place he had lived with Cara.

"It was always a midnight flit, nothing planned, just grabbed their stuff and left. And I think he set their New York apartment on fire the night he fled."

But it was when John described how he had found Richard bound and gagged and left alone that Julie really opened up. In fact, she then got up, walked through to another room and returned with a laptop.

"This is his," she said. "I was so upset that he didn't pay me or give me any notice about my job that I took it. He always kept it in the safe but the day he phoned me and told me to take it out and take it with a load of money from the safe to some place down by the harbour, I decided I had had enough. He was a pig to work for. One day, he would be charming and nice and we would have a laugh and the next he would be as rude as they come and treat me like dirt. I knew when he wanted me to empty the safe that he was going and I probably wouldn't see him again. I felt bad about taking it. I've never used it.

"I couldn't really tell the police about it when they came asking questions, so I just hid it in my bedroom."

John thanked her and told her she had probably saved Cara's life. He took the laptop and said he would not mention the money in the safe to anyone. As he left, he gave her a big hug as she said, "Let me know will you? How Cara gets on. I didn't really know her, in fact I didn't really like her when she accused me of having an affair with her husband, but she didn't deserve what you have told me. I know that."

John didn't bother going to the hospital; he thought he had enough evidence now to get Cara out of prison. He just hoped the laptop would tell all. If the gun was on the Buccaneer, that would top it all off.

He was back to the airport within the hour and flying north the following morning. Again he realised he had eaten very little.

Chapter 20

Overnight, John drew up his plan. He would keep Richard safe with Rosie. She was not connected in any way with Cara or Ian, and no one could ever link him to her either. That way Richard was safe—Ian would know it was him who had taken his son, but he could hardly report him to the police.

He then called the penitentiary where Cara was being held and said he was her husband and wondered how she was getting on. On hearing that she was now in the infirmary and in a critical state, John asked to be put through to the prison governor. In a rapid fire of words, John tried to explain how the police had got it all wrong and that he now had evidence to prove it. He asked for the name of the senior policeman investigating Cara's so-called crimes. Within the hour, he was sitting in his office showing all of Karen's e-mails to and from Cara, detailing his meeting with Ian so long ago in Portland marina, and finally producing the laptop.

At first, the policeman didn't seem interested, saying such things as, "They never are guilty. It's always someone else's crime," until he read the e-mail about the two men visiting the New York apartment looking for Ian.

He sat up, slowly read all the rest of the e-mails and then turned to the laptop. He pressed the intercom button on his phone and asked for the duty officer in the technical office to come in. The laptop serial number was written down and a sheet filled out detailing where it had come from. It was then taken away and John felt uneasy he had not been able to back up whatever was on it, but time was crucial now. He had to trust the police to do the right thing and eventually release Cara.

The next six hours saw John going through every detail he knew of Ian and Cara since he had met them; Cara's bruises on the first day, Ian's instant mood swings, Cara finding the gun in the Buccaneer's stern cabin, his visits to their apartment outside town and his eventual involvement in Cara's escape. He did not mention Richard, apart from to say he knew Ian had also beaten him and that he was very concerned for his safety. He also did not say he thought the gun could still be on the Buccaneer.

When the police told him he could go but stay locally, he went straight to the penitentiary and on to the infirmary. When he got there, Cara already had a police officer next to her bed but she was unconscious with numerous monitors wired up to her. The police officer and a doctor were talking in whispers which John could not hear, but he soon realised they were planning to move Cara to the town's hospital intensive care unit. But time was running out for his friend. If the monitors hadn't shown her pulse was still beating, he would have thought she was dead. She was motionless, pale and looked gaunt. Her eyes were sunk into their sockets and her cheekbones protruded in an ugly angle, almost making her look skeletal. What was the difference between life and death? Just a very slow heartbeat which skipped occasionally, making John feel wretched and tense because he could do nothing for her. He knew Cara's only hope was to know Richard was safe, but how could he explain to her what had happened, how he had kidnapped him from his prison near Yonkers when his father had left him caged like an animal, sitting in his own faeces?

John weighed up the consequences of saying nothing more to the police, or of telling them everything to try to persuade them who was the real criminal here—but it would be Ian's word against his and they could construe whatever they wanted to, or whatever Ian persuaded them to.

He couldn't take the chance of the police arresting him—then he could not help Cara at all. It would be the end instantly and with both he and Cara locked up, there would be no one on the outside, except Ian.

He phoned Rosie and told her the situation—Cara would not last very long unless they could get Ian arrested and show her Richard was safe. He told her to prepare to go to the hospital with Richard as soon as he told her to—it may be the next day or it could be in a few days' time, but it was urgent as soon as he phoned her.

John then hired a car and drove as fast as he could to the Buccaneer. On the way, he stopped at a camera shop and picked up a digital camera. He wasn't really sure why but just thought he might need to gather evidence for the police. Ian might be the planner here but John was not in the league of the master criminal.

He then phoned the policeman in charge of the investigation and told him he was going to the Buccaneer and that he thought the gun could still be hidden there. He said he would call him again if it was and would not touch it or anything else around its hiding place until the police got there. He then rang off. He didn't wait to hear the policeman tell him not to go to the boat on his own.

As soon as he stepped on to the Buccaneer, he knew something was wrong. Maybe it was the way the boat didn't tip to the extent it usually did when his weight was on the side deck, or that the ropes were not coiled neatly, the way he usually left the boat. He couldn't quite put his finger on it or really acknowledge things were not right. Subconsciously, he knew.

In an instant, he heard the police siren at the same time as Ian appeared in the companionway, gun in hand aimed directly at him.

John felt the hot liquid through his tee shirt before he realised it was his blood oozing from his stomach, and before he really felt the excruciating pain as the bullet ripped through his skin. In what seemed to be like a slow-motion repeat of a soccer game, John stumbled backwards over the guardrails, hitting his head on the pontoon before his body finally slumped into the water. He lost consciousness but not before hearing a second shot, its destination unknown.

The Buccaneer's mooring warps had been thrown on to the pontoon and the engine started before the second policeman reached the top of the slipway. Hitting the stern of the yacht moored in front, Ian clumsily manoeuvred out of the marina and into the channel leading to the open sea. By the time the police had recovered John from the water, realised their colleague had also been shot and called an ambulance, Ian was almost out of sight. They commandeered a speedboat from a nearby pontoon, taking the owner with them to helm, but the channel was packed with sailing and powerboats of every shape and size. They went in the direction they thought the Buccaneer had gone, but didn't really know what they were looking for. Every boat looked the same to them.

Ian's mind was racing. Now the whole situation would change. Cara would be seen to be the victim and his story would never be believed. He had just shot a policeman and John in daylight, in front of witnesses. Why had he not made some excuse to John as to why he was on the boat? It would have been easy but he had the gun in his hand and he knew it was John who had taken Richard. There was no one else who could have done it. But he should have planned John's demise, not just acted like a gun happy unprofessional hoodlum. That could be his downfall.

The more distance he put between himself and the marina, the safer he would be. And the more he was in the middle of the whole armada of yachts out on the water, the less likely the police would find him. Just as he was thinking through his options, an alarm sounded inside the boat and when he looked down into the cabin, what appeared to be smoke was coming from the engine compartment. In his haste to get away and start the engine, he hadn't turned the water inlet on to cool the engine. He had no option but to turn the engine off, or get help. He shouted to a nearby yacht that he thought the engine might be on fire.

As the crew from the yacht came on board the Buccaneer to help, Ian swiftly hopped across on to their boat and was away, but there was another man down below whom Ian hadn't expected. Things were going badly wrong again. He needed to escape, be alone, and take stock—once more. In a swift leap over the stern of the yacht, Ian found himself in the tender. Cutting the dinghy loose, Ian pulled the start cord on the outboard motor and was away in seconds.

In half an hour, he was ashore just south of Portland. He had jumped out at the shore but not before turning the boat around and winding up the throttle so the dinghy set off back towards the throng of boats, leaving no tracks of where Ian was. He walked up to a small road running along the coast. Hitching a lift a few miles south, he then took a motorbike from outside a general store and was free again, heading inland, well away from boats, marinas and the police.

By the time the police had caught up with the Buccaneer, then the rescue yacht, the dinghy, the car which gave him a lift, and then the motorbike owner, Ian was miles away.

He was an expert.

Chapter 21

Cara woke up in the hospital to find Richard sitting on her bed holding her hand, a confused and frightened expression on his face. The woman holding his other hand, Cara didn't know. Was she a policewoman, a carer, an official of some sort? Not that it really mattered—Richard was safe and there was no sign of Ian.

It took her a long time to work out how Richard had come to be at the hospital. There seemed to be no link between any of the people around her bed, in the hospital or from the police station. She took to Rosie instantly—a rounded woman in her mid-fifties, originally from England, Cara guessed, but now apparently living in Portland running a small café, as well as looking after her little boy.

How had she come to have Richard living with her? And then she thought of John. The last time she had seen him was when she was first arrested and was held at the local police station. She couldn't remember seeing him since, but she was sure if he could be there to help her, he would be. She realised then that John must love her, and that although she didn't love him in the same way, he was her only rock in a raging sea that swept her along from one nightmare wave to the next.

It was another two days before Cara could even speak—her illness had left her devoid of most human actions, but she now knew she could survive. Richard was alive and well and whatever torture he had been through, surprisingly, he was a survivor too. Occasionally, he would point to his arm or to hers and draw a picture on it. Cara didn't know what he wanted or what it was he was trying to tell her, but she knew it wasn't a game. Eventually, a young cleaner came into the ward carrying a bucket and mop. As he prepared to clean the floor he pulled his sleeves up as it was a warm day. Richard immediately reacted and ran to the young man, a smile on his face. It was when he pointed at the man's tattoo on his forearm Cara, and Rosie too, realised he was asking about John.

Cara didn't know what to say and looked helplessly to one of the nurses. But it was Rosie who spoke.

"When I heard there was a shooting at the marina, I knew it must be John. He told me to bring Richard to the hospital as soon as he phoned me, but he never called. I waited and waited and eventually phoned the police and said I was worried about my husband. Well, they wouldn't tell me anything, would they, if I wasn't a relative?

"They told me there had been two shootings—one a boat owner and one a policeman—and asked me to go to the mortuary to identify my husband."

At this news, Cara shrieked. "No, no, not John, it can't be true. No. Please God, no." Richard looked frightened when he realised how distressed his mother was, and began to cry. Everyone in the ward looked at Cara for some sort of clue as to her state, but she couldn't enunciate any words.

Just then, two more policemen arrived and asked to speak to Rosie. She left Richard sitting with his mother and went with the policemen. They asked her about her 'husband' and she had to admit he was just a friend and explained she needed to know what had happened to him because of Richard.

Then there, began hours and hours of questioning about Richard, about how he had come to stay with her and how she had got involved.

"Well, you backed the wrong horse, didn't you?" she said to the police. "Isn't right, leaving a young child so vulnerable to his monster father. You should have got your facts straight before you handed him over."

The police began to protest and to suggest she might keep her remarks to herself when she didn't know the full facts, when she continued, "And yet you were told the full facts, but you didn't listen. Seems as if he conned you, too. Ian, that is, that criminal who has duped you, drugs people, the police down in Miami and Lord knows who else."

Rosie had just begun to feel that maybe she had said too much when the police countered her scrutiny of them with questions about why she was keeping a child whom she knew had been kidnapped from his father.

They were going around in circles, but the police seemed to believe Rosie's story and had begun to warm to her. They didn't get many witnesses, or even possible criminals, treating them in this way. And, after all, Richard was safe, and she had brought him back to his mother whom they had wrongly imprisoned.

Eventually, the conversation came back to John and what had happened to him.

"Was hit right in the stomach," said one policeman. "Lucky, it wasn't a bit higher—maybe because Ian wasn't at the top of the companionway down to the saloon. He's still unconscious—not sure if he'll make it."

Rosie was suddenly overcome, tears started to flow down her cheeks, and her neck flushed a bright turkey-neck red. From her quiet, boring life of a few weeks ago, so much had happened. She knew John was a good man; she felt it in her bones. And to hear that he had been close to death after all he had done to keep the boy safe, was just too much. The policemen were surprised—they had obviously thought of her as a tough old bird. This was not a side of the strange English woman they had expected.

Just as they were wondering what to do, whether to try to comfort her or wait until she had composed herself, their radios crackled into life. They both left the room, leaving Rosie still sobbing and wringing her hands, and Rosie heard them talking in low whispers outside the room. She couldn't quite hear enough to work out what was happening—whether it was good news or bad, so she got up and walked over to the door, putting her ear against it.

"Okay, we're on our way. Probably be there by nightfall. Don't take your eyes off him; he's a master."

It must be Ian they were talking about, thought Rosie. It couldn't be John as he was in hospital just down the road. It couldn't be Richard as he, too, was nearby in the hospital, and anyway neither of them could be described as a 'master.'

She returned to her chair just as the policemen came back into the room. They told her she could go but that she must not leave town, she must report to the police every morning in person, and that she could continue to look after Richard if his mother allowed it.

So good of them, Rosie thought sarcastically. *If it had been left to them, Richard and his mother could well have been dead by now.* But, this time she kept her thoughts to herself.

Chapter 22

Cara continued to improve over the next few weeks and became stronger, both physically and emotionally. At first, Rosie came just for an hour each day with Richard but within a few weeks she could leave Richard with his mother for the day and collect him later when she had finished work.

Cara began to put on weight and her strength slowly returned. Although, she now knew she was safe, and so was Richard, all she thought about was going home. Going home to England, to safety and to normality—she would never again think her life was humdrum.

The police visited Cara frequently but were never allowed to stay for more than an hour as she just would not be able to cope with the questioning. As it was, the short bursts of interrogation exhausted her.

She came to realise they knew far more than she had thought—they had been in touch with Karen in New York, with Joanne and even her university tutors in Sheffield. They intimated they had mistakenly arrested and imprisoned her but never actually apologised. It was then that Cara became quiet and sorrowful. If it wasn't for John she would have died in prison, and she could only imagine the horror Ian would have put Richard through. It was just so wrong that John had become the victim—it should be Ian who had met his end at such a young age.

Eventually, Cara was discharged and she moved in with Rosie and Richard until she could put her life back together enough to fly home. It was only then she realised she had nothing—no job, no money, no home, no husband...not even any clothes.

But Rosie had realised her predicament and had subtly asked her to work in the café sometimes. Within three months, Cara was fit enough to face the next chapter in life and asked Rosie if she could borrow enough money to get home. Getting herself a new passport had not been simple—her spell in prison had marked her as a possible threat and despite assurances from the local police, it had taken many weeks to persuade the passport office in England and the US immigration authorities that she was a simple UK citizen wanting to go home and just needed a passport.

Rosie drove her into New York and to JFK airport for her final flight back to England. Cara could not actually imagine herself ever-leaving England in the future. She planned to start all over again—get her degree and settle down to a quiet life bringing up Richard. It was an emotional farewell when she said goodbye to Rosie; this woman had looked after her son and had taken her in when she was homeless without asking for anything in return. A truly generous person.

Arriving at Heathrow early in the morning, Cara and Richard made their way through the commuters to Kings Cross station to take the train to the midlands. Although, it would be sad going home without her parents there to welcome her in, offer her great quantities of food and to make a fuss of Richard, it was still home, still her bedroom, still the familiar green front door. She couldn't wait, her excitement welling up with every mile the train moved northwards.

Richard felt her excitement too. He had no idea really why his mother was so excited but he loved the way she kept hugging him and smiling and telling him they were starting a new life. He knew they were safe now; he didn't know what had happened to his father but he just knew he and his mum were safe and he was far away from them.

They got off the train and waited for the bus—as Cara had done so many times before. In the past, she had never felt excited about going home, just felt it was her duty, and although she had loved her parents, she had grown up and was living her own life. The bus pulled up outside the 'open all hours' shop on the corner of the road and Cara and Richard hopped out on to the pavement. They had no luggage, just a few clothes in a small holdall. They walked along the road and Richard could feel the excitement in his mother's hand. He felt eager for whatever it was making his mum so happy.

It took many minutes for Cara to work out what the problem was. She reached the garden gate and looked up the path to the front door. It was red. There was a car parked on what was her father's vegetable garden and part of the front hedge had been ripped out to make way for a drive. There was another family living in her home.

Various thoughts raced through her mind; were they tenants and Ian had rented out the house while they were away—in which case at least she would have some sort of income—were they friends of Ian's staying there for a while, or who were they?

Cara tentatively walked up the path to the front door—it wasn't just red, it was a completely different door. UPVC and double-glazed with a gaudy floral design in the small window in the top half of the door. There was no letterbox, just a copy of an American letterbox on a post in the ground next to the front door with a lever at the side. As Cara looked around her, at this strange pretence of her former home, she noticed the windows—white PVC double-glazed everywhere. More gaudy floral patterns in the top opening lights. Where were the old wooden sash windows? Then, she noticed the curtains. Her mother always had all the curtains for the windows in the front of the house the same—deep red with a beige stripe in a heavy, almost tapestry material. These were all different for each window—different colours, different patterns, different material. This wasn't the empty home of her late mother.

Just as she was wondering whose house this was, the door opened and a woman with a cigarette hanging out of the corner of her mouth stood there in her mother's hallway, holding a toddler on her hip. Richard moved to stand behind Cara, unsure of the scene in front of him, but sensing from his mother's change in mood, that things were not right.

"Can I help you?" said the woman, managing to blow smoke out of the corner of her mouth without removing the cigarette or even holding it. At least she blew the smoke in the opposite direction to her daughter, thought Cara subconsciously.

"Err, I'm not sure," said Cara. "I just wondered, err, how long you had lived here?"

"Well, what's it to do with you," said the woman, immediately defensive.

"It's just that this used to be my parents' home and I haven't been in this area for a while."

"Been here two years, I suppose. Yeh, just before Kate here was born. We've done a lot to the house since we bought it—new windows, doors etc. Very old fashioned, it was. Bit of a state."

"Bought it?" said Cara. "You mean you own this house?"

"Yeh, we own it. Hey, I'm not sure I like where this is going. What do you want?"

And with that she yelled at the top of her voice, what was presumably her husband's name, because a scruffy, unshaven man wearing tracksuit bottoms and a grubby vest appeared in a few seconds, sensing his wife needed him urgently.

Her daughter then began to cry, obviously frightened and shocked at her mother's screech in her ear.

"This woman claims she used to live here and is asking all sorts of odd questions," the woman told her husband.

"What sort of questions?" he answered, and then turning to Cara, said, "What's your business with us. We don't know you. You from the council?"

"No, I'm not from the council," said Cara, "I hadn't realised the house had been sold. I thought we still owned it. My husband and I, that is. Do you remember the name of the person you bought it from?"

Two years ago? How? This time Cara wasn't really shocked. She knew Ian was capable of anything, so selling her parents' house was insignificant compared to all he had done.

At first, she wanted to contest the purchase, hire a lawyer, claim it back. But she knew she wouldn't get anywhere. She married Ian so everything that was hers, was also his to do with what he wanted to. Why would he have bothered to tell her; there was no reason. He had intended her to never find out, never come home, never return to the sanctuary she now sought. He had, after all, taken her passport and kept her in a prison he thought she would never be able to escape from. She wasn't strong enough or wily enough. But then, he hadn't bargained on John coming to her rescue.

Cara simply apologised to the couple for disturbing them, took Richard's hand and walked back down the path.

"It's all legal like," the husband shouted after her, but she was no longer listening. She was walking away from her home forever.

Right, time to get real. Get a grip. No point in dwelling for too long, thought Cara. She had been too weak for too long. It was time to move on, move into the next era of her life. Try to forget about the past.

She rang Julia's mobile and forced herself to sound cheerful and excited to be home.

"You still in Sheffield?" she asked her friend. "It's just that I have a little boy with me who I am dying to introduce you to."

They were heading north again on the train within the hour, getting off at Sheffield Midland station and taking the bus to Julia's digs. She had finished her degree, went on to do a masters and then taken a job in town. She rented a small flat with her boyfriend. Cara felt a tiny pang of jealousy she didn't deserve to allow herself to indulge in. She had made her choice all those years ago, despite her best friend's warnings and feelings.

When the two friends met, there were hugs and tears for a very long-time, leaving Richard to look a bit embarrassed. He wasn't used to seeing his mum like this—happy and sad at the same time. She hadn't been like this with Joanne or with Rosie in Portland. His mum was a bit strange, but he loved her, anyway.

Julia poured out the questions, not taking a breath, and then she realised Richard was there and she hadn't even acknowledged him. "I'm so sorry, little man. I haven't even said hello," she put out a hand to him.

He flinched a little as he hadn't heard anything she had said but realised she was trying to be friendly. Cara gave him a little nudge and told him it was all right. Over the years, they had both learned to 'sign' a little, but did not communicate conventionally. They were just very happy together and didn't need words to express themselves to each other.

Julia looked a little confused and looked from Richard to Cara and back to Richard again. Cara had never told her friend Richard lived in a silent world or the reason for it. In fact, she had not really told her anything of the nightmares she had lived through since leaving Sheffield. There had never been the right moment and it wasn't something you could write in an e-mail. "Oh, and by the way, my husband beats me, had an affair with my only friend where we lived, killed my mother etc. etc." No, there was never a proper time, until now.

Julia had even more questions and this time, demanded to know the answers.

"What's been going on, Cara? Where's that wonderful husband of yours? There were months on end when you just didn't stay in touch. I thought we were soul mates?" But she didn't mention that Cara was almost unrecognisable as her college mate—she now looked twice her age and the sparkle, which was always around her, had gone.

"Well, I don't really know where to begin," said Cara. "How long have you got?"

"As long as it takes," said Julia, sensing it was going to be a very long conversation, and also sensing it was not going to be a happily ever after sort of story either.

While Julia prepared a meal for Richard, Cara began to tell her only real friend in the world her very sorry story. But she felt it was too awful to tell her everything. Julia remained silent and let her friend talk, only interrupting her occasionally to ask what Richard liked and disliked and after his meal, if he would like a bath before bed.

She grew more and more incredulous as Cara poured out the drug dealing, the arson and the shooting of the policeman.

When Cara finally finished, she felt drained and exhausted—just ready to sleep and do nothing else. Julia realised what Cara was thinking and quickly made up a spare bed for her and Richard and told her to get a good sleep.

Then, Julia sat for a very long time into the night thinking about the nightmares her friend had endured. She would be strong for her now and help her put her life back together.

When her partner, James, came in, he found her sitting looking out of the window. It was 6 am and he had just finished his shift taxi driving.

"Hey Jules, what you doing up? Anything wrong? What's going on? Nothing serious, is it?"

Julia couldn't begin to explain it all to him and just said, "Cara is here and we need to help her." James knew Julia well enough not to need to ask anything else—for the time being.

Even though Julia had only managed a couple of hours' sleep, she was focused. A woman on a mission. First of all she logged on to her bank account and checked her finances. She would need to provide for Cara and Richard for some time. Then she e-mailed her father in Ireland and explained she needed to borrow £5,000 straight away and possibly more at a later date. She said it was for a very close friend and that she would explain everything when she was home at the end of the month. She knew her father would help—he never needed to know why; he just trusted her to do the right thing always.

Next, she showered, dressed and left the flat, leaving a note for Cara on the kitchen table saying she would be out for a couple of hours. Her first visit was to the letting agency she rented her flat through. After just a ten-minute conversation, she was out on the street again with a list of addresses to view. She hoped James would not mind moving to a bigger flat which Cara and Richard could move into with them. She could not see any other way of Cara being able to start again on her own.

Her next visits were to the council offices and social services. Cara had no money, no home, no income, but she had a child. Surely there could be some help for her. After a very frustrating two-hour wait she was told Cara's situation could only be discussed with Cara and that they could not tell her anything.

Finally, she phoned her former university tutor and asked to speak to him urgently. She had worked hard at university and had built up a very good relationship with her tutor so she knew he would listen. But she also knew he had very little time for Cara because of the place she had wasted in her few weeks at college, a place another student could have taken.

"So why would I want to help her. Didn't she just dump her course, dump her friends and chase some guy?" said Stephen. "What makes you think she wouldn't just do it again?"

"It's different now," said Julia. "You wouldn't believe what has happened to her since she left here. If you would just meet her you would understand—she is not the person she once was, not in any way."

"But didn't you say she just turned up without warning with a young boy in tow. No money, no home and no prospects? No, I don't see why I should bend the rules to take her back. There are other students far more determined to succeed. She's just a waster."

"But she's not," pleaded Julia and then raised her voice. "She made one mistake—she fell in love with the wrong person—and believe me, she has paid the price over and over for it."

The lecturer was taken aback by Julia's outburst—it was not like her at all to be so demonstrative and forthright with him. She was usually a focused, hardworking student. Maybe he should think about this, but maybe he would just be wasting his time again.

By the time Julia returned to her flat, Cara and Richard were up and dressed and sitting playing with a puzzle. They looked a picture of contentment and happiness, thought Julia, but she now knew otherwise.

"Right, we're moving," Julia announced, hoping James would just go with the flow and not ask too many questions yet. She glanced at him as he appeared at the door from their bedroom, and hoped he would realise she just needed him to go with it until she had time to explain everything to him when they were alone.

"We're what?" said James. "Where, when, why?"

"Tell you later, James," Julia said praying to herself he would realise it was a delicate situation and that she hadn't gone mad.

"But I like it here," he went on, "It's near to the town, the local's great and we've signed up for another six months."

Cara instantly realised she and Richard were the reason for her friend's sudden action and tried to protest, but she also knew Julia was the only person who could help her, help Richard, and keep them safe—until at least she had time to sort something out.

She began to protest but Julia jumped in straight away and announced to the room she had already decided, already taken on a bigger flat, and that she would make sure everyone was happy, even though she felt far from confident after seeing the look on James's face.

She explained to Cara that she had made two appointments for her—one with the local district council's housing department and one with her university tutor.

"Really," said Cara, "already? We only arrived last night."

James started to speak again but Julia just put her palm up towards him and he thought better of it. Her Irish temper could be very persuasive—he knew from experience—so he just said he was off to the pub and would see them all later.

Julia moved towards him and went to put her arms around his neck but he brushed her away.

"I love you, James. Remember that and trust me."

He snorted as he shut the door behind him.

"I'm so sorry, Julia. I shouldn't have come. It's just that I had nowhere else to go and no-one else I could ask for help."

"Ach, he'll be okay. Just a man. Doesn't like his peace disturbed but as it's me who does everything around here, he'll just have to put up with it until we can get you settled. Don't worry about him. I'll be *nice* to him tonight!"

Cara smiled at her Irish friend's confidence and humour and wondered if she would ever feel confident again.

"Right, I think you and Richard need to register with a local doctor's practice and I really think you should both have a comprehensive medical. It's hard to take in what you two have been through and I'm sure you haven't told me the whole lot—just précised it."

Cara felt weary. Although, she knew everything her friend was saying was right, it was hard to take in all the appointments and organisation. She had drifted from nightmare to nightmare for so long she just couldn't get her brain to work in an ordered manner.

Julia read her thoughts and gently said to Cara what she had said to James, "Trust me. It will be okay."

Two hours later Cara, Richard and Julia were on their way to the district council offices.

They walked into the waiting room and sat down on the stained, torn chairs. The walls were drab and the paint was peeling. Even the long rubber mat which was supposed to protect the floor was torn and the corners turned up. Two broken chairs lay in the corner while others had arms missing. There were signs all over the room telling you not to be aggressive—they would prosecute—not to smoke, not to drop litter, not to approach the counter until asked to do so, and to make sure you had your social security number with you and proof of identity.

Half a dozen people sat waiting to see how they could improve their lives; how they could have somewhere they could call home. But their faces showed a resigned look which meant they would never really be able to get out of their situation. They needed to go back to school, learn to read and write properly, and get some qualifications. But how could they do that without some sort of income, somewhere to live and some hope?

It was a depressing place, to say the least and Cara didn't really know what she needed to do or what she needed to say. She needn't have worried. Julia was still a woman on a mission.

"Right, this is the woman I told you about. She's been through hell. She's been abroad for a few years. She has no money. She has no job. She has nowhere to live. But she has a son who can't hear. How can you help her?"

"What references do you have?" the council official said to Cara.

"Didn't you hear me?" said Julia. "She has nothing!" Cara jumped when Julia raised her voice.

"But she must have something," said the council official.

Julia sighed loudly and tutted at the same time. She didn't have much patience at the best of times and this woman was really trying what little she had.

"Look, let's start again."

"Okay, I get the picture," the woman behind the counter said. "There's no need to be so aggressive. I don't have to put up with it, you know."

This wasn't going very well.

Cara interrupted the two women scowling at each other.

"I have just returned from America where my husband is on the run for murder, drug trafficking and God knows what else. I was arrested and thrown into jail because my husband persuaded the police it was me. My little boy is profoundly deaf because of his father who also happened to tie him up and leave

140

him alone covered in his own excrement for God knows how long. I returned to the UK when the American police realised they had got it wrong and let me go. I came home to find my husband had sold my parents' house—after killing my mother, by the way—and so, you see, what my friend has told you is the truth. Sounds farfetched, I know, but that is my predicament."

Both Julia and the council official stared at Cara open-mouthed, but said nothing.

Eventually, Julia said, "Oh my dear, dear friend, Cara. I had no idea. What you told me last night was bad enough but I cannot begin to imagine how you have got through all of that. Why…"

But Cara didn't let her finish her sentence.

"What was the point in telling you? I was too weak to pack my bags and leave, and when I eventually did, I was arrested and thrown into jail. I have ruined my life but I am determined that Richard's life will not be ruined, also. I will get somewhere to live. I will go back to university and finish my degree, and eventually, while he is still young enough to enjoy his childhood, we will have a happy home."

The council official asked the two friends to return to the depressing room with broken chairs housing people with broken dreams while she went into a back office.

Julia and Cara sat side by side saying very little. The others in the waiting room had heard Cara's outburst and, at first, also said very little.

Then, a young man who looked in his early 20s turned to them. "Well, that's the best story I've heard in this place and I've been coming here for four years. It's too farfetched not to be true. You should write a book!"

Cara could not look at him; she just stared down at her grey, scuffed trainers with the sole of the right shoe hanging down.

"Go on, tell us a bit more. Brightens this place up. Gets a bit boring sitting here for hours waiting for the Gestapo to decide not to give us a decent place to live."

"I'd be grateful if you would mind your own business and leave my friend alone," Julia growled at him.

"Only trying to be friendly," the young man countered. "Didn't mean to upset anyone."

"Well, best you just shut it," Julia snapped at him.

"Look," Cara said. "I didn't mean for you to hear any of this. I just need somewhere to live. I'd be grateful if you would just let me be."

"Ark at her," said a woman with three children causing chaos near the toilet door. "Don't ere that sort of hoity toity voice in ere much, do yer?"

"Don't believe any of that stuff, do you? Some people will say anything to jump the queue."

Julia leapt off her chair and stood in front of the woman with her feet apart, arms crossed.

"I suppose you have some sad story about all the different dads of your bastards leaving you in the lurch," she yelled at her.

"Just look at you. Filthy hair, dirty clothes, snotty-nose brats. No wonder you wear sweat pants!"

The rest of the room fell silent. No one dared say a word. Even the woman with the three children seemed in shock.

Cara was about to try to calm the situation down when the council official reappeared behind the counter and ushered her and Julia into the back room—just in time as the woman got to her feet and started towards Julia.

"You little…" But the woman's voice trailed off as Cara and Julia quickly moved around the end of the counter and through the door. For the first time in a very, very long time, a smile appeared over the two friends' faces, as they conspiratorially grabbed each other's hands and escaped the onslaught of the mother's tongue.

The council official told the two women they could offer Cara a small flat because she had Richard, but the only one available was on the 'wrong side of town.'

"I know, I shouldn't say this but it might not be a good place for a woman on her own. I can only believe your story because, as the oik outside in the waiting room said, it's too farfetched not to be true."

"My advice is to live with your friend here for a few months and if there is anything at all on our housing list which comes up in a better area I'll give you a call. I'm not supposed to do this, but I think you've been through enough not to live in almost a squat with drug dealers on your doorstep."

It was as if Julia and the council official had been friends for years. Julia stood up and hugged the woman and said she thought she was doing a wonderful job—if only all councils could be like this.

Nothing more was said.

The next visit was to the doctor's surgery where Cara registered herself and Richard and made an appointment to have a medical.

"Right, that was easy," said Julia. "Now the difficult bit. We're off to the university."

"I'm not sure I can do this now," Cara began to say. "I just feel very tired and would like to be a bit more with it before I see him. The last time he saw me I was driving out of the campus with Ian and things were a bit sour."

"He'll be putty in your hands," Julia replied. "No worries. I tell you, as soon as he sees you, there won't be a problem." Cara was unaware how awful she looked—and how much older than her years.

As she sat outside Professor Stephen Smith's office, she looked around at the décor. A bit shabby, but nothing like the housing department's waiting room, she thought. You could almost go back in time sitting there. Wood panelling everywhere, book cases, old yellowing pictures on the walls of people from a different era.

"I wonder what they are all doing now," she though absent-mindedly, when the door opened and a middle-aged man with round spectacles on the end of his nose looked up and down the corridor. He glanced briefly at Cara, looked at his watch and tutted.

"Typical," he muttered under his breath. "Can't be that desperate to come back if she can't even be here on time."

He returned to his office and Cara heard him on the telephone. "So much for her ladyship wanting to come back and get on with her degree. Hasn't even turned up. Tell her not to bother wasting my time again." The office was quiet again.

"But I've just looked out of my office and she's not here I tell you. The only person out there is a woman who I think must be here about her son or daughter but she hasn't made an appointment, so she won't be lucky today."

Quiet again. And then the office door opened once more and the professor looked over his glasses at Cara. "It can't be," she heard him say to the telephone. "It's been what, three years, four years? This woman must be 50 if she's a day." Julia told him to take another look.

Stephen Smith returned to the corridor and stood in front of Cara. He was visibly shaken at the sight of the young woman before him. He put out both hands to her, took hers and pulled her to her feet.

"Oh my god. It is you Cara. What on earth…" But his voice trailed off as Cara leaned against his chest and silently let tears fall.

"I'm so sorry. So Sorry. I should have listened to you. I've been a fool."

The professor and his former student talked for a very long time in his dark office which was full of books and piles of papers strewn across his desk and which were spilling on to the floor. He gently asked her what had happened to her but soon realised she needed to look forward, not back. Cara could not begin to tell this man what she had been through. She needed to talk about normal things, studying, work placements, possibilities. Not the hell of her life since she was last here when the world was hers, she was free, single and loving life. How could she have got it so wrong?

"Cara," said the older man, "Please, just call me Stephen. I think I have been very mistaken over you. I now realise you are very serious about doing a law degree and I will help you in any way I can. It will not be easy with a young son but I know Julia will help—and she won't let anyone cross her; or you for that matter!"

When Cara finally left the professor's office, she knew exactly what she needed to do to get her degree—and whatever it took, she was going to do it. She had three months before the course started which would give her time to settle somewhere, find Richard a nursery school, and hopefully find some sort of job. She felt lucky. And she hadn't felt that for many years.

Julia was sitting outside the office with Richard, and in her usual way, said, "About time. How long does it take to decide whether you are going to offer her a place?" But with her strong Irish accent and her wry smile, both Stephen and Cara knew she was just being Julia.

Chapter 23

By the time Christmas came, Cara felt her life was at last going in the right direction. The council official had been true to her word and had called her as soon as a small flat became available. It was really a bedsit but had a tiny garden and was in a quiet area. It was a safe haven. Julia and James had given her and Richard a room in their slightly bigger flat and James had decided he liked the move and did not want to go back to their old area of town.

Cara had taken on three jobs—stacking shelves at night in a big supermarket around the corner from her flat, word processing reports for a chartered surveyor and cleaning the nursery where Richard went on a Saturday. All three jobs fitted around her life with Richard and the university. An old lady lived in the flat below hers and babysat in the evenings when Cara was at work. Although none of the jobs paid well, she could pay the bills—just—and do her degree, which was what really mattered.

She used whatever time she had keeping up with her studies and coursework—she would not and could not let her tutor down again. He knew she was working as hard as she could and he helped her with whatever she struggled with.

Although, she was still skinny and gaunt, her complexion looked better and her eyes were not so dull. She had even put on a couple of pounds over the few months back in England. Richard was very happy at the nursery and had made a friend, Peter, whose mother had invited him home for tea a couple of times.

One day, she had a letter from the police department in Portland, re-directed from the university, the only point of contact the police thought could trace her. Her first thoughts were that maybe the police had changed their minds again and perhaps they wanted her to return to Portland. Maybe they thought, once more, that she was guilty, she was the one involved in all the drug dealing and murders. But she took hold of her thoughts and forced herself to breathe slowly and calmly and read the letter properly.

It was just telling her that they were still looking for Ian but there was no other news. They asked her to let them know her address or e-mail address in case they needed to contact her. She duly obliged, secretly hoping she would never hear about Ian ever again.

Cara knew her student debt was building up but that was ok. She could deal with that later. All she needed was to get through her degree. Julia had given her all her textbooks and more, including an old laptop computer, so she needed very little other than food and to save whatever she could to pay Rosie back. She had been so busy she hadn't thought very much about her time in Portland, but now that the university had closed for the Christmas break, she spent some time catching up.

She wrote a long letter to Rosie telling her all about her life and telling her she would never be able to thank her enough for all the help she had given her and Richard. She enclosed a cheque as a first instalment for repaying the money she owed and sent her a small present for Christmas.

When she had finished she sat quietly in her small sitting room. There was just one lumpy sofa, a small table where she did her work and a lamp. Richard was fast asleep in their tiny bedroom.

For the first time, she thought about John. Thought about Ian. And thought about her life on a sunny island in the Caribbean. Was that really her? She felt so far removed from it all now, she could almost not take in that it was her who had lived through it. She then thought about Ian. Who was that man? Was it really the beautiful young man she met in the university bar on the first night at college? Was it really the same man who killed her mother? The same man who shot a policeman in broad daylight. And the same man who had shot John?

She felt a sudden sadness, almost desperation, for the loss of her friend. He had saved her and he had saved Richard. But why did he have to pay the ultimate price for it? He was a good man. She felt her throat tighten and the tears began to flow. Until now she had not allowed herself to indulge in self-pity, a feeling of loss, sorrow or melancholy. Christmas just brought all the memories back— good and bad.

She cried for two hours—at times almost wailing—and when she finally stopped, she felt better but exhausted. She dragged herself into the bedroom and lay down next to Richard, not bothering to wash or clean her teeth.

As she curled up next to the warm little body of her son, she realised that without him, she really didn't have a reason to live. There would be no point in doing her degree, no point in working every hour she could. No point in anything.

As she drifted off to sleep, a picture of John formed in her mind—smiling with the sun shining down on him at the helm of the Buccaneer. He had been a good friend.

Chapter 24

The next morning Richard was up early—as usual—giving his mum a nudge to wake her to come and play. He had a new kit space ship his friend Peter had given him and he wanted to build it.

Cara sat up and looked at the eager face on her son. There was no question. She would get up as she always did and play with Richard.

She put her dressing gown on and wandered through to the kitchen/diner/sitting room. She put the kettle on and came back to Richard who was sitting on the floor, legs splayed with the kit spaceship between his knees. He picked up each of the big pieces and looked at the diagram on the instruction leaflet. He placed them on the floor in front of him in the exact sequence the diagram described and then looked for the smaller pieces to be glued to the fuselage. He didn't really need Cara to help him. He just loved her to be part of his game.

Cara picked up the instructions and tried to work out what was needed but Richard was always ahead of her. "This piece next", he mouthed at her. No-one else would have understood him, but she knew his every sound and movement.

Two hours later, Cara was on her third cup of tea, they hadn't had breakfast, but the spaceship was beginning to look like the picture on the box.

It was still only eight in the morning and she heard the postman drop her mail through the letterbox. She padded down the hall to pick up the post and saw there were a couple of Christmas cards and a letter with an American postmark. Rosie was the only person she knew in the States, so assumed it must be from her.

As she opened the envelope, something made her stop and look at the envelope again. A cold fear crept up her spine. It was a formally typed letter and before she read it she somehow felt it was bad news.

The letter was again from the Portland Police Department.

Her hands shook as she held the letter between her right thumb and first two fingers—so much so she could hardly read it. She sat down on the wobbly chair next to the table and put the letter on the table so she could read it properly.

It was almost just a formality—an update on their hunt for Ian. Reading between the lines, it was obvious they were no nearer to catching him than they were when she was living with Rosie. They merely wanted her to contact them if she had any communication whatsoever from him—and to update her contact details. They had sent their first letter via her university students' office asking them to pass it on. She thought she had replied to their first letter via e-mail. She breathed more calmly now and realised Richard had been trying to attract her attention. She stared out of the window and thought for the first time that she actually loved the grey skies of England. She felt safer here than anywhere she had been in the last few years. As long as she stayed focused, got on with her life and left Ian far behind, everything would be ok, wouldn't it?

She returned to building the spaceship but was still deep in thought about the letter and about where Ian was. Just then the doorbell rang and a very chirpy Julia called through the letterbox.

"Come on you two, it's almost Christmas. Time we went shopping and met Santa."

As Julia entered the room, Richard looked up from his spaceship and realised she was there. He ran to her; Julia had become one of Richard's favourite people, probably because she didn't really behave like most adults did. She was fun and didn't feel the need to conform to being a sensible grown-up. Once, she had even hidden in a wardrobe in a shop and jumped out on the salesman when he was showing it to his mum.

Although, he adored his mum, he secretly wished she could be more like Julia. His mum was a bit too serious sometimes.

Julia whisked Richard up in the air and gave him a big hug.

"Shall we go and see Santa then, little man? He's in the Co-op today. Bit odd that he should choose the Co-op to visit when he comes all the way from Lapland, but that's men for you."

She grinned across at Cara and noticed her friend was quieter than she had been of late.

"What's up? It's Christmas, you're supposed to be jolly and singing awful carols all day."

"Oh, nothing really. Just a reminder in the post," she passed the letter to Julia.

"Well, no surprises there," Julia said. "Ian's far too clever for the average American cop, isn't he?"

"I mean, look at how they treated you. It's obvious to anyone you couldn't possibly get involved in drug dealing, murder or any of the stuff that husband of yours got into."

She realised she had maybe gone too far so changed the subject.

"Right, time you two got up. Get your kit on and we'll have brunch in town. My treat."

They walked into town with Richard swinging between the two women—no care in the world. They passed the Starbucks and Costa and headed for what Julia described as the greasy spoon on the corner near the bus station.

They ordered the works—bacon, eggs, mushrooms, tomatoes, beans and even fried bread. Cara and Richard shared—neither of them could eat anywhere near as much as Julia could.

"Now, this is what I call a proper Saturday morning," said Julia.

"After this, we're off to the Co-op to find Santa for Richard."

"I'm not sure he will be too keen," said Cara. "Having to meet a strange man dressed in strange clothes, sit on his lap and try to work out what he's saying," Cara trailed off.

"Nothing new then," replied Julia. "Sounds like James the morning after he's been out drinking and he's trying to be nice to me so I don't get grumpy with him. And don't forget the dodgy beard."

Cara laughed. Her friend was so laid back about life and just seemed to go from strength to strength. She wondered how her life would have been if she had stayed with Julia, got her degree and followed convention. But there was no point in dwelling.

Santa turned out to be better than expected. He realised Richard was a bit shy and reticent so sat on the floor of his grotto and persuaded Richard to do the same. He then opened his sack of presents and asked Richard to choose one. Richard wasn't sure if he should but the sight of his mum and Julia egging him on helped him.

His new kit model brought a big smile to his face and a sigh to his mum.

"Oh, no. Not another kit to build. I'm just not cut out to do these. I don't have the patience to read the instructions and Richard doesn't have the patience to wait for me."

The three wandered around more shops looking at all the gaudy decorations and having to listen to the tinned Christmas music.

"If I hear 'Don't Stop the Cavalry' one more time, I'm not going to be responsible for my actions," said Julia. "That Jona Lewie has probably caused more bad feeling at Christmas than any other song. Even 'Hark the Herald Angels Sing' is better than that."

Cara laughed and suggested they went home for a cup of tea and muffins.

"Oh, but I was so enjoying the festivities, the shop girls wearing their Santa hats, the men sporting the worst sing-along ties imaginable. Do we have to go?"

As they entered the front door, Richard ran ahead, clasping his new kit from Santa, eager to start building it.

"Hang on there," said Cara. "We've got to finish the spaceship first."

But as she went towards her son, she stopped dead. He was standing in their sitting room, his face contorted in terror and urine was running down his legs, making a puddle on the floor.

"Richard," she screamed. "What's..." But she couldn't finish. Ian had grabbed their son, putting his hand across his mouth and dragging him towards Cara.

"You didn't really think you could escape from me, did you? You underestimate me, my darling. There's nowhere you can go where I won't find you."

Julia backed off down the hall, praying Ian did not know she was there. In an instant, Cara realised she needed to stop Ian seeing Julia so ran towards him, leaving Julia shielded by the door. She was stronger now. She could deal with him, but she wasn't expecting the gun butt which knocked her to the floor. As she lay in the puddle of urine, her own blood trickling into it, the picture before her made her physically sick. Her son, again held by his father, again terrified, again looking totally lost in the nightmare of his father's actions, stood rigid on the spot, his father's hand still grasping his mouth and jaw.

Cara tried to get up but her husband's leather brogue shoe came up and kicked her stomach.

"Get down where you should be," Ian growled at his wife. "I'm in charge again and this time there's no way out for you or for the brat.

"Did you really think you had seen the last of me? You must have thought you had died and gone to heaven when they let you out of prison. The American plods are even more stupid than they are here.

"I walked straight into their police station and found out who it was who had collected you from prison. Easy. Then I dealt with her. Nice of you to send her a Christmas card with your new address. Saved me the trouble of visiting the police station again to find your address. And that, my darling, is how I found you. Much easier than paying your friend from university a visit. I knew I could find you through her.

"Did you like my letter on police department stationery? Knew you would fall for it. So naive. So stupid. You didn't even spot the e-mail address I'd written wasn't the police."

Cara gaped at him. Why did she not realise it was from him. She never could read his next move. Yes, she was naïve. After all these years she should be able to guess some of his moves. She had yet again given him everything he wanted—the route to get back to her and Richard. Another blow came from his fist.

Cara slowly lifted her head again and tried to focus on her husband. He looked very different—he had died his hair darker and grown a beard which changed the shape of his face completely. He was thinner and stooped slightly, but other than that, he was the same. His face seemed more intense somehow, maybe the beginnings of downward lines from the edges of his nostrils and the sides of his mouth accentuated his features. He had aged. But nothing like Cara had aged.

"How" she began to ask him, "did you get out of America? How did you escape? What do you want from me? There is nothing left, Ian. Nothing I can give you. Can't you just let me be. I won't cause you any harm. I won't tell the police anything. Please, Ian, just leave us to get on with our lives."

"Oh, that would be too easy, my darling Cara. You betrayed me and you must know by now that I don't forgive. Never. You are going to help me get back on my feet. For some reason even I cannot fathom, I need you. I can't exist without you. You will be my wife again. But this time, without the brat."

With that, he grabbed Richard and held the gun to his head.

"No!" screamed Cara. "No, Ian, no. He's been through enough. Leave him alone. Take me, but not him. Please Ian. He doesn't deserve this. He can go and live with Julia. Please, I'll do anything."

But Ian just said, "Stop your snivelling. You sound even more pathetic than you are. I'll do what I want to do. You should know that by now. You are coming with…"

But he didn't finish his sentence. A policeman appeared at the doorway with Julia standing behind him. As soon as the policeman saw the gun, he pushed Julia back and tried to call for back up, but it was too late. Ian calmly lifted the gun, aimed at the police constable and shot him at point blank range. He then aimed the gun at Julia and fired, but she had been protected by the policeman's body and had fled down the hall and out into the street in an instant, missing Ian's bullet. Ian ran after her but couldn't see her hiding behind the wheelie bin outside the house next door. He looked up and down the street but knew he had very little time. The police radio had responded instantly to the constable's attempted call, so back-up was obviously on its way.

He grabbed Cara's hand and tried to pull her out of the flat. She clung to Richard and desperately tried to shield him from his father but she still wasn't very strong and Ian's grip on her arm was unresisting. Ian turned to see why Cara was struggling so hard and saw his son. Without a moment's hesitation, he pulled Richard from Cara, threw him to the floor and put an end to his misery with one bullet. Cara fainted and collapsed almost on top of Richard's little body.

Ian heard the police sirens and knew he was trapped. He just had one way out. He pulled Cara up on to her feet and threw her over his shoulder, running to the front door as the first police marksman ran down the path.

"Christ, thank god you're here," Ian shouted at the officer. "Quick, there's a total nutter in there. Be careful he's got a gun and he's used it. Shot your mate."

The marksman looked over his shoulder and beckoned to his colleagues to follow him.

"Let this man through. Says there's a nutter on the loose in there. Already shot Andy. Get him to the ambulance."

As Ian climbed into the back of the ambulance, the driver and his colleague took Cara from him and laid her down on the trolley inside. Ian knelt beside her and told them to be quick. "She took a major blow from that bastard." As the ambulance doors shut Ian saw Julia shouting and waving at a policeman and pointing at the ambulance.

"Quick," he shouted again. "She needs to get to a doctor." The ambulance sped away from the flat, the driver on his own in the cab and his colleague in the back with Ian and Cara.

As soon as Ian thought they were a safe distance away, he pulled out his gun and told the ambulance woman to tell the driver to stop. "And don't do anything stupid," he added. "I hold the trump card," he said, waving the gun in the air.

The ambulance stopped and the driver got out and came round to the back doors. As he opened them, Ian pushed the ambulance woman out on top of the driver and they both fell to the ground. Ian aimed his gun again but the driver lunged at his feet, knocking him over. The gun went off, missing both his intended victims. He aimed again and this time he shot the driver, but as he tried to shoot the ambulance woman, he was pushed from behind and missed again. Cara had come around and had woken up to the scene before her. She pulled herself up and threw herself at her husband, knocking him to the ground.

As he struggled to get Cara off him and to deal with the ambulance woman, a car screeched to a halt behind the ambulance, the driver getting out and hiding behind his open car door. Ian aimed his gun yet again, but this time it was empty. He had used all his bullets. In a second, he ran around to the front of the ambulance and got into the driver's seat. The wheels spun, throwing up a black rubber smoke as he desperately tried to get away. Eventually, they took hold and Ian had escaped again, but this time he had a tail. The car driver took chase behind him, swerving around the two-ambulance people still lying in the road.

Sweat poured down Ian's face and into his eyes, blinding him periodically. He wiped his brow with the back of his hand and poked at his eyes with his fingers.

"Damn that bloody bitch," he yelled at himself. "Damn her. Why did I come back? She has to die."

The car was still tailing him and he knew he could not get away from it—the ambulance was no match for an Audi TT. He couldn't shoot the driver. If he stopped, he might not even be able to overpower him. So he let him overtake and when he had, he slowly pulled to a halt in the middle of the road behind the Audi. As the driver got out, Ian carefully stepped down from the cab of the ambulance, hiding his gun in his jacket pocket. He raised his arms and walked quickly towards the driver.

As soon as he was within a few feet, he took his gun out and pointed it straight at the driver's face, telling him to get to his knees. "But you've run out of bullets, remember?" said the driver.

"Are you willing to take the chance I didn't reload or there was one more random bullet in the barrel?" Ian retaliated. The driver looked confused and then dropped to the ground, allowing Ian to step around him. He could hear the police car coming up behind them but it couldn't get past the ambulance. Ian leapt into the driver's seat and sped away.

He was just too clever for them all.

Chapter 25

When Cara arrived at the hospital she continually told the doctors there was nothing wrong with her, it was her son who had been shot and she needed to go to him. It was only when the police from the flat arrived that she realised Richard was dead. They whispered amongst each other and occasionally looked sideways at her.

There were no cries, no noise, no tears, just an old resigned look which had become Cara's trademark. Just another tragedy in her life she could have done nothing about. Or could she?

Julia arrived in the next police car and ran to her friend.

"Cara, dear Cara, I am so sorry. I should have warned the police what he was capable of—they should never have gone without back-up. Come home with me. Please come. We'll take care of you."

"I want to see him," Cara replied. "I need to see Richard. To make sure. To realise this is the end."

"It's never the end," shrieked Julia. "It isn't, Cara. Please. We're here for you. We'll make you strong again."

"Why?" was all Cara replied.

Cara was taken to see Richard after waiting for more than two hours, by which time she was like a rag doll. Limp and lifeless. No sign that she was alive apart from the fact she was standing up and could move. Richard looked a lot better than she expected. His face was no longer in pain emotionally, the nurse had cleaned him up and he was just calm. But dead.

She later had to spend what she felt was a totally worthless time with a counsellor introduced to her by a policewoman. She didn't reply to any questions or make any comments—just sat waiting until she could leave the room.

It was the evening before Julia could take Cara home to her flat with James who had been told the full story by Julia on the phone.

"I've made up the spare bed for you, Cara," he told her. "And I've made a lasagne for us all." Cara did not reply, just walked through to the spare bedroom and closed the door behind her.

"Christ, I don't know what to do," Julia told James. "How can she pick herself up from this? Richard was her sole reason for living." She burst into tears and sobbed on James' shoulder. He had never seen her like this. She was the strong one. The one who could juggle her life, and his, with all the balls in the air, and never drop one.

"First of all, we'll talk to her tutor and between us all we'll work out a way; she is never on her own," said James. "She is very vulnerable right now and will be for a very long time."

"I am owed a few days off so I'll take them now until we can sort it out. I think we should also plan to do lots at weekends—walks, cycle rides, anything to keep us fit, give Cara something to do away from all this crap, and maybe even plan to decorate this place."

Julia lifted her head from his shoulder. She had never heard him so positive and so in charge and she knew everything he had said was absolutely the right thing to do.

"You're amazing," was all she said.

The days that followed were pure torment for Cara. She had to organise a funeral for Richard but she just couldn't. She couldn't bring herself to say a final goodbye to him, her little boy who had seen more horror in his short life, than most people did in 80 years. They had been through so much, almost from the time he was conceived, but they had survived it all, despite his disability. The people he had got to know had all disappeared in some way or another—the people at the nursery, Joanne, their neighbour, Rosie in Portland, and John. John, the man who became their true friend who rescued them and eventually gave his life for them.

Cara had no tears—just a resigned look which Julia and James thought would never leave her.

Although, she could not bring herself to organise anything, she went along with whatever Julia and James suggested because she was not capable of thinking of doing anything else. In some ways, it made it easier for her friends to get her out of the flat and engaged in something. But they knew she could not live her life like that.

Her tutor at university gave her more and more work every week without fail but the work she handed in was poor and would never gain her any sort of qualification, let alone a degree.

He decided one day to take his task a step further so asked her to come in for a chat.

"I know it is very early days since Richard died, but…"

"Murdered. He didn't die," Cara replied. "He was murdered by his father, my husband."

"Yes, of course," said Stephen. "I'm sorry."

"Don't be," said Cara. "He was nothing to you."

Her tutor was surprised at her directness. Usually, she was so meek and never countered anything anyone ever said.

"Look, I need you to focus more on your studies."

"Why? What is it to you whether I fail?"

This was going nowhere.

"Well, because you are taking up a place someone else could be using and because I know you are capable of becoming an excellent lawyer, of achieving far more."

"Okay, I'll leave," replied Cara.

"No, you will not leave. Not this time. It matters greatly to me that a student of your potential achieves the highest she can. It reflects on me if you don't."

Cara was a little surprised at his directness this time and sat quietly for a few minutes pondering her situation and what he had said.

"I don't know how to study any more," she said. "I just can't seem to concentrate and retain any information. I just sit there like a zombie and don't get anywhere. I try to do the work because I feel beholden to you, no other reason. You gave me a second chance."

The professor felt totally overwhelmed by Cara's little speech, so much so he could not reply for some time. This poor woman had lost everything, but she had to find a reason to live, a reason to carry on and put all her tragic life behind her. One day, he knew she would succeed and be happy but he had no idea how to help her get there.

"Have you seen a bereavement counsellor?" he eventually said.

Cara, who had been staring at her feet, lifted her head and looked at him.

"I know you are trying to be kind to me and I know I really don't deserve your kindness. I threw away the good chance I was given, but I have to find a way to believe I want to carry on and not just because I feel beholden to you. Everything goes round and round in my mind all the time—my father's death, my mother's murder, John, and now Richard."

Her throat became tight and she didn't think she could carry on, but it was the first time she had felt she could talk about it all, so took a deep breath and went on, "I am trying to remember all the reasons I came here in the first place, but I keep coming up against all these stumbling blocks. I wanted my parents to be proud of me, to know all their hard work to give me a good education had paid off, but they will never know now, will they? They are not here to see me get my degree. No one is. So I just end up thinking, what's the point?"

"Then I start again and remember my teachers at school and how they encouraged me. I think I'll do it for them but they probably wouldn't even remember me, so again, what's the point."

"I know Julia and James would love me to be happy again but I honestly don't know how I can be. You see, I really don't have anybody and that's not just me feeling sorry for myself, it's the truth. Everyone needs someone, don't they, to make them get out of bed in the morning and get to grips with life. But I can't see how.

"I don't want to be part of Julia and James' lives. They are a couple and need to be together. Just together. Not with me tagging along for the ride. They have done so much for me, but sometimes I wish even they weren't here so I could just disappear. No one would miss me or think, 'Could I have done more to help.'

"The doctor would probably just put me on anti-depressant pills, but that's not the answer. They would just put everything on hold until I came off them. I really just don't know how to move forward or whether I really want to."

Her tutor stared at her and for the first time in his professional life, his throat tightened, his eyes filled up and he reached across and took her in his arms.

He held her tightly to him and neither of them said a word. They just stood in his dark study surrounded by his piles of papers and books and silently cried.

Chapter 26

It was another three hours before Cara finally left Stephen's office. She had been shocked by him. Shocked by his strength of emotion. Shocked by his care. But above all, it made her realise there really were people in the world who cared. And if she continued to dwell on what was and what could have been, she would never be able to see the good around her. He had made her realise, too, that it really mattered to Julia and James what happened to her. They were not just being kind friends. She mattered to them and if she was no longer around, their lives would be affected—and not in a good way.

Maybe she should start thinking about them. About her tutor. And not about everything in the past. Perhaps, there could be a future for her.

She walked home slowly and on the way stopped at a shop. There really wasn't anything to celebrate, but life itself, so she bought a bottle of champagne, Julia's favourite crisps, James' favourite dry roasted and walked into the flat.

She could hear them talking in the sitting room but there was someone else there—the sound of their voices was muffled so she could not really hear properly. She walked through the door holding the champagne to see John sitting on the sofa talking to Julia. Her grip on the champagne slipped and her head spun. As the champagne hit the carpet, John was up on his feet in an instant and caught her before she fell.

"Is it you, John? Really you?" she said. "But I thought you were dead."

"No, almost dead. I had a 20/80 chance of survival—the odds not in my favour—but somehow I came through it. I was unconscious for 11 weeks and then had no memory for a long time after that, but eventually it all came back and here I am.

"It took me a long time to find you. The police were absolutely useless in the States, and not much better here but eventually you wrote to Rosie. Dear Rosie. I suppose you've heard?"

"Not really," replied Cara. "Ian said he had dealt with her, but I didn't ask how. I really didn't want to know any more about what he had done."

"Well, she's alive, but in a wheelchair so she's had to sell up and move to a much smaller place on the ground floor. She's okay but she'll never be the same dear Rosie who helped us so much."

Cara sighed a long sigh and just shook her head.

"Well, what's the champagne for?" said Julia. "I know we are celebrating John being here but you bought it before you knew."

"Just life," replied Cara. "I talked to Stephen for a very long time and he made me realise I had to stop thinking about me and what had gone on before. It's time to look forward, not back."

"Wow! That's great. James and I have been trying to find a way to get through to you but failed."

"You didn't fail in any way, my friend," said Cara. "I know I would not be here if you had let me be on my own for one minute."

"Told you so," said James, beaming across the room.

John and Cara didn't quite understand the looks crossing between Julia and James but they didn't need to. Things were at last moving in the right direction.

John and Cara talked and talked for hours, well into the night, filling each other in on the missing pieces of the jigsaw; how Ian had escaped from America; how she had found her parents' house; how Julia had just organised her life since the day she arrived.

From what John had found out from the police and others he knew at home, Ian had killed someone else and basically stolen his identity. The man had died just because he happened to look a bit like Ian—darker hair and with a beard and glasses, but the same height, build and age. Ian had stalked him and followed him home. He had taken his passport, social security card, driving licence, bank cards and anything of use after killing him at his flat. The man was found after the police broke in when he hadn't turned up for work—but it was two weeks later because, as Ian's luck would have it, he was supposed to be on holiday. By that time, Ian had left the country and come back to England. He just used the man's money to buy his plane ticket, turned up at the check-in desk with a week's beard growth, wore a pair of glasses he bought in a chemist's shop, and just walked away from his trail of death and destruction. As cool as that.

When Julia got up the next morning, she found John and Cara both asleep on the sofa, Cara's head on John's chest. It brought a smile to her face and made her feel good.

Chapter 27

When Cara woke, she knew she was lying on the sofa with a man but it took her a few seconds to remember the events and discussions of the night before. She felt strange feeling a man's breath on her face and his warm body close to hers and at first, felt a little embarrassed. As her body stiffened and she began to pull herself upright John stirred and opened his eyes.

"It is just so good to see you, Cara, and to be with you. I have thought so much about you and Richard over the last few months. If only I had found you earlier…" But he didn't finish.

"We have to look forward now John. We just can't go over all the horror of the past few years any more. It is totally destructive and will get us nowhere. I was ready to just give up after Richard died. I couldn't find a way forward but I feel a tiny thread of hope now. Hope that I can have a future. I will never be able to get over Richard's death, but I know I have to learn how to deal with it, not to let it engulf me as I have done.

"I can never tell you how pleased I am that you are alive. I thought I had lost you, John. I love you—not in the way of lovers, but just because you are so unselfish and generous and gave Richard and me so much.

"Ian is still out there and I know he will come looking for me but I can't continue to live in fear. I have to be positive. I will be careful but I can't let him ruin my life any more."

The four friends decided to go out for the day—drive out into the countryside, find a nice walk by a river and enjoy a long, leisurely pub lunch. Cara couldn't remember when she last did that—it just seemed such a beautiful thing to do.

Julia and James walked hand in hand, feeling better than they had for a very long time because they knew at last that Cara was coming out of the darkness of the last few months. They both also secretly hoped Cara and John would eventually get together—they liked him and knew he would always be there for their friend. But that was, maybe, hoping for too much.

Their day was perfect. The sun shone and the gentle breeze made the trees sway with their branches silhouetted in the river. They sat down on the river bank and watched a couple of teenagers trying to row an old wooden dinghy unsuccessfully. The oars seemed too long so knocked against each other where they met in the middle. Eventually, one of the rowlocks pulled up out of its socket and plopped into the water, rendering the boat stranded in the middle of the river. The teenagers both tried to grab the rowlock at the same time and ended up tipping the boat over. Their laughter seemed to echo across the water as they swam, towing the boat to the bank.

John got to his feet and went to help them. "Looks like you guys are having fun," he said to them.

"Not really got the hang of this," said one. "Got any tips?"

"You could maybe do with some shorter oars."

As John and the teenagers chatted and pulled the boat up on to the bank to empty it, Cara turned to James and Julia and said, "I just feel normal today. Just a normal person having fun with normal friends. It's great. I actually want to get back to my studies—the first time I have felt that for ages. Thank you so much you two—I could never have got here without you. And, now I know John is alive, I just feel everything's eventually going to get back to normal and I can begin to live again. Richard's death will always be with me, but I know now I can learn to live with it."

Julia burst into tears and hugged her friend.

"Women! Unbelievable. One says she's happy and the other one cries."

John joined them again, bringing the teenagers with him.

"These two are Jack and Jonny and they have enlisted my help in teaching them to row, so if it's ok with you, I'll meet you at the pub in a little while."

The two groups of three set off—one by boat, and one by foot—and met up again at the Rowers Arms. John had invited Jack and Jonny to join them and the six of them spent the afternoon enjoying lunch.

As they parted, John said, "I'll definitely be in touch with your dad. Thanks."

"What's that all about?" James asked.

"Their dad has a carpentry workshop and is looking for someone to do some work so I thought I might see if I would do. I'd just like to stay around for a while—or at least until the authorities pack me off back to the States," he replied. "Well, if that's okay with you three?"

Cara couldn't have been more pleased. She had missed her friend so much so she certainly didn't want him to go again so quickly.

"If they take me on, I'll find a flat and stay awhile."

Within two weeks John had got himself a job helping the boys' father at the workshop building window frames, doors and bespoke kitchen cupboards. He had also found a flat half a mile from Julia and James and had enjoyed spending as much time as he could with Cara, asking her to help him choose furniture and fittings.

He had come to realise he loved her and wanted to spend the rest of his life with her, but now was not the time to do anything about his thoughts. She was still in emotional turmoil and he didn't want her to make a mistake they would both regret later or he could end up losing her friendship too. He was ten years older than her and wanted to make sure the age difference would not matter in years to come.

John started work with the boys' father and felt his life at last had a purpose. He had drifted for years, chartering the Buccaneer but never feeling he wanted to settle anywhere.

He had always said he could never do a 9-5 job; he just wasn't a routine person, but his life now was more routine than ever before.

He tried very hard not to invade Cara's life; she was trying to get back into studying and her tutor was seeing her almost daily to help her. But John knew this idyll he had found could not last. He had a visitors' visa and his job could never be official—just cash in hand at the end of the week.

He was fortunate enough not to need to earn very much—his parents had died when he was a teenager and had left him enough money and a house to never really have to work. But without work of some sort he had little purpose in his life.

Cara had changed everything. The day he met her was a turning point in his life. He had seen her vulnerability—and her bruises—but had believed Ian's story of her falling, at first.

He had soon realised that the doting husband was actually a bully, and that there was a particularly dark side to him. He had never realised the real extent to that dark side until the day he turned up at their house and found Cara and Richard.

165

From that day, he had promised himself he would always be there for her.

At weekends, he would meet up with Cara, Julia and James and they would repeat their walk and pub lunch every Sunday. Cara had continued to live with James and Julia until one day she called at John's flat one Saturday morning and said she wanted to ask him a favour.

"I sort of feel I shouldn't abuse their hospitality any more. I needed to be there with them for a long time but I think I should move out. They are a couple and need to have time on their own. The threesome is great—we are all very close—but I think the time has come to make a change. I wondered what you might think about me renting your spare room? I'd pay you rent and we could share all the bills. We know we get on well, but I don't want you to feel you have to take me in. I need to be more independent now, but still don't think I can live alone. I still have very low swings when something reminds me of Richard."

John wanted to leap up and pick her up—he had thought about this for months but had never dared to suggest it.

"I, um, don't want you to read anything into my suggestion," Cara went on. "It just seems a perfect solution."

John, at first, had thought that maybe she had begun to think of him in the same way he thought about her—so felt a little disappointed at her comment.

"Of course not," said John. "We are mates, that's all, and we know we always will be. Sounds a perfect set-up to me. Shall we go and get your stuff?"

"Er, not quite so fast. I need to talk to Julia and James first—just explain what I feel. I don't want them to think I am dumping them in favour of you. I'm sure they won't because I know they really like you, but I just want to make sure."

When Cara left John's flat, she too felt a little disappointed. She had never thought she could be with anyone ever again after Ian, but the last few months had been great with the four of them doing things together and just having simple fun. She now knew John didn't think of her in that way so she would not upset anything by hoping for something that would never happen.

Julia and James began to protest when Cara told her what she had been thinking, but soon stopped when she said she was going to move into John's flat.

"That's brilliant," screamed Julia. "We've thought for ages you and John were great together and this is just perfect."

"No, Julia, it's not like that. We were both honest with each other and I now know he's not at all interested in me in that way. And anyway, I think I'm better off being on my own. Relationships like that just upset the equilibrium. We're just great friends and that's how it always will be."

"But that's nuts," said Julia, never one to hold back. "You were made for each other. I don't believe you when you say you're better off being on your own."

Cara smiled. Julia was so open and confident, she sometimes wished she was like that.

"But we talked about it and we both agreed that wasn't on the agenda and never would be."

"Well, we'll see," continued Julia. "You can be so stubborn sometimes." She wanted to point out that it was her stubbornness which had led her to leave university in the first place and run off with Ian, but thought better of it.

"Well, we'll miss you but I think it's great you and John will be sharing a flat. Ignore my girlfriend—engages mouth before brain sometimes," said James.

"When do you want to move in? I can get a van from work and give you a hand."

"Thanks James," said Cara, "But I really don't have that much stuff. I'll talk to John and see when it's convenient for me to move in."

"Yesterday, I would imagine," said Julia grinning. "No need for more furniture, especially in the bedroom."

Cara remembered why she liked Julia so much. She had the ability to say anything at all and never insult her.

Within a few days, Cara had moved in. John had suggested he cook dinner and invited Julia and James and the four had a great evening together. The more time they spent together the more funny times they had and could recall over dinner. Cara loved it. And John secretly hoped that the stronger Cara became, and the more she thought about her future, and what she would do once she had her degree, perhaps he would be part of it all.

But one day, a letter came addressed to John from the immigration department.

He knew that one day it would come and he would have to deal with it. It was a form asking about any work he had done, if he paid tax on it and when he planned to leave the country.

Before he replied, he spoke to his boss and asked if he had declared any work he had given John, and if so, how he had dealt with the PAYE liability, tax etc. His boss said he had never disclosed anything about John and as far as anyone was concerned, he didn't work there and never had. But he added that it might be better if he stopped working for him for a while if the immigration department was beginning to investigate him.

Although John was disappointed, he knew it was the right thing to do. He returned the form saying he was not working and was sharing a flat with a friend and that he hadn't any immediate plans to return to the US, but politely said he knew the regulations and realised he could not stay beyond his visa limitations.

He could not think about leaving now. For the first time since he lived at home with his parents as a teenager he felt settled, content and without need to explore the world or do anything else. But he had little choice.

As he sat quietly pondering his situation, Cara noticed he had not spoken for a while.

"Everything okay?" she said. "Not like you to be so contemplative. Anything wrong?"

"Well, not really wrong," he replied. "Immigration people are asking a few questions."

"What sort of questions?"

"Well, I am only here on a visitors' visa—maximum of two years, so they are just checking I am following the rules."

"And?" she said.

"Well, they won't let me stay here permanently, but I don't ever want to leave. This is the happiest year I have had since I was a child."

He actually sounded down—not something Cara had ever seen before.

"But can't you apply to extend your visa?"

"I could apply but I don't think they will allow it."

"Worth trying though," she said, trying to sound nonchalant.

He had shocked her. She couldn't bear to think about life without John there. She had come to rely on him, to love living with him, to begin to live her life over again. With Stephen's help, she had really started studying again and, apart from an underlying sadness over Richard which she knew would always be with her, she was moving forward. She has passed her first year's exams and was working very hard now as Stephen and Julia always thought she could with the right help. John had come back into her life at just the right moment.

The thought of him not being there worried her.

"Well, I'll have a think and talk to Stephen. He has a lot to do with the foreign students so he might be able to come up with something to help."

Cara decided to go and talk to Julia before she let her thoughts take over and make her panic.

"Well, it's easy," said Julia. "You just have to marry him and live happily ever after."

"Please, be serious, Julia. I really don't know what I would do without him now. He does everything to make it as easy as possible for me to study. Washing, ironing, cooking, cleaning. And above all, he makes me feel good."

"So why not marry him then?"

"JULIA! I am serious."

"And so am I!"

"But I couldn't. We love each other as great mates, but that's all. He made it clear to me ages ago that that was all it was and it's the same for me."

"Bollocks!" said Julia. "Why are you both pretending? You, above all, should know life is too short not to make the most of it. You were made for each other."

Cara began to object but gave up and sat quietly thinking about Julia's outburst. Were she and John pretending? She knew what he had said when she moved in with him and she had agreed totally.

"Okay," said Julia. "So you wouldn't be at all bothered if he met someone else and announced he was getting married?"

"What?" said Cara. "Do you know something I don't?"

"Give me strength," said Julia. "It's a hypothetical question. Of course, he hasn't met someone else. He only ever sees you. Yes, I know that sounds yucky and what you and I would have put our fingers down our throats about a few years ago, but, I'm sorry my friend, it's true."

Cara was quiet again. "Do you really think that?"

"God, you can be so obtuse sometimes. A bright law student, but totally stupid in the love department."

"Julia, do you have to be so blunt?"

"Blunt, I may be, but totally wysiwig—what you see is what you get. I say it how it is. Maybe you would like it more wrapped up, but I'm Irish. We don't mollycoddle."

Cara was quiet again.

Eventually, she looked up at her friend and said, "Yes, I would be devastated if he met someone else but I really do not think you are right. He said we would just be friends when I asked if I could rent his spare bedroom and I agreed."

169

"But you only agreed because you couldn't let yourself be put into the situation where you could be hurt again. He didn't think you were ready to fall in love again, so he didn't want to pressure you. I tell you, the guy's a saint. He will wait for as long as it takes for you to realise you could love again and it will be okay this time."

"Really? How do you know all this? Have you talked to him?"

"Course I haven't. I tell you, James and I are desperate for you two to finally come out. How could either of you ever be with anyone else? And it's not natural to live as you do when it's obvious you love each other. Know what we call you?"

"Call us?" said Cara. "What do you mean?"

"For god's sake, Cara! The nun and the monk! It's only a joke but we keep thinking one of these days you two will get drunk, fall into bed and finally get it together."

"Really?"

"I know I am sounding as if we treat it as a big joke, but honestly, we do feel you are just great together but you are both too scared to take that big step in case it all goes wrong and you end up losing each other's friendship.

"John is a good man, so that would be a good enough reason given your past, for you two to get together. But there's a lot more than that. He adores you. Why would he have travelled all over the world to rescue you so often?"

"It wasn't so often," Cara protested.

"Well, three times is a lot more than the average damsel in distress!"

"I'm not sure if you are right, Julia, and so I'm not sure what I can do about it. We live together so companionably that the subject never comes up. How could it if you are right? We couldn't take the risk of one of us declaring our love for the other and it not being reciprocated."

"Well, you need to do something about it. You should know life is too short to let things drift. I don't mean to be flippant, Cara, but I mean it.

"If you knew he loved you, would you marry him?"

Cara was quiet again.

"Well? I know you would."

"But what if…"

"Cara, don't think about what if. You could say that for the rest of your life and on your deathbed finally tell him you love him. What a waste that would be."

"Okay, yes, I do love him in that way. Every night when I go to bed I think about him and want him. I want him more than those ridiculous early days with Ian. That wasn't love. That was a crush that sort of turned into love, but it wasn't the same.

"Sometimes the need is too great and I can't see how I can live with him as we do without being with him. Yes, I love him."

"Well, thank the lord for that!"

"I can't believe you are my best friend and you have never told me that. We used to share everything. Why have you not told me?"

"I don't know. I think I just stopped telling anyone anything. I kept it all to myself and just thought I didn't deserve the things I could see other people have. I sort of made my bed by running away with Ian and thought I couldn't go back to a normal life. I'm sorry."

"Oh God, enough of that. Don't go all-maudlin on me. That's not you any more. You are my fun friend again.

"As I see it," Julia continued, "The only way John can stay here is if he married an English woman. Not the most romantic of reasons to get married, but what does that matter? No, don't answer that, you'll go maudlin again!"

"You are forgetting one thing," said Cara.

"What's that?"

"I'm already married—to Ian."

"Well, divorce him then. I think you can do that without him having to be around to agree, can't you?"

"Don't know. I thought you could divorce after two years if you both agreed, but it has to be five years if you don't agree.

"Anyway, I think we are getting a bit carried away here. Don't you think maybe John and I need to talk about this first? Don't know how I'm going to broach the subject really.

"Oh, by the way John, I thought it was time we jumped into bed together and then let's get married."

Julia laughed.

"Yes, a bit random I agree, but needs be. Maybe you two should just get drunk and get the polite bits out of the way."

Chapter 28

Cara went to college the next day and went straight to the library to look up divorce law. She had said nothing to John but Julia had made her think that just maybe it would be possible. The more she thought about John the more she knew she could not bear to be parted from him again. He was the strong man she needed now, the caring, sensitive man who just did everything for her and didn't even notice he did. A very rare breed.

She found out that divorce papers needed to be served to Ian and if he didn't respond, she could ask the court to grant a divorce. But really she knew it could not be as simple and straightforward as that. If the police on both sides of the Atlantic couldn't find him, what hope had she? And she didn't think the court would do very much if she merely said she didn't know where he was. The immigration authorities were also very sceptical about quickie divorces followed by quickie weddings when a visitor's visa was about to expire. But there had to be a way.

She decided to talk to the police inspector who had led the hunt for Ian following Richard's death. He had been easy to talk to and she felt she could be open with him—without actually saying she wanted to get married to John. Maybe that was going a bit too far when she and John weren't even together—yet.

She still had his card so in her lunchtime she called him and arranged to go to the station to meet him.

Inspector Clements explained there had been no sightings at all of Ian. The car he escaped in had been found very soon after with no trace of him. He had abandoned it outside the railway station, hopped on a train without buying a ticket so no one could trace which direction he travelled in and just disappeared, again. There had been no ticket inspector on any of the trains that afternoon—cutbacks meant the inspectors tended to only travel on the commuter peak-time trains and not on Saturdays.

There had been no reported sightings, nothing, but he was such a master at changing his identification, who knew what he looked like now—blonde, brown, black hair. Stations north and south of Sheffield with CCTV cameras had been checked and checked but there was absolutely no trace, as if he had never got on the train, but everyone involved in the investigation was sure that's how he left Sheffield.

"The real reason I need to know where he is, is because I want to divorce him. While I am still married to him I can't move forward. I need to be rid of him altogether," Cara told the inspector.

"I can understand that and I am very sorry I can't offer you any information. Believe me, I want to find that bastard just as much as you do. He killed one of my best friends remember, as well as your little boy. Never came across such a cold-blooded killer before. He seems to have no normal feelings, and from what I have heard from the US police, he would have been on death row without a doubt if they had caught him."

Cara sat and listened to the policeman describing the man she thought she had been in love with—a man described as having no normal feelings. Where did that bright college student go, playing tennis on a sunny Sunday morning appearing to have no cares in the world? It wasn't so many years ago and yet it seemed to Cara a lifetime ago. Would she ever really be able to forget him?

And then a thought struck her. "Maybe we should stop looking for him and persuade him to come looking for me. He said he couldn't live without me, so maybe I should give him real reason to come back for me."

"That sounds pretty dangerous to me," said Inspector. "You, of all people, know what he's capable of."

"Yes, but we would have to be ready for him. I've got to start thinking the way he does. How would he come back? What would he plan to do? How would he plan to get me and get away again?"

"But Cara, you couldn't be more different from his personality than if you were an alien from Mars. I still can't really see how you two ever got together."

"He was different in the beginning. Not a sign of the monster he became."

"Can people really change that much?"

"I'll talk to my friend and see what he thinks. He knows Ian. He knows what he has done and how he has done it," said Cara. "I'll give you a call next week."

Cara left the police station and did something she had never done before. She went to a wine bar, ordered a large glass and sat in a corner to think. She got out a notepad and wrote down her thoughts. Her thoughts about John, whether he felt the same, about Ian and about how she could trap him. While he was still free he would always be a threat, both to her and to John. If she was ever to really begin again, he had to be caught and kept behind bars for the rest of his life. She even thought about what the inspector had said. In America, he would have been on death row. Did she really want him dead?

No, she could never feel that strongly. There was a flaw in his character, a brain dysfunction. That was why he was like that. That was why he could kill cold bloodedly and walk away, seeming to not give the murder another thought. If he could kill his own son like that, there had to be something wrong—something he couldn't help.

But that was the old Cara thinking—always finding some sort of excuse for him. There was no excuse, and she had to begin to realise that. While he was still free, she never would be.

She went back to thinking about John and how she could show him what she felt about him. But she was scared, too scared to take the chance. If Julia was wrong, she would lose him. She was sure of that. He couldn't stay knowing she wanted him but he didn't feel the same. He would realise it would be too much for her. They couldn't continue to live together as they have done. But how could she be sure?

Cara had another glass of wine and decided to write him a letter. She wrote page after page and realised what she was writing was not a letter to John, but a letter to herself. She was at last pouring out everything she felt. She suddenly needed to empty her thoughts out, to clear the way for what was to come—whatever that was.

She revisited so many old horrific memories—her imprisonment on the island when she allowed Ian to rape her time after time in some sort of attempt to pacify his anger, to make him return to the man she once knew, to be a father for Richard. How could she have thought that? There was no sense to it at all, she realised now. But she was never thinking properly then. She couldn't; she was numb to her situation, her life.

Then she thought back to the night she saw Ian and Joanne together, the accident, Richard's birth, the realisation of his impairment. Her imprisonment in America was just a blur; she couldn't really remember much about those months. But she knew she had nearly died. Since she had come back to the UK she had never allowed herself to think too much. She just didn't know if she could cope with it. But now she realised that she couldn't just push it away any more. She had to deal with it all in order to compartmentalise it. To put it into some sort of perspective, some sort of order—and in the past.

Page after page poured out—at times tears rolled down her face but she was not aware of them. The barman watched her and at times wanted to ask her if she was okay but he could see she was writing and didn't want to disturb her. Instead he took her another glass of wine and a bottle of water.

Hour after hour Cara wrote, filling her notebook. She began to feel tired and realised she hadn't eaten since breakfast time. Eventually, she looked up from her notebook and saw that it was very dark outside. She noticed the clock behind the bar and was surprised to see that it was after 10 pm. The barman smiled at her and came over to her.

"Can I get you a sandwich or something? The kitchen is closed now but I could do you a sandwich. Ham, cheese, prawns, beef, white or brown?"

"That would be nice. Thanks. I hadn't realised it was so late. Prawns on brown, please, with mayonnaise."

"Well, looks like you've been writing the sequel to 'War and Peace'," he went on.

Cara said nothing, just looked down at her notebook with the pages curled from the weight of her pen's nib.

"I'll get your sandwich," he said, as he returned to behind the bar.

Cara sat back against the velour bench seat and felt a strange sense of satisfaction. A freedom she had not felt in many years.

She got up and went to the toilet. When she saw her face in the mirror it was the first time she realised she had been crying. Her eyes were red and blotchy and she looked a mess. Her hair was pushed back off the left side of her face which had crumple lines as she had rested her head on her left hand there as she wrote. She had obviously wiped the tears away without noticing because the remains of her make-up was smeared across her temples—a few black streaks making her look like a Halloween character.

She pulled some sheets of toilet paper from the cubicle and returned to the mirror, dampening the paper to try to remove the smears. It took her a few minutes to clean her face and she grabbed more paper which she soaked with cold water to dab at her puffy eyelids.

When she returned to the bar, her sandwich was on the table and the barman was hovering, asking her tactfully if she would like more wine or a coffee.

Twenty minutes later, Cara was out on the street again, walking purposefully back to her flat. She knew she had achieved something she should have managed to do a long time ago, and she felt almost exuberant.

As she entered the front door, John appeared instantly from the sitting room.

"God, Cara, where have you been? We have all been so worried."

Cara hadn't even thought that her coming home so late was totally out of character and that John would be worried. She had been engrossed in her writing.

"I'm so sorry, John. There was something I just needed to do."

He could see she was different. Lighter, less intense, happier.

"Am I allowed to ask what?" he said. "I tried calling you but you had left your phone on the kitchen table."

"Well, I just needed to put a few ghosts to rest. Should have done it long ago, but I didn't really know how to do it. A few glasses of wine helped."

John knew whatever Cara had done, however she had put her ghosts to rest, was a very positive move for her. He was dying to ask more but didn't want to spoil the moment—Cara just looked happy and he would be satisfied with that for the time being.

"I'll just call Julia and James," he said. "We've all been worried and they've been all over the place looking for you."

"I'll call her," Cara replied.

Before Cara could say anything, Julia was almost shouting down the phone. "Where are you? Are you okay?"

"Sorry, Jules, just had to sort things. I'm fine and I'm going to do something I should have done a long time ago. Call you tomorrow."

Julia had started to reply but had realised Cara had ended the call. She hadn't called her Jules for years.

Cara then told John she was going to have a soak in the bath and not to wait up for her. John felt a little as if he had been dismissed and felt a bit disappointed but didn't ask any questions. As he heard the bath taps running, he got up, turned the lights off, closed the sitting room curtains and went to bed.

He lay in the dark trying to work out where Cara had been and what she had been doing, but got nowhere. He had never seen her so untroubled and happy. Then a thought struck him. Maybe she had met someone and had spent the evening with him. The thought twisted his gut and he realised he could never cope with thinking of Cara with another man, but he didn't know what to do about it. Perhaps it was time he showed his hand, showed her he loved her and the thought of ever having to leave her, he could not contemplate.

As he was turning over his thoughts in his mind, there was a light knock on his bedroom door and Cara appeared next to his bed, wearing just a bath towel.

The moonlight outside silhouetted Cara's body in the room and as she let the towel drop to the floor, he could see her full shape, her breasts pert and her nipples large and erect.

He lifted the sheet covering his naked body and she slid into the bed beside him, her arms sliding around his neck as her lips met his. His lips hungrily enveloped hers, their tongues twisting together, both their bodies rhythmically beginning to respond to each other. She felt him grow hard against her and she moved one hand away from his neck and down across his chest, further to his stomach and eventually to his groin. He moaned into her neck, kissing her ears and moving one hand across her shoulder and down to her breast. His thumb and forefinger lightly rubbed her nipple and he felt it grow harder and bigger. He moved his mouth down, kissing her soft skin as he found her breasts, opening his mouth. This time, she moaned and began to stroke him. His mouth moved further down across her stomach. Subconsciously, she arched her back. Their lovemaking found no bounds.

It was dawn when they finally slept, both spent, exhausted and happier than either of them had ever felt.

Chapter 29

It was almost ten o'clock when they finally woke, their arms and legs still entwined.

Cara woke first, immediately remembering every detail of what had happened since she stepped out of the bath. She smiled to herself and silently kissed John's nose as he lay in her arms, his beard tickling her chin.

He stirred and slowly opened his eyes, nuzzling into her neck.

"How long. How long I have waited for this moment," he said.

"Well, it took me to make the first move," she replied, "I wasn't going to wait any longer."

But before he could answer, she kissed him again, this time on his mouth, eating his words. They wrapped each other again, their arms locking each to the other and their legs taking a hold on the other as if they were moulded that way.

They made love again, this time slowly but just as passionately, both reaching climax simultaneously, both uttering sounds only lovers could make, before lying back on the bed, again spent, again deliriously happy.

The doorbell rang and they both knew straight away it was Julia, and possibly James, too.

"You going to answer it," said Cara. "Or shall I?"

"Think you'd better go," John said. "Not sure I can at the moment," with that he pushed her out of the bed.

Cara grabbed John's dressing gown on the way out of the bedroom and reached the front door as her mobile started ringing. The letterbox was pushed open and Julia shouted through it. "Come on, we know you are in there. The curtains are still closed. It's nearly 12 o'clock. I thought we were walking to the pub for lunch."

As Cara opened the door, wrapping the dressing gown tightly around her, Julia launched herself into the hall and grabbed her friend.

"Yippee, yippee," was all she said.

James looked slightly confused behind her and just uttered a hello as he followed Cara and Julia down the hall.

"Having a lie-in?" he said. "Well, why not. Chance would be a fine thing," he finished, aiming a mocking glare at Julia.

"Well, that's one way to put it," Julia said, shouting through to the bedroom, "Come on John, time to face the music."

James still looked a little confused.

Cara glared at Julia and grabbed her arm, pulling her through to the kitchen.

"Please. You'll embarrass him. And me!"

"Oh, come on," said Julia. "You know I'm only kidding. I think it's great. I worked out what you meant on the phone last night at about 3 am this morning. Poor James is still wondering. Bless him."

An hour later, the four left the flat and headed off to their favourite river walk.

Over the next few weeks, Cara gained a spring in her step, a smile permanently on her face, and a new demeanour everyone around her could not help but notice.

Her tutor saw a younger Cara, again optimistic, looking forward, rarely back. She was working well, always on time with her work, and now gaining As and Bs, instead of the earlier Fs.

He didn't ask why.

One day, Cara asked John about the letter he had received a few months earlier from the immigration authorities. She guessed what it had said but wanted to hear it from John, to see if he had thought of a solution.

"I've been meaning to talk to you about it," he said. "But I didn't want to spoil the great times we have had. I have never been so happy Cara and I have tried to have my visa extended, but there is no way."

"Well, there is one way," she said. "But, I'm not sure how to say this."

"I know what you have in mind but I just wish the timing was different. It's not exactly the most romantic way in the world, is it? And anyway, you are not free.

"I would have married you the day I arrived in the UK but I was too scared to take the first step and now it will look like I only want to marry you so I can stay here."

"I know, all that has been through my mind too, but you and I both know what we want, and surely we should do whatever we have to, to get it.

179

"I looked into trying to divorce Ian without him being present but papers need to be served on him and only if he doesn't respond can we take it further. As we have no idea where he is, it's not that easy.

"I even spoke to the police inspector to try to think of some way of trapping Ian into coming to find me, but we never took it further. He thought it would be too risky for me, and probably for you, too."

"Well, we should think about it," replied John. "Assuming you would never want to live in the States with me?"

"I don't think I could," said Cara. "When I was in prison, I vowed I would never leave England again if I ever managed to get back here. This is home and I want to finish my degree and work as a lawyer. I know that might be a bit selfish, but that's what I set out to do all that time ago when I first met Julia.

"I never want to be without you, John, so we only have one option. Trap Ian into coming to find me and then divorce him."

"But how?" said John. "I just can't see a way."

"Well, he told me he could not live without me for whatever reason, so if he thinks I am marrying someone else, especially you, maybe he will come back and try to find me.

"It's a big risk for him but he's done it before and this time we'll be ready for him.

"We need to publicise our engagement or something. I have no idea how, but maybe Inspector Clements can come up with something."

Chapter 30

John and Cara spent many hours planning how to goad Ian into coming out of hiding, how to force her divorce, and how to leave her past behind.

She wanted to be with John for the rest of her life, but she also wanted to finish her degree. It mattered to her now, as it had mattered to her parents those years before. Each day, she grew stronger and more determined to put Ian behind her and behind bars. He should never get away with what he had done, to any of his victims, but more so to his son. She wanted him to rot in jail and be forced to face his crimes, his total disregard for others and for life. Before, she had just wanted to get away from him, but now she wanted him caught. That way, she would not have that underlying feeling that he could still get to her; still hurt her.

She needed publicity, but how? She was nobody and so was John. The papers would never be interested in anything they did.

But then it came to her. She knew how she would do it, how she would get Ian to notice. Perhaps she was just as masterful as he was...

She went to the library to do a bit of research on line. Everything had to be planned down to the slightest detail—the timing, the place, the event, the net.

She looked up companies which towed banners behind light aircraft. It took her a while but she eventually found the perfect company. She quickly e-mailed them and asked if they could tow a banner for her over the university.

Armed with their details and possible dates, depending on weather, she returned home to talk her plan over with John.

"We have a banner towed around the city saying something like, Cara, marry me. I love you, John."

"Then," she went on, "We have a Sunday Love Songs request on Radio Two with Steve Wright, from you to me, telling me to go to the university at a particular time. We make sure he reads both our names out and mentions something about the Buccaneer."

"And then, just to make sure, we get the local paper to cover the banner proposal with pictures of us. That must surely bring him out of his den!"

"It all sounds great, Cara," said John, "But we both know what he is capable of. Anything could happen."

"Yes, I know," Cara said slowly, "But there will be armed police waiting for him."

"We have to do something to get rid of him or he will always be there, always make us look over our shoulders. He's evil, John, and we have to catch him."

Over the next few weeks, Cara was totally engrossed in her plan; this time she would be the victor, and he would be the victim. She felt confident and strong with John helping her. She had to think how Ian would think. He could realise it was a trap and if so, she had to think what he would do about it. But if he really was obsessed with her, maybe jealousy would take over and that would make him careless. Even after all these years, she wasn't quite sure of him.

She talked to the police and to Stephen at college and between them all they tried to dot every i and cross every t. Her's and John's lives together depended on the plan working.

The police decided they would deal with the radio show part of the plan to make sure it was read out on the right day and at the right time. If the whole thing didn't work, they didn't want it to be seen as a police bungle again. That would be too much for the superintendent to cope with.

John and Cara talked about how Ian would react, what he might do, and how they would all react. There was always the possibility he had fled the country so might not even see the banner or hear the radio show, but Cara had a feeling he was still around. He didn't get what he came for last time so she was sure he would try again. There were times he could easily get her, but maybe he didn't really want her that much. But if he knew John did, he would not be able to accept that; he would do something.

One weekend, John and Cara decided to have a break from it all and go away for a couple of days. They drove to the coast, found a B&B overlooking the sea, and enjoyed two days of total relaxation. They walked and talked and knew then they would always be together. In a strange way, Ian was a bond which brought them together and made them strong in their resolution to catch him and have him locked up either in the UK or US.

"The day you arrived at the marina and came along the jetty with Ian, I knew there was something about you which made me want to know you more. I saw the bruises and when Ian explained you had fallen, I sort of accepted his explanation, but there was a silence which told me more. You were not happy even though you pretended to be. When you found his gun hidden in the stern cabin, I knew then that I would always want to protect you, to be there for you."

Cara, John and Inspector Clements met regularly to make sure the plan was failsafe. If it was going to work, they had to have every angle covered; where Ian might turn up, including their flat, what he might do, where he would escape to once he realised it was a trap, and how.

The plane was booked and the banner made. Radio Two had been contacted frequently to go over the script and the local papers had also been given as much detail as possible to try to ensure they turned up.

As the day grew near, Cara started to worry. Then the worry turned to panic, to the point she was ready to call the whole thing off. But John was determined that Ian had to be caught. The torture Cara had endured for so long had to come to an end. She had to be free of him, free to live her life the way she wanted to, not the way Ian dictated. No one had the right to control anyone else so much. He had caused her more pure grief in just a few years than most people didn't have to endure in a lifetime.

Even if Cara wanted to back out of the plan, John decided he would go ahead with it. He wanted to live the rest of his life with Cara. He had seen how carefree she could be sometimes; he wanted her to feel like that all the time—with him.

He rang Inspector Clements and asked if he could make an appointment to see him to go over the plan one last time. John knew Ian more than anyone else except for Cara. He knew what he was capable of and no one could ever really accept what a monster he was; how he could cold-bloodedly kill his son and walk away. How he had fooled so many people and managed to escape so many times. He was going to find Ian and make sure he could never again bring Cara to her knees.

When he walked into Inspector Clements' office, the inspector was busy on the telephone.

"Yes, it's covered. Yes, we have marksmen organised all around the building and on the top. There is no way he will be able to do anything without us being there on top of him."

John thought about what the inspector was saying and had a bad feeling about it. He knew the policeman didn't know Ian and therefore had no real idea of what a monster he was. He sometimes seemed a little condescending to Cara and

John—he was the man with police experience. He was the one who could deal with anything. And he was the one who would deal with this man they all seemed to be scared of.

He didn't seem to take into account the bungle at Julia's flat when Richard was shot and Ian calmly walked out carrying Cara, stole the ambulance and got away in a bystander's car. But however much John tried, Inspector Clements seemed unable to accept any advice from him without becoming defensive which was no good to anyone.

John asked if he could see the plans the police had for the position of the marksmen, the escape routes around the buildings and the contingency plans if anything was to go wrong.

Inspector Clements went over the details, but John knew he was just humouring him; he really didn't want some American tourist telling him how he should run his operation. After all, if the Americans hadn't messed up totally, Ian would be in jail over there, Richard would be alive and Cara would not be the highly-strung mess that she was. But, of course, he couldn't say that.

British police knew what they were doing. Yes, it was a mistake when Richard was shot, but that just happens, doesn't it? They can't always get it right.

John left the police station feeling worse than before he had arrived. He decided to take himself off for the day and to think the whole plan through. The radio, the newspapers, the plane. How Cara might react when she saw Ian—if he turned up. And what if he didn't? What then?

He decided he couldn't rely on the police. They were too sure of themselves—they really didn't know what they were up against. He had to find some sort of guarantee they wouldn't bungle it all again. But what and how?

He went into town and found the seediest bar he could. He bought a pint and sat propping up the bar for more than two hours. Eventually, the barman asked him how he was, where he was from, and what was he doing in the UK. They chatted for half an hour and then John decided this was going nowhere. He decided to come right out with it.

"Look, I need to find a professional thug. I can't tell you why, but I just do."

The barman was a bit taken aback but saw from John's expression, he was not joking.

"Mmm, okay, I think I might know someone. Give me your mobile number and I'll get back to you."

As John left the pub, he wondered if he had done the right thing but then decided nothing to do with Ian would be the right thing, He wasn't clutching at straws, he needed as much force as he could muster to deal with Ian and the police had left him feeling they were not quite up to the job.

Two days went by and there was no call from the barman so John decided that maybe he had just been humouring him and that he really didn't know a hit man. Well, how many people would? But then, just as he was thinking that he had no choice but to go along with the police's plan, he had a text asking him to meet him outside the city, at a lay-by near a local reservoir.

The text just gave him the place and time. Nothing else.

John felt he had nothing to lose so he went, telling Cara he needed to go and see someone for work. He didn't want to worry her more—a hit man wasn't really in Cara's scope of knowledge and experience.

He drove south and arrived at the lay-by with 15 minutes to spare. For the first time in years, he wanted a cigarette. He had given up many years before but today, he wanted either a good whisky shot or a cigarette. Nothing else would do. He knew his pulse was high; he could feel it pounding in his neck. His hands were clammy and his breath was shallow. But none of that mattered. He had to go through with it.

When the man turned up, he took John by surprise. He was wearing an expensive suit, a very smart shirt and tie, and carried a soft leather briefcase. He spoke well and merely said, "And how can I help you? Steve, at the pub, said you needed some professional help."

John looked at the man and all his thoughts of how to deal with the situation evaporated. He wasn't sure how to go about this.

"Not what you expected?" said Mr Smith.

"I assume there is someone who you need me to deal with. Someone, shall we say, who needs to be removed?"

John looked at the man and slowly answered.

"I am not sure I should be doing this, but the 'person' has made my partner's life intolerable to say the least. The police and I have formed a plan to try to trap him—he is wanted on both sides of the Atlantic for murder—but I don't have much confidence in the police.

"This man is a monster, not a thug or a gangster. An evil monster."

"They usually are," replied Mr Smith calmly.

185

"Don't worry, I believe you. And I also understand your concerns over the police. Tell me the background."

It was three hours before John finished. All the time he was talking, he thought Mr Smith should be making notes, but he sat with his hands in the lap, listening and never interrupting.

"I need to be sure the police don't bungle it again. Cara cannot go through another episode. It would finish her."

Mr Smith then asked for a photograph of Ian which John had brought along, and asked if he knew what sort of disguises Ian had used in the past, if any. He asked if Ian had a particular gait which might distinguish him, or anything else which might help.

After another hour had gone by, Mr Smith said he would be in touch.

"But it's all supposed to be happening on Sunday. We don't have much time," said John.

"I know it is Sunday—five days away—and be assured, I will be in touch before then to tell you what I will be doing. I will need £10,000 in cash before Sunday and another £20,000 once he is deactivated."

With that, he walked to his car, got in and drove off leaving John sitting slightly bewildered.

He had confidence in the strange and aloof Mr Smith, more so than in Inspector Clements, but he still wasn't sure it was the right thing to do. But what choice did he have?

When he returned home Cara was out and she hadn't left a note. It wasn't like her to go out without saying anything, but he needed to stop molly coddling her. She was so much stronger now and he knew if he continued to think for her and try to do everything for her, she would never be the person he knew she could be. He resisted the temptation to call her mobile.

Chapter 31

Cara had also lost confidence in the police. She felt they patronised her and didn't really take on board what she was saying; her real anxieties about what Ian might do if he was caught. Even though they knew it was their fault Ian had got away after shooting their son, they still did not seem to grasp the intensity of what could happen.

She decided she would try to add her bit to the operation. Whatever happened, she would protect herself and John. Ian was not going to take anything or anyone else from her.

She bought a copy of Exchange and Mart and looked through the section at the back.

She was amused and amazed to find you could buy anything from sex toys to garden implements, to fishing tackle, to guns.

She had no idea what to look for but decided she would arm herself with a gun.

She rang a few numbers but ended up feeling she was out of her depth. This wasn't the right way to do it. She googled gun and rifle clubs in the Sheffield area and eventually found what she thought must be the way to go about it.

Within a couple of days, she had been for her first lesson and knew the difference between a 9mm snub nose revolver and a Magnum.

But time was running short, so she skipped a few university lectures and had another four lessons to make her feel more confident of the gun she was about to buy.

The day drew near and she thought she was ready—ready to tackle her bully of a husband in whatever way it took to make sure he would never hurt her or anyone else again. She wasn't sure why, but she didn't tell John.

It was just 24 hours until the plan was to be put into action. One day, which could change all their lives completely—Cara's, John's and Ian's. More so Ian's—he had to be trapped and put away forever.

They had checked the weather forecast almost every hour for days—it just had to be good. The plane had to fly.

"Think we should go out somewhere today," John told Cara. "We can't just sit here and wait for something to happen. I know, let's go and look at houses. I've thought for a while we should move into something more permanent."

"Okay, sure," Cara replied distractedly. "Where to?"

An hour later, armed with estate agents' details and brochures from development companies, John and Cara found themselves looking around a new house on the outskirts of the city.

"Pretty good, isn't it?" John said. But Cara wasn't listening. She was engrossed in her thoughts and worries about what might go wrong. She just knew it would.

Just then John's mobile phone rang and she heard him answer, "Yes, Mr Smith. Yes, all is in order." But that was all he said.

She had never heard him mention a Mr Smith and something told her it wasn't anything to do with work.

"Who was that?" she asked him.

The second he replied, she knew he was hiding something.

"You don't have to lie to me," she said, more curtly than she had intended to.

John was a little surprised and reacted just as curtly.

"Not a lie, just bending the truth a little," and then added, "For your benefit."

"Please don't bother for my benefit."

After ten minutes of bickering, they both realised it was a pointless exercise.

"Look, it's just the stress of all of this. Let's just stop this and go and have lunch somewhere," said John.

"I just need to drop something off so we'll order and then I'll go. Won't be long."

Cara didn't have time to reply before she saw John heading out of the door of the restaurant. She knew whatever he was doing, it would be for her benefit, and it would be honourable, but she hated the secrecy. She needed to trust him.

John was back at the table before the food arrived and looked a little flushed. He was sweating and slightly out of breath.

"Look, I need to be able to trust you totally, John. What's going on? I need to know."

"I'm sorry, Cara. You should trust me. I don't want to tell you. It's just a sort of insurance policy, nothing else.

"It's all going to be okay. Tomorrow. You wait and see. He'll be out of our lives forever."

Although, Cara knew John meant what he said, she didn't believe him. She knew Ian was stronger and wilier than John. He would stop at nothing to get himself out of any situation. John would never step over that line. She made a mental note to get Mr Smith's telephone number from John's phone. Just in case.

They ate their lunch in silence, not even daring to look at each other. They both knew the other was scared of what might happen the next day. As much as they both tried to be positive and believe their plan would work, they also knew they could never count on Ian doing anything anyone else thought he might. They were both beginning to doubt what they and the police had put into place. As much as they both tried to face each obstacle, work out what could go wrong, and find a structured solution to it, they could not count for the unknown—the reaction Ian would have to being cornered. Last time he had simply shot his son, picked Cara up and carried her out past the police and away to freedom.

When the waiter returned to their table, neither had eaten very much of their lunch. The plates and food were now cold and they had lost their appetites.

John said nothing, just passed his credit card to the waiter and sat with his hands in his lap. The waiter offered the ATM machine to John who punched in his pin number, still saying nothing, and not looking in any particular direction.

He felt drained at that moment. Had they done the right thing to try to trap Ian? If it didn't work, Cara could be killed, and then his life would end, too.

He took Cara's hand and led her out of the restaurant. He knew he should be strong for her then, but as much as he tried to sound optimistic, he knew she could see through it.

They returned home and sat in silence for a very long time, the darkness creeping in through the open curtains as time went on. Neither could think of anything to say.

When John was asleep, she crept out of bed and took his mobile phone to the bathroom. She didn't want to mistrust him but something told her she needed to know who he had been talking to. She looked through the list of received calls and ones he had made. Most of them were from or to her, a couple to James and then two to a Mr Smith. She made a note of his number and went back to bed.

Cara was up at 6 am, pacing up and down the hall. The day had dawned bright and she knew the plane would fly. She showered and dressed in her best jeans and jumper. She was likely to have her photograph taken by the local paper, so she didn't want to look too scruffy. Some things mattered.

She put the kettle on and turned on the radio. It was already tuned to Radio 2. Aled Jones was interviewing a missionary from a small African country and, although she heard the words, she didn't take them in. Her mind was too full of the day's plans to allow anything else to interfere.

John appeared at 7.30 am looking sleepy and tired. He walked over to the window and noticed two undercover policemen already in place across the street watching their flat just in case Ian turned up. Cara looked at him and realised for the first time he was beginning to look old. Their age difference had never been noticeable before; it had never been an issue, but today she wondered if she had put him through too much since she met him all those years ago in Portland.

Maybe she was wrong to fall in love with him. It was never going to be easy; they both knew that. Ian would always be in the background.

She walked over to him and put her arms around his neck and laid her head on his shoulder. His arms enveloped her and they stood there without the need to say anything. They both knew this could be the last morning they woke up together.

Eventually, she took his hand and led him back to the bedroom.

Chapter 32

They called the police inspector and checked that all was in place. They listened to the radio and smiled when they heard their request read out. DJ, Steve Wright, had really gone overboard with the story, telling everyone to go to Sheffield University to watch the plane towing the banner and to cheer if they saw John and Cara.

The trap was set. If Ian didn't take the bait this time, they would never be able to catch him. It had to work.

John suggested they went to the university together and liaised with the police inspector there as to where they should stand to be as noticeable as possible. A tannoy announcement over the university grounds relayed the Radio Two show so that no one could possibly miss what was going on. Cara felt excited and worried at the same time. She looked around her at the crowds of students who had gathered in the grounds and wondered whether that man she had met on their first night at university was there: the man she had married, whose son she had borne, and the man who had wrecked her life. She heard nothing, not the crowds milling in the grounds, not the radio show, not the people next to her. She noticed the trees and the grass in the grounds and for the first time realised how beautiful the university was, not the concrete blocks she had seen at other universities. There was an eerie silence around her even though the crowds were cheering as the plane was first spotted.

It came from the south of the city and its low drone drew nearer and nearer, eventually turning across the university grounds to show the full length of the banner—"Cara. Marry me. Buccaneer John."

She was suddenly aware that John was pulling at her sleeve. She looked to her side and realised he was on his knees.

"I mean it, Cara. Marry me."

The crowds all turned towards them and shouted, "Say yes, Cara." For a moment she forgot all about the plane and looked down at John. He was smiling up at her as he said, "Forget him Cara. It's our turn now…"

But before he had finished a shot rang out followed by screams and shouts from the crowd. Some ran for cover and others dived to the ground, their hands covering their heads.

In a moment, four policemen surrounded John and Cara, protecting them from every angle. But no one knew where the shot had come from or who it was aimed at. Cara heard the police radios crackling out orders from the inspector, "Information, now! Who fired?"

Within five minutes, the situation was under control. One of the marksmen had seen a man running at speed towards Cara and John, pushing people out of his way to clear a path. The marksman thought he had seen a gun in his hand and had fired a shot into the air as a warning shot.

In the confusion that followed, the marksman had lost sight of the gunman but was adamant he was heading for John and Cara and that he was brandishing a gun.

No one knew quite what to believe. Had the marksman been mistaken—the police inspector didn't think so. They were highly trained and knew to shoot only if there was no other option. John thought otherwise. He felt the police were under so much pressure after their bungled attempt at catching Ian the last time that the marksman had tried to be a hero. Maybe it had been Ian. Maybe it hadn't. But now they would never know and they were still searching for him in vain.

The reporter on the local paper who had written the story about them appeared and tried to talk to Cara, but was held back by an armed policeman. There were police with guns all over the grounds and the crowds were looking scared and confused. It was a shambles.

Eventually, all the students left and wandered off to their halls of residence or to the local pub, leaving just John and Cara and the police inspector to walk to their cars.

No one said a word. It had not been a good morning for any of them.

"We'll talk tomorrow. Can you come to the station at 10 am, please?"

John slowly turned to look at the inspector and said, "Is there any point? I don't think so."

Just at that moment, his phone rang in his pocket. It was Mr Smith.

"Doesn't look like he showed, does it? Call me if there's anything else I can help you with." Then he cut the call.

Cara didn't want to go home but she also didn't want to be anywhere near other people. She just wanted to sit quietly with John. They walked for two hours, wandering around the city streets, not talking and not noticing anything. Both deep in thought.

John spoke first. "Well, it didn't work, but there will be another way. He can't hide forever. There will be a time. Believe me, Cara. We will get him."

Cara stopped walking and turned to face John. "Maybe. Maybe he will be caught one day and maybe I will be free to marry you but the longer we keep looking for him, the less time we have together. He's still with us, John, and I think he always will be. I think the only thing we can hope for is to be together as much as we can. I am not being realistic thinking I can just find him, divorce him and marry you. Of course, I can't do that. I will just have to accept that we can't marry so I will just have to let you go home to Portland and we will see each other whenever we can. One day, I will have finished my degree and then I will be free to go wherever I want to. Until then, we will have to accept we can't be together."

John started to contradict her but she put her fingers up to his lips and just shook her head. "No, John. There really isn't any other way. It doesn't mean we will never be together. It just means we can never marry and so we can never be together in England.

"I have been stupid to think there was a way. If Ian is watching us, as I am sure he is, he will have seen through our plan and he is probably laughing at us at this very minute, thinking how naïve we are and how stupid. I'm sorry John, but you have to go home."

Chapter 33

On their way to their flat, John suggested a pizza as they hadn't eaten since the day before. Breakfast hadn't really happened. They sat quietly eating, neither of them saying very much. They felt flat, deflated and resigned. There were about ten other people in the restaurant but John and Cara didn't notice them. They were blind to the world outside of themselves. They ate their meal very slowly, saying very little. What was there to say now?

"It isn't really awful," said Cara. "It could be worse. We might not be together or maybe he would have shown up and something dreadful would have happened again. Come on, let's go home and plan how we are going to be able to make the best of it all."

They paid their bill and got into the car. Their mood lifted a little and they began making plans around term times, holiday times, birthdays and anniversaries.

"As soon as we get home, I'm going to book flights for our first reunion after I'm settled back in the States," said John.

"Maybe it won't be so bad after all," he continued, forcing himself to be cheerful. When they pulled up outside their flat, it was beginning to get dark. He leaned across and kissed Cara.

"Yes, it's going to be fine," she said. "Just not what we planned."

By the time they had unlocked their front door and walked down the hall they were in each other's arms and heading for the bedroom door, all thoughts of their disappointment gone for the time being.

John kicked open the door, still hugging Cara, their lips together and their bodies vibrant with expectancy. Cara's arms were around John's neck as they fumbled in the dark, neither wishing to put the lights on. Whatever happened, they were still together, alive, in love and had a future, even though it was not how they had wanted it. Their unity would make them stronger.

"How sweet," growled Ian from the bed, shining a torch at them.

"Had a good day?"

Cara froze, taking a sharp breath as she did.

She felt John try to push her back into the hall, but Ian was on his feet in an instant, lashing out at John's face with the butt of his gun. The weight of John's body hit the floor with a heavy thud. He made no noise.

Ian told Cara to put the light on and to sit on the bed, all the while pointing his gun at her.

"You didn't really think I would fall for that, did you?"

"You really are so stupid, Cara. And to think I thought you were bright all those years ago. You are just a bimbo, pathetically hanging on to any man who will have you. And yes, I had you over and over whether you liked it or not. Remember? On that paradise island in the Caribbean." He laughed as he spat the words at Cara.

He bent down, took a dressing gown cord from the back of the door and tied John's hands behind his back. He then yanked his body so that he sat up, leaning against the chest of drawers. Cara heard a crack as one of his arms broke. She felt sick.

Ian walked over to her and pushed her legs apart with his right knee.

"You know what I'm going to do, don't you? But this time lover boy over there is going to watch. I want it etched on his memory as he dies. Yes, Cara, I'm going to kill him, but I want you to suffer it, too. You should never have left me."

Cara's mind was racing. Her mind had been shocked into focus. Why hadn't she realised that even if the police watched their flat Ian would find a way past them. But this time, he was not going to win. She had to work out how she and John could get away, even if it meant, going through another rape by her husband. She needed time to think.

John murmured something and opened his eyes to see the end of Ian's gun.

Ian kicked him as he sat on the floor.

"Don't say a fucking word," he shouted at him. "Just watch."

Ian walked back to the bed and grabbed at Cara's jumper, pulling it up over her head and yanking it back, leaving her defenceless with her arms stuck in the jumper.

"Don't," John shouted. "Ian, you don't have to hurt her any more. What do you want of us? We have nothing to give you."

195

"Wake up, Yank," shouted Ian. "You've stolen my wife and I never forgive. You both have to suffer for that."

As Ian had turned to shout at John, Cara rolled backwards over to the other side of the bed, pulling her jumper back down as she did. She pushed herself off the bed and crouched on the floor, desperately fumbling in her bag which was still on her shoulder as she did. Ian turned to face her as she pulled her revolver out of her bag and pointed it at him. She was shaking and couldn't hold it very steadily.

John tried to get to his feet but Ian was on top of him in a second. As Ian tried to bring the gun butt down on his head again, the bedroom door was shoved into his back, pushing him over and across John's legs. A gun went off as Mr Smith leapt across John and grabbed Ian from behind. He wrestled the gun from his hand, forcing it to drop to the floor and skid across the floorboards under the bed.

In a second, Mr Smith had knocked Ian out, handcuffed him and tied his feet together.

He then left the room, saying before he went, "The police are on their way."

It was then Cara realised, it was her gun that had gone off. She had shot John.

Chapter 34

Two police officers took Ian away in the back of a patrol car, leaving two other officers with John and Cara. They had called an ambulance when they found John—blood was pouring from his chest and he was unconscious. The police officers looked at each other and shook their heads. They hadn't seen many gunshot wounds before, but they had seen enough to know this one was bad.

Cara was clinging to John, willing him to wake up, to show her he was all right. But deep down she knew he wasn't. He was dying and she had killed him.

"What is there to say," said Cara. "You bungled it again, but this time you caught him, or rather we caught him for you."

"I have nothing more to say to you, Inspector. Please, don't bother me again."

"But we will need you to make a statement and to appear in court as a prosecution witness. Okay, I admit, we got it wrong again, but at least we have him in custody now."

Cara stopped walking, turned to face Inspector Clements, and simply said, "Not now. You can subpoena me when the time comes. Right now, I have nothing more to say to you. Please, get out of my way."

With that, Cara carried on walking out of the car park and into the night. She knew John would not make it and she knew she hadn't really killed him, but she had fired the gun. She felt empty with nothing more to think, do or say. There was no point in thinking of taking her own life. What good would that do? She just had to get on with it, work and grow old and then eventually die. All that she once loved had gone. There was no one else left—not Ian, not her parents, not Richard and not John. Yes, he was still alive, but she knew there was no hope. He was not conscious. He could not hear. He could not respond in any way. It was just a matter of time. That was all.

As the hospital lights began to dim in the night behind her, Cara kept walking. Past the bus stop and taxi rank, past the gates out of the hospital grounds and eventually down the hill towards the outskirts of the city. She didn't have a plan; she just knew she had to breathe fresh air and try to collect her thoughts. Her mobile phone rang in her pocket but she didn't acknowledge its ringing. She just kept walking. Hour after hour, step after step. The phone rang again and again and eventually Cara stopped and took it out of her pocket. As she held the small shiny device in her hand, her eyes focused on the screen but she felt no connection between what she was looking at and anything she knew before. It was as if her life had been swept clean. No real memories. Nothing of any significance. There was no path through her past life, no real direction, just a jumble of faces and vague recollections which had resulted in her walking along this dark road.

She felt the vibration of the phone in her hand and heard the Jingle Bells ringtone which now seemed ridiculous to her. This stupid jaunty sound piercing her ears in the stillness of the hour. She raised her arm and threw the phone as hard as she could. Still it rang. Jingle Bells continued to ring out, annoying her and breaking into the silence she longed for in her mind. Eventually, it stopped. At last there was nothing—just the blackness of the night and the sound of the nighttime creatures going about their business. At last she could stop. She sat down on the grass verge, leaning up against a tree trunk. She wondered what sort of tree it was—oak, ash, beech. She had never been very good on nature. She guessed it wasn't an oak as it wasn't very big. She felt a strange comfort in thinking about the tree. It was a simple problem to solve, nothing complicated, nothing which would tear into her heart—again.

She pondered the problem of the tree for a long time until her eyes began to close. She had no idea where she was or how long she had been there, but so what. There was no one left to wonder about her whereabouts, her health, her being. No one. She felt she could actually be the last human being on the planet.

Chapter 35

Julia shrieked at Inspector Clements. "You just left her out there, alone? Walking? You didn't think she may be needed someone to look out for her? For god's sake man, if anything has happened to Cara, I will hold you personally responsible. It is because of your total incompetence Cara has no one left. First Richard and now John.

"But John is still alive," said the inspector.

"Yes, but with zero chance of recovery. I have spoken to his doctor and it is just a matter of a few hours. He can't do anything. He is deeply unconscious; he can't even hear anyone which we all know is the last sense we have before death."

"I am sorry," said the inspector. "We tried to cover every angle. We had an officer watching the house 24 hours a day for the last three days. We tracked their car, their movements and checked out the whole of the university and grounds. I am afraid he got the better of us again. I need to know who this Mr Smith was though. We are not keen on vigilantes."

"Yes, but he saved the day, didn't he?" said Julia. "Without him maybe even Cara would be in the mortuary or hospital, too."

"At least he got that bastard for you. Please, make sure you don't cock it up again and let him go."

With that, she stood up, glared at Inspector Clements and walked out.

The inspector sat motionless for a few minutes. He felt wretched. How had he got into their flat without being seen? No one had gone in or out apart from John and Cara. It was then that it slowly dawned on him.

He grabbed his coat and car keys and ran to his car, grabbing a police radio on his way.

"Get me back-up to the flat," he shouted. "Now!"

It took him just five minutes to reach the flat, slamming his blue flashing light on the roof of the car. He jumped out of the car and ran to the flats' entrance.

The blue and white police tape across Cara's front door was still intact and her neighbour's front door to the left side was as it should be. No sign of broken glass, or attempted break-in. But he knew in his gut that it was this flat that gave Ian his entry to Cara's flat. He stood back and looked up at the roof and it was then that he realised how Ian had got past the police.

The tops of scaffolding poles were just visible at the apex. His heart sank as realisation crept up on him. A back-up police car pulled up next to him.

"Round the back," shouted the inspector.

The two uniformed constables joined Inspector Clements as he sprinted down the road until he reached the alleyway that led to the backs of the houses. He was in Cara's back garden in a flash where he saw the whole scaffolding and a ladder up to the roof. There were a lot of roof tiles broken in a heap on the ground and others piled up on small stilts of wood on laid tiles. Then he saw it. At the back corner of the chimneybreast, he could see there were no tiles and no roofing felt or battens. He climbed the ladder and scurried up the roof to the chimney breast. He cursed himself for being overweight and unfit as he struggled to climb around the chimney to the back. As he managed it, he could see how Ian had got in. The six feet from the bottom of the chimneybreast to the top of the roofline had given him the hiding place he needed until it was dark. He must have disguised himself to get himself up there during the day when the policemen on watch had just assumed he was one of the builders and then made his way into the upstairs flat at night.

He radioed down to the constables and told them to break into the neighbour's front door.

By the time he was down from the roof and back to the front of the house, they were in and climbing the stairs. The place smelt musty and old. The carpet was threadbare and worn in the middle as though it had been there for many years. Wallpaper curled at the bottom edges and was faded; signs of an elderly person's flat or maybe just a temporary home to many tenants over many years. Three newspapers lay on the floor just inside the front door—today's and the previous two days, plus a few letters and brown envelopes. Inspector Clements knew what he was about to see.

As the three policemen reached the door at the top of the stairs, the first one knocked, but the inspector said, "I don't think there is any point. Break the door down."

The scene which greeted them was stomach-turning. The old lady was still sitting in her armchair in front of the television but her throat was cut. Her body sat as if it was a wax dummy—no colour, just clammy and pale, her clothes a dark maroon stain of dried blood.

Inspector Clements told the constables to call for the coroner's office and the crime scene investigators before telling them to leave and stand by the front door to make sure no one else came in. He then quietly and methodically stepped around the flat until he found what he was looking for—the hole in the floor which Ian had cut to access his wife's home while she and her fiancé waited to trap him at the university. He knew they would be there and not at home. Ian had once again outwitted the police and once again there were more dead bodies.

Chapter 36

Cara woke up and wondered where she was. She couldn't at first remember the previous day's events but then slowly it all came back to her. She knew in her heart John had died. She had suffered so many losses of those she loved, it almost felt natural to her. She didn't feel pain or heartache or loss—just another vacuum, just another death she would eventually come to terms with.

She stood up and looked around her. She thought the trees and countryside looked beautiful—another world which was filled with beauty and serenity, but a world she would never be a part of.

She walked the few steps back to the road and looked up and down the road. How had she ended up here? She instinctively knew which way was back to the city even though she did not remember the route she had taken from the hospital.

She started walking and after about 20 minutes reached a junction in the road—a main road which had traffic flowing both ways. As she turned to walk along the side of the road, a car pulled up next to her and the driver asked her if she would like a lift.

Without a thought for safety or who the driver was, she opened the car door and got in.

"Long way out of the city," the driver said. "Your car broken down?"

"No," Cara replied adding nothing more.

"Are you the woman from the university proposal," said the driver. Cara didn't answer.

"I saw you in this morning's Star. You and John, isn't it?"

"He's dead," was all she said.

The driver didn't know what to say so carried on driving and said nothing more until they reached the city.

"Shall I drop you in the centre," he said. "I'm going past the centre."

"No," Cara replied, "Just near the hospital."

She didn't feel the need for unnecessary etiquette.

Cara walked back up the road leading to the hospital entrance and walked into the main reception.

"I am here to see John, the man shot dead yesterday," she told the receptionist.

"Which ward is he in?" asked the receptionist.

"He's not; he's in the mortuary," Cara said, without any emotion at all.

"Oh, I see. If you would like to take a seat, I'll make a few enquiries."

"No, I don't want to sit down. I just want to see him and then I'll be on my way."

"But it might take me a while…"

But Cara didn't want to hear what she had to say.

"Look, my name is Cara Campbell. I was his fiancé. I shot him yesterday and I just want to make sure he is dead. That's all."

The receptionist looked aghast and quickly telephoned security and said, "Main reception, now." In a matter of seconds, Cara was surrounded by the hospital security guards and a policeman had been called.

"Could you come with me," he said. "My boss, Inspector Clements, wants to speak to you."

"But I have nothing to say to him. I merely want to make sure John is dead. Nothing else."

"But it's not that simple," said the policeman. "We need…"

But before he had finished, Cara pushed him out of her way and started walking to the front door.

"Hold on there. You can't just do that."

"Why not? He knows I have not committed a crime, so what's your problem?"

The policeman was not sure what to say or do. "But I have been asked to detain you until he can be here if you turned up."

"Detain me?" said Cara. "Detain me! And why should I be detained? I merely came here to make sure John is dead so that I know I have to just get on with my life. If he isn't, then he'll be a cabbage so he'll need looking after, but I know in my heart he's dead. I killed him."

The policeman had never come across anyone like this before and didn't know how to handle it. She seemed so cold and callous. Was she really the person his inspector had said was the sad and vulnerable victim of a catalogue of murders, crimes and torment? To him, she seemed a hard-nosed bitch. His inspector must be losing his marbles, he thought.

"Now, look here," he told her. "You will wait with me until Inspector Clements gets here, and if you resist, I will handcuff you." He began to raise his voice and reach around to his back to grab the handcuffs. As he went to grab Cara's wrist, his inspector's voice bellowed in his ear.

"Out, you idiot. I'll deal with you later."

"Cara, I'm sorry."

But before he could say why, she retorted, "Why? What have you cocked up now?"

"Look, can we go and have a coffee and talk a few things through."

"Tell me if he's dead."

"But we need to talk."

"No! Tell me. Did he die?"

Inspector Clements looked at the floor and said in a quiet voice, "Yes, he died less than two hours after he came in. He didn't suffer."

"Oh, that's good then," she said. "Well, I'll be on my way."

"Please, Cara. I know this is awful but it isn't the end."

"No?" she said. "Of course, it is. My parents are dead. Richard is dead. John is dead and you have my bastard husband in custody. What else is there? Oh, don't tell me he's escaped from you already?" Her voice was harsh and bitter without any softness or the real Cara in it.

"No, he hasn't escaped. He will go down for a very long time but we need you to help us put him there. We need your evidence."

"You've got enough to convict him of murder and so have the Americans, so what happened yesterday doesn't really come into it, does it?"

"But it does," the inspector said. "He could be out in five years unless we nail him for everything this time. Please, Cara, help us to put him away forever."

Cara turned and looked at him. She didn't see the tranquil colours of the corridor any more, the ambulance people in their green uniforms pushing trolleys up and down, the nurses in their blue dresses, physios in their white tunics and navy trousers or the doctors in their white coats, stethoscopes dangling around their necks. She just saw Inspector Clements and at that moment she hated him. He had promised Ian would be caught and that he would never again be able to hurt her. But he had let her down. Again.

"No," she said. "I will not help you any more."

With that she turned around and walked out of the hospital.

Inspector Clements knew he had to bring her in. Knew he had to get a statement about the shooting yesterday, but he also knew for Cara, there was no point, so he let her be. For the time being.

As Cara walked back along the hospital road again Julia was driving in. She screeched to a halt next to her and leapt out of the car. "Cara, Cara, I am so sorry. Come with me, please. We'll work something out."

"Julia, my dear friend. There is nothing to work out. John is dead. Ian is in custody. I just need to begin my life again. I have thought of suicide but that would be letting John down again, and my parents. And, of course, Richard. So I will not stoop to that, which leaves me no option but to pick up the pieces and begin again. But this time, I will be harder. I will not let my natural being get in the way of living my life the way I need to now.

"Please, let me go Julia. Maybe one day I will get in touch, but I want to leave my past behind. And I mean all of my past."

Julia's cries behind her diminished the further she walked. She went to the nearest bank, drew out £500 and took the train to London.

Chapter 37

Cara woke up in the small hotel room she had rented in Earls Court. It was tiny, really, but clean and was all she needed for the time being. She was still wearing the clothes she had worn since Sunday and she knew she looked a sight. She got up and left the room, walking to the nearest cafe where she ordered an Americano and two croissants. She was hungry but croissants would do for the time being.

After her breakfast, she took the tube to Oxford Circus and headed for the nearest Primark where she bought cheap underwear, two pairs of jeans, a couple of jumpers and a cheap parka-type coat. That would do.

She then went to the nearest newsagent's and bought a Loot, Metro and London Evening Standard which she scanned for cheap flats and jobs. She still had John's credit card he had given her so long ago in the Caribbean, so before it could be cancelled by his bank when they were informed of his death, she took out as much as she could in cash and then went into the nearest HSB bank and opened an account. She transferred all of the money from her joint account with John and put it all in her new account. She knew once the 'authorities' had been informed of John's death it would not be easy to sort out any money, and right now she had no other income.

She then bought a cheap mobile phone, put £50 of credit on it and sat down at the nearest Costa to scan the newspapers for flats. It wasn't long before she realised her money would not last more than a few months and that she needed to think smaller—bedsits or studios.

In the nearest internet café, she typed out a few reference letters, making up various business letterheads and printed them out, photocopying them each a few times on different paper.

By the end of the day, she had viewed a few bedsits, all of them tiny with a hint of squalor about them. But, so what, she thought. She didn't need anything other than a bed and table.

She chose one and paid the first month's rent as deposit and a further month's rent in advance. Now she had to find a job.

Cara walked miles for the next few days, looking in every shop window, every cafe and every Evening Standard for any job.

There was very little choice, if any. This was not going to be easy but she had to keep busy to stop her dwelling on everything that had happened. She would not allow herself any time to grieve—she had been there before and it had not helped.

After a week, she decided she needed to raise her aspirations higher. How could she live the rest of her life working in some two-bit job which would just pay the bills?

She needed to find a job which raised her status, and therefore her income and esteem. But first she needed to look the part—her Primark jeans and jumpers were not going to get her anywhere. She found herself sitting in the foyer of the Savoy hotel where she had spent her first night with Ian—not from nostalgia, but for research. She needed to see what sort of clothes the women who stayed there wore and what sort of business people she could meet.

Just in the first morning she had gathered enough information to speed her towards her next goal. So many women came and went without a thought for their luggage. They just handed the odd £20 or even £50 note to the uniformed bell boys or concierge to 'deal with it'.

She decided they didn't deserve their lives. They took it all for granted without a thought for how they came to be there. By the second morning, she had checked out other expensive hotels and found out where the hotel staff had their tea breaks and therefore where their uniforms were kept. And by the third morning she had managed to steal a uniform of about her size in a very up-market hotel, hidden her hair in a bellboy's cap and 'snaffled' a couple of suitcases dumped on her by guests.

She quickly changed back to her old clothes, grabbed a taxi and was off with her prizes. At home, she discovered she not only had two very expensive Gucci dresses, but a couple of necklaces, a very smart jacket and numerous pairs of shoes, plus a very expensive handbag. What a strike!

Now, she could look the part for the next part of her plan.

She picked up a City magazine and looked through to find the perfect job. There were numerous big companies based at Canary Wharf—she just needed to find the right one. She had been reading the Financial Times for a while and had begun to pick up bits and pieces of information about some of the finance houses in the city. She just needed to find out a bit more. She was about to give up and move on to the next magazine when an article caught her eye. Bingo! There was a profile on a City corporate gaining momentum in the finance world with plans to take over a smaller company. A big blue chip company was their targeted customer. She then dressed in one of the Gucci dresses and went to a few wine bars in the City where she intended to find out more information. She ordered a glass of champagne in each of them but was careful not to drink more than a sip of them. She needed to be focused. It didn't take long to begin to pick up the threads of the gossip among the financiers.

The next morning saw Cara dressed for the part and in a cab to Canary Wharf—well, she couldn't take the train dressed like that. Although her pulse was racing and her confidence dwindling, she was determined to land the perfect job for her. She walked into the offices mentioned in the magazine, took the lift to the top floor and walked straight up to the woman behind the front desk and dumped her jacket on top of her keyboard, merely telling the woman not to disturb her meeting with Heinrik. Before the receptionist could close her mouth, Cara had walked through the nearest door to the woman, praying it was Heinrik's office. He was on the phone.

"Cut the call, Heinrik," she said in her best Queen's English accent. "We have business to sort." Even Heinrik's mouth fell open.

But before he could say anything Cara was beginning her well prepared speech.

"Right, Heinrik. I am working for the Bell Corporation, your main competitor, handling all the deals with their main client, Cameron, for my boss, Rick Ansty. He is an arrogant, misogynist and, quite frankly, I have had enough so I thought I would do better for myself and work for you.

"I want £100,000 a year, a generous expenses account, a car at my disposal, and your undivided attention. Do I make myself clear?"

Heinrik began to splutter a reply when Cara continued, "I don't have time for small talk. Don't tell me about your marriage problems or that your kids don't understand you. I am not interested. I am only interested in making this company more money than the Bell Corporation."

She then sat back in the chair opposite Heinrik's desk and waited with bated breath for his reply.

"But I don't need anyone like you. My company is on a roll and doing very well, thank you."

"Then why is there talk of you being taken over by another company in which case you will be removed and replaced immediately?"

"How do you know about that?"

"I didn't but you just confirmed a few suspicions circulating in all the city wine bars."

The next hour saw Heinrik telling his receptionist to bring coffee and to hold all his calls while he discussed what he and Cara could do about the takeover bid.

Cara introduced snippets of information—which was all she actually had—she had heard in the wine bars and read in the financial press, and Heinrik picked up on each bit and elaborated on it all.

The next two hours saw Heinrik agreeing to Cara's demands and telling her to be back at 7 am the next day for a breakfast meeting with his directors. She was in.

When Cara left the offices she smiled at the receptionist when she picked up her jacket but guessed she wasn't the flavour of the month in that direction. She would soon need to change that but for time being she needed to keep Heinrik eating out of the palm of her hand.

When Cara arrived home she was exhausted. The adrenalin had been in full flow for most of the day and she just needed to switch off for a while. She wasn't hungry but knew she should eat so she just opened a can of tuna and ate it straight out of the tin. That would do. She drank a couple of cups of coffee and sat down to make notes. She needed to stay one-step ahead of Heinrik if possible so that he would not suspect her as the total fraud she was. But she no longer cared—she was a different Cara to the one that had gone before. She would get what she wanted and walk all over anyone who got in her way. She needed to live a different life—one of hype, energy and glamour; just anything to the opposite extreme of her previous life, because she knew one day Ian would be back and she would deal with him once and for all.

Chapter 38

Working with Heinrik proved to be a lot better than she had thought. He seemed open to any suggestion she made—often to the annoyance of other directors—but Cara had had one very lucky break in her first week working with him which had cemented his belief in her. She had gone to a wine bar after work and had overheard two pinstripes talking about the Bell Corporation boss. It was rumoured he was having an affair with the wife of the Managing Director of their main client. One word in the right ear and Bell Corporation was dumped.

Cara didn't take long to get her feet under the table. She stayed late in the office which pleased Heinrik when actually she was reading as many files as she could get her hands on to keep up to date with his business. She couldn't believe how easy it had been to land the job she had; how she had hoodwinked Heinrik. He had obviously never checked up on her claimed previous experience.

Things were going in the right direction for Cara. She felt secure earning what she was, living an anonymous life as she was and getting satisfaction out of securing big money deals with Heinrik. Even the other directors were beginning to soften towards her. She had won over the receptionist in the first few weeks by giving her tickets to see Mumford and Sons which she said she had planned to go and see but had to cancel at the last minute. She had overheard the receptionist talking to a friend about wanting to see them so it was a simple job of buying tickets and giving them to her.

Home life was still lonely and sad—especially at weekends. Each week she tried to conjure up a reason to work at weekends, flying off to Frankfurt, Brussels, New York or wherever, just so long as she was not at home alone. She had the Sheffield Star sent to her each week to try to keep track of Ian. She also knew that if at all possible, Inspector Clements would get her to court to testify against him. Despite all that had gone before, she could not bring herself to see Ian. It could take her back to the quivering unconfident mess she had been before. And this time, there was no John in shining armour charging up to rescue her.

No, she needed to build her life with work and Heinrik had turned out to be just what she needed: a successful businessman who needed a strong back-up.

The months went on and the only thing that changed in Cara's life was her continued success in the business. She put deals together that none of the other directors had managed and had helped to turn the company from a weak contender for a merger or takeover to a strong player in the field. Heinrik was pleased and at the end of the financial year her bonus was more than she had earned.

One Saturday, she got up and made herself a coffee while she opened the week's Sheffield Stars to scan for any snippets about Ian and the trial. At once, she sat up straight, spilling her coffee as she did so. There was a photograph of Ian on the front page and a headline, 'Murder trial begins' with a secondary sub-heading reading, 'Wanted in the US and UK on charges of cop killing.'

Cara looked at the photograph and memories, good and bad came flooding back. She had married him out of adoration and love. She had left him out of terror and hate. Then she thought of little Richard and she cried for her son. How much his young life had seen torture and devastation at the hands of his father. Then she longed for him, longed to hold him and cuddle him. Longed just for his being. She had not allowed herself to dwell since she had arrived in London, but today, just for today, she would allow herself to let it all out. The tears started to flow and then she howled, wailing like a tortured animal until she was exhausted, totally spent. She thought about the times in the sun when she took Richard swimming and how he loved wearing his mask and watching the colourful fish, how he cowered from his father when Ian shouted and raged. But she wouldn't let herself think about everything else Richard might have seen. That was too much to deal with.

She then thought about John and how things could have been. He had been her saviour. She wondered how things might have been if he hadn't come back to see her. Would she still be alive? And it was this reason and this reason alone why she hadn't ended her life last year when she had nothing left. All John's perseverance to help her and Richard would have been wasted. She had to carry on.

Eventually, she stopped crying and went through to the bathroom to wash her face. She looked in the mirror and couldn't see a 30+-year-old. Instead, she saw an old woman, drawn and tired, lines embedded in her once pure skin, dark circles under her eyes, no sparkle in her eyes or sign of the vibrancy she once had. But she knew, with the right make-up, she could change all that, if only a pretence for whomever happened to want to look.

She went back into the kitchen and put the kettle on. As she waited for it to boil she looked out of the window. It was a summer's day with the sun streaming through the branches of the trees in the distance, creating shadows moving around on the ground. A young child was playing with a ball while his mother sat on a bench in the park.

Cara lived in an ugly dark grey tower block in the east end of London, but it was only ugly to the people looking at it. She was looking out from it and could pretend she wasn't in what her parents would have described as a slum. The other tenants were resigned to living there—especially the older ones who had been there for more than 20 years. They no longer smelt the stale urine in the hallways, no longer saw the rubbish blown into the nooks and crannies of the stairwells. That was their life and that was where they would be for the rest of their lives.

Cara was just passing through, though to where, she had no idea. She had come to like her job and Heinrik, although she thought of him as a weak person, no one she could really respect. But that suited her because she did not want to be anywhere near a dominant male. One of the directors at work, Paul Wingard, had asked her out for a drink when they worked late one evening, but she declined, pretending she still had work to do. That was a direction she would definitely avoid.

She went back to the newspapers and started reading about the court case, the prosecution laying out their case. But as she read she realised Ian had a very good chance of being acquitted. The prosecution witness was detailing the case against Ian Campbell but Ian had sworn on oath that he was not the man they were looking for. He claimed he was Tom Read, an agriculturist from Surrey and he could prove it if they would just let him get his passport and other documents The prosecution counter claimed they could prove the defendant was Ian Campbell and there was no need to get passports or anything else from Surrey. The barrister proceeded as if there was absolutely no doubt in his mind that the defendant was Ian and began his opening speech.

Cara sat back, saying to herself as she did, "God, he's clever. He could actually get away with it. There were no witnesses to the events in the flat and only her word against his that he had broken in, knocked John out, tied him up and then been caught by a so-called Mr Smith. And she had walked away without giving a statement or anything else the police had asked of her."

She continued to read about the events of the day at the university and also about the events in America and how Ian had escaped the police after the shooting.

As she read, she found she didn't agree with some of the scenario being told to the court.

"No, that's not right," she said to herself. "He didn't do that. He went to the Buccaneer for the gun."

She was soon irritated to the point of discarding the newspaper to one side and sitting deep in thought for more than two hours. "How could the police get everything so wrong, and how could they convict Ian if they couldn't prove who he was?" she asked herself. "This is just ridiculous. He'll get off at this rate." And then the thought struck her that if he did get off, he would be free to search for her again, and even though she had left no trail—not even with Julia—he would find her. He always did.

She knew she had to go and see Inspector Clements and maybe even be a prosecution witness if need be or she could be forced to spend the rest of her life looking over her shoulder.

But first, she would see for herself what her husband looked like and how he was in court. She showered and dressed and went to Oxford Street where she bought her disguise including a wig, pair of glasses and skirt and jumper to suit a middle-aged woman. She also bought a second mobile phone and put £100 of credit on it, just in case. She would make sure both phones were always fully charged with all her contacts backed up to each. She would also back everything up to iCloud. She came home and tried all her clothes on, meticulously applying her make-up to suit the image she wanted. She then looked up the times of the trains to Sheffield, packed a small case and left for the station. She would be there late but that suited her. She didn't want to risk being seen by anyone.

As she got off the train, she looked around her and took in her surroundings. How many times before she had been there, over so many years. From her first time at university before she had even met Ian, to the time after her father died—so many times. But this time, she hoped it would be her last. She booked into the nearest hotel and paid with cash. She wanted to leave no trace.

She left her bag in her room and walked out of the hotel to find somewhere to eat—anything would do.

Once she had demolished a plate of penne pasta and a nondescript sauce, she ordered a glass of wine and got out her mobile phone.

"Julia, it's me! I'm so sorry I disappeared. I had to. Are you okay?"

Julia cried as she heard her best friend's voice but she soon recovered and reverted back to her strong Irish upbringing. "Jesus, Cara. Where the fuck have you been? Don't you realise James and I have been tearing our hair out worrying about you."

"I know and I am really sorry. I just had to get away—from everything. It was the only way I was going to make it."

"Well, that was bloody selfish of you, but we still love you. I assume you know he's been in court?"

"That's why I'm here. I've read the stuff in the Star and so much of it is wrong. How can they be so stupid?"

"Yeah, I know but not much we can do about it, is there?"

"Can you meet me, Julia, now?"

"Christ, it's nearly 11 o'clock at night, Cara. Yes, of course, where are you?"

"I'm at a little Italian place near the station, Bella something or other, I think. I'm staying at a hotel nearby."

"No you are not, Cara. You'll be coming home with me."

"No, Julia. It's best this way, for both of us. If Ian ever escapes again, he'll come looking for you first. If there is no trace of me and if I have not set foot in your place since John died, there will be no trail. Believe me Julia, I know him. This time he will not get the better of me."

"Okay, be there in 15."

As Cara ended the call, a small smile crept over her face. Julia was a good friend and would always be there for her, no matter what happened. She hadn't changed in all the years she had known her.

She thought about what she should do. She didn't want to go to court or to be a witness; that would mean she would be up against Ian and she was not sure she would be strong enough not to wilt at his stare. And she could be sure he would use everything he could to bring her down, to stop her from testifying against him. She decided to make a plan and work backwards from it. If things got out of hand, she needed a fool proof escape plan—a car maybe parked near the courthouse, some form of transport definitely. She would need to get as far away from the courthouse as she could in the shortest possible time. Ian would not hold back if he was to get away. Anyone who got in his way, he would simply dispose of. But she had to think as he thought. He would guess she would go straight to the railway station, so where else could she go? She was still

214

pondering her runaway plan when Julia came into the restaurant. She looked up and watched her friend scrutinise all the other diners, looking at each table and each person swiftly, moving on quickly to try to find her friend. Eventually, when Cara knew her disguise was good she raised her hand and beckoned Julia over.

"Christ Cara, is that you?"

Cara stood up, held out her arms and held Julia close to her. She stayed like that for more than a minute, soaking up the smell and aura of her best friend, her only friend.

When she released Julia and looked at her, she saw Julia's eyes had filled with tears. Cara's were dry.

"Cara, Christ, I have missed you. Where have you been, what have you been doing?"

"I'll tell you briefly but the more knowledge you have of me, the more dangerous it is for you if Ian gets out."

"Well, I'll deal with that," Julia said. "I won't hold back. You know that. And you also know that I never have been taken in by his charms. Not once. Remember back in the early days I told you not to go there?"

"Yes, I do, but I did, and there's no point in going back over my mistakes. We can only look at the future now."

"I didn't mean that. I just meant I will never trust him whatever he says."

The two friends sat sipping a glass of wine and talking for a very long time until eventually the restaurant owner politely told them he was closing. They hadn't realised it was already nearly 1 am so they apologised and left. They went back to Cara's hotel room and carried on talking until almost dawn when they both fell asleep.

Chapter 39

Cara woke first and looked across at Julia. Her friend looked her age, still young and vibrant. No signs of ageing. No signs of a heavy heart. But she realised she would get nowhere thinking that way. She had spent too much of her life harping back at the past. Today was her future and she was going to make it positive.

She got into the shower and stood for a long time under the jet, feeling better the longer she stood there. There was a bang on the bathroom door as Julia shouted, "How long are you going to bloody well spend in there? You're worse than James."

Cara loved her friend, loved her accent, her ways and how she was just Julia—no airs and graces and no ceremony.

"Okay, be out in a minute."

"Before the well runs dry, hopefully."

As Cara dressed and positioned her wig carefully, she told Julia they must leave the hotel separately. They must not be seen in public together. They could go to the big Catholic church which would be packed and sit towards the back where they could talk quietly without being noticed.

"Church! Christ me mother would be delighted. Haven't been to church since the last time I went home. Yeh, okay, see you there in half an hour."

Cara left the hotel room ten minutes after Julia and went down to the front desk where she left her room key and walked out.

It was a beautiful morning and she wished she could have suggested having a picnic with Julia and James near the river where they used to go with John instead of huddling in the back of a church talking about Ian.

She walked slowly, enjoying the warm sun on her back, watching all the people coming and going on their day off, some walking their dogs, some just strolling home after buying their Sunday papers. Their lives seemed easy to Cara.

She met Julia at the back of the church and they sat quietly working out a plan. Cara had brought a lot of cash with her so gave Julia £300 to hire a car in her name. She would text her to say where to leave it and where to leave the keys.

Secretly, Julia thought Cara was being too cautious. Ian was in jail, for goodness sake. He couldn't just walk out and grab her.

Cara then asked Julia where there would be an internet cafe open on a Sunday and before the two friends parted, they agreed to meet again the following evening after the courtroom adjourned for the day.

By the afternoon, Cara had formulated her plan. She had bought open rail tickets to Edinburgh and had found out where the nearest airport was for a quick flight to anywhere. Eventually, she would be back in London but only when she knew she was not being followed by anyone.

She had e-mailed Heinrik, telling him she had had to go away for a few days but had contacted everyone she was diaried to meet this week and had rearranged appointments.

By the evening, she felt everything was under control, and more importantly, her control. She found another hotel not far from the courthouse and ate in a small brasserie nearby. When she went to bed that night she knew she would not sleep. She had visions of Ian's face each time she closed her eyes. She knew then that the only way she could ever be rid of him totally from her life was if he was dead.

Monday morning saw her up and dressed before 8 am, wig and make-up in place and glasses perched on her nose. She left the hotel and sent a text to Julia, asking her to leave the car two streets away from the courthouse, Green Avenue, and to leave the keys under the driver's floormat. She might not have time to go anywhere else to collect the keys.

Julia replied saying she was just at the car hire place and would do as she asked and text her the make of car and registration number. Cara felt stupid that she had not thought of the most basic fact—the registration number. She had to be better than that.

She found a small cafe and sat down to a cup of coffee and a bagel although she did not feel like eating. She would wrap it in a serviette and keep it in her bag, in case she couldn't get food later. Cara got up twice to cross the road to the courthouse but she felt scared. She had never wanted to see Ian again and she knew he would still be able to control her, disguise or no disguise. Her pulse raced and she felt her breaths come in short gasps. The waitress approached her and asked her if she was all right.

"Yes," gasped Cara. "Thanks, I'll be okay in a minute. Just a bit of asthma."

The waitress brought her a glass of water and asked her if she would like anything else.

"No, honestly, I'm fine." But the waitress persisted so it was another 20 minutes before Cara left the cafe. By this time, she felt her pulse was racing and she was ready to implode.

She paid her bill and walked out of the café. She could almost feel Ian's close presence to her and because of that, she felt scared. She knew that whatever happened she had a route to escape. She just wanted to sit in the courtroom and listen to all the reasons her husband had to be put away. Away from her, away from all the people he had swindled and away from anyone else he could hurt. She stood on the pavement looking across at the courtroom wondering if this was really the day she could finally put him behind her, well into her past so she could get on with her life. She silently thought through what she would do; sit at the back of the courtroom in the public gallery, quietly listen to the evidence being given and make notes which she would pass on to Inspector Clements if need be. There had been so many errors in the evidence she had read in the papers that she wanted to correct anything which might reduce the prosecution case, or maybe even reduce his final sentence. At last, she was ready to go into the courtroom and face Ian. She prayed he would not see through her disguise. She wanted no eye contact with him.

As she began to cross the road, she stopped short in the middle, right in front of a taxi, its bumper stopping just as it touched her leg. She folded over the bonnet, her skirt riding up her legs as she fell to the ground and her wig sliding off the back of her head. "You blind or summat?" shouted the taxi driver. "You'll get yourself killed if you carry on like that."

But Cara didn't hear anything. She just stared in front of her at her husband. Ian was nonchalantly walking down the courtroom steps with a man Cara presumed was his defence barrister at his side. Ian was smiling and shaking his hand before he turned and continued down the steps, turning and smiling at the press photographers as he did so.

It was too late for Cara to run; he had seen her and seen through her disguise. She had drawn attention to herself by making the taxi do an emergency stop. He leapt across to her in a split second, took her arm, picked up her bag and said, "Come with me, dear. You look a bit shocked. Let me help you."

He hailed a taxi and, in just a few seconds, Cara's life was back to her prison on the Caribbean island, back to the beatings and back to hopelessness.

Chapter 40

Cara's phone bleeped a message alert just at that moment. Ian grabbed it out of her bag and saw the message from Julia.

"Great, the bitch has come up trumps!" he said and told the taxi driver to turn around and go to Green Avenue. In the space of five minutes Ian had walked free from court, caught Cara and was away in a car hired by Julia and paid for by his wife. *What a scoop,* he thought.

His barrister had produced evidence to the judge as soon as proceedings had begun proving that Ian was Tom Read and asking that the case be dismissed. The judge had been told before he closed proceedings the previous Friday that the defence intended to claim there was no case to answer against their client and the judge had warned the police and prosecution barrister to prove otherwise. They had no witnesses and absolutely nothing to prove Ian was the man being sought on both sides of the Atlantic—there was no DNA on record. The police in Portland had been asked to send fingerprints electronically, but they had failed to do so, apart from sending the wrong set initially. The judge threw out the case, told the court they could not detain a man any more just for breaking and entering the flat in question and Ian was told he was a free man but he would be bailed to appear before magistrates on the lesser charges.

Ian pulled Cara out of the taxi and slowly walked towards the hire car, pretending to be putting his arm around Cara's shoulder as he did so. He pushed her into the back seat, secured the child locks on both sides and drove off.

Cara regained her composure and sat quietly in the back seat, desperately trying to think of a way out. He had won again, but not for long. She was a changed person and he didn't know that. He thought she was the same quivering wreck he had claimed she always was. She thought it best to let him carry on thinking that while she tried to think.

He drove out of the city and towards the A1 where he headed south and just kept driving. Cara's phone had rung a few times and she knew it must be Julia trying to get in touch. Eventually, Ian just threw it out of the window.

"Well, isn't this cosy," he said to Cara. "Just the two of us again. I must say I was a bit shocked you killed lover boy. What were you thinking?" He then laughed a long cackle sort of a laugh which went through Cara to her soul.

"But he will not win. Not this time," she said to herself. "I'll bide my time until I can work out a way to escape and then I will deal with him finally." This time she would be strong.

Ian carried on driving and stopped at a Little Chef on the A14 just after leaving the A1. "Behave yourself in here or you'll know what I'll do. Remember?"

Cara just nodded and followed Ian when he opened the back door of the car.

Ian ordered a full English breakfast for himself and a pot of coffee. He then turned to Cara and said, "Hungry?" The waitress looked at Cara, expectantly. Cara just shook her head.

"Okay," Ian continued. "Just for me then."

The waitress walked away tutting and shaking her head. "Those two should go on Mr and Mrs," she said to her mate behind the counter. "Why do people like that stay together?"

Cara heard but stayed silent. Ian was amused. "Hear that?" he said. "We should go on Mr and Mrs. Always said we were the perfect couple."

Then Cara spoke. "Why Ian? What's the point? You don't love me and I certainly don't love you. So why?"

"You are my wife till death do us part," he replied. "Believe it or not, I need you, Cara. I'm not very good on my own. Now that you have dealt with John, we can work things out. Believe me, it will be okay. Maybe we could even have another baby."

Cara looked at him incredulously. He really thought they could be together as man and wife. He seemed incapable of seeing reality.

But she needed to guard her true feelings for this man; the man who had killed each and every person in her life who had really mattered to her. She had to stay strong but at the same time make Ian still think he could control her.

"But, Ian. It wouldn't be easy to go back, would it? So much has happened."

"Yes, but we can put it all behind us. Start again. I have money and passports—yes for you, too. I knew one day we would meet up again. You should know by now, I leave nothing to chance."

He ate his full English heartily, swallowing gulps of coffee between mouthfuls. Cara tried not to look at him. Everything about him disgusted her. The way he chewed with his mouth open. The way he started talking before he had swallowed his food and worst of all, his smile. His smile which once made her weak and long for him, but now just made her despise him and wish he were dead.

She tried to unfurrow her brow to look as though she could love him again. Hard as it was, she was going to deceive him; make him really believe they could start over again.

When he had finished, he pretended to cover a belch, holding his stomach as he did so, grinning like a naughty schoolboy as he did so.

"Revolting," said the waitress to her mate. "These men always think it is so funny when they pass wind from either end. Why doesn't the missus tell him?"

Cara heard but again ignored it. The waitress was right, but Ian's table manners were the last thing she should take him to task for.

"Where to?" she asked him. "Where are we heading for?"

"Ah, my dear, you wait and see. Another 24 hours and we will be snuggled up in a little place I know which is pure romance."

The thought repulsed Cara but she tried not to show it, instead forcing a half smile.

"That's my girl," her husband said. "You'll see, it will work out. Now that John is out of the way and you are not fussing excessively over our cabbage of a child, we have room to breathe."

Cara wanted to stab him with his own fork. To kill him there and then. But she knew that would not be enough. She had to remain calm, focused and thinking straight.

"Yes, maybe," she forced herself to say.

"Of course, we can," he replied. "Once we have got out of this godforsaken country, we can really go for it and enjoy life again. Maybe buy a boat and do the sort of sailing we talked about when we left Portland the first time."

He stood up, almost bowing as he held out his hand to her.

"Come on, Cara. Lighten up and we'll have a great time."

He took her hand and they walked towards the till near the entrance.

She pulled away from him, saying, "Just need to nip to the loo," as she did so.

Ian glared at her, whispering under his breath, "Don't try anything silly, Cara. You know I will always win."

Cara walked away knowing he was right.

When she got into the cubicle she burrowed into the bottom of her bag to find the second hidden mobile phone. Thank god, she had had the sense to hide one and copy all her contacts across to it.

She switched it on and clicked on Julia's name to send her a message:

"He's free, got me and the car. Don't bother with the police. Ian's too good. Will be in touch when I can. Don't worry. This time it will be different."

She then sent a text to her boss. "Sorry, big family crisis. Will be in touch asap."

As soon as the messages had been sent, she switched the phone off to save the battery. She didn't know when she might be able to charge it again.

She hid the phone again, flushed the toilet and left the cubicle to find Ian standing right outside. "Just thought I'd better check you weren't climbing out of the window," he said. "Can't quite weigh you up at the moment, Cara. Not sure I can trust you yet."

"Look Ian," said Cara, as calmly as she could. "I have no one else, do I? I loved you once, maybe I could love you again. It will take time, and I don't know if it will happen, but I will try. That's all I can say."

Ian looked pleased. "Yes, I suppose that's all you can say for now. I will try, Cara. I will try to make you love me again. I need you and I have no one else either."

This time it was Cara who smiled, but not for the same reason as Ian.

They left the restaurant and carried on along the A14 for another hour, heading east towards the coast.

Chapter 41

They took the overnight ferry from Harwich to the Hook of Holland, leaving the hire car in Ipswich. Ian bought train tickets to London but they got off at Manningtree, changing trains to take the link to Harwich International. In the space of 24 hours, Ian had again turned Cara's life around—and again in the opposite direction she wanted to go in.

Overnight, Ian and Cara sat in the bar talking—to anyone watching them they seemed like an ordinary, everyday couple setting off on a trip to Europe. When they slept they sat in armchairs, their heads lolling towards each other. Who would have known?

In the morning, Cara woke first. She had slept restlessly, shaking her head to wake herself up and stop leaning towards Ian. Fleetingly, she thought of getting up, walking out on to the deck and jumping over the side. But what good would that do. That would be the old Cara, the weak, controlled Cara who fell for every trap Ian set. No, this time she would be the one controlling their lives, but Ian would not be aware of it. Not for a while anyway. She could see they were about to dock in Holland.

As she stood up to go to the bathroom to freshen up, Ian stirred and grabbed her arm. "Not thinking of doing anything stupid, are you," he said.

"Ian, I am just going to wash my face and clean my teeth. Where do you think I could go on a ferry across the North Sea?"

"Okay, but don't be long. I'll be waiting for you. Remember that."

Two minutes later, Cara was again in a toilet cubicle. Again sitting on some public toilet trying to keep in touch with the rest of the world while her evil husband waited for her. As soon as she got a signal on her phone, it vibrated to show her she had two messages. Her boss just wished her well and told her to take as much time as she needed to. Julia's was not quite so docile.

"What the fuck, Cara? How did that bastard get out? How did he get to you? Tell me how I can help you. Tell me where you are?"

Cara quickly told her 'Holland' but couldn't give her any more details. She switched off the phone, hid it and returned to the washbasins. She couldn't make Ian suspicious. She had to look as if she was towing the line.

She made sure she left a tiny bit of toothpaste on her chin and splashed water on her blouse before returning to the bar.

"Right, time to head off," said Ian. "Follow me."

Cara followed him down the narrow, steep stairs leading to the lower deck, smelling the pungent diesel and feeling the heat of the engines as she did so. It made her feel nauseous. As she reached the deck, the cold air hit her and she pulled her cardigan tighter around her and hugged herself with both arms. She carefully stepped around the puddles of seawater mixed with spilt oil on the deck where the lorries had been parked. She looked up and saw Ian beckoning her to hurry up and join him on his way off the ferry.

She rushed to join him, not wishing to stir his anger.

"Where are we going?" she asked him as calmly as she could.

"Train station," was all he said.

The silence between them as they walked to the station seemed to hang over Cara's whole being. She hated it. Hated the fact that once again she was scared to speak, and at the same time, scared to stay silent in case it angered him. She tried to sound light-hearted but she knew he wouldn't fall for it. He had, after all, abducted her and it was not a natural reaction, whoever he was.

She tried another tack. "Look, Ian. You and I both know this situation is impossible. What's the point in running any more?

"You know I can never love you again. You know you will always have to watch me. And deep down, you know there is nowhere you can really go."

"No ,Cara. We can work this out. A lot has happened since we met, but we really can put it all behind us. Begin again."

She started to reply but felt too emotional to utter anything. He believed what he said. She would never be able to understand him.

They reached the train station and Ian booked two single tickets to Amsterdam, paying from a wad of Euros he produced from his laptop case.

Cara wondered when he had changed money, where he had done it, how he had done it when he had hardly left her side since he was freed from court.

The hour-and-a-half train journey took them to Amsterdam where they arrived in beautiful sunshine outside Amsterdam Central. Pigeons, bicycles, trams and people going in every direction gave the central square a buzz, a sense of excitement you could only find in a city. Cara's mood lifted slightly; she had never been to Holland and, despite, her traveling companion, she immediately felt better.

"Come on," said Ian, sensing her mood. "Let's go and have some breakfast."

They left the station and left the square to cross Prins Hendrikkade towards the Crowne Plaza hotel where they found a small café offering fresh coffee and croissants as well as a full cooked breakfast.

As they sat at a table by the window, Cara looked out at the throngs of people passing by, mostly business people on their way to work, most carrying laptop bags. She noticed how smart they all looked, and how tall many of them were.

There were also a couple of backpackers staring at a city map and a family all on bicycles. Cara noticed how happy they looked, how light their expressions were—no cares, she thought. Her thoughts drifted back to Richard, as they often did when she saw other children. But instantly, she checked herself. Self-indulgence was not the right way for her to go.

She turned to Ian. "Right, what now?" she said, finding it impossible to hide the harshness in her voice. "Got any ideas as to where you are going to run to next?"

Ian reacted immediately. "You will go wherever I decide we are going to. And don't think of trying to get away from me. You should know by now, Cara, you will never be able to leave me."

He paid the bill, grabbed Cara by the arm and marched her back into the street. The city didn't seem as exciting any more. She was back to reality.

In a few minutes, they were back at Amsterdam Central and Ian was again buying tickets—this time to Paris.

"Told you, I would be taking you to somewhere romantic," he said in a loud voice, playing to the audience of the queue behind him.

A couple of women smiled and one whispered something to her friend.

Stupid bitches, Cara thought to herself, surprised at her strength of reaction to two women she had never even met. She looked at the rest of the queue and saw that no one else had taken the slightest bit of notice of Ian's performance.

They walked to the platform and stood behind the yellow lines, waiting. *It would be so easy,* Cara thought. Just push him a second before the train passes them, but Ian read her thoughts.

"You couldn't do it, darling, so don't even think about it."

She gave him a sarcastic smile and stood quietly next to him. The train rolled in and they were away on the next stage of their journey to who knows where.

By mid-afternoon, Cara found herself following Ian across the concourse at Gare du Nord station in Paris to get the metro to St Michel on the Charles de Gaulle—Saint Remy les-Chevreuse line.

He dragged her up the steps from the metro to the pavement, appearing in the sunlight with the Notre Dame cathedral behind them.

"Look Ian, I'm not going to run. Without money, a passport, clothes or anywhere to stay I am not likely to be able to do much, am I."

"Okay, let's just try to enjoy ourselves for a couple of days before we move on."

The next two days saw Cara back in the blackness of her life on the island being used and abused by her husband.

Each time he raped her, she felt her resolve to be strong, getting weaker. But each time he left the hotel room, she struggled to regain her strength, to stick to her plan. To make sure he was out of her life, forever.

On the second morning, Ian showered and dressed and walked over to where Cara was still lying on the bed, her knees bent up and her arms hugging them in a desperate attempt to ward off anything which would hurt her. He yanked her hair back, put his mouth close to her ear and growled at her not to try to do anything stupid. He then left the room, locking her in again and telling the staff at reception that on no account was anyone to disturb his wife whom he said was suffering a terrible migraine.

As soon as she heard the lift begin to descend, she walked over to the window, hiding herself from being seen behind the curtain, and watched him walk away from the hotel. She grabbed her bag and unzipped the pocket at the bottom, retrieving her mobile phone. Julia answered on the second ring, recognising the number from the earlier text messages, "Cara, where are you?"

"Paris. Can't talk for long. I need you to do something for me."

"Anything, Cara, anything."

"I need you to call my boss and ask him to pass a message to Paul Wingard, one of the other directors. Tell him to call me on this number. Don't say anything else."

"Okay, but who's Paul Wingard? How can he help?"

"Sorry, I can't explain yet. Please, just do it. I'll be in touch again."

She switched off the phone and quickly hid it again, in case Ian returned quickly.

She hoped Paul Wingard would try to call her on his mobile so that she could get his number. He seemed to be her only hope.

Ian returned an hour later and told Cara to follow him. She did as she was told.

They left the hotel, Ian smiling to the receptionist and saying they were just popping out for a bit of sightseeing and he would see her later.

"He just can't help himself," thought Cara. "Just swans in and out of hotels, doesn't pay, and moves on."

They walked along the lane next to the small St Michel church, the restaurants preparing for the evening's business. Soon they were back on the Metro going in the opposite direction they had come in, heading for Charles de Gaulle airport.

God, where to now? thought Cara. *Are we ever going to stop?*

The flight was uneventful—just the usual drinks, food, duty-free and headset servings by the cabin staff. Cara immediately put the headset on, desperate not to have to talk to anyone, especially Ian. She plugged in to the in-flight movie and sat staring motionless ahead of her for almost nine hours until the plane landed at Cape Town International Airport.

When they walked through to the arrivals area, a very tanned, blonde woman screamed, threw her arms up in the air and ran over to them.

"Ian, you are here. It's so good to see you. And you must be Cara. I have heard so much about you."

"Cara, meet my sister, Janine. Janine meet Cara."

Chapter 42

Janine lived with her husband Mike, their two children and two dogs on the outskirts of Cape Town at Beaumont, a sleepy little town in False Bay. Janine ran an antiques shop, making frequent visits to the city as well as to Europe to buy stock, while Mike ran a company, building, repairing and renting small catamarans to visitors.

Theirs seemed an idyllic life, Cara thought. And they obviously knew nothing of Ian's 'business' activities. Cara found she liked Janine and felt at ease in her company. But she never let her guard down—not even when Ian was away working with Mike.

She kept up Ian's pretence of their marriage and to Ian, she pretended to be the warm, welcoming wife when he returned each evening. No one would ever know she was plotting the ultimate murder—her final escape from Ian.

"I think at last our life is going in the right direction," Ian said to her one evening after dinner. "For the first time in a very long time, I don't feel I am having to watch my back. I have decided to buy into Mike's business. He wants to release some capital from the business and the best way is to sell me shares.

"I am also going to ask him to find us a plot of land so we can build our own house. Won't that be great, Cara. I know we have had our ups and downs, but I really feel things are starting to go well for us."

Cara just smiled. She could not show her contempt for him or ask who he had killed or conned to get the money. No, one day she would get her chance, but for now, she just had to bide her time and wait for her opportunity, which she knew one day would come.

Ian seemed satisfied with her response and said nothing more.

The next day, Ian and Mike went off to work and Janine said she had to go into the city. Cara at last had some time on her own. It had been three days since they had arrived in Cape Town and there hadn't been any time for her to escape and check her phone. She went upstairs to their bedroom and switched her phone on. The battery was almost flat. There were three messages and two voicemails. One message was from Julia but the others and the voicemails were from another number she didn't recognize. She hoped it would be Paul Wingard's.

It was. He seemed very keen to meet up with her and had suggested different times and dates in the messages. She replied quickly, saying she was still stuck sorting out a family crisis but would be back at work very soon. Flirtatiously, she suggested a romantic evening somewhere nice. She then replied to Julia saying she was now in Cape Town with Ian's sister, that she was okay and hoped to be home soon. She added that any communication between them had to be treated in confidence.

She switched the phone off again but plugged it in to charge the battery, covering it with a cushion in case someone came home before it was charged.

She sat pondering her situation over a cup of coffee. There was no point in trying to escape from Janine and Mike's house. She had no means to survive and no means to buy a plane ticket home.

She knew she just needed to build Ian's confidence in her, make him think she was growing to love him again and that they had a future together. Otherwise, she would never be able to escape.

As the weeks went on, Ian and Cara settled down to, what to the outside world, appeared to be a peaceful life. Ian seemed content working with Mike and while he was content, she knew he would not be chasing the big deals.

One day, Janine came home with bag-fulls of shopping and announced she was going to book a trip to Europe. She missed home sometimes and used the Portobello market in London as an excuse to return and buy stock. The two women sat chatting for a long time, Janine explaining how she got into the antiques market, how she had met Mike and how they had come to live in Beaumont.

Cara took in as much information as she could; she didn't know why, she just knew she had to know all there was to know.

They ate lunch and then went for a walk along the beach with the dogs. Cara really liked Janine and wished things were different, but there was no point in thinking like that. She had done that for too many years and it had got her nowhere. They came to the local sailing club where they met a friend of Janine's.

"Out again with the beach cats?" her friend said. "Yes, Mike and my brother, Ian, left early to get the boats out. Good day for racing. Should be back early evening."

"And they call it work!" said her friend, laughing.

They continued their walk, the dogs running in and out of the sea, barking at them to throw more stones and shells for them. Eventually, they reached a sand dune with long, wispy grass blowing almost horizontally across the sand. Janine and Cara sat down to enjoy the view.

"This is such a beautiful place," said Cara. "You are very lucky."

"Yes, we are. We don't earn a fortune but we both enjoy what we do. Ian says you were doing a law degree when you met."

"Yes. That seems a lifetime ago. I left university when we went to the States and did go back briefly, but I don't suppose I'll ever finish it now."

"That's a shame," said her sister-in-law. "You should do it one day. Finish it, I mean."

"Maybe. I don't know. I'll see where we eventually settle," Cara said cagily. She didn't want to have to say any more about her life with Ian. How could she?

"Well, while you are here, why don't you come and work with me? I'd love the company. Gets a bit lonely sometimes in the shop, but I can't really afford more staff."

Cara didn't know how to answer. She didn't want to commit herself to anything in case it upset Ian. She couldn't afford that. She needed him to think she was happy, content and going back to him. She was still scared that anything he didn't control or plan could tip him over the edge and turn him back into the monster he had shown himself to be.

"Yes, I'll talk to Ian," was all she could say.

The next morning at breakfast, Janine asked Ian what he thought. "What I think about what?" he replied. "Didn't Cara tell you. She's coming to work with me at the shop."

Cara held her breath without realising it. She knew the hairs on her arms had stood up and that her breathing was shallow in sharp breaths.

"You okay, Cara?" said Janine.

"That's a great idea, Janine. Cara will love it, won't you, darling," Ian replied. Cara breathed again but not before Mike had noticed her stress.

After breakfast, the two women went to the shop and Cara found herself reading books on historical clocks, 18th century chairs, 17th century candlesticks and leather-bound volumes.

"There is so much here," she said to Janine. "I wouldn't know where to start. How do you know what to buy?"

"Well, there's one way to find out. I am going to Belgium next month. There are so many dealers there, so many shops and so many wholesalers. Want to come with me?"

Cara nearly jumped. She knew this was her way out. The way to start the rest of her life.

"Yes, please," she replied. "I would love to—if Ian will let me."

"Let you?" said Janine. "I will tell my dear brother that you are coming with me and that's that."

Cara felt a warm glow creeping through her. She felt excited and scared at the same time. She had to play this right with Ian or it wouldn't work. She had to make him feel she was back, that she loved him and that they had a future together.

Her mind was racing. She had to plan her escape carefully, leave nothing to chance. The day went by and Cara could think of nothing else.

On their way home, Janine said, "Just leave this to me. I'll deal with Ian."

But Cara knew she had to talk to Ian first—she had to make him think she wanted to be with him, wanted to stay and be happy with him. It would never work if Janine just jumped in with both feet as she had over her working with her.

As they walked in the door, Ian looked up as Cara walked towards him.

"Come with me," she whispered in his ear. "I just need to tell you something."

Before Janine could interrupt or Ian could question her, she took his hand and led him upstairs to their bedroom, all the while hugging him and showing the world she loved her husband.

"What's going on, Cara," Ian said as they reached the bedroom.

"Oh, it's nothing really, Ian. It's just that for the first time in ages, I have had a great day and I just wanted to show you I had. Janine is lovely and I think I could really enjoy working with her. I have realised since we got here that the old you is still there. The one I met all those years ago in the university bar. I think I am falling in love with you again, Ian. Life just seems to be good here and I really like Mike and Janine."

Ian blew a whistle through his teeth and smiled at his wife.

"You sure?" he said. "It's not that long ago that you still hated me."

"It's all in the past now, Ian. Everything that happened has happened. There's nothing anyone can do about it now. Let's just try and forget it all and move on. You are happy here, too, aren't you?"

"Yes, I am, but can I believe you? It's a fairly big change from where we were just a couple of months ago."

"Yes, I know. I didn't think I could love you again, but here you are different. Here you seem happy, content and no longer chasing big deals and planning your fortune. You are back to the person you were when we first met."

She then kissed him, sliding her arms around his neck and stroking the back of his head.

All the time they lay on the bed, Cara felt repulsed by him. Sickened by this revolting man grinding away inside her. But she would put up with it if it meant she could escape, get away forever from this man and then deal her final trump card.

They went back downstairs and Cara quickly whispered in Janine's ear not to mention the trip to Belgium yet. She then whispered to her, "And don't mention what we have obviously been doing upstairs. It will embarrass him."

Janine giggled and looked over at Ian who picked up on the wrong reason for his wife giggling with his sister. *Thank goodness,* thought Cara.

Chapter 43

Cara could hardly contain her feelings. Her feelings that she could again be free to live her life—what was left of it without Richard or John. Janine and Mike were nice people but as long as she was near Ian she would never be safe and never be free.

Over the next few days, she learned as much as she could about the antiques business to try to show Ian she really meant to settle in Beaumont with his family. He seemed to relax as the days went by and appeared to believe she really was coming back to him. While he was busy working with Mike and planning on how they would build their own house, he rarely thought of the deals he had spent the last few years plotting. Maybe it was because he was a bit older, and maybe he still thought of Cara as weak and unable to contrive anything behind his back.

Eventually, Cara brought up the subject of a trip to Belgium with Janine. She had waited until exactly the right moment when they were sitting on the porch watching the sun go down one evening. Everyone was mellow and happy.

As soon as she mentioned it, Janine took her cue to explain the whole trip; where they would go, what sort of stuff they would buy, how long they would be and how she really needed Cara there to help her. All the while she was talking, Cara did not realise she was gripping the edge of her chair and staring directly at Ian. Again, she didn't see Mike watching her.

Ian looked at his sister and then at Cara. "I'm not sure," he began to say. "It's a bit of a long trip and I am not sure if Cara is really up to it. When we came here she was very weak after not being well for a long time so I did everything for her. It would be an enormous burden on you, Janine."

"Nonsense, Ian. She's fine. As strong as an ox now. You should see her moving all the heavy furniture around in the shop. And even if she wasn't, do you think I wouldn't be able to help?"

Cara listened to the conversation but felt as if she was removed from it. She could hear the waves of the sea in the distance and the occasional car driving along the coast road. She began to focus on the fence which separated Janine and Mike's garden from the path at the side of the road. She hadn't really looked at it before—the paint just beginning to peel, the latch on the gate bent from being slammed in the wind too many times.

"I could give that a lick of paint," she said absent-mindedly, not really directing the words at anyone. The other three stopped talking at once and turned to look at her.

"What?" said Ian. "What are you talking about?" his voice beginning to show irritation.

But before she could reply, Mike came to her rescue. "Yes, Cara. It's what I was saying earlier. Hardly get time to do the bits of maintenance around the place."

Cara came back to the gathering in the porch immediately and realised she had let herself drift in another direction to subconsciously push Ian out of her mind. She was surprised at Mike's help and saw at once that he must know something, or at least sense her tension. She gathered her wits about her and brought the conversation back to Belgium, trying desperately to be upbeat, enthusiastic and energetic, to cover her real feelings.

"Yes, see, Ian. Course she's fine. We'll have great fun together."

Cara knew she had to do more to divert Ian's thoughts so she got up and walked over to him, stroking his hair and saying, "We won't be away very long, darling. I'm sure you can do without me fussing over you for a week."

"Course, he can," said Janine. "And he will."

Cara was not sure how Ian was feeling. Was his temper welling up because he was being pushed in a direction he didn't want to go in, or was he just accepting what Janine was saying. She knew she had to be very careful. After months of smoothing the way towards her escape, she couldn't blow it now.

"Well, my friends, I am tired and in need of my bed. And, of course, in need of one of my husband's great hugs, so if you don't mind, we'll leave you to it."

She took Ian's hand and gently pulled him out of his chair. He seemed to resist at first but she smiled at him and squeezed his hand, not daring to look in Mike's direction. Something told her he suspected their great pretence of the perfect marriage didn't really ring true.

When they reached the bedroom, she pre-empted what she thought Ian might say.

"I don't need to go, you know. Janine just wants a companion and we happen to get along very well. If you are not happy about it, I'll be very happy to stay here with you. You know I like this place; I feel happy here and I think you do, too."

She felt she had chosen the right words. Ian seemed to listen. She put her arms around his neck and kissed him softly on the lips.

"I mean it, Ian. There's no need to go. I'll stay here with you."

Ian seemed happy at that and decided to say nothing more. He gently pushed Cara on the bed, and once more, she endured her husband's abuse of her body.

The next morning, Cara came out of the shower, grabbing a towel from the back of the chair in their bedroom. She never thought she would ever feel clean after Ian's abuse. Ian was sitting on the bed looking at her. She forced a smile and said very lightly, "Another great day in paradise. Have you looked out of the window?"

"Look, Cara," Ian replied. "I am just not sure you really are back with me. We have had so many ups and downs, I sometimes find it hard to believe you have put it all behind you."

Cara felt like swinging a cricket bat across the side of his head. How can he put the murders, the lies, the torture, the hell down to 'ups and downs?'

But again, she controlled herself, not letting Ian see the slightest sign of her hatred of him.

"Oh, let's not talk about that. Let's just enjoy the day," she said.

"But I don't want to cause an upset. You and Janine get on so well. I want to be able to trust you totally and believe we are back together for all time."

Cara knew the truth was that he didn't want Janine and Mike to ever think badly of him. He needed their support, their friendship. After all, who else did he have?

"Ian, of course we are back together. This is our new life now. Don't worry, everything will be fine."

She walked over to the window and sat down on the window seat, looking out across to the sea. How beautiful it looked; the sun giving it life with a shimmering glow over the waves. She heard Ian close the shower door and the water flow. She sat watching the waves for a long time, resigned to her fate of being with Ian for longer. But one day, she would get her chance. Her thoughts drifted as they often did, to Richard. He would have been half-way through primary school by now, she thought. Sometimes it made her feel better to think of him and to remember his smile and his love of the sea. But other times, like now, it made her more determined than ever to take revenge for his life. She would do it.

She awoke from her thoughts when she heard the bedroom door close and Ian go downstairs. She slowly stood up, picked up her shorts and tee shirt and dressed for breakfast. As she reached the bottom step, she heard excitement coming from the dining room. "Yes, it will be wonderful, Ian. Cara and I get on so well. I have not had a friend like her since I was at school. We'll have a great time buying in Belgium"

Cara didn't dare to ask anything. Had Ian said something or had Janine continued her conversation from the porch the previous evening?

She sat down at the table and just smiled at her friends. Mike was the first to speak.

"Ian's just been telling us how pleased he is you are joining Cara on her trip to Belgium. You two will have such a good time."

Cara caught her breath. Had she heard him correctly? Was he really saying she could go? She could escape and never have to see Ian again?

She had subconsciously put her hand to her mouth and taken a sharp breath. Her heart was pounding at the realisation of what could now happen. She tried hard not to let anyone see but couldn't look anyone in the eye.

She got up from the table and said in as light-hearted way as she could muster, "Anyone for more coffee?"

She escaped to the kitchen, letting the door slam behind her. She breathed slowly and hung on to the counter edge until she had recovered. The door opened behind her.

"Looks like you need a bit of a break." It was Mike.

"Oh, I'm fine," she replied. But before she could say anything else, he continued. "He's always been a bit heavy going. Even as a kid, Janine says. Must be a bit hard sometimes—wants most things his way."

Cara was surprised but felt she had a bit of an ally in Mike.

"Oh, he's okay. Just doesn't like me going away without him. A lot of men are like that, but you don't seem to mind."

"No, I enjoy the peace when Janine's away," he laughed. "And it's always nice when she comes home again."

Cara was pleased Mike had come out to the kitchen. She didn't want to face Ian. She didn't want him to suspect her total excitement at her future escape.

As soon as she could, she left the house saying she was just going to have a short walk along the beach before driving into town with Janine. As soon as she was sure she was out of sight she sent a text to Julia and one to Paul Wingard. She might need him to give her an anonymous home for a few days, so wanted to keep him hooked.

As soon as she had finished, she switched the phone off and hid it again in the bottom of her bag. Now all she had to do was book the flights with Janine and wait for her moment.

Chapter 44

The next three weeks dragged by—Cara couldn't contain her excitement or her fear. She didn't know how to get through each day. She had planned so much in her head, been through every possible scenario, every possible problem. Ironically, the person closest to Ian who actually loved him as a brother, was the one person who would be his downfall.

Cara felt the need to go to the toilet 20 times a day—her stomach was in turmoil and her bladder seemed to feel full all the time.

"You okay, Cara?" Janine said one day. "You seem to go to the loo all the time. You're not pregnant, are you?"

As the words left her lips, Cara knew that would be her escape. Her reason to leave Janine in Belgium.

"Oh god, you are, aren't you?" Janine went on. "Does Ian know?"

"No, I haven't told him. He'll just fuss too much and I definitely don't want him scuppering our Belgium plans. Please, keep it to yourself. I'll tell him as soon as we're back."

"You've never told me about your son, Richard. Terrible thing. Ian told me all about it when it happened. Did they ever catch him?"

Cara realised, at once, that Ian had again denied himself the truth, pushed it away from his mind and eventually persuaded himself that it was someone else who had killed their son.

"I still can't really talk about it much," Cara replied, not wanting to risk losing her cool and telling Janine what sort of a murdering bastard her brother really was. But it made her more determined than ever to put an end to him.

Eventually, the morning came for Janine and Cara to go to the airport to fly to Europe. Ian had been very quiet the previous evening and over breakfast and Cara knew he was wondering if she would really escape or whether she really had come back to him.

She made a big show of cuddling him, running her fingers through his hair and kissing him in front of Janine and Mike. She would play the part.

The KLM flight landed at Brussels on time and the two friends headed for the Sheraton hotel nearby, both very tired from the long flight.

Cara felt comfortable again being in Europe—just a short hop from her roots. Somehow, she felt safe being near to home, even though there was no home anymore. Brussels was only 80 miles away from the Hook of Holland where she had landed with Ian by ferry from Harwich, just a few months earlier.

The two women had planned to go to an antiques fair in the city the following day and Janine had hoped to meet up with a friend from London who was also going to the fair.

They both slept well after their long journey, waking early to the grey morning meeting Brussels.

Cara tagged along with Janine, knowing her chance would come when she could have a reason for going home to England. She didn't yet know how, but she was certain it would happen.

They found a few items at the antiques' fair which Janine felt could be good for her shop so took the dealer's number to contact him at the end of the week, when she would have seen hundreds of antiques of interest.

By the evening, they were tired and hungry and ready for dinner and bed. They walked to a Thai restaurant near their hotel and enjoyed a set meal for two, having a couple of glasses of wine, too. Janine tucked into a green curry while Cara had a Tom Yum soup which proved to be a lot hotter than she had anticipated. By the time they left the restaurant, it was dark and beginning to rain so they hurried along to the hotel.

Over the next four hours, Cara found herself in the en-suite bathroom, being very sick and feeling very dizzy. She knew it was just the chillies in the soup, but she also knew it was the excuse she had been searching for to be on her own. By the morning, the sickness had gone and she felt ready to put the first part of her plan into action.

She told Janine that she would stay in bed as she was worried about the baby—it wasn't like her to be sick. Janine immediately said she would stay with her but Cara's protestations won. She would just stay in bed and try to sleep.

As soon as Janine had left and was well out of the way, Cara was up and on the phone to Julia.

"I'm on my way," she said. "I'll be back in England later today."

She also sent a text to Paul Wingard asking if he would like to meet her for a drink in Covent Garden the following evening. She got an immediate positive response.

She then called reception and asked if they would book her a flight to London as soon as they could. She explained she was pregnant and had been very unwell and needed to get back to England to see her consultant in the afternoon. She ignored their pleas to get a local doctor, saying she had a previous condition and it was best to see her consultant.

They called her back within ten minutes saying she was booked on the KLM flight to Heathrow that morning.

Cara then left the hotel, taking a taxi to the airport. She sent a text to Janine telling her what had happened and said she would call her as soon as she had seen the consultant but asked her not to mention anything to Ian yet as he would go into panic mode and hop on the next flight. She hoped Janine would keep her word and not tell Ian. She had taken a chance giving Janine her mobile number, but she knew she had to stay in touch, if only to keep tabs on Ian in case she told him. She then switched her phone off, asked the taxi to divert to the railway station and took a train to the Hook of Holland. She was not going to leave a traceable trail via Heathrow.

Cara arrived at Liverpool Street Station in London the following lunchtime, booking herself into a small hotel just off The Strand. When she later checked her phone she found numerous missed calls from Janine. She was sorry she had been forced to lie to her friend, but as she was Ian's sister, she could do nothing else.

She phoned her at once and said the consultant had advised her to do very little and rest for a few days as she was in danger of losing the baby. She had decided to stay with a friend and hoped to meet up with her again as soon as she could.

"I am so sorry to have messed up our week," she said to Janine.

"Oh, don't be sorry," her friend said. "It's just such bad luck, but it's so good you could see the consultant straight away. Do as he says and I'll see you in a few days."

Cara marvelled at how easily she could lie. *It was catching being with Ian,* she thought. She then moved her plan towards the next move. Mr Smith.

Although, she had never met him, she had his number and because John had trusted him, she knew she could. She called him and arranged to meet him the

241

following day at 4 pm near Sheffield railway station. Then she went out, walked through Covent Garden and along to Leicester Square. As she walked on to Piccadilly Circus and up Regent Street, she breathed in the fresh air and found herself smiling and beginning to feel better about herself than she had in a very long time. She turned right at Oxford Circus and crossed over to the other side of the street to a bank where she withdrew £1000 after checking her balance. Her thoughts turned to her job and she felt very guilty she had just upped and left. At first, she had thought she would return after she had seen Ian go down for a long jail term, but then events had overtaken her and once again, she had had to put her life on hold. Maybe one day she would be able to return but she didn't think Heinrik would want her back. He had trusted her totally against some of the other directors' advice, and although at first she had proved them all wrong, she had in the end left him in the lurch.

She thought of Paul Wingard and felt guilty again. She would use him as she needed to and then dump him. She needed a place to stay and somewhere no one would think of looking. Her own flat was too dangerous in case Heinrik had given out any information to anyone. She couldn't leave anything to chance. Paul, on the other hand, was putty in her hands. He was so keen, he would do whatever she wanted him to. All she had to do was to keep him sweet. Simple.

Her next stop was to a phone shop to add another £100 to her mobile and then to clothes' shops to stock up on whatever might be necessary in the days to come.

As she walked through the crowds of tourists she felt totally alone—but this time she enjoyed her anonymity. She could be whomever she liked and she didn't have to answer to anyone. She enjoyed people watching and saw couples walking along next to each other, no closeness between them, just familiarity. They didn't even talk. Then she saw young people with their arms around each other, stopping every couple of minutes for a lingering kiss. Such innocence. Such purity. They hadn't yet taken the knocks life was no doubt going to give them. They exuded happiness and didn't have a care in the world.

That was how she used to feel all those years ago. And now here she was, planning her husband's murder. How did that happen?

She wasn't the carefree 18-year-old she had been on that first night in the university bar any more. She saw herself in a shop window and stood for a while staring at her image. She didn't even recognise herself any more. There were a lot of lines on her face—even her cheeks had begun to sag. Her figure still looked okay with clothes on—maybe a little thinner than was healthy, but there was certainly no sign of heading towards middle-age spread. She was tanned, though, from the South African sun, which always helped, but today she stood wondering how she had come to be in the situation she was in. Lying her way through any situation, having no one to really confide in for fear of Ian extracting information from them. She was alone in the world, but she didn't really mind that. What mattered more now was to finally take revenge for all the wrong doings her little boy had suffered because of Ian. She had taken the course of action which led her to their Caribbean island. But Richard was a young innocent boy who had not only been treated appallingly by his father but had paid the ultimate price for being his son.

In the past, Cara had not allowed herself to dwell on Richard's death; there had been no positive reason to think about it, but now thinking about him made her stronger, more determined than ever to finally rid herself of Ian—and rid the world of Ian. There was no point in going to the police here, across the Atlantic or in South Africa. He had been acquitted of whatever crime the English police had decided to charge him with and they had let him go. The American police were unlikely to ever catch him again.

As Cara stood pondering on the busiest shopping street in the world, thousands of people passed her by and didn't even notice her. She was anonymous and that was the way she wanted it to be. As she moved away from the shop window, her phone bleeped; it was a message from Paul just checking she was still okay to meet later. At the end of his message, he had keyed two kisses.

God, why are men so shallow? she thought. She knew Paul was married with children but he just fancied a bit on the side. *Well, that was what she would give him,* she thought, *but it would be on her terms and only because it suited her final plan.*

She sent one kiss back.

Over the next couple of hours, Cara bought clothes for the evening as well as an outfit very different from her usual character—outdoor wear including hiking boots, waterproof trousers and a cagoul. If she was returning to Sheffield, she did not want anyone at all to recognise her. She must never be linked to "Mr Smith."

As she wandered back to her hotel room, she consciously lifted her mood. She needed to be fun, frivolous and outgoing. Paul would not be interested in someone who would dwell on the past, dwell on the present and never dare to look into the future. She had to be a 'live for the day' woman to hook Paul, use him for her needs and then throw him back in the pond. And she never wanted to care for any man again. She would live her life her way from now on.

She showered, dressed in the outrageous underwear she had bought and put on her figure-hugging black dress. An hour later, with make-up and hair in place, she was ready to meet Paul. As she walked out of the hotel entrance, she looked up and down the street seeing still more tourists meandering around the capital. She had made sure she had left nothing in her hotel room that could ever be traced back to her—and then she had just walked out with no intention of paying the bill. How she had learned from Ian. It was so easy. She arrived at the wine bar where she had arranged to meet Paul 15 minutes later than their plan just to make sure he would be even keener. And if he wasn't and was angry with her, then he would not suit her plans at all. As she went in, she handed a holdall to the waiter and asked him to keep it for her.

Paul was at her side in an instant, taking her jacket and steering her towards a quiet table at the back. As they sat down, a waiter arrived in an instant with a chilled bottle of champagne and a dish of nibbles.

"Thought we would start the evening as we mean to go on. I've booked us a table at the Savoy," he said.

Cara had to catch her breath and control her reaction. She couldn't go back there, not now. But then, after a few seconds, she realised how ridiculous it was not to go there. "Great," she said. "Sounds wonderful."

"Room service?" she flirted with him, all the while pulling him in to her trap.

She drank very little during the evening because she wanted to make sure she was always on her guard. Paul poured the champagne down his throat and then ordered another bottle, slurring into her ear, "I've waited so long for this."

"You don't have to wait much longer, Paul," she replied. "Shall we bother with dinner?"

The next morning, Cara thought she had played her part very well. She had made sure he was so drunk he fell asleep as soon as he got into the room, and she had left soon after making sure he was unlikely to wake until breakfast time.

As she walked back along the Strand, London was just waking up. The sun was just coming up and she thought the city looked beautiful without thousands of people with cameras around their necks. The sun threw long shadows down the buildings, giving the streets an almost cardboard cut-out film set look. She strolled along to a coffee shop where she had a croissant and large mug of black coffee. She hadn't had any sleep and needed to stay awake—until at least she got on the train at St Pancras station where she left her luggage in a locker.

An hour later, she was asleep on the train heading north to meet Mr Smith.

Chapter 45

Like John, Cara was surprised at Mr Smith's appearance. She had expected some sort of hooded bouncer. Instead, she was pleasantly surprised to meet a well-spoken, articulate professional man who just happened to be a criminal. They sat on a park bench talking, passers-by taking no notice of the couple who just seemed like any other. An old lady walked past with her small dog who sniffed at Cara's shoes, looked up expecting a stroke, and then moved on. Two young boys roller-skated along the path, chatting away, taking no notice of the two people plotting a murder. The tranquillity of the scene was a strange paradox.

"My guess is that you want him out of your life once and for all. The police had him in their cells but he managed to get away again. Quite an expert your Mr Campbell," said Mr Smith.

"He's not my Mr Campbell," Cara was quick to point out.

Mr Smith noticed the aggression in her manner—not quite the person he had thought her to be a few months ago after his discussions with John. But then, if everything John had told him was true, she had two choices—go down or fight back.

"Where is he now? Do you know?"

Cara talked almost without interruption for almost an hour telling him how Ian had grabbed her outside the courtroom, their escape from the UK and their subsequent flight to South Africa. She explained how she had managed to get away and how urgent it was to deal with him straight away before he was told she was no longer with her sister-in-law. She said she just had four to five days maximum before he would flee South Africa and once again find her. As she spoke, her level of stress was obvious. Her breathing was normal when she detailed how he had managed to get her, but it came in gasps when she told how she knew he would find her again, but this time he would never let her out of his sight. He would not be fooled by her again. She told Mr Smith she did not have any idea how to go about having Ian killed, but she knew John had confided in him and, although she didn't know the details, she knew it was him who had managed to capture Ian and hand him over to the police. He was all she had—but this time there would be no police, no great publicity stunt to draw him out. She needed him dealt with efficiently and swiftly, without any trace back to her.

Eventually, Mr Smith stood up and suggested they took a walk. They strolled through the park, talking in hushed voices—just in case. When they reached the park gate, he held it open for her and ushered her through, pointing to his car and suggesting she got in.

Cara didn't waste any time wondering if it was safe to get into his car—she had no other choice. She wanted Ian dealt with and Mr Smith was the only possible way to make it happen.

He drove her into town, parked the car outside an Italian restaurant and said, "If this is going to work and work quickly, we have to move fast so I need every tiny detail you can give me. This place is safe and there is a quiet room at the back where we can talk properly."

Before he locked the car, he took a small briefcase out of the boot and followed her into the restaurant, leading her by the arm to the back room. As they passed the bar, the waiter acknowledged him and suggested he brought a platter of food and a bottle of water. He seemed to be aware that Mr Smith did not want any conversation, just food and somewhere private.

They spent the rest of the day talking and pouring over an iPad with a Navionics app of the coast around South Africa, homing in on Beaumont. They looked at all the inlets within five miles and then used Google Earth to pinpoint Mike and Janine's house. Although the photograph had been taken two years before, it was still current, with very little changed. By the time they had everything detailed, it was dark and too late for Cara to get a train back to London.

"You can use a room here," Mr Smith said. "It's safe and no one will ask any questions. I will contact you tomorrow at 6 pm to tell you what I will have put into place."

His voice softened slightly—maybe he could see how desperate Cara was to end this nightmare once and for all. "It will be done by the end of the week."

"What you must do is keep in close touch with your sister-in-law to make sure she has not told Ian you are not with her. Let me know the instant anything changes."

Cara went upstairs and was shown her room and the bathroom by the waiter she had seen when they arrived a few hours earlier. She felt terrified and excited at the same time. She knew this time it would be the end, but how she would cope between now and the final act, she did not know.

She sat down on the bed and took her phone out of her bag. She had ten missed calls, two from Julia, one from Janine and seven from Paul. She listened to her voicemail messages. Julia and Janine both sounded worried and pleaded with her to call them. Paul's messages were full of apologies.

She immediately phoned Janine who answered straight away. "I am so sorry Janine. I have been asleep most of the day and had my phone on silent."

"I was so worried, Cara. I didn't know where to find you or what to do. I spoke to Mike but don't worry I didn't say anything to Ian because I think you are right. He would be on the next plane to be at your side."

Cara felt the hairs on her neck rise up. Janine might not have said anything to Ian, but had she mentioned anything to Mike? How could she ask her without sounding odd?

She felt almost out of control. This time it had to work. Ian had to be out of her life for good. She forced herself to calm down and try to talk to Janine in a calm manner.

"Thanks, Janine. I just know he will panic. I'm sure I'll be fine again in a couple of days and maybe join you at least for the last couple of days of our trip."

"Well, you must just do exactly what the consultant says. When will you see him again?"

"I'm seeing him the day after tomorrow when they will do another scan and a few more tests to make sure all is well. Don't worry about me. I am just staying in bed and only getting up to have light meals. I'm not taking any chances, Janine, believe me."

"I do believe you, Cara. I just feel desperate you are having to deal with this on your own. Maybe I should come to London."

The panic rose again. Cara felt contempt for Janine at that moment. How could she say she was desperate—she couldn't possibly know the real meaning of the word. But again, she calmed herself.

"I am fine. Stop fussing. I'll call you tomorrow and update you. Don't worry, everything will be okay."

Janine seemed to accept what Cara had said and rang off.

Next, she phoned Julia.

"Where the fuck are you?" Julia would never change.

"Actually, I am in Sheffield but only for the night. I am back in London tomorrow. I'll be in touch as soon as I can. There's a lot going on at the moment. Be patient. I'll see you soon."

Then she had to deal with Paul. She needed him so had to tread carefully.

She called him and made the right noises to pacify him and make him realise he had not blown it. He had no idea how much she needed him at that moment—just to give her somewhere to live while she waited for Mr Smith to do his work.

She arranged to meet him for a late lunch the following day.

When she finally got into bed, although she was exhausted, she could not sleep and knew she would not be able to over the days to come.

Chapter 46

When Cara arrived back in London she met Paul for a coffee and persuaded him she did not think badly of him and that she had enjoyed the evening with him. She sat chatting to him for more than an hour and arranged to meet him later that day for dinner.

She returned to the station and collected her luggage before finding a small hotel near Earls Court tube station where she showered and tried to sleep for an hour. She knew she was getting very tired, but she just had to hold on—just for a few more days.

She phoned Janine and tried to work out whether she had told Mike, and if so, if there was any danger Ian would realise she had managed to escape. She chatted for nearly ten minutes and eventually decided she was safe for the time being.

She made sure she was awake, alert and off the phone for her 6 pm call from Mr Smith.

When the call came, she listened, writing herself notes of timings and plans. Eventually, Mr Smith stopped talking and Cara asked him where she needed to transfer money to him.

"That won't be necessary yet," he said. "Let me do the job properly this time and then we'll talk." That was the last he said to her before he ended the call.

Cara sat motionless on the bed, staring into space. She knew that this time, it would happen. Ian would be out of her life and that Mr Smith would leave no trace. As she sat in silence, she could hear sirens wailing in the distance outside—emergency services racing to save someone's life as she sat planning to end one. She knew she felt nothing—no fear, no guilt, not even sadness. To her now, Ian's death was a necessity, simply that. She had only contempt for him and thought she would never again feel any love or warmth for any man. But that didn't matter to her. She was a very different person to the young, excited under graduate who had seen Ian in the university bar on her first night in Sheffield.

Paradoxically, she was now as hard-bitten and scheming as Ian. If she could have pulled the trigger on him, she would, but she didn't want his death to become the beginning of the end of her life. She had to distance herself from the murder.

As her thoughts moved slowly from Ian, to home, to her parents and back to Ian, Cara didn't move. Until her phone rang, launching her back to reality. It was Ian.

As Cara saw his name appear on the screen, she froze. Should she answer it? Could she put on the show she needed to for her husband?

She knew she must answer and quickly, before it went to voicemail. She eventually pressed the green button and managed to say, "Darling, I was just thinking about you."

She knew her voice sounded shrill, but she managed to calm herself down.

"Everything okay, Cara? I hadn't heard from you so I just wanted to make sure."

"Of course it is, darling. Why wouldn't it be? Janine and I are having fun finding lots of bits and pieces for the shop. How are things in the sunshine?" She tried desperately to stay calm.

"How long have you had this phone? Why haven't you called me?"

Cara realised immediately Janine must have given him the number so she must have talked to him. Her heart rate raced and the sweat on her palms almost made her drop the phone. Stay calm. Answer calmly, she shouted at herself in her head.

"Ian, I bought it the other day because Janine has been meeting with different dealers while I have been searching through the antiques' fairs here. There were a couple of times we couldn't find each other. These fairs are enormous—far bigger than I thought."

She prayed silently to herself that he would buy her answer, believe her.

"I really miss you, you know," she added, a sick feeling growing in her stomach.

"Why didn't you call me then?"

"I only put £20 on the sim card, and as I only bought it to stay in touch with Janine while we were here, I didn't want to run out of call time. Sorry, Ian.

"Can't wait to get home to you," she added quickly, hoping to move the subject away from the phone. "Got lots to tell you. I could really get into this business. It's so interesting and exciting. I can see why Janine loves it so much."

Ian stopped talking about the phone and chatted about the work he had been doing with Mike during the day.

"Well, glad you are having a good time. I can't wait to see you on Sunday. You are my life, Cara. I knew it would all work out for us in the end." With that, he rang off.

It was only then that Cara realised that she was supposed to be in Belgium and she would have paid in Euros, not Sterling for the Pay as you Go sim card.

She found herself shaking uncontrollably, the fear in her growing by the minute. What if Ian realised, too? He wasn't stupid. If he didn't realise now, he would eventually work it out.

She forced herself to have a bath, drinking two large glasses of wine from the bottle in the mini bar as she did so. She had to calm down and see her plan through. This would be her only chance. If Ian started to suspect something was wrong, he would catch up with her instantly and she would never again be able to run away.

As she lay in the bath, her thoughts raced through the plan Mr Smith had outlined. Eventually, the warmth of the water and the wine began to calm her down. She decided she needed to speak to Ian again—to try to steer him away from her mistake. She called him while she lay in the bath and he answered immediately.

"I forgot to say, I love you, Ian."

Ian responded as she wanted him to, letting his ego outweigh reality.

"Silly, Cara," he said. "I know that. I've always known that."

She then flirted with him on the phone, teasing him about what she was doing and what she wasn't wearing. It worked. He was putty in her hands.

When she rang off, she felt better but knew that he could still see through her. How could she have been so stupid?

She dressed and got ready to go out to meet Paul. She felt slightly guilty about using him, but she didn't really care. She would do whatever was necessary to see her plan through.

As she went out into the bustling streets, she realised she was slightly drunk. She hadn't eaten at all during the day and had only snacked at the plateful put in front of her when she was with Mr Smith in Sheffield. She would make sure she didn't drink any more until she had eaten a decent meal. She almost staggered across the street and bumped into a young couple, arms around each other, not noticing anyone else near them. As she apologised, she realised they hadn't even noticed. She cursed herself for wearing high heels which made it even harder to walk in a straight line. The evening air made her head feel very woozy and she wished she had not drunk the wine.

She met Paul in a Thai restaurant and as she walked in, he appeared with a large bunch of flowers for her.

"I am so sorry about the other night and I am very glad you haven't held it against me."

"I've forgotten all about it, Paul. Don't worry, I don't take offence that easily."

As the evening went on, Cara's mind drifted in and out of their conversation. She needed Paul purely as an alibi and to give her some sort of base that no one else would know about. She knew she had to act quickly to make sure everything she and Mr Smith had planned was put into place within 48 hours.

As her mind slowly drifted back into focus, she put her hand out and touched Paul's cheek.

"I don't really know you," she said. "But you have a very trustworthy face. Can I trust you?"

Paul seemed surprised but pleased. "Of course, you can trust me. I know we don't really know each other but all the time you were working for Heinrik, I watched you. I admired the way you were so focused, the way you made Heinrik so successful without claiming the glory. I liked the peace in your face, the calmness, the total professionalism. I liked you and wanted to know more about you."

He took Cara's hand and said, "Yes, you can trust me."

As they left the restaurant, Cara felt a fraud. Here she was, yet again, with a kind man, a man whom she no doubt could trust, but whom she would use for her own needs. She knew this time she could not escape the eventuality of ending up sleeping with him, but she could do that. If she could endure Ian's abuse, she could endure anything. It was merely a means to an end.

As he turned the key in the lock to his flat in Pimlico, he pushed the door open and stepped back to let Cara enter first. She surprised herself at how calm she felt. She could transport herself into thinking it was someone else there in the flat, not Cara. As she walked into the sitting room, she was impressed by the décor, the tidiness and the unusual mementoes—obviously from places Paul had visited around the world. He simply used the flat during the week, going home to his family at weekends.

Paul put his hands on her shoulders and turned her around to face him. He was gentle and caring and Cara felt even more of a fraud. She only had to get through this one night and she would be prepared for what would happen over the next few days.

As he kissed her, she forced herself to put her arms around his neck and return his kiss.

His arms enveloped her and his breathing became heavier as she knew he was becoming aroused. She tried not to think about him, about what she had to do to remain safe, about Ian, or about anything. She responded as slowly as she could, wishing she was more confident and easy about sleeping with men, but her up-bringing stopped her short.

As his hands moved around her and stroked her breasts, she wanted to run. Why couldn't she have just holed up in a hotel room somewhere until it was all over? But that way she would not have had a witness as to her whereabouts—in case she needed one.

He led her to the bedroom and slowly and gently pushed her down on to the bed, climbing on to the bed next to her and moving his leg between hers, raising his knee slowly to gently rub her groin.

"God, I've wanted you for so long."

Cara was almost in a panic. She couldn't go through with it; she couldn't sleep with this man whom she didn't know and whom she was merely using to give herself an alibi. She felt nothing but panic. She had to get away, but she didn't know how to without blowing the whole plan. Without knowing how or why, she burst into tears.

Paul stopped immediately and sat up, pulling her up towards him and holding her close to him.

"What on earth is wrong? I am so sorry if I have hurt you or upset you. I would never want to do that."

Cara was relieved that he was not angry, but furious at the same time with herself for being so stupid.

"I am sorry, Paul. I can't really explain. I am sorry."

"It's okay, we don't have to. Maybe it's too early in our relationship."

Relationship? thought Cara. *We don't have a bloody relationship.*

Paul stood up and said he would make a cup of tea. When he left the room, Cara wanted to run but instead sat quietly pondering her situation.

She might think she was stronger and a match for Ian, but deep down, she knew she wasn't. Deep down, the strong values her parents had instilled in her from the day she was born, always prevailed.

When Paul returned, she looked at him and simply said. "I am sorry Paul, I can't do this. I thought I could, but I can't."

Fortunately, Paul misunderstood her meaning and just said he would make up the bed in the spare room and would sleep in there.

"We'll talk in the morning, but it really isn't a big deal if you need more time. I can wait, if it means I can be with you."

Cara felt relief flow through her body, drank her tea and said a simple, "Thank you, Paul. You are a good man."

By the morning, Cara had formulated a story to tell Paul which she felt was plausible, would not make him want her to leave, but would give her the extra time she needed while Ian was dealt with. Although the guilt crept back into her thoughts, she was pleased with herself.

Paul accepted her story that it was a very long time since her husband had died and although she was very keen on him, she needed more time to get to know him.

He said she could stay as long as she liked and hoped that she would not go and give up on him. Cara felt even guiltier.

As he left the flat to go to work, she asked him not to mention he had seen her to Heinrik. She would contact him soon and hopefully return to her job.

When the front door shut, Cara let out a long, slow breath and lay back on the pillow, feeling more tired than ever. This was not going to be easy because she was not as strong as she thought she was.

Chapter 47

The next morning, Cara got up, showered and made herself a cup of coffee. She sat looking out of the window and saw a dishevelled old man shuffling along the street with a torn carrier bag spilling bits of dirty clothing out. His life looked simple and far from Cara's, as if they didn't live on the same planet. She suddenly realised she would happily swap her life for his. Walk away with her only worry being where to pick up the next morsel of food to eat.

Her phone bleeped a text message—it was from Mr Smith saying all was in line for a final solution that night. He would confirm early the following morning.

Cara's pulse raced again. She was on a roller-coaster and knew she couldn't get off until Mr Smith switched off the power.

She knew she couldn't sit in the flat all day and think about what might be happening in Beaumont. She had to find something to do, something to engage her brain, her thoughts, her whole being. She felt on the edge of a very high precipice—and at any minute she could fall off.

She quickly dressed and left the flat, picking up her phone as she did so. She stepped out into the sunshine and walked to the nearest tube station, aiming to go to a museum or art gallery to disappear into the crowds of tourists. She needed anonymity, and if at all possible, peace.

She found herself at the Tate Modern and joined a guided tour of what they called, Poetry and Dream. Again her thoughts drifted from what was in front of her, to what the guide was explaining. She had started to relax a little when her phone rang, causing others on the tour to tut and glare at her. It was Ian.

She walked away from the group and pressed the green button.

"Where the fuck are you?" he yelled at her. "And don't lie. I know you are not with Janine."

Cara shook and let out a sound like an animal caught in a trap. She tried to speak but couldn't enunciate any words.

Ian's onslaught continued. "It took me a while to realise you were not in Belgium and then I eventually got it out of Mike that you were in London. You will never escape, Cara. You must know that by now. Janine and Mike see me as the over caring husband, and that's exactly how it is going to be. I am coming to get you and bring you back."

Cara suddenly felt the blood rush to her head. She was sweating and freezing cold at the same time. As she crumpled to the ground, two people in the group were at her side, just stopping her from hitting her head on the cold, hard floor.

Cara woke up to see a lot of strangers' faces peering down at her. Her head was in someone's lap and her handbag had emptied its contents over the floor next to her.

Her lipstick was still rolling across the polished surface, quietly escaping between the feet of the onlookers.

"You okay, dear?" Cara's gaze followed the sound to an old lady standing above her. "You just fainted. It's hot in here. Always is. I've told them before to turn the air-conditioning up."

Cara slowly got to her feet, thanking her rescuers and confirming that she was okay and would just go to the Café 2 to sit down with a cold drink.

She edged away from them, slowly picking up her bag and its contents as she did so.

When she sat down with a glass of water, she fumbled in her bag for her mobile phone but couldn't find it. Then she remembered what had happened just before she had collapsed. She ran back to the tour, desperately searching for her phone. She could not communicate with anyone, especially Mr Smith, if she couldn't find it.

It was no-where to be seen. She caught up with the group and asked all of them if they had seen it. She was greeted with blank looks.

Cara began to panic. She had to speak to Mr Smith. Had to warn him Ian was on his way to London but she couldn't. She cursed herself for not writing his number down anywhere else, but she thought she was doing the right thing, not leaving anything to chance that could connect her to him.

She ran from room to room, almost shrieking to the groups of people looking at the exhibits. "Have you seen a phone? I've lost my mobile."

The people seemed to be in a trance, none of them answering her, just staring in amazement at this highly-strung, screeching woman disturbing their peaceful visit to the gallery.

Cara ran out of rooms to search. She sat down on a chair, trying to take in her new situation—again feeling Ian was getting closer and closer to imprisoning her for life. She tried to think logically but the fear creeping through her body prevented her from rational thought. She couldn't fail now, not for the sake of losing her phone.

Then she remembered she had e-mailed her entire contacts list from her phone and e-mail address book to Livedrive cloud storage. She left the gallery and ran along the street, desperately looking for an internet café.

It took her what seemed like hours to find one and when she did, there were no terminals free. She walked up and down behind the people sitting, chatting on line to friends, e-mailing or just searching, willing them all to finish what they were doing.

Eventually, a woman stood up, having closed her e-mail account and headed for the door. In one quick step, Cara sat down and tried to access her files.

"You need to pay at the counter first," said the man sitting next to her. "Bit behind the times here."

Cara leapt off her chair, throwing money on the counter, almost screaming at the man that she wanted an hour. He was in the middle of serving someone else and ignored Cara's pleas.

"Look, this is urgent. Please, give me the code or whatever you do. I need to get on-line."

"Please, just wait your turn. You are not my only customer."

As Cara was about to scream at him again, she turned round to see a man sit at the terminal she had tried to use, and log on.

The man behind the counter noticed, too, and a half smile appeared on his face.

Cara ran out of the internet café, and tried to find another one, all the while knowing Ian could possibly be boarding a plane in Cape Town, escaping his fate and on his way to find her. She knew she didn't have much time to warn Mr Smith.

Cara ran faster, turning into a small lane, the end of which had an internet sign hanging outside a small doorway.

She was breathless when she reached the door, but carried on, barging her way in past a couple of people on their way out.

"Hold up, lady. No rush," said the young man she had run into.

"Sorry," said Cara, "Urgent!"

Five minutes later, she was printing the contact numbers she needed—Janine, Paul, Mr Smith, Julia, and finally Ian. She needed to buy another phone with another sim card, and if he got hold of the number via Janine, she needed to be prepared if he phoned her.

She left the shop and went in search of a phone shop.

It was another hour before she could phone Mr Smith, by which time she was almost out of control, running from street to street, knocking tourists out of her way. "Why are there so many Carphone Warehouses, Phones 4U, O2, Orange and T-Mobile when you don't need them, and yet when you are desperate, there isn't one to be found," she muttered to herself. Eventually, she bought a phone, paid for a sim card and called Mr Smith.

"He's on his way back to London," she screeched at the phone when he answered. "He knows I am not with Janine and he's coming to get me."

"Try to stay calm," he said. "Your husband does not know where you are so he is not going to turn up just like that."

"I have been watching the house since I got here and as far as I can see, he's still here, so please go to wherever you are staying and calm yourself down. Buy yourself a bottle of wine and go to bed." With that he ended the call.

Cara was not convinced. "What does he mean, as far as he can see, he's still in the house?" she asked herself. He doesn't seem to realise the true situation. Ian could have escaped out of a window, gone out of the back door or any which way if he thinks someone is after him.

Her thoughts were scrambled and absolutely neurotic. She couldn't think clearly or logically and could only think that at any minute, he would be there, grabbing her, just as he did outside the courtroom a few months ago.

She shivered at the thought of him and was almost sick when she thought of how her life would be if he really did find her.

"For god's sake, get a grip," she shouted at herself as she walked to the tube station. "He doesn't know where you are, so he can't just turn up tonight, can he?"

Cara arrived back at Paul's flat and spent the rest of the day sitting by the window watching the street. She phoned Janine and tried to tell her calmly she had seen the consultant and everything was okay. She said she would get a plane back to Brussels the next day and meet her for their final couple of days before flying home. She couldn't tell from anything her sister-in-law said whether she had spoken to Ian.

She then sent a text message to Mr Smith telling him she was back at her flat and would await his calls or messages. She pleaded with him to let her know the instant anything changed, whether Ian was still in the house or where he was.

Finally, she phoned Paul to explain she had lost her phone and had bought another one. She was delighted to hear he had been told to go to a conference in Liverpool which started early the following morning so he would not be home that night.

At least, that was one piece of good luck. Now, all she had to do was wait.

Chapter 48

Cara couldn't sleep at all. She tried to think through how Ian could possibly find her and concluded he could never find her where she was in Paul's flat. There was nothing to trace her to there. Or was there? Had she missed anything?

She desperately wanted to call Mr Smith again but knew she shouldn't. Was Ian still in Cape Town? Had he managed to get away to find her before Mr Smith had caught up with him?

She could stand it no longer. She had to speak to Mr Smith. She grabbed her phone just as it started ringing. It was Mr Smith.

"Thank god, it's you," she shrieked at the phone. "Tell me what's happening. Is Ian dead?"

The line crackled and the call was disconnected without Mr Smith replying.

She tried to call him but without success. Surely he would try to call her again—she couldn't stand it any longer. Her body trembled and her fingers shook as she tried to press the green button again to connect to Mr Smith. Just then a text message bleeped, 'Everything is in hand. Don't worry, Cara. I'll be in touch again soon.'

She breathed more slowly and sat back and decided she was being irrational. Mr Smith had it all in hand. All she had to do was stay where she was until the job was done. She didn't notice that the text included her name which Mr Smith would never do!

She walked back into the kitchen and made herself a coffee. She needed to keep her brain awake and alert and not dive down every dark alley whenever fear crept in. The next few hours were the longest in her life. She couldn't concentrate on anything; she tried watching television but every programme was just an irritation. Do people really put themselves up in front of the whole country to air their dirty washing in public? She tried the radio but that was no good either. Every song just seemed to be either a love song which she thought was shallow and unreal, or a black poem, describing the nightmares going through the singers' minds. She picked up a magazine on the coffee table and flicked through the pages, not one article taking her attention. Every time she started to read, a thought came into her head, wondering if Mr Smith was following Ian at that very moment. Had he committed the crime? Was that the end of Ian?

The hours slowly ticked by but there was still nothing from Mr Smith. She looked back at the text messages she had received from him in the past few days and slowly, realisation dawned that the last message was not written in his usual succinct, staccato style, simply detailing moves and timings. This was slightly different but she couldn't quite put her finger on why. Then she saw it. Her name, Cara. Mr Smith would never use her name on his phone. They had agreed there would be nothing to link them—no names, no addresses, no mobile numbers associating their joint plan.

Then she heard a window smash. The noise shattered her silence and sent a fear through her body she was not capable of removing. She shook and her breathing seemed to choke her. She was devoid of all reasonable thoughts. She threw herself to the floor and under the kitchen table. Slowly, she crept through the flat towards the sound of the breaking glass, her breath coming in gasps as though she was drowning in a raging sea pulling her down to the seabed.

She could hear someone in Paul's bedroom—it had to be Ian. Who else would be breaking into the flat at that moment?

Cara tried to see into the bedroom but the half-closed door prevented her from seeing very much. She could hear him creeping around the bed, but couldn't work out what he was doing. Just as she was working out how she could get out of the flat quickly, she heard her phone bleep a message in the kitchen. She was torn between going back to the kitchen, trying to see what was happening in the bedroom and trying to escape. In the next few seconds, she realised she had to act and had to act swiftly and positively. Her life depended on it. She decided to run for it just as the man in the bedroom returned to the hall.

She saw the hooded youth running towards the front door with Paul's laptop under his arm. A simple burglar had sent shock waves through her body, leaving her completely drained and unable to think anything. She slowly slithered down the wall, sitting in a heap on the floor, her body shaking and her pulse beating so loudly she felt a hammer was banging on her head. She felt as though this was her end, not Ian's. It was her life that was ending. The fear he had cemented in her could not be pushed aside. He would always be able to control her, even if he was on the other side of the world.

She sat on the hall floor for a very long time, trying to breathe slowly and take control of her body. She felt her legs could not support her if she stood up. She finally crawled back to the sitting room and pulled herself up on to an armchair, where she slowly began to calm down. It was another two hours before she got up and walked back to the kitchen to her phone.

When a message bleeped, Cara jumped, not believing the two words that meant it was finally all over; 'Job completed.'

What did that mean? Was it from Mr Smith? Was it from Ian? If it was from Ian, how did he have Mr Smith's phone? If it was from his killer, how had he made a mistake in his last message, naming her?

She didn't know what to think, who to believe, where to go from here.

She thought about it for a very long time. She had to send a message back which would confirm who had the phone.

"Text me John's mobile number."

No reply.

Cara stared at her phone and wondered how the situation she was now in, had come about. What was going on at Mike and Janine's house? Who was in control?

She decided she could wait no longer. She had to know. She called Mr Smith who answered in his usual efficient manner.

"It's me, Cara. What's happening? Why did you send me a text with my name in it?"

"Is he dead? I need to know now, from you."

Mr Smith ended the call saying it was not convenient to talk but he would explain very soon.

Cara's nightmare continued. At least she knew Mr Smith was alive. But that was all. She spent the rest of the night pacing up and down the hall, into the kitchen, the bathroom and back down the hall. Every now and then she stopped and listened. Listened for any noise at all beyond the normal city sirens. She drank another coffee and waited.

It was 5.30 am before the explanation came by text message.

"Ian picked my pocket, took my phone and worked out our plan. He sent you a text from my phone. It changed nothing, so continued to conclusion. Saw to the brake pipes on his car and followed him towards the airport until the car went off the road at Hill Top Bay.

"As I said, job completed.

"You will not hear from me again."

That was all.

Was that it? Was that really the end?

Where was the climax, the uproar, the explosion? Where was the full stop at the end of the long sentence she had endured?

Hours passed by as Cara disappeared into a crevasse of black thoughts, remembering how her life had swung from love to torture, from care to rape, from murder to betrayal. Had she really survived all of that? What should she do now? Where should she go?

Chapter 49

After hearing the details of the accident from Janine, she booked her flight to Cape Town and left Paul's flat, hoping that maybe one day she would be able to see him again, but knowing that would not really be possible. She had to start a new life, leaving everything and everyone behind her.

The flight passed quickly and on arrival at the airport, Cara re-applied her make-up, rubbing her eyes hard before she did so to make them red and sore. She hadn't slept for what seemed like days, so she didn't have to try hard. Mike met her and told her Janine's flight from Brussels would arrive in a couple of hours' time.

She let him hold her and made all the right noises a grieving widow in shock would.

She had been over and over in her mind whether Mr Smith was right. Had he checked it was the right man? Had he assumed? She would not believe it until she saw the body.

But when she did, she still could not be sure. The fire which engulfed his car on impact had burned the body so badly there was nothing left to identify him. She stared at the black remains for a long time, not crying, not thinking, just looking into a coffin which held a body.

She didn't sit down, she didn't lean, just stood looking for something that would tell her it was Ian. She felt nothing.

After an hour, she turned and walked out of the chapel of rest.

Mike and Janine were outside waiting for her, wrapping her up with their outstretched arms as they approached her.

"Come home, Cara. Come with us and we'll take care of you. This is your home now."

Cara heard the words but felt nothing towards them, just a complete emptiness. She turned towards them and slowly shook her head.

"No, this is not my home. Nowhere is."

As she got into the taxi to go to the airport, she didn't notice the bent, bearded old man with the walking stick watching her every move.

The End